PERSUASION

JANE AUSTEN

PERSUASION

An Annotated Edition

EDITED BY

ROBERT MORRISON

The Belknap Press of Harvard University Press

Cambridge, Massachusetts

London, England

2011

Frontispiece: *Lyme Regis, Dorsetshire: A Squall,*
by J. M. W. Turner, circa 1812. In *Persuasion,* Anne Elliot
and her party stay at Lyme Regis in November 1814,
only a few years after Turner visited the area and
painted this highly evocative picture of its
color, light, and atmosphere.

LIBRARY OF CONGRESS CATALOGING-IN-PUBLICATION DATA

Austen, Jane, 1775–1817.

Persuasion : an annotated edition / Jane Austen ;
edited by Robert Morrison.

p.   cm.

Includes bibliographical references.

ISBN 978-0-674-04974-1 (alk. paper)

1. Young women—England—Fiction.   2. Motherless families—Fiction.

3. Rejection (Psychology)—Fiction.   4. Ship captains—Fiction.

5. England—Social life and customs—19th century—Fiction.

I. Morrison, Robert, 1961–   II. Title.

PR4034.P4   2011b

823'.7—dc22   2011013150

For Glenn and Joyce, David, Janet, and Helen

The England of *Persuasion*.

Contents

Note on the Text

Jane Austen completed *Persuasion* in July 1816, but within three weeks she had rejected her final two chapters and replaced them with three new ones. The two cancelled chapters are the only portion from any of her published novels extant in manuscript, and they are reprinted here in Appendix A.

The manuscript of *Persuasion* as published does not survive, and Austen died before the novel was sent to press. Nothing is known of the proofs, though it seems likely that they were checked by Austen's sister, Cassandra, and her brother Henry. The only legitimate text of the novel, then, is the first published version, which appeared in December 1817 as volumes 3 and 4 of a four-volume set that was dated 1818 on the title page, and that featured *Northanger Abbey* as volumes 1 and 2. John Murray was the publisher. The cost of the four volumes was 24 shillings. The print run was 1,750 copies.

At the time of her death, Austen seems not to have decided on a title. Cassandra later reported that the name of the novel "had been a good deal discussed between Jane and herself, and that among several possible titles, the one that seemed most likely to be chosen was 'The Elliots.'" In the event, however, it was probably Henry who decided to call the novel *Persuasion* (William Austen-Leigh and Richard Arthur Austen-Leigh, *Jane Austen: A Family Record,* revised and enlarged by Deirdre le Faye [London: British Library, 1989], 214; David Gilson, "Jane Austen's Text: A Survey of Editions," in *Review of English Studies,* 53 [2002], 62).

The copy-text for the present edition is volumes 3 and 4 of the four-volume edition of *Northanger Abbey: and Persuasion* held in the Houghton Library, Harvard University (*EC8.Au747.817n v. 3 [B] and *EC8.Au747.817n. v. 4 [B]). I have also examined three other copies of *Persuasion:* a second copy held in the Houghton Library (*EC8. Au7.817n. v. 3 [A] and *EC8.Au7.817n. v. 4 [A]); the copy held in the Thomas Fisher Rare Book Library, University of Toronto (B-10 5073); and the copy held in the British Library (Cup. 403.bb.13).

All four copies carry the same irregularities in spelling, punctuation, capitalization, and hyphenation: for example, "favor" and "favour"; "dropped" and "dropt"; "connection" and "connexion"; "Great House" and "great house"; "Kellynch-hall" and "Kellynch hall" and "Kellynch Hall." Typographical errors—letters that are upside down, for example, or words that have been run together—are also consistent across the four editions, as are spelling mistakes such as "againt" and "blesssed." Yet there are differences among the four copies. In volume 1, page 265, lines 8–9, of the 1818 text, Austen states that Captain Harville and "his wife decided what was to be done." In the copy-text, as well as in the British Library copy, the "s" in "his" is plainly visible. But it is missing in the second Houghton copy, as well as in the Fisher copy. Similarly, in volume 2, page 227, line 8, Austen writes that "the gentlemen were richer." In the copy-text, the second Houghton copy, and the Fisher copy, the first "r" in "richer" is missing. But in the British Library copy it is plainly visible. These differences suggest that certain letters dropped out over the course of the printing, and that other copies of the novel probably contain letters that are similarly faded or missing. Substantive variations among the 1818 printings, however, seem unlikely.

I have retained many features of the 1818 text, including the double quotation marks (and the single quotation marks within the double), the inconsistencies in spelling and punctuation, the ligatures, and the periods following "Mr.," "Mrs.," "Dr.," and so on. I have corrected obvious printer's errors ("the mall" has been amended to "them all," for instance) and added a letter when it is clearly missing ("means a are" has been corrected to "means as are"). Like many of the editors who have come before me, I have altered the text on a small number of occasions to improve the sense. In volume 1, chapter 1, however, I have broken from previous texts of *Persuasion* by amending "she" to "he," so that it is Mr. Elliot, and not Elizabeth Elliot, who is in mourning for Mr. Elliot's wife. All emendations and corrections are listed in Appendix C. Substantive changes to the text are also cited in the marginal notes.

PERSUASION

Introduction

"What throbs fast and full, though hidden," wrote Charlotte Brontë, "what the blood rushes through, what is the unseen seat of Life and the sentient target of death—*this* Miss Austen ignores."[1] Brontë's criticism is based on her frustration with Jane Austen's narrative restraint and with the codes of propriety that structure the business of her novels. Ironically, Brontë's indictment also speaks to Austen's enduring appeal, for it highlights the wit, smooth elegance, and highly mannered emotion that both draw us to her world and reveal our distance from it. Yet below the glittering surfaces that have so often preoccupied both her detractors and her admirers, all six of Austen's published novels display a broad and intimate awareness of the inner rush and throb of life, an awareness that links her with a host of later nineteenth-century writers including George Eliot and Brontë herself, and that is nowhere more evident than in *Persuasion*.

Underwritten by the principal events of the French Revolution and Napoleonic Wars, as well as by a wide range of literary sources and biographical experience, the novel tells the story of the isolated and unloved Anne Elliot, whose sense of duty to others does not prevent her from wishing to take control of her own fate, and whose thoughts and actions repeatedly highlight the ways in which the lives of those around her are blunted by spurious societal conventions, from the dictates of "feminine" behavior to the prescriptions designed to safeguard the distinctions of rank. Anne and her former fiancé, Captain Frederick Wentworth, share a sorrowful past that at once divides and unites them, and when circumstances bring them

NORTHANGER ABBEY:

AND

PERSUASION:

BY THE AUTHOR OF " PRIDE AND PREJUDICE ;"
" MANSFIELD-PARK," &c.

WITH A BIOGRAPHICAL NOTICE OF THE
AUTHOR.

IN FOUR VOLUMES.
VOL. III.

LONDON:
JOHN MURRAY, ALBEMARLE STREET.
1818.

The title page of the first edition of *Persuasion*. The novel
appeared as volumes 3 and 4 in a four-volume edition that
also included *Northanger Abbey*. Though dated "1818" on
the title page, the edition actually appeared in December
1817, five months after Austen's death.

back together again, their confusion and interest in others continually thwart their attempts to understand both themselves and each
other. *Persuasion* is Austen's last published novel, and a moving love
story of despair, anticipation, missed opportunities, and second
chances.

    "The French Revolution" is "the master theme of the epoch in
which we live," declared the radical poet Percy Bysshe Shelley in Sep-

tember 1816, just four weeks after Austen finished writing *Persuasion*.[2] Touched off by the storming of the Bastille prison on July 14, 1789, the Revolution marked the end of the ancien régime and set in motion a series of momentous events, including the abolition of feudalism and the establishment of the French republic. By 1792, however, the relative peace that had marked its opening months began steadily to give way to factionalism and violence. A year later, England went to war with France, plunging the two countries into the center of a fierce international conflict that raged almost without intermission for the next twenty-two years. Napoleon Bonaparte led the French, and his military genius brought him close to his goal of unifying Europe. England's campaign against him was spearheaded on the sea by Horatio Nelson, Viscount Nelson, who scored decisive victories over French fleets in the Battle of the Nile (1798) and the Battle of Trafalgar (1805), and on the land by Arthur Wellesley, the future duke of Wellington, who guided the British to victory in the Iberian Peninsula (1808–1814) and then went on to join the allied forces that were attacking France on all its frontiers. Napoleon, who had been badly weakened by his disastrous invasion of Russia in 1812, unconditionally surrendered to the allies on April 11, 1814, and was exiled to Elba, an island off the west coast of Italy. He was not done yet, however. In an astonishing move, Napoleon broke from the island ten months later and returned to France, where he quickly set about trying to rally support and rebuild his empire. Britain, Prussia, Austria, and Russia mobilized against him, and on June 18 Napoleon was routed at the Battle of Waterloo. Four days later he abdicated for a second time and the allies took him into custody. On August 8, 1815, the *Times* announced that Napoleon was soon to be put on board the *Northumberland* and sent into exile on St. Helena, an island that lies 1,200 miles west of the southwestern coast of Africa. On that same day, Austen began to write *Persuasion*.[3]

The events of her novel are woven tightly round these vast political and cultural upheavals, for as is so often the case in Austen, public actions burden the apparently private, familial decisions made by her characters. Anne Elliot's father, Sir Walter Elliot, is the current head of the family and a vain, petty man who values his hereditary title as a baronet above all else, and who takes great delight in reading about his family history in his beloved *Baronetage,* though he is oblivious to his own public responsibilities as the owner of his Kellynch estate and as a titled member of the gentry. In 1789, the year the French Revolution cast a long shadow over the wealth and privilege enjoyed by landed elites like Sir Walter, he and his wife also lose their only son, whose stillborn death substantially increases the possibility that Sir Walter's cherished title will pass out of his immediate family and to an estranged relation, Mr. William Elliot. Further difficulties arise for Sir Walter when, following his wife's death in 1801, he cannot keep himself out of serious debt, and by 1814 he is forced to move to Bath after renting Kellynch to Admiral Croft, a highly successful naval officer who has amassed a considerable sum in prize money, and who fought alongside Lord Nelson at the Battle of Trafalgar. Although he does not fully comprehend it, Sir Walter's life changed dramatically in the year of the French Revolution, while that same event gave men such as Admiral Croft the opportunity to make their fortune and to advance far up the social scale through merit and courage.

Admiral Croft's wife, Sophia, has a brother who is also a naval officer. It is not clear when Frederick Wentworth first went to sea, but it may have been as early as eleven or twelve years of age. He is "lucky in his profession" but spends freely what comes freely, and realizes nothing. In 1806, he is promoted to commander for his part in the economically crucial Battle of St. Domingo in the West Indies, and while he awaits his next posting he returns to England, where he meets Anne Elliot, and the two fall "rapidly and deeply in love." Anne, however, is convinced by her father and more especially by her closest friend, Lady Russell, to break off her engagement to Wentworth, for she comes from privilege, and she is not to throw herself away on a "headstrong" man who has "no hopes of attaining affluence, but in the chances of a most uncertain profession." Badly shaken, Wentworth returns to the sea. He commands a sloop to the West Indies, where he makes money fast ransacking "privateers enough to be very entertaining." In August 1807, on his first passage back home in a year, he has the "good luck" to "fall in with the very

French frigate I wanted," and he brings her into Plymouth. Within months he is posted again, this time as a captain on the frigate *Laconia,* and he takes a "lovely cruise" off the Azores in the North Atlantic Ocean, where he conducts another series of raiding expeditions on enemy ships and makes a great deal more money, a trend that continues in the summer of 1809, when he has "the same luck in the Mediterranean." By the time of Napoleon's first abdication in April 1814, Captain Wentworth has built up a fortune of £25,000 and risen "as high in his profession as merit and activity could place him." Memorably, V. S. Pritchett described Austen "as a war-novelist, formed very much by the Napoleonic wars, knowing directly of prize money, the shortage of men, the economic crisis and change in the value of capital."[4] Croft and Wentworth are similarly formed by the war and its consequences, both as private individuals and as commanding officers.

Peace with Napoleon meant demobilization in the British navy. Wentworth returns to England, where in the autumn of 1814 he pays a visit to his sister and Admiral Croft at Kellynch. He again finds himself in company with Anne, a spinster now at twenty-seven years old, who is living just three miles away at Uppercross Cottage as a temporary guest of her hypochondriacal younger sister, Mary, and her husband, Charles Musgrove. Time has not dimmed Wentworth's vivid remembrance of the day eight years earlier when Anne shattered the "exquisite felicity" of their engagement and rejected him; nor has time dulled the pain she still feels at their separation. When Lady Russell urged her to refuse Wentworth, it was because she worried that marrying him would sink Anne "into a state of most wearing, anxious, youth-killing dependance!" Not marrying him, it turns out, has had the same effect. Anne continues to believe that she did her duty in following Lady Russell's advice, for "to me, she was in the place of a parent." But she needs Wentworth now even more than she did then.

Anne's longing for him is shaped by a variety of literary sources. Austen borrows from Shakespearean comedies such as *Twelfth Night* (*c.* 1601), where Viola's plight presages Anne's as she sits like patience on a monument smiling at grief, and *The Winter's Tale* (*c.* 1609), another story about love come thrillingly back from the dead. Samuel Johnson's writings on sorrow, fortitude, and female isolation, especially as collected in the essays of *The Rambler* (1750–1752), have clearly helped to sustain Anne through barren years when she could learn of Wentworth's whereabouts only by anxiously reading navy lists and newspaper accounts of battles with the French. The major Romantic poets—Austen's immediate contemporaries—loom larger in *Persuasion* than in any of her other novels. "Its emphasis on memory and subjectivity have been called Wordsworthian, its emotional tone has been likened to Shelley and Keats, and its epistemological strategies compared to Coleridge's conversation poems," Adela Pinch observes.[5] Coleridge's "Kubla Khan" (1816) seems also to inform Anne's heightened response to the landscape when she and a group from Uppercross venture to the coastal town of Lyme Regis, "with its green chasms between romantic rocks." It is an appropriate setting for Anne's grieving heart and the intensity with which she yearns for her lost lover. Most strikingly, Anne has a highly ambiguous response to the poetry of Walter Scott and Lord Byron, two of the most famous figures of Austen's day. During a walk through Lyme, she discusses the two poets with Captain Benwick, a friend of Wentworth's who is in mourning over the recent death of his fiancée, but who Anne is sure cannot possess "a more sorrowing heart" than her own. Benwick is "intimately acquainted" with "all the impassioned descriptions of hopeless agony" in Byron, and he repeats to Anne, "with such tremulous feeling, the various lines which imaged a broken heart, or a mind destroyed by wretchedness." Anne gently reproves him for his morbidity and recommends less impassioned poetry and more moral and religious prose in his daily reading regimen. Yet her own fate is powerfully evoked in some of Benwick's favorite Byron poems, including *The Giaour* (1813) and *The Bride of Abydos* (1813), where Byron engages in penetrating analyses of anguish and loss, female agency, and the constancy of both men and women.

Austen also roots *Persuasion* in her own experience. Her mother was unquestionably a *malade imaginaire,* and Austen seems to have vented some of her frustration with her in her portrait of Mary, who is "so ill" she can "hardly speak" when Anne arrives for her sojourn at Uppercross, and whose "sore-throats, you know, are always worse than anybody's." Austen's beloved older sister, Cassandra, lost her fiancé to yellow fever in St. Domingo, where Wentworth fights in 1806. Further, two of her brothers were in the navy, and they both provided her with much detailed information on the war effort: "I believe that no flaw has ever been found in her seamanship . . . in *Persuasion,*" her nephew boasted many years later.[6] Francis and Charles Austen had already joined the navy when war broke out between England and France, and both went on to have distinguished military careers. Francis fought mainly in the Mediterranean and the Baltic and was intimately involved with British naval operations throughout the Napoleonic Wars. He dined with Nelson on the afternoon before the Battle of Trafalgar, but on the following day Nelson dispatched his ship from Cadiz to Gibraltar for resupplying, and Francis missed the actual fight, unlike Admiral Croft. Charles was actively engaged in the Mediterranean, where, like Wentworth, he cruised for privateers and made prize money. Later he served on the North American Station, and in 1815 he was again sent to the Mediterranean following Napoleon's escape from Elba.

Other circumstances in the novel are even more personal. Like the party from Uppercross, Austen herself visited Lyme, and in the summer of 1804 she wrote a vivid letter to Cassandra describing what she did ("the Bathing was so delightful this morning"), where she went ("we . . . walked together for an hour on the Cobb"), and the people she saw ("a new, odd looking Man . . . had been eyeing me for some time").[7] Austen's circumstances when she wrote the novel, including her declining health and straitened financial position, parallel those of Mrs. Smith, Anne's school friend whom she meets again in Bath. Austen herself has also frequently been taken for Anne. Her friend Ann Barrett declared that "Anne . . . was herself; her enthusiasm for the navy, and her perfect unselfishness reflect her completely," comments echoed many years later by the novelist Elizabeth Bowen, who asserted that Austen enveloped Anne, "unconsciously, in the greatness she had herself as a woman, the poeticness, the submissiveness, the courage that the younger novels had not yet brought into play."[8] Virginia Woolf went even further when she suggested that *Persuasion* proved "not merely the biographical fact that Jane Austen had loved, but the aesthetic fact that she was no longer afraid to say so. Experience, when it was of a serious kind, had to sink very deep, and to be thoroughly disinfected by the passage of time, before she allowed herself to deal with it in fiction." But now, in this last completed novel, "she was ready."[9] When, for example, Anne declares, "all the privilege I claim for my own sex . . . is that of loving longest, when existence or when hope is gone," do we hear something of Austen's own voice?

In addition to its debts, *Persuasion* looks decidedly to the future, for it is at once revolution and revelation. Like all of Austen's novels, it is a comedy of manners in which courtship is the foremost interest and marriage the highest ambition. But Anne is older and much closer to despair than any of Austen's other heroines, though she is also the most passionate. Austen renders Anne's consciousness—its integrity as well as its dark misgivings—in a prose style that is much more lyrical and impressionistic than anything in the earlier novels, and that gives to *Persuasion* an intense subjectivity. Further, the social commentary in this final novel is more acerbic and impatient than what has come before, as Austen contends much more overtly for a society that prizes openness, professionalism, and mobility. In *Pride and Prejudice,* Elizabeth marries into the upper echelons of the traditional gentry and retires to the magnificent grounds of Pemberley. In *Persuasion,* it is different. Darcy's seat is replaced by Wentworth's sea, and Darcy's land by Wentworth's landaulette. "In narrative mode, social view, and character conception, [*Persuasion*] marks a radical change from all that has gone before," asserts Judith Prewitt Brown. "Its debilitating ambiguities and hatreds, its conception of society, its surrender to disgust" point the way toward George Eliot, Henry James, and beyond.[10]

Missing Wentworth has not been the only burden that Anne has had to shoulder. Her elder sister, Elizabeth, is her father's favorite, as Anne was almost certainly her mother's. But Lady Elliot's death thirteen years earlier has left Anne almost entirely alienated within her own family. Her father and Elizabeth care nothing for her. She is "only Anne," and her opinions on what the country owes to the navy, or how to pay back her father's debts, or why Elizabeth's sycophantic friend Mrs. Clay is intent on hovering near Sir Walter, count for nothing. Mary treats Anne marginally better, but she is primarily interested in her sister as the companion who seems most willing to listen to her incessant whining, and there is a callousness about her even when she does not fully realize the import of her words. Following the first meeting between Wentworth and Anne in eight years, Mary cannot wait to report back to Anne with the painful news that Wentworth found her "so altered he should not have known you again." Lady Russell is Anne's dearest friend, but as it was her advice that led Anne to reject Wentworth, the two "never" allude to him, and Anne must close her heart to her on the sorrow that is steadily consuming it. Anne is also friendly with Mary's in-laws, the Musgroves, and while they treat her kindly, they have no real sense of her worth. Her proficiency at the pianoforte escapes them—"Lord bless me! how those little fingers of yours fly about!"—and they fail to notice the tears in her eyes as she sits at evening parties and plays the instrument so that the others can dance. Often she wishes for nothing more than "to be unobserved," though on occasion this means she is simply ignored or forgotten. "Is not this one of the ways to Winthrop?" she asks a party from Uppercross as they walk together through the fields. But "nobody heard, or, at least, nobody answered her."

In the face of such isolation, and with the pain of her broken engagement unmitigated by a "second attachment," or a "change of place," or "any novelty or enlargement of society," Anne has retreated into herself and done her best to be useful to those around her. When Sir Walter and Elizabeth prepare to leave Kellynch to take up residence in Bath, she busies herself "making a duplicate of the catalogue of my father's books and pictures," working "several times in the garden with Mackenzie," and "going to almost every house in the parish, as a sort of take-leave," for while her father is uninterested in his own duties, Anne is anxious that they be fulfilled. But when she leaves Kellynch to stay at Uppercross, she submits to "another lesson, in the art of knowing our own nothingness beyond our own circle," for the events of such paramount concern at Kellynch are of virtually no interest just three miles down the road, and while Anne "had expected rather more curiosity and sympathy" from the Musgroves, she recognizes that "every little social commonwealth should dictate its own matters of discourse," and she gratefully takes on "any thing marked out" to her "as a duty" in Mary's home. Soon she is the chief confidante to most members of the Musgrove family in matters of domestic dispute, though "she could do little more than listen patiently, soften every grievance, and excuse each to the other." More significantly, in a novel in which ill health and broken bones play such a large role, Anne is a companion and nurse to Mary, as well as to her small children. When Mary's eldest son, Charles, is brought home one day with a dislocated collarbone, it is Anne who has "every thing to do at once—the apothecary to send for—the father to have pursued and informed—the mother to support and keep from hysterics—the servants to control—the youngest child to banish, and the poor suffering one to attend and soothe."

Yet self-sacrificing as she habitually is, Anne also works hard to shield herself from the insensitivity that surrounds her and to ameliorate at least some of the conditions under which she lives. She evades unpleasantness as best she can, happy to find "a pretence for absenting herself" from a dinner party, or to contrive "to evade and escape from" a visit she does not wish to make, just as she tries to put herself in the way of her own happiness when an opportunity presents itself, as when she resorts to "a little scheming of her own" in Bath to attract Wentworth. What is more, since refusing him Anne has been much more willing to brook disapproval and stand up for her own better interests. When Charles Musgrove makes an offer to her three years after Wentworth's, Lady Russell is keen on the match and attempts to persuade Anne to accept him. "But in this case, Anne . . . left nothing for advice to do," and she refuses Charles. Later in Bath, Anne also defies her father when she pursues her friendship with Mrs. Smith, who turns out to be such a valuable ally. When Sir Walter first learns of the relationship, he snootily informs Anne that rather than spending time with "every thing that revolts other people," such as "low company, paltry rooms, foul air," and "disgusting associations," she is to postpone a scheduled meeting with Mrs. Smith in order to accompany him and Elizabeth on an evening visit to their cousins, Lady Dalrymple and Miss Carteret. Anne declines: "I do not think I can put off my engagement, because it is the only evening for some time which will at once suit her and myself. — She goes into the warm bath to-morrow, and for the rest of the week you know we are engaged." In part because she means so little to her father, but also in part because her bitter past has made her intent on shaping her present as fully as possible, Anne carries the day: she "kept her appointment; the others kept theirs."

According to Rebecca West, Austen "put the institutions of society regarding women through the most grueling criticism they have ever received."[11] In *Persuasion,* some of this criticism comes from Anne, but more frequently and stridently it comes from the narrator, who has the freedom to voice what decorum and the interests of family harmony prevent Anne from saying, especially as regards Sir Walter's vacuity, Elizabeth's conceit, Mary's carping, and Lady Russell's "prejudices on the side of ancestry." Austen's primary satiric target in the novel, however, is not the hypocrisy and selfishness of the gentry but the sentimentality and affectation that characterize so much "feminine" behavior, and that she sees as undermining the authenticity of feeling so crucial to productive human relationships that animate and heal. The narrator lambastes Mrs. Musgrove's "large fat sighings" over the death of her son Dick, not because her feelings are entirely absurd but because too much of her grief is performative. Dick Musgrove, who joined the navy at a young age, "had been very little cared for at any time by his family, though quite as much as he deserved; seldom heard of, and scarcely at all regretted, when the intelligence of his death abroad had worked its way to Uppercross, two years before." Captain Wentworth's visit to the neighborhood understandably revives Mrs. Musgrove's thoughts of her dead son, who had served under Wentworth on the *Laconia.* But her memories of him are overheated and inaccurate, for she recalls a "poor dear fellow . . . grown so steady, and such an excellent correspondent." If "nobody had cared for" him when he was alive—including presumably Mrs. Musgrove herself—Austen insists that it is damaging now to pretend otherwise, all that is "real and unabsurd" in Mrs. Musgrove's feelings notwithstanding.

A similar kind of caustic forthrightness colors her account of Louisa Musgrove's accident on the Lower Cobb. When Wentworth misses her outstretched hand and she falls hard to the pavement, he raises her up lifeless, and her friends recoil under "the horror" of the moment: "'She is dead! she is dead!' screamed Mary, catching hold of her husband, and contributing with his own horror to make him immoveable; and in another moment, Henrietta, sinking under the conviction, lost her senses too, and would have fallen on the steps, but for Captain Benwick and Anne, who caught and supported her between them." Meanwhile, as word of the accident spreads, "workmen and boatmen" gather on the Cobb "to be useful if wanted," but more readily, it seems, "to enjoy the sight of a dead young lady, nay, two dead young ladies, for it proved twice as fine as the first report." Austen's recourse to black humor in the middle of such a distressing scene comes somewhat unexpectedly. But in emphasizing that Mary's screaming and Henrietta's swooning have confused onlookers to the point where they cannot distinguish between who is genuinely injured and who is not, Austen highlights the absurdity of the two women's behavior. They do not need to act in this way. Anne does not. While chaos breaks out all around her, she takes command of the situation, tending to Louisa, rallying Wentworth, and sending Benwick for a doctor. Mary's and Henrietta's actions are in accord with the kinds of behavior prescribed in female conduct books and enacted in scores of contemporary novels, but Austen works in *Persuasion* to explode such sentimental extravagance. Anne's decisiveness under pressure highlights her freedom from patriarchal convention and hits back at representations of women as simpering and frail.

Yet at the same time Anne herself is not immune to lapses into sentimentality. When Mrs. Smith describes the instruction and aid she has received from nurse Rooke, Anne is quick to romanticize the role of nurses, though her own experience with Mary might have given her very different views: "What instances must pass before them of ardent, disinterested, self-denying attachment, of heroism, fortitude, patience, resignation—of all the conflicts and all the sacrifices that ennoble us most," she enthuses in an "elevated style." Mrs. Smith cannot agree: "Here and there, human nature may be great in times of trial, but generally speaking it is its weakness and not its strength that appears in a sick chamber; it is selfishness and impatience rather than generosity and fortitude, that one hears of." Similarly, on the way to another visit with Mrs. Smith, Anne luxuriates in the contemplation of Mr. Elliot's flattery and Captain Wentworth's jealousy, and she swears to love Wentworth forever: "Their union, she believed, could not divide her more from other men, than their final separation." Romantic notions such as these undoubtedly helped to sustain her in bleaker years, but they have also made her much less able to penetrate Mr. Elliot's character, and they seem grotesquely self-indulgent as well. Given her choice of two affluent lovers, both of whom can ensure the continuation of her privileged lifestyle, Anne would choose Wentworth alone. Her close friend Mrs. Smith, on the other hand, has no lovers, little money, few friends, and fewer options, and she has to rely on a remarkable "elasticity of mind" to face the burden of most days. The narrator responds to Anne's ruminations with an irony that is openly indignant: "Prettier musings of high-wrought love and eternal constancy, could never have passed along the streets of Bath, than Anne was sporting with from Camden-place to Westgate-buildings. It was almost enough to spread purification and perfume all the way." Anne's romantic idealism is informed by good luck, financial security, and a highly respectable social position. The narrator is at pains to emphasize that not everyone is so fortunate, including Mrs. Smith and of course Austen herself.

Austen's assault on sentimentality in *Persuasion* is matched by the vigor with which she assails the conventions of rank. Sir Walter is a fading Regency dandy, born just two years before the prince regent, and utterly invested in the traditions and inherited dignities of the aristocratic system that the French Revolution put under such severe pressure. Elizabeth is similarly hidebound, wholly uninterested in the state of the nation and still insistent that any marriage proposal must come from "baronet-blood," even as her thirtieth birthday and the realities of spinsterhood press down upon her. Yet as Austen makes exhilaratingly clear in *Persuasion,* the world enshrined in the *Baronetage* is beginning to collapse. Charles Musgrove is untitled but from the same class as Sir Walter, and good enough to marry his youngest daughter, though he has not the least deference for rank. "Don't talk to me about heirs and representatives," he tells Mary after she insists that he meet Mr. Elliot. "I am not one of those who neglect the reigning power to bow to the rising sun. . . . What is Mr. Elliot to me?" In the same way, when Sir Walter and Elizabeth decamp to Bath and the Crofts move in to Kellynch, Anne cannot "but in conscience feel that they were gone who deserved not to stay, and that Kellynch-hall had passed into better hands than its owners." It is a strikingly provocative assertion, especially given Austen's affection for the gentry in previous novels. But in *Persuasion* she changes course and throws her unqualified support behind the women and men of the navy. Their professionalism and commitment to the concept of a meritocracy constitute a thoroughgoing challenge to the distinctions of rank, while the warmth, patriotism, and courage that unite them stand in stark contrast to the fixation with class that has deformed the lives of the Elliots, with the exception of Anne. Sir Walter may survive his debt crisis in Bath and move back to Kellynch, but Austen's critique in *Persuasion* shows him to be bigoted, arrogant, and profoundly superfluous. He and others like him will remain in the *Baronetage,* but they are slipping steadily from the history books.

As rank binds and divides people, so do socially constructed notions of gender, and in *Persuasion* Austen boldly contends for a conception of men and women that sees them as equals rather than as occupants of two distinct spheres, with men committed to the public world of politics, war, economics, and adventure, and women relegated to the private sphere of purity, piety, and submissiveness. In the novel, role reversals abound, as women do men's work, men do women's work, and both sexes benefit. Lady Elliot was devoted to the domestic sphere—"her duties, her friends, and her children"—but she also performed the masculine role of managing the Kellynch estate, to its advantage and her own. Wentworth's good friend Captain Harville inhabits the public sphere as a sailor who fights and is wounded in the Napoleonic Wars. Yet when he returns to England he is also heavily involved in domestic concerns, for his "ingenious contrivances and nice arrangements . . . turn the actual space" of the family cottage "to the best possible account," and he spends a great deal of his time with his children, whom he loves and has missed terribly during his time away. Mrs. Croft is as feminine as she is expected to be: "a very well-spoken, genteel, shrewd lady," and "without any approach to coarseness." But she is also very much at home with a variety of concerns traditionally associated with men. When discussing the possibility of renting Kellynch with Sir Walter's agent Mr. Shepherd, she "asked more questions about the house, and terms, and taxes, than the admiral himself, and seemed more conversant with business." Out for a ride with the admiral in their carriage, she and her husband both have hold of the reins, but she has the firmer and cooler hand, and Anne imagines "their style of driving . . . no bad representation of the general guidance of their affairs." In a conversation with her brother Captain Wentworth, he dares to suggest that women do not belong aboard naval ships. Mrs. Croft quickly takes him to task. "I hate to hear you talking so, like a fine gentleman, and as if women were all fine ladies, instead of rational creatures," she tells him, before going on to declare that she has "crossed the Atlantic four times" and has been "once to the East Indies" with the admiral as he performed his duties in the Napoleonic Wars. Indeed, "the happiest part" of her life has been "spent on board a ship," and the only time in her marriage when she "really suffered in body or mind" was when she and the admiral were separated and she was confined at home, for during the winter that she passed by herself "at Deal, when the Admiral . . . was in the North Seas," she lived "in perpetual fright . . . and had all manner of imaginary complaints from not knowing what to do with myself, or when I should hear from him next." Mrs. Croft is a new woman who acts as her husband's collaborator, guide, supporter, and confidante—on the land and on the sea, in peacetime and in wartime, across private and public realms—and the admiral's relationship with her thrives as he redefines masculinity in terms that respect women as equals and that embrace partnership with them rather than power over them. At the close of his 1821 *Defence of Poetry,* Shelley declares that "poets are the unacknowledged legislators of the World."[12] Three years earlier in *Persuasion,* Austen endorses such a view. In Admiral and Mrs. Croft, she dismantles the notion of separate spheres for men and women and gives us the future of gender relations.

Wentworth and Anne have the Crofts' successful marriage before them as an example, but whereas the admiral and Sophia came swiftly to an understanding, Wentworth and Anne have to struggle much harder. Wentworth has deeply confused notions about love. He is confident when he returns to Kellynch that, when it comes to women and marriage, he has "thought on the subject more than most men." Yet after it is clear that he has allowed himself to become too closely involved with Louisa, he concedes that he has "not thought seriously on this subject before." Wentworth arrives at Kellynch with "a heart . . . for any pleasing young woman" who comes "in his way, excepting Anne Elliot." But it is plain almost from the start that she preoccupies him. When young Walter clambers up onto her back, Wentworth notices her distress and acts promptly to relieve it, coming up behind her and removing the child in a moment of close physical contact that leaves him avoiding conversation and her with "most disordered feelings." Again, on the hill above Winthrop, Wentworth declaims on the strength and richness of the hazelnut, and though speaking directly to Louisa, he is clearly thinking primarily of Anne and her willingness to end their engagement at the encouragement of others. "This nut," he tells Louisa, ". . . is still in possession of all the happiness that a hazel-nut can be supposed capable of. . . . My first wish for all, whom I am interested in, is that they should be firm." What is more, on the walk back to Uppercross, Wentworth spends his time alone with Louisa, and yet he also watches Anne closely enough to determine that she is tired and in need of a rest. When the party meets the Crofts and they offer Anne a ride, she demurs but they insist, and Wentworth, "without saying a word, turned to her, and quietly obliged her to be assisted into the carriage. . . . Yes,—he had done it. She was in the carriage, and felt that he had placed her there, that his will and his hands had done it."

It is another instance of Wentworth's seeking physical intimacy with Anne, and this time on the same walk in which he intensifies his interest in her chief rival. All may be fair in love and war. But while Wentworth is decisive in war, he works at cross-purposes in love, where he must battle "the blindness of his own pride, and the blunders of his own calculations," both of which greatly impede his attempts to understand Anne.

Wentworth's confusion over love may in part be derived from the fact that Austen bases him most clearly on Lord Nelson and Lord Byron, both of whom were notorious for their infidelities and *amours*.[13] Nelson, like Wentworth, came from modest beginnings, joined the navy at a young age, rose rapidly up the ranks, displayed great boldness in battle, and enjoyed impressive success capturing prize money. But Nelson was also infamous for his longstanding love affair with Lady Emma Hamilton when they were both married. Similarly, Byron stands behind Wentworth's restless and resentful individualism, as well as his proud, bright eyes and contemptuously curled lips, but he was equally well known for his many love affairs and turbulent domestic life. Indeed, as Austen wrote *Persuasion,* Byron's ill-fated marriage to Annabella Milbanke collapsed after less than a year, and he himself was hooted out of England as rumors swirled regarding his affair with his half-sister Augusta Leigh. Further, both the sailor and the poet shape Wentworth's declaration that "any body between fifteen and thirty may have me for asking," his simultaneous pursuit of both Louisa and her sister, Henrietta, and his painful disregard of the suffering he is causing Anne even as he subtly indicates that he is interested in her, too. As the authorial voice, Austen chastises Anne for her overwrought idealism concerning love and romance, but Anne is not the only romantic in *Persuasion.* Austen herself engages in a good deal of elevation and elision in order to turn Nelson and Byron into the faithful and domestic Wentworth, though the scandal that followed both men can still be felt in the portrait, and their presence adds a deeply unstable element to Wentworth's character.

Anne is in many ways no less confused about love than is Wentworth, for though she speaks eloquently of unswerving constancy, she too pursues her interest in others. To be sure, when she sees Wentworth again after eight years she is filled with longing: "the years which had destroyed her youth and bloom had only given him a more glowing, manly, open look." But when she meets Captain Benwick in Lyme, he also interests her, for even at the end of the very distressing day on which Louisa falls on the Cobb, Anne turns her thoughts to Benwick and "continuing their acquaintance," thoughts that stay with her when she travels back to Kellynch and cannot "return from any stroll of solitary indulgence in her father's grounds, or any visit of charity in the village, without wondering whether she might see him or hear of him." Anne is also attracted to Mr. Elliot, who gains a much firmer and deeper hold on her affections than Benwick, as she does on his, and this despite the fact that Anne views the lack of frankness in his character as "a decided imperfection": "Mr. Elliot was rational, discreet, polished,—but he was not open." Like Benwick, Mr. Elliot first catches her eye at Lyme, and she soon decides that "she should like to know who he was," a feeling that only increases when she—"smiling and blushing"—meets him again in Bath and begins to spend a good deal of time with him. He considers her "a most extraordinary young woman" and "a model of female excellence," opinions that Lady Russell quickly conveys to Anne, who "could not know herself to be so highly rated by a sensible man, without many of those agreeable sensations which her friend meant to create." Within weeks he and Captain Wentworth are virtually tied in her affections, as Mr. Elliot's "manners were so exactly what they ought to be, so polished, so easy, so particularly agreeable, that she could compare them in excellence to only one person's manners. They were not the same, but they were, perhaps, equally good." Shortly thereafter, in the concert room, Anne and Mr. Elliot flirt with each other in front of Wentworth (as he had done with Louisa in front of Anne), to the point where Anne cries, "For shame! for shame!—this is too much of flattery," and Mr. Elliot feels confident enough in her affections to float an informal proposal of marriage: "The name of Anne Elliot . . . has long had an interesting sound to me . . . and, if I dared, I would breathe my wishes that the name might never change."

Anne is as unguarded in her attachment to Mr. Elliot as Wentworth was in his to Louisa. Lady Russell watches them closely and is so encouraged by what she sees that she starts to angle for their marriage. During one conversation, she is particularly persuasive on the advantages of such a match, and Anne is "obliged to turn away, to rise, to walk to a distant table, and, leaning there in pretended employment, try to subdue the feelings this picture excited. For a few moments her imagination and her heart were bewitched. The idea of becoming what her mother had been; of having the precious name of 'Lady Elliot' first revived in herself; of being restored to Kellynch . . . was a charm which she could not immediately resist." Yet when Mrs. Smith announces to her that "all" her "acquaintance" consider her as intended for Mr. Elliot, Anne is surprised and announces flatly that she is "not going to marry" him, and that she "should like to know" why Mrs. Smith imagines that she is, even though she herself had been imagining that very circumstance only a short while before! Indeed, though she repeatedly protests otherwise, until Mrs. Smith exposes Mr. Elliot as "hollow and black," Anne can "just acknowledge within herself such a possibility of having been induced to marry him," a striking admission and one that presumably speaks to Lady Russell's enduring sway over her. Similarly, only a few days later Wentworth also confesses to her that he was almost certain that she and Mr. Elliot had reached an understanding, and that it was "agony" to watch them sitting together in the concert room, especially as Lady Russell was of their party, and he bitterly recalls what "her influence . . . had once done." Bafflingly, Anne assures him that he had nothing to worry about. "You should have distinguished," she instructs, ". . . . You should not have suspected me now; the case so different, and my age so different." But Wentworth was distinguishing, and he had good reason to be concerned. Anne does not know her own heart or her own situation as well as she claims she does, while Lady Russell exerts an influence on her that remains remarkably strong, and that can still move Anne to consider possibilities that would undermine both her own happiness and Wentworth's. According to David Monaghan, Anne "has achieved maturity by the time the novel opens."[14] On the contrary, she has as much to learn about love as Wentworth does, and her journey contains as much confusion as his.

Yet it is part of the enormous appeal of *Persuasion* that Wentworth and Anne seem destined for each other even as they wander from each other, and that the errors and misjudgments that define their relationship upon Wentworth's return from the war only heighten the enormous sense of relief that they and we feel when the reconciliation scene finally arrives. To a certain extent, it is difficult to blame either of them for the delay. *Persuasion* is a novel about the power of love, and while Wentworth believed in it when he first proposed to Anne, she decided they should part on the basis of her "conscience" and her "strong sense of duty." "She had been forced into prudence in her youth, she learned romance as she grew older—the natural sequel of an unnatural beginning." At the same time, however, it is difficult to blame Anne for enjoying the attention of handsome and available men, especially given Wentworth's interest in others, and the fact that she has been for so many years confined at—and isolated within—Kellynch. Yet even as their relationship founders, the two seem to recognize that they are connected to each other by what Harold Bloom characterizes as "something of an occult wavelength," for while they speak only on topics that do not transcend the trivial, they read each other's bodies and voices and minds with astonishing perceptiveness.[15] When during an evening at Uppercross Wentworth surveys his naval experience and discusses his various activities in 1806, Anne knows that he is also recalling that they met and separated in that same year, and she feels "the utter impossibility, from her knowledge of his mind, that he could be unvisited by remembrance any more than herself." Later that same evening, Wentworth and Mrs. Musgrove discuss Dick Musgrove's service aboard Wentworth's frigate, and while Wentworth does not speak of his displeasure with Dick, his "bright eye" and the "curl of his handsome mouth" convince Anne that "he had probably been at some pains to get rid of him." Anne can lock on to Wentworth's voice "in spite of all the various noises of the room, the almost ceaseless slam of the door, and ceaseless buzz of persons walking through," as Wentworth can lock on to hers when she speaks: "You sink your voice, but I can distinguish the tones of that voice, when they would be lost on others." Although they seem often to be moving in opposite directions, and in some instances even to feel justified in doing so, Anne and Wentworth are subtly in touch with one another almost from the moment of his return. In fact, in many ways they know each other better than they know themselves.

Their reunion is the most moving scene in all of Austen. They do not speak face to face, as Austen understood that mediated and misdirected messages frequently carry a far greater charge than explicit declarations. For eight and a half years, Anne has suffered in silence and spoken to no one about her grief over Wentworth. Now, in the White Hart Inn, as she and Harville look at a portrait of Benwick that is to be reset for Louisa in preparation for their upcoming nuptials, Harville mentions his dead sister Fanny, who had been engaged to Benwick less than a year earlier, and who had asked him to sit for the portrait as a present to her, though she did not live to see it and he seems to have forgotten about her with disarming ease. Anne and Harville agree that Fanny would not have forgotten Benwick so soon, but they take opposing sides in an ensuing discussion of men, women, and constancy. Although Anne responds to him in generalities, she also seizes the occasion to voice her very specific sadness, and before long eight years of pent-up anguish over Wentworth flood out of her. "We certainly do not forget you, so soon as you forget us," she tells Harville. "It is, perhaps, our fate rather than our merit. We cannot help ourselves. We live at home, quiet, confined, and our feelings prey upon us."

Wentworth, sitting nearby and writing a letter, overhears this conversation and knows immediately that Anne is revealing her deepest feelings of alienation and commitment. Seizing another sheet of paper, he begins a second letter, which records his feelings toward her as she utters hers toward him, and which he leaves behind on the desk for her to read. Ralph Waldo Emerson objected to Austen's novels because he found them "imprisoned in the wretched conventions of English society, without genius, wit, or knowledge of the world."[16] But Austen knew that love is the very largest concern of life, then as now, and in *Persuasion* she makes "all which this world" can do for

Anne hang on a single letter. It is a moment that demonstrates both the superb compression and the enormous appeal of her art, as well as the fundamental role that personal preference and individual desire play in the course of our lives. If Wentworth loves Anne, she has a future that stretches as far as the seas. If he does not, she has only a past that will steadily imprison her. She reads the letter. He does. Her joy is inexpressible, and so is ours. What is more, Austen has contrived to tell us both at the same time, and with a passionate frankness that far transcends the "wretched conventions of English society." "You pierce my soul," Wentworth's letter reads. "I am half agony, half hope. Tell me not that I am too late, that such precious feelings are gone for ever. I offer myself to you again with a heart even more your own, than when you almost broke it eight years and a half ago." Anne is overwhelmed. Over the course of the novel she has been transformed, from faded to blooming, from nobody to somebody, from "only Anne" within her family to Wentworth's "only Anne." He approaches her a few moments after she finishes his letter, and they are reunited.

It will not, however, be simply clear sailing from this moment forward. Even after all the grief of the past, Anne is still convinced that she was "perfectly right" to follow Lady Russell's advice and reject Wentworth's first proposal, though she makes it plain that if he had asked her again two years later she would have instantly accepted him. "Anne is steadfast in refusing to apologize," Claudia Johnson points out, and her certainty about her own behavior sits awkwardly beside Wentworth's willingness to adapt his.[17] Further, Anne and Wentworth must face almost immediate alarm, for as they reconcile and plan their life together, Napoleon breaks from Elba and marches toward Paris to begin his "Hundred Days" of rule. Anne glories "in being a sailor's wife," but the present is uncertain, and the "dread of a future war" there to "dim her sunshine."

Charlotte Brontë disparaged *Persuasion* because she felt it lacked the fast and full throb of our inner lives. But in 1862 the novelist and biographer Julia Kavanagh saw much more clearly when she astutely linked it to Brontë's own *Jane Eyre.* In *Persuasion,* Kavanagh argued, "we see the first genuine picture of that silent torture of an unloved woman, condemned to suffer thus because she is a woman and must not speak, and which, many years later, was wakened into such passionate eloquence by the author of *Jane Eyre*. Subdued though the picture is in Miss Austen's pages, it is not the less keen, not the less painful."[18] Anne's devotion to Wentworth sustains and haunts her through years of sorrow, while her shimmering sense of her own integrity enables her to rise above the insensitivity and superciliousness of those around her, as her frequent disregard for the injunctions of rank and gender allow her a more unfettered pursuit of her own happiness. Her second chance with Wentworth is perplexed by miscalculations and by attractions to others, as his is with her. But while these forces separate them for several months, the strength of their initial love and their ability to remain committed to it at the deepest levels, even as they entertain the possibility of relationships with other people, enact a peculiarly modern distress: amid whirling cultural changes and vast shifts in the political and social landscape, our best alternative is to devote our most vital energies to an intense personal relationship such as Anne has with Wentworth, a relationship that structures and redeems our lives even as it concentrates them in ways that leave us dreadfully vulnerable. *Persuasion* is Austen's saddest and most impassioned novel, and in its blend of the public and the personal it explores both the anguish of silence and the value of hope.

Notes

1 "Charlotte Brontë on Jane Austen," in *Jane Austen: The Critical Heritage,* ed. B. C. Southam (London: Routledge and Kegan Paul, 1968), 128.

2 *The Letters of Percy Bysshe Shelley,* ed. Frederick L. Jones, 2 vols. (Oxford: Clarendon Press, 1964), I, 504.

3 "Buonaparte," in the *Times,* Tuesday, August 8, 1815, p. 3, issue 9594, col. E; Deirdre Le Faye, *A Chronology of Jane Austen and Her Family* (Cambridge: Cambridge University Press, 2006), 513.

4 V. S. Pritchett, *George Meredith and English Comedy* (London: Chatto and Windus, 1970), 28.

5 Adela Pinch, "Lost in a Book: Jane Austen's *Persuasion,*" in *Studies in Romanticism,* 32 (1993), 99.

6 J. E. Austen-Leigh, *A Memoir of Jane Austen and Other Family Recollections,* ed. Kathryn Sutherland (Oxford: Oxford University Press, 2002), 18.

7 *Jane Austen's Letters,* ed. Deirdre Le Faye, 3rd ed. (Oxford: Oxford University Press, 1995), 94–95.

8 "Copy of part of a letter from G. D. Boyle, Vicar of Kidderminster," in Austen-Leigh, *A Memoir of Jane Austen and Other Family Recollections,* 197; Elizabeth Bowen, "Jane Austen," in *The English Novelists,* ed. Derek Verschoyle (New York: Harcourt, Brace, 1936), 110.

9 Virginia Woolf, "Jane Austen," in *The Essays of Virginia Woolf,* ed. Andrew McNeillie and Stuart N. Clarke, 5 vols. (London: The Hogarth Press, 1986–), IV, 154.

10 Judith Prewitt Brown, *Jane Austen's Novels: Social Change and Literary Form* (Cambridge, MA: Harvard University Press, 1979), 128–129.

11 Rebecca West, "Preface," in Jane Austen, *Northanger Abbey* (London: Jonathan Cape, 1932), vii.

12 *Shelley's Poetry and Prose,* ed. Donald H. Reiman and Neil Fraistat (New York: Norton, 2002), 535.

13 Jocelyn Harris, *A Revolution Almost Beyond Expression: Jane Austen's "Persuasion"* (Newark: University of Delaware Press, 2007), 91–108.

14 David Monaghan, "The Decline of the Gentry: A Study of Jane Austen's Attitude to Formality in *Persuasion,"* in *Studies in the Novel,* 7 (1975), 76.

15 Harold Bloom, *The Western Canon* (New York: Harcourt, Brace, 1994), 254.

16 *Emerson in His Journals,* ed. Joel Porte (Cambridge, MA: Belknap Press of Harvard University Press, 1982), 495.

17 Claudia Johnson, *Jane Austen: Women, Politics, and the Novel* (Chicago: University of Chicago Press, 1988), 155.

18 "Julia Kavanagh on Jane Austen," in *Jane Austen: The Critical Heritage,* 195.

Abbreviations

Auerbach	Emily Auerbach, *Searching for Jane Austen* (Madison: University of Wisconsin Press, 2004)
Austen, *Letters*	*Jane Austen's Letters,* ed. Deirdre Le Faye, 3rd ed. (Oxford: Oxford University Press, 1995)
Austen-Leigh, *Memoir*	J. E. Austen-Leigh, *A Memoir of Jane Austen and Other Family Recollections,* ed. Kathryn Sutherland (Oxford: Oxford University Press, 2002)
Brown	Julia Prewitt Brown, *Jane Austen's Novels: Social Change and Literary Form* (Cambridge, MA: Harvard University Press, 1979)
Brydges, *Autobiography*	*The Autobiography, Times, Opinions, and Contemporaries of Sir Egerton Brydges,* 2 vols. (London: Cochrane and M'Crone, 1834)
Buchan	William Buchan, *Domestic Medicine, A New and Enlarged Edition* (Edinburgh: Nelson, 1820)
Bush	Douglas Bush, *Jane Austen* (New York: Macmillan, 1975)
Butler	Marilyn Butler, *Jane Austen and the War of Ideas* (Oxford: Clarendon Press, 1975)
Byron, *Poetical Works*	*Lord Byron: The Complete Poetical Works,* ed. Jerome McGann, 7 vols. (Oxford: Clarendon Press, 1980–1993)

Cecil	David Cecil, *A Portrait of Jane Austen* (London: Book Club Associates, 1978)
Collins	Irene Collins, *Jane Austen and the Clergy* (London: The Hambledon Press, 1994)
Critical Heritage	*Jane Austen: The Critical Heritage,* ed. B. C. Southam (London: Routledge and Kegan Paul, 1968)
Deresiewicz	William Deresiewicz, *Jane Austen and the Romantic Poets* (New York: Columbia University Press, 2004)
Duffy	Joseph Duffy, "Structure and Idea in Jane Austen's *Persuasion,*" in *Nineteenth-Century Fiction,* 8 (1953–1954), 272–289
Edgeworth, *Works*	*The Novels and Selected Works of Maria Edgeworth,* gen. ed. Marilyn Butler, 12 vols. (London: Pickering and Chatto, 1999–2003)
Egan	Pierce Egan, *Walks Through Bath* (Bath: Meyler, 1819)
Feltham	John Feltham, *A Guide to All the Watering and Sea-Bathing Places . . . A New and Improved Edition* (London: Longman, Hurst, Rees, Orme, and Brown, 1815)
Felton	William Felton, *A Treatise on Carriages,* 2 vols. (London: Felton, 1794)
Gomme	Andor Gomme, "On Not Being Persuaded," in *Essays in Criticism,* 16 (1966), 170–184
Grey	*The Jane Austen Handbook,* ed. J. David Grey (London: The Athlone Press, 1986)
Harris	Jocelyn Harris, *A Revolution Almost Beyond Expression: Jane Austen's "Persuasion"* (Newark: University of Delaware Press, 2007)
Hazlitt, *Works*	*The Complete Works of William Hazlitt,* ed. P. P. Howe, 21 vols. (London: Dent, 1930–1934)

Hopkins	Robert Hopkins, "Moral Luck and Judgement in Jane Austen's *Persuasion*," in *Nineteenth-Century Literature,* 42 (1987), 143–158
Johnson	Claudia Johnson, *Jane Austen: Women, Politics, and the Novel* (Chicago: University of Chicago Press, 1988)
Johnson, *Rambler*	*The Rambler,* in *The Yale Edition of the Works of Samuel Johnson, Volumes III, IV, V,* ed. W. J. Bate and Albrecht B. Strauss (New Haven: Yale University Press, 1969)
Lavery	Brian Lavery, *Nelson's Navy: The Ships, Men and Organisation, 1793–1815* (London: Naval Institute Press, 1995)
Mansford	John Mansford, *The Invalid's Companion to Bath* (Bath: Meyler and Son, 1820)
OED	*Oxford English Dictionary*
Phillips	M. Phillips, *Picture of Lyme-Regis, and Environs* (Lyme-Regis: Tucker and Toms, 1817)
Pope	*The Twickenham Edition of the Poems of Alexander Pope,* gen. ed. John Butt, 11 vols. (London: Methuen, 1938–1968)
Richardson, *Grandison*	Samuel Richardson, *Sir Charles Grandison,* ed. Jocelyn Harris, 3 vols. (Oxford: Oxford University Press, 1972)
Sales	Roger Sales, *Jane Austen and Representations of Regency England* (London: Routledge, 1994)
Smith, *Works*	*The Works of Charlotte Smith,* gen. ed. Stuart Curran, 14 vols. (London: Pickering and Chatto, 2005–2007)
Smollett, *Humphry Clinker*	Tobias Smollett, *The Expedition of Humphry Clinker,* ed. Thomas R. Preston (Athens: University of Georgia Press, 1990)
Southam	Brian Southam, *Jane Austen and the Navy* (London: Hambledon and London, 2000)

Tanner	Tony Tanner, *Jane Austen* (Cambridge, MA: Harvard University Press, 1986)
Tave	Stuart Tave, *Some Words of Jane Austen* (Chicago: University of Chicago Press, 1973)
Tomalin	Claire Tomalin, *Jane Austen: A Life* (London: Viking, 1997)
Trusler	John Trusler, *A System of Etiquette* (Bath: Meyler, 1804)
Waldron	Mary Waldron, *Jane Austen and the Fiction of Her Time* (Cambridge: Cambridge University Press, 1999)
Wiltshire	John Wiltshire, *Jane Austen and the Body* (Cambridge: Cambridge University Press, 1992)
Wollstonecraft, *Works*	*The Collected Works of Mary Wollstonecraft,* ed. Marilyn Butler and Janet Todd, 7 vols. (London: Pickering and Chatto, 1989)

Volume I

I

Sir Walter Elliot, of Kellynch-hall, in Somersetshire,[1] was a man who, for his own amusement, never took up any book but the Baronetage;[2] there he found occupation for an idle hour, and consolation in a distressed one; there his faculties were roused into admiration and respect, by contemplating the limited remnant of the earliest patents;[3] there any unwelcome sensations, arising from domestic affairs, changed naturally into pity and contempt, as he turned over the almost endless creations of the last century[4]—and there, if every other leaf were powerless, he could read his own history with an interest which never failed—this was the page at which the favourite volume always opened:

"Elliot of Kellynch-hall.
"Walter Elliot, born March 1, 1760, married, July 15, 1784, Elizabeth, daughter of James Stevenson, Esq. of South Park, in the county of Gloucester;[5] by which lady (who died 1800)[6] he has issue Elizabeth, born June 1, 1785; Anne, born August 9, 1787; a still-born son, Nov. 5, 1789;[7] Mary, born Nov. 20, 1791."

Precisely such had the paragraph originally stood from the printer's hands; but Sir Walter had improved it by adding, for the information of himself and his family, these words, after the date of Mary's birth—"married, Dec. 16,[8] 1810, Charles, son and heir of Charles Musgrove,[9] Esq. of Uppercross, in the county of Somerset,"—and by inserting most accurately the day of the month on which he had lost his wife.

1 Somersetshire is a county in southwestern England, bordered on the northwest by the Bristol Channel. Kellynch-hall is fictional.

2 King James I of England (1566–1625) created the baronetage in 1611, ostensibly as a means of raising funds for a war in Ireland. It is a hereditary dignity, but one at the lower end of the aristocratic hierarchy, Sir Walter's enormous pride in the title notwithstanding. Baronets were ranked above knights but below barons and were technically classed as commoners (not members of the peerage). Several lists and accounts of the baronets of England were published from the late seventeenth century onward, but the reference here is most likely to the *Baronetage of England* (1808), a two-volume edition published by John Debrett (*d.* 1822).

3 "Titles" were also referred to as "patents." Sir Walter is full of "admiration and respect" for the families whose titles date back to the early seventeenth century, though he acknowledges that of these families, only a "limited remnant" endures.

4 The "almost endless creations of the last century" refer to those peers and baronets whose titles were created in the eighteenth century. Sir Thomas Bertram in *Mansfield Park* (1814) may well be one of them. Many of these men came from the lower ranks of society, and their ascension to the peerage was a source of considerable irritation to conservatives such as Sir Walter Elliot. Austen may have based Sir Walter in part on Sir Egerton Brydges (1762–1837), a man of literary and antiquarian interests, who was the brother of Austen's

favorite mentor and close friend Anne Lefroy (1749–1804). Like Sir Walter, Sir Egerton combines supercilious attitudes with a keen interest in physical appearances. "When I knew Jane Austen I never suspected that she was an authoress," he declared with typical pomposity; "but my eyes told me that she was fair and handsome, slight and elegant, but with cheeks a little too full. The last time I think that I saw her was at Ramsgate in 1803: perhaps she was then about twenty-seven years old. Even then I did not know that she was addicted to literary composition." Sir Egerton also aligns himself with Sir Walter when he grumbles about "the greater part of the men who have been advanced from nothing in the last fifty years—they are a miserable set—they have neither had virtues, nor talents, nor knowledge, nor even manners. The nobility who take a leading part in society and public business are almost all new nobility." In 1818 Sir Egerton fled to the continent because he—like Sir Walter—was deeply in debt (Brydges, *Autobiography,* II, 41, 49).

5　Gloucester is a county in southwestern England, lying at the head of the River Severn estuary on the Welsh border.

6　If, as Austen states later in this chapter, Elizabeth was sixteen and Anne was fourteen when their mother died, this date should be "1801." Thus thirteen years have passed since Lady Elliot's death. Sir Walter is now fifty-four years old. Elizabeth is twenty-nine, Anne has just turned twenty-seven, and Mary is twenty-two.

7　The death of Sir Walter's only son falls on a highly charged date that conflates at least two different political events, both of which threatened England's monarchy and its landed Protestant elites. On November 5, 1605, English Roman Catholics including Guy Faux attempted to blow up the parliament buildings and kill James I. In 1789, a mob stormed the Bastille prison in Paris, touching off the French Revolution and plunging Europe into war until 1815.

8　This date is one of several private jokes in the novel. Austen's birthday was December 16.

9　Musgrove is a name that Austen clearly liked for fictional purposes, as she employed it in the fifth of her *Collection of Letters,* which was written as early as 1791, and which centers on the Musgrove family.

10　Cheshire is a county in northwestern England, bordering Wales to the west.

11　Austen's reference is to the medievalist and antiquary Sir William Dugdale (1605–1686) and his *Antient Usage in Bearing of such Ensigns of Honour as are commonly call'd ARMS. With a Catalogue of the present NOBILITY of England* (1682). In the section entitled "Catalogue of the Baronets of this *Kingdom* of England; From the first Erection of that Dignity until the 4th of *July* 1681 inclusive," Dugdale is particularly concerned with distinguishing between authentic and bogus claims to the honor of baronet, for "no person whatsoever ought to take upon them this Title of dignity, but such as have been really advanced thereto by Letters Patent under the great Seale of England." It is thus especially important to Sir Walter to be "mentioned in Dugdale."

12　The "High Sheriff" was the Crown's chief officer within a county and was elected from among the principal landowners. He was in charge of elections and the administration of justice.

13　The "ancient and respectable" Elliot family was awarded a baronetcy in 1660, the year Charles II (1630–1685) became king of Great Britain and Ireland. During his reign, Charles II created 408 baronets, far more than his grandfather James I, who created 204, and his father, Charles I (1600–1649), who created 250.

14　"Duodecimo pages" were small (approximately four-by-seven inches) and were formed by folding a large printer's sheet into twelve sections.

15　In *Pride and Prejudice* (1813), Mrs. Bennet tells her husband, "I do think it is the hardest thing in the world, that your estate should be entailed away from your own children" (I, 13). Sir Walter's annotation indicates that his estate, too, is entailed away, meaning that it is subject to strict settlement in the male line. William Walter Elliot is a distant relation, but as the most senior male in the Elliot family after Sir Walter, he legally supplants Elizabeth, Anne, and Mary and is heir to Kellynch-hall. In his seminal treatise *The Wealth of Nations* (1776), the Scottish philosopher and economist

Then followed the history and rise of the ancient and respectable family, in the usual terms: how it had been first settled in Cheshire;[10] how mentioned in Dugdale[11]—serving the office of High Sheriff,[12] representing a borough in three successive parliaments, exertions of loyalty, and dignity of baronet, in the first year of Charles II.,[13] with all the Marys and Elizabeths they had married; forming altogether two handsome duodecimo pages,[14] and concluding with the arms and motto: "Principal seat, Kellynch hall, in the county of Somerset," and Sir Walter's hand-writing again in this finale:

"Heir presumptive,[15] William Walter Elliot, Esq., great grandson of the second Sir Walter."[16]

Vanity was the beginning and the end of Sir Walter Elliot's character; vanity of person and of situation.[17] He had been remarkably handsome in his youth; and, at fifty-four, was still a very fine man. Few women could think more of their personal appearance than he did; nor could the valet of any new made lord be more delighted with the place he held in society. He considered the blessing of beauty as

Haldon Hall, near Exeter, by Francis Towne (1739–1816), 1780. Kellynch Hall is fictional, but it may well have resembled a home such as Haldon Hall.

Adam Smith (1723–1790) pointedly condemns entails as "the natural consequences of the law of primogeniture," which stipulate that "the male sex is universally preferred to the female," and "the elder everywhere takes place of the younger," for "nothing can be more contrary to the real interest of a numerous family, than a right which, in order to enrich one, beggars all the rest of the children" (Smith, *The Wealth of Nations,* eds. R. H. Campbell and A. S. Skinner, 2 vols. [Oxford: Clarendon Press, 1976], I, 383–384).

16 Walter Scott (1771–1832) was the most popular novelist of Austen's age, and Austen begins *Persuasion* by comically rewriting an early scene from Scott's enormously influential first novel, *Waverley* (1814). As Sir Walter pours over the *Baronetage,* so too does Scott's baronet Sir Everard Waverley examine "the tree of his genealogy, which, emblazoned with many an emblematic mark of honour and heroic achievement, hung upon the well-varnished wainscot of his hall. The nearest descendants of Sir Hildebrand Waverley, failing those of his eldest son Wilfred, of whom Sir Everard and his brother were the only representatives, were, as this honoured register informed him, (and indeed as he himself well knew) the Waverleys of Highley Park, com. Hants; with whom the main branch, or rather stock, of the house had renounced all connection since the great law-suit in 1670" (Harris, 112–113; Walter Scott, *Waverley,* ed. Peter Garside [Edinburgh: Edinburgh University Press, 2007], 8).

17 Vanity was frequently censured in contemporary political and moral tracts, and in ways that clearly suggest Sir Walter's shortcomings. "In a small degree, and conversant in little things, vanity is of little moment," the great political philosopher and orator Edmund Burke (1729–1797) observed in his *Letter to a Member of the National Assembly* (1791), which he wrote amid a deepening crisis over the direction of the French Revolution. But when "full grown, it is the worst of vices, and the occasional mimick of them all. It makes the whole man false. It leaves nothing sincere or trustworthy about him. His best qualities are poisoned and perverted by it, and operate exactly as the worst." Similarly, the novelist and essayist Elizabeth Hamilton (c. 1756–1816) asked pointedly, "Does [vanity] sympathize

in the sorrows of the afflicted? Does it glow with the honest warmth of gratitude? Is it capable of making a generous sacrifice for another's good?" Her response was blunt: "No: Vanity, so far from partaking of these characteristics of benevolence, is ever *cold* and *selfish,* alike incapable of tender sympathy and generous affection" (*The Writings and Speeches of Edmund Burke: The French Revolution, 1790–1794,* ed. L. G. Mitchell [Oxford: Clarendon Press, 1989], 313; Hamilton, *Letters on the Elementary Principles of Education,* 6th ed., 2 vols. [London: Baldwin, Cradock, and Joy, 1818], I, 128).

What is more, Sir Walter's vanity aligns him with dandies such as George "Beau" Brummell (1778–1840), who made physical appearance an important societal concern during the Regency (1811–1820). Sir Walter lacks Brummell's youth and especially his wit, but he shares with him an enormous conceit about his own person, as well as an inability to stay out of debt. Roger Sales also allies Sir Walter with the future George IV (1762–1830), who was for many years a close friend of Brummell's, and who acted as prince regent during the time frame of *Persuasion.* "The head of the estate, or state, cares more for complexions and capes than he does about the great issues of war and peace," Sales remarks. "He is hopelessly in debt but is much more concerned with the arrangement of hair than with the fact that the war may have had a profound effect on social arrangements. There are clear echoes and reminders throughout of the world of the Regent and Brummell" (Sales, 178).

18 Sir Walter is deeply enamored of "his good looks and his rank," and while these "attachments" are at the heart of his overmastering vanity, they also have one positive "claim," for they turned the youthful head of the "excellent woman" who became his wife, despite the large gap between her "very superior character" and his own.

19 "Awful" here means "terrible," "dreadful," "awe-inspiring."

20 As Sir Walter has three daughters, some editors have amended "daughter's" to "daughters'." But the location of the apostrophe is probably correct, for it is clear that he values only Elizabeth.

Elizabeth Hamilton, by Henry Meyer (circa 1782–1847), after Sir Henry Raeburn (1756–1823), circa 1812. In 1813, Austen heard a rumor that *Sense and Sensibility* was attributed to Hamilton. The news did not trouble her: "It is pleasant to have such a respectable Writer named," she said (Austen, *Letters,* 252).

inferior only to the blessing of a baronetcy; and the Sir Walter Elliot, who united these gifts, was the constant object of his warmest respect and devotion.

His good looks and his rank had one fair claim on his attachment; since to them he must have owed a wife of very superior character to any thing deserved by his own.[18] Lady Elliot had been an excellent woman, sensible and amiable; whose judgment and conduct, if they might be pardoned the youthful infatuation which made her Lady Elliot, had never required indulgence afterwards.—She had humoured, or softened, or concealed his failings, and promoted his real respectability for seventeen years; and though not the very happiest being in the world herself, had found enough in her duties, her friends, and her children, to attach her to life, and make it no matter of indifference to her when she was called on to quit them.—Three girls, the two eldest sixteen and fourteen, was an awful[19] legacy for a mother to bequeath; an awful charge rather, to confide to the authority and guidance of a conceited, silly father. She had, however, one very intimate friend, a sensible, deserving woman, who had been brought, by strong attachment to herself, to settle close by her, in the village of Kellynch; and on her kindness and advice, Lady Elliot mainly relied for the best help and maintenance of the good principles and instruction which she had been anxiously giving her daughters.

This friend, and Sir Walter, did *not* marry, whatever might have been anticipated on that head by their acquaintance.—Thirteen years had passed away since Lady Elliot's death, and they were still near neighbours and intimate friends; and one remained a widower, the other a widow.

That Lady Russell, of steady age and character, and extremely well provided for, should have no thought of a second marriage, needs no apology to the public, which is rather apt to be unreasonably discontented when a woman *does* marry again, than when she does *not;* but Sir Walter's continuing in singleness requires explanation.—Be it known then, that Sir Walter, like a good father, (having met with one or two private disappointments in very unreasonable applications) prided himself on remaining single for his dear daughter's sake.[20] For one daughter, his eldest, he would really have given up any thing, which he had not been very much tempted to do. Elizabeth had succeeded, at sixteen, to all that was possible, of her mother's rights and consequence;[21] and being very handsome, and very like himself, her influence had always been great, and they had gone on together most happily. His two other children were of very inferior value. Mary had acquired a little artificial importance, by becoming Mrs. Charles Musgrove; but Anne, with an elegance of mind and sweetness of character, which must have placed her high with any people of real understanding, was nobody with either father or sister: her

21 Following her mother's death, Elizabeth would be regarded as Sir Walter's "lady," meaning that she would preside over his dinner table, superintend the running of his household, and accompany him to social events.

Sir Egerton Brydges, from an unattributed engraving. Brydges wrote novels such as *Mary de Clifford* (1792) and *Arthur Fitz-Albini* (1798), but he is best known for his self-serving *Autobiography* (1834). Austen read *Arthur Fitz-Albini* shortly after it appeared and was unimpressed: "There is very little story, and what there is told in a strange, unconnected way" (Austen, *Letters,* 22).

22 Amy King writes that "we might today assume that bloom is simply a reference to complexion, health, or physical beauty," but in fact in Austen's day it also carried connotations of courtship and sexual attractiveness, so that Anne's "lack of bloom" means, in effect, the "lack of a marriage plot." Seven months after completing *Persuasion,* Austen asserted of herself, "I must not depend upon being ever very blooming again" (King, *Bloom: The Botanical Vernacular in the English Novel* [New York: Oxford University Press, 2003], 5; Austen, *Letters,* 335–336). Compare *Sense and Sensibility* (1811), where Elinor tells John Dashwood that Marianne has been suffering from "a nervous complaint." "I am sorry for that," he replies. "At her time of life, any thing of an illness destroys the bloom for ever!" (II, 11).

23 Anne would appear on another page of the *Baronetage* if she married a baronet, for her name would then be listed under her husband's family's name as well.

24 "Miss Elliot" identifies Elizabeth specifically as the eldest daughter. As a younger daughter, Anne would usually be addressed as "Miss Anne Elliot," though she herself is sometimes called "Miss Elliot" when Elizabeth is absent or not the subject of conversation, or "Miss Anne," as a "convenient half-way stage towards informality" (K. C. Phillipps, *Jane Austen's English* [London: Deutsch, 1970], 209).

25 "Worsting" means that it is "getting worse."

26 The chaise was an enclosed carriage drawn by four horses. The vehicle could be powered by two horses, but Sir Walter delights in extravagance.

word had no weight; her convenience was always to give way;—she was only Anne.

To Lady Russell, indeed, she was a most dear and highly valued god-daughter, favourite and friend. Lady Russell loved them all; but it was only in Anne that she could fancy the mother to revive again.

A few years before, Anne Elliot had been a very pretty girl, but her bloom had vanished early;[22] and as even in its height, her father had found little to admire in her, (so totally different were her delicate features and mild dark eyes from his own); there could be nothing in them now that she was faded and thin, to excite his esteem. He had never indulged much hope, he had now none, of ever reading her name in any other page of his favourite work.[23] All equality of alliance must rest with Elizabeth; for Mary had merely connected herself with an old country family of respectability and large fortune, and had therefore *given* all the honour, and received none: Elizabeth would, one day or other, marry suitably.

It sometimes happens, that a woman is handsomer at twenty-nine than she was ten years before; and, generally speaking, if there has been neither ill health nor anxiety, it is a time of life at which scarcely any charm is lost. It was so with Elizabeth; still the same handsome Miss Elliot[24] that she had begun to be thirteen years ago; and Sir Walter might be excused, therefore, in forgetting her age, or, at least, be deemed only half a fool, for thinking himself and Elizabeth as blooming as ever, amidst the wreck of the good looks of every body else; for he could plainly see how old all the rest of his family and acquaintance were growing. Anne haggard, Mary coarse, every face in the neighbourhood worsting;[25] and the rapid increase of the crow's foot about Lady Russell's temples had long been a distress to him.

Elizabeth did not quite equal her father in personal contentment. Thirteen years had seen her mistress of Kellynch Hall, presiding and directing with a self-possession and decision which could never have given the idea of her being younger than she was. For thirteen years had she been doing the honours, and laying down the domestic law at home, and leading the way to the chaise and four,[26] and walking

The prince regent, oil on canvas, by Thomas Lawrence (1769–1830), circa 1814.
Sir Walter is only two years older than the regent and shares with him many of the
qualities associated with dandyism.

27 Elizabeth follows Lady Russell out of the room because the exacting rules of social etiquette dictate that the daughter of a baronet ranks below the wife of a knight (Charles Roger Dod, *A Manual of Dignities, Privilege, and Precedence* [London: Whittaker, 1843], 83–84). Much of the action of the novel is governed by similarly strict rules of behavior and decorum. Here, and throughout *Persuasion,* "country" means "county" or "neighborhood."

28 Country dances were led by the couple of the highest rank. As Sir Walter is the only baronet in the neighborhood, and both he and Lady Russell are too old for dancing, the honor of opening the proceedings falls to Elizabeth and her partner.

29 "Shewn" is an obsolete form of "shown."

30 Sir Walter and Elizabeth journey to London to enjoy the "season," a fashionable round of plays, balls, concerts, and sporting events that took place each spring.

31 In 1766, Richard Tattersall (circa 1725–1795) founded a horse auction mart near Hyde Park Corner. It became the leading place for fashionable men to buy, sell, and bet on horses. In 1798, the dramatist and novelist Thomas Holcroft (1745–1809) "went to Tattersall's" and found "the usual group there of horse-dealers, jockeys, and gentlemen" (Hazlitt, *Works,* III, 172).

32 Sir Walter's appearance in the House of Commons may suggest that, like some of his ancestors, he is a member of Parliament.

33 This passage on Elizabeth, Mr. Elliot, and mourning has elicited a good deal of commentary. The published text reads "she was at this present time . . . wearing black ribbons for his wife," and various critics and editors have labored to explain why Elizabeth would be in mourning for her estranged cousin's dead wife. John E. Grant cuts the Gordian knot by arguing that "she" is a misprint for "he," and that it is Mr. Elliot, and not Elizabeth, who is in mourning. As Grant points out, "the paragraph in question begins by declaring the 'anger' still felt by Elizabeth and the very sentence which appears to declare that Elizabeth was in mourn-

immediately after Lady Russell out of all the drawing-rooms and dining-rooms in the country.[27] Thirteen winters' revolving frosts had seen her opening every ball of credit[28] which a scanty neighbourhood afforded; and thirteen springs shewn[29] their blossoms, as she travelled up to London with her father, for a few weeks annual enjoyment of the great world.[30] She had the remembrance of all this; she had the consciousness of being nine-and-twenty, to give her some regrets and some apprehensions. She was fully satisfied of being still quite as handsome as ever; but she felt her approach to the years of danger, and would have rejoiced to be certain of being properly solicited by baronet-blood within the next twelvemonth or two. Then might she again take up the book of books with as much enjoyment as in her early youth; but now she liked it not. Always to be presented with the date of her own birth, and see no marriage follow but that of a youngest sister, made the book an evil; and more than once, when her father had left it open on the table near her, had she closed it, with averted eyes, and pushed it away.

She had had a disappointment, moreover, which that book, and especially the history of her own family, must ever present the remembrance of. The heir presumptive, the very William Walter Elliot, Esq. whose rights had been so generously supported by her father, had disappointed her.

She had, while a very young girl, as soon as she had known him to be, in the event of her having no brother, the future baronet, meant to marry him; and her father had always meant that she should. He had not been known to them as a boy, but soon after Lady Elliot's death Sir Walter had sought the acquaintance, and though his overtures had not been met with any warmth, he had persevered in seeking it, making allowance for the modest drawing back of youth; and in one of their spring excursions to London, when Elizabeth was in her first bloom, Mr. Elliot had been forced into the introduction.

He was at that time a very young man, just engaged in the study of the law; and Elizabeth found him extremely agreeable, and every plan in his favour was confirmed. He was invited to Kellynch Hall; he was talked of and expected all the rest of the year; but he never came. The following spring he was seen again in town, found equally agreeable, again encouraged, invited and expected, and again he did not come; and the next tidings were that he was married. Instead of pushing his fortune in the line marked out for the heir of the house of Elliot, he had purchased independence by uniting himself to a rich woman of inferior birth.

Sir Walter had resented it. As the head of the house, he felt that he ought to have been consulted, especially after taking the young man so publicly by the hand: "For they must have been seen together," he observed, "once at Tattersal's,[31] and twice in the lobby of the House of Commons."[32] His disapprobation was expressed, but apparently very little regarded. Mr. Elliot had attempted no apology, and shewn himself as unsolicitous of being longer noticed by the family, as Sir Walter considered him unworthy of it: all acquaintance between them had ceased.

This very awkward history of Mr. Elliot, was still, after an interval of several years, felt with anger by Elizabeth, who had liked the man for himself, and still more for being her father's heir, and whose strong family pride could see only in *him,* a proper match for Sir Walter Elliot's eldest daughter. There was not a baronet from A to Z, whom her feelings could have so willingly acknowledged as an equal. Yet so miserably had he conducted himself, that though he[33] was at this present time, (the summer of 1814,)[34] wearing black ribbons for his wife, she could not admit him to be worth thinking of again. The disgrace of his first marriage might, perhaps, as there was no reason to suppose it perpetuated by offspring, have been got over, had he not done worse; but he had, as by the accustomary intervention of kind friends they had been informed, spoken most disrespectfully of them all, most slightingly and contemptuously of the very blood he belonged to, and the honours which were hereafter to be his own. This could not be pardoned.

Such were Elizabeth Elliot's sentiments and sensations; such the cares to alloy, the agitations to vary, the sameness and the elegance, the prosperity and the nothingness, of her scene of life—such the feelings to give interest to a long, uneventful residence in one country circle, to fill the vacancies which there were no habits of utility abroad, no talents or accomplishments for home, to occupy.

ing for the dead wife of Mr. Elliot also states that 'she could not admit him to be worth thinking of again.' Together, these statements are hardly compatible with Elizabeth's alleged show of mourning." Grant concedes that it is possible that the customs of mourning within an extended family occupying the Elliots station in life "might be so stipulative that Elizabeth would be obligated to exhibit signs of mourning for the loss of a male relative's wife." But "is it not immensely more probable . . . that Elizabeth would never condescend to recognize the loss suffered by her unworthy, almost unspeakable, cousin?" Grant asks. "What could be gained by the Elliot family in this tiny community by observing mourning for a bereaved relative who did not reside there, who seems indeed never to have visited there, though he was eventually to inherit Kellynch? Does it not become certain that the Elliots of Kellynch-Hall are too proud to seem to care? Would not Sir Walter himself have to set the pattern of family mourning for his heir apparent? Can we suppose that the second daughter, Anne, would not join in the observance of family mourning in the unlikely event that her sister did?" The answers to these questions seem to me to demonstrate convincingly that "she" is a misprint, and that it is Mr. Elliot who is "wearing black ribbons." I have amended the text accordingly (John E. Grant, "Shows of Mourning in the Text of Jane Austen's *Persuasion,*" in *Modern Philology,* 80 [1983], 284–285).

34 The summer of 1814 was a remarkable moment of false security. Napoleon Bonaparte (1769–1821) abdicated as emperor of the French in April 1814 and was exiled to the island of Elba. A month later France and the Allies (including Great Britain, Prussia, and Russia) signed the first Treaty of Paris, restoring peace in Europe after nearly a quarter century of war. The following spring, however, Napoleon broke from Elba and marched on Paris, where he ruled for the so-called Hundred Days before the duke of Wellington (1769–1852) and the Allies finally defeated him at Waterloo in June 1815. "Subtly, covertly, without announcing as much, Austen makes the events of the novel coincide precisely with the period of Napoleon's first exile," William Deresiewicz remarks. "To put it differently, *Persuasion* is a novel that takes place in the shadow of

Napoleon's return—the shadow of Waterloo." Perhaps the most telling consequence of this chronology is that it synchronizes "the novel's personal drama of loss and love with the national drama of war and peace" (Deresiewicz, 146–147).

35 Mr. Shepherd is the manager of the Kellynch estate and probably supervised everything from the farming of the land to the hunting and access rights of the tenants. Sir Walter himself has little interest in his respon-

Edmund Burke, after James Barry (1741–1806), circa 1774. Burke is most celebrated for his *Reflections on the Revolution in France* (1790), in which he championed conservatism and denounced the radical doctrines of the French revolutionaries. Suggestively, in 1795 he also published his "Letter to William Elliot, Esq." Perhaps Austen took note of his use of this name.

But now, another occupation and solicitude of mind was beginning to be added to these. Her father was growing distressed for money. She knew, that when he now took up the Baronetage, it was to drive the heavy bills of his tradespeople, and the unwelcome hints of Mr. Shepherd, his agent,[35] from his thoughts. The Kellynch property was good, but not equal to Sir Walter's apprehension of the state required in its possessor. While Lady Elliot lived, there had been method, moderation, and economy, which had just kept him within his income; but with her had died all such right-mindedness, and from that period he had been constantly exceeding it. It had not been possible for him to spend less; he had done nothing but what Sir Walter Elliot was imperiously called on to do; but blameless as he was, he was not only growing dreadfully in debt, but was hearing of it so often, that it became vain to attempt concealing it longer, even partially, from his daughter. He had given her some hints of it the last spring in town; he had gone so far even as to say, "Can we retrench? does it occur to you that there is any one article in which we can retrench?"—and Elizabeth, to do her justice, had, in the first ardour of female alarm, set seriously to think what could be done, and had finally proposed these two branches of economy: to cut off some unnecessary charities, and to refrain from new-furnishing the drawing-room; to which expedients she afterwards added the happy thought of their taking no present down to Anne, as had been the usual yearly custom. But these measures, however good in themselves, were insufficient for the real extent of the evil, the whole of which Sir Walter found himself obliged to confess to her soon afterwards. Elizabeth had nothing to propose of deeper efficacy. She felt herself ill-used and unfortunate, as did her father; and they were neither of them able to devise any means of lessening their expenses without compromising their dignity, or relinquishing their comforts in a way not to be borne.

There was only a small part of his estate that Sir Walter could dispose of; but had every acre been alienable, it would have made no difference.[36] He had condescended to mortgage as far as he had the power, but he would never condescend[37] to sell. No; he would never disgrace his name so far. The Kellynch estate should be transmitted whole and entire, as he had received it.

Their two confidential friends, Mr. Shepherd, who lived in the neighbouring market town, and Lady Russell, were called on to advise them; and both father and daughter seemed to expect that something should be struck out by one or the other to remove their embarrassments and reduce their expenditure, without involving the loss of any indulgence of taste or pride.

sibilities as a landholder, and in several key areas he is prepared to be guided by the aptly named Mr. Shepherd.

36 There is only one small part of the estate that Sir Walter may sell (that is, that he may "alienate"). The rest of the property must pass intact to Mr. Elliot.

37 "Condescend" in this context means "to descend to a less dignified level."

The title page of John Debrett's famous *Baronetage of England,* the only book that Sir Walter ever reads.

Napoleon Bonaparte on Board the Bellerophon *in Plymouth Sound,* by Charles Lock East-lake (1793–1865), 1815. Dressed in the uniform of the Chasseurs, Napoleon leans his right elbow immediately below a Union flag to emphasize Britain's victory and his defeat at the Battle of Waterloo in June 1815. Within weeks the British government dispatched Napoleon into exile on St. Helena.

2

Mr. Shepherd, a civil, cautious lawyer, who, whatever might be his hold or his views on Sir Walter, would rather have the *disagreeable* prompted by any body else, excused himself from offering the slightest hint, and only begged leave to recommend an implicit reference to the excellent judgment of Lady Russell,—from whose known good sense he fully expected to have just such resolute measures advised, as he meant to see finally adopted.

Lady Russell was most anxiously zealous on the subject, and gave it much serious consideration. She was a woman rather of sound than of quick abilities, whose difficulties in coming to any decision in this instance were great, from the opposition of two leading principles. She was of strict integrity herself, with a delicate sense of honour; but she was as desirous of saving Sir Walter's feelings, as solicitous for the credit of the family, as aristocratic in her ideas of what was due to them, as any body of sense and honesty could well be. She was a benevolent, charitable, good woman, and capable of strong attachments; most correct in her conduct, strict in her notions of decorum, and with manners that were held a standard of good-breeding. She had a cultivated mind, and was, generally speaking, rational and consistent—but she had prejudices on the side of ancestry; she had a value for rank and consequence,[1] which blinded her a little to the faults of those who possessed them. Herself, the widow of only a knight, she gave the dignity of a baronet all its due;[2] and Sir Walter, independent of his claims as an old acquaintance, an attentive neighbour, an obliging landlord, the husband of her very dear friend, the

1 "Consequence" is "social status."

2 A knighthood is conferred by the sovereign for particular services. It ranks below a baronetcy and is non-hereditary. In *Pride and Prejudice,* for example, "Sir William Lucas had been formerly in trade in Meryton, where he had made a tolerable fortune and risen to the honour of knighthood by an address to the King, during his mayoralty" (I, 5).

A watercolor of Jane Austen painted by her sister, Cassandra, around 1802, when Austen was twenty-seven years old, the same age as Anne Elliot in *Persuasion*. It is one of only two authentic portraits of Austen; the other one is also by Cassandra.

father of Anne and her sisters, was, as being Sir Walter, in her apprehension entitled to a great deal of compassion and consideration under his present difficulties.

They must retrench; that did not admit of a doubt. But she was very anxious to have it done with the least possible pain to him and Elizabeth. She drew up plans of economy, she made exact calculations, and she did, what nobody else thought of doing, she consulted Anne, who never seemed considered by the others as having any interest in the question. She consulted, and in a degree was influenced by her, in marking out the scheme of retrenchment, which was at last submitted to Sir Walter. Every emendation of Anne's had been on the side of honesty against importance. She wanted more vigorous measures, a more complete reformation, a quicker release from debt, a much higher tone of indifference for every thing but justice and equity.

"If we can persuade your father to all this," said Lady Russell, looking over her paper, "much may be done. If he will adopt these regulations, in seven years he will be clear; and I hope we may be able to convince him and Elizabeth, that Kellynch-hall has a respectability in itself, which cannot be affected by these reductions; and that the true dignity of Sir Walter Elliot will be very far from lessened, in the eyes of sensible people, by his acting like a man of principle. What will he be doing, in fact, but what very many of our first families have done,—or ought to do?—There will be nothing singular in his case; and it is singularity which often makes the worst part of our suffering, as it always does of our conduct. I have great hope of our prevailing. We must be serious and decided—for, after all, the person who has contracted debts must pay them; and though a great deal is due to the feelings of the gentleman, and the head of a house, like your father, there is still more due to the character of an honest man."

This was the principle on which Anne wanted her father to be proceeding, his friends to be urging him. She considered it as an act of indispensable duty to clear away the claims of creditors, with all the expedition[3] which the most comprehensive retrenchments could secure, and saw no dignity in any thing short of it. She wanted it to be prescribed, and felt as a duty. She rated Lady Russell's influence highly, and as to the severe degree of self-denial, which her own conscience prompted, she believed there might be little more difficulty in persuading them to a complete, than to half a reformation. Her knowledge of her father and Elizabeth, inclined her to think that the sacrifice of one pair of horses would be hardly less painful than of both, and so on, through the whole list of Lady Russell's too gentle reductions.

How Anne's more rigid requisitions might have been taken, is of little consequence. Lady Russell's had no success at all—could not be put up with—were not to be borne. "What! Every comfort of life knocked off! Journeys, London, servants, horses, table,—contractions and restrictions every where. To live no longer with the decencies even of a private gentleman! No, he would sooner quit Kellynch-hall at once, than remain in it on such disgraceful terms."

"Quit Kellynch-hall." The hint was immediately taken up by Mr. Shepherd, whose interest was involved in the reality of Sir Walter's retrenching, and who was perfectly persuaded that nothing would be done without a change of abode.[4]—"Since the idea had been started in the very quarter which ought to dictate, he had no scruple," he said, "in confessing his judgment to be entirely on that side. It did not appear to him that Sir Walter could materially alter his style of living in a house which had such a character of hospitality and ancient dignity to support.—In any other place, Sir Walter might judge for himself; and would be looked up to, as regulating the modes of life, in whatever way he might choose to model his household."

Sir Walter would quit Kellynch-hall;—and after a very few days more of doubt and indecision, the great question of whither he should go, was settled, and the first outline of this important change made out.

There had been three alternatives, London, Bath, or another house in the country. All Anne's wishes had been for the latter. A small house in their own neighbourhood, where they might still have Lady Russell's society, still be near Mary, and still have the pleasure of sometimes seeing the lawns and groves of Kellynch, was the object of her ambition. But the usual fate of Anne attended her, in having

4 The clergyman and religious writer Thomas Gisborne (1758–1846) explicitly condemned those like Sir Walter who had run up debts through self-indulgence and carelessness: "Justice and every moral principle concur in reprobating that pride and false shame which sometimes impel men to persist in a mode of life far more expensive than they can afford, in defiance of all the duties owing to their family and to their creditors, rather than submit to lessen the parade and retrench the extravagance of their household." What is more, Gisborne's instructions on how to address the problem are very much in line with Mr. Shepherd's advice. "When considerable retrenchments are to be made, it is not uncommon for the family to remove to some distant quarter. This practice is prudent and right, either when the new place of residence is in a much cheaper situation, or when the heads of the family have reason to doubt whether they shall have the honest resolution to persevere in their new plan of life, if they remain subject to the temptations of the old neighbourhood" (Gisborne, *An Enquiry into the Duties of Men in the Higher and Middle Classes of Society,* 7th ed., 2 vols. [London: Cadell, 1824], II, 476–477).

5 Bath is a city in Somersetshire, founded by the Romans and famous for its hot mineral springs. In the eighteenth century, it was immensely popular, both as a resort for the sick and as a pleasure ground for the rich. By Austen's day, however, its reputation was in decline. Austen herself moved there with her family in 1801 but was glad to leave five years later. "It will be two years tomorrow since we left Bath," she wrote on July 1, 1808, ". . . with what happy feelings of Escape!" (Austen, *Letters,* 138).

Thomas Gisborne, by Henry Meyer, after John Jackson (1778–1831), after John Hoppner (1758–1810). Austen read Gisborne's *Enquiry into the Duties of the Female Sex* (1797). "I am glad you recommended 'Gisborne,'" she wrote to Cassandra in August 1805, "for having begun, I am pleased with it, and I had quite determined not to read it" (Austen, *Letters,* 112).

something very opposite from her inclination fixed on. She disliked Bath, and did not think it agreed with her—and Bath was to be her home.[5]

Sir Walter had at first thought more of London, but Mr. Shepherd felt that he could not be trusted in London, and had been skilful enough to dissuade him from it, and make Bath preferred. It was a much safer place for a gentleman in his predicament:—he might there be important at comparatively little expense.—Two material advantages of Bath over London had of course been given all their weight, its more convenient distance from Kellynch, only fifty miles, and Lady Russell's spending some part of every winter there; and to the very great satisfaction of Lady Russell, whose first views on the projected change had been for Bath, Sir Walter and Elizabeth were induced to believe that they should lose neither consequence nor enjoyment by settling there.

Lady Russell felt obliged to oppose her dear Anne's known wishes. It would be too much to expect Sir Walter to descend into a small house in his own neighbourhood. Anne herself would have found the mortifications of it more than she foresaw, and to Sir Walter's feelings they must have been dreadful. And with regard to Anne's dislike of Bath, she considered it as a prejudice and mistake, arising first from the circumstance of her having been three years at school there, after her mother's death, and, secondly, from her happening to be not in perfectly good spirits the only winter which she had afterwards spent there with herself.

Lady Russell was fond of Bath in short, and disposed to think it must suit them all; and as to her young friend's health, by passing all the warm months with her at Kellynch-lodge, every danger would be avoided; and it was, in fact, a change which must do both health and spirits good. Anne had been too little from home, too little seen. Her spirits were not high. A larger society would improve them. She wanted her to be more known.

The undesirableness of any other house in the same neighbourhood for Sir Walter, was certainly much strengthened by one part, and a very material part of the scheme, which had been happily engrafted on the beginning. He was not only to quit his home, but to see it in the hands of others; a trial of fortitude, which stronger heads than Sir Walter's have found too much.—Kellynch-hall was to be let.[6] This, however, was a profound secret; not to be breathed beyond their own circle.

Sir Walter could not have borne the degradation of being known to design letting his house.—Mr. Shepherd had once mentioned the word, "advertise;"—but never dared approach it again; Sir Walter spurned the idea of its being offered in any manner; forbad the slightest hint being dropped of his having such an intention; and it was only on the supposition of his being spontaneously solicited by some most unexceptionable applicant, on his own terms, and as a great favor, that he would let it at all.

How quick come the reasons for approving what we like!—Lady Russell had another excellent one at hand, for being extremely glad that Sir Walter and his family were to remove from the country. Elizabeth had been lately forming an intimacy, which she wished to see interrupted. It was with a daughter of Mr. Shepherd, who had returned, after an unprosperous marriage, to her father's house, with the additional burthen of two children. She was a clever young woman, who understood the art of pleasing;[7] the art of pleasing, at least, at Kellynch-hall; and who had made herself so acceptable to Miss Elliot, as to have been already staying there more than once, in spite of all that Lady Russell, who thought it a friendship quite out of place, could hint of caution and reserve.

Lady Russell, indeed, had scarcely any influence with Elizabeth, and seemed to love her, rather because she would love her, than because Elizabeth deserved it. She had never received from her more than outward attention, nothing beyond the observances of complaisance;[8] had never succeeded in any point which she wanted to carry, against previous inclination. She had been repeatedly very earnest in trying to get Anne included in the visit to London, sensibly open to all the injustice and all the discredit of the selfish arrangements which shut her out, and on many lesser occasions had endeavoured to give Elizabeth the advantage of her own better judgment and experience—but always in vain; Elizabeth would go her own way —and never had she pursued it in more decided opposition to Lady

6 Many commentators have seen Sir Walter's precarious financial position as representative of the social and spiritual disintegration of landed society in early nineteenth-century England. But as David Spring has argued, not only did men of Sir Walter's class remain politically powerful right through the nineteenth century, but leasing their "country houses to someone who paid a good rent and going to live elsewhere more cheaply . . . was an ancient expedient" for many of them: "Sir Walter . . . was doing what prudence and custom dictated. . . . In a year or two, perhaps longer, he would be able to scale down his debt and return to Kellynch" (Spring, "Interpreters of Jane Austen's Social World," in *Jane Austen: New Perspectives,* ed. Janet Todd [New York: Holmes and Meier, 1983], 65).

7 The "art of pleasing" was a stock expression in this period, and often intended—as here—in a negative sense. The novelist and poet Mary Robinson (1758–1800) uses the phrase in *Walsingham* (1797), where the tutor Mr. Hanbury describes "the art of pleasing" as "fawning, sycophantic, servile adulation, which only knaves bestow, and none but fools delight in." Similarly, in *Patronage* (1814), the Anglo-Irish novelist Maria Edgeworth (1767–1849) describes the scheming Mrs. Falconer as "mistress of the art of pleasing, and perfectly acquainted with all the shades of politeness," which she knows "how to dispose . . . so as to conceal their boundaries, and even their gradation, from all but the most skilful observers" (Mary Robinson, *Walsingham,* ed. Julie A. Shaffer [Peterborough, ON: Broadview, 2003], 91; Edgeworth, *Works,* VII, 3).

8 Austen uses the word "complaisance" often and in a number of different senses. Here it means "politeness." Elsewhere in *Persuasion* she uses it to mean "ease" or "compliance."

9 Mrs. Clay's surname is evocative, suggesting every-thing from low social status, to a malleability that will harden with time, to an idol's feet of clay.

Russell, than in this selection of Mrs. Clay;[9] turning from the society of so deserving a sister to bestow her affection and confidence on one who ought to have been nothing to her but the object of distant civility.

From situation, Mrs. Clay was, in Lady Russell's estimate, a very unequal, and in her character she believed a very dangerous compan-ion—and a removal that would leave Mrs. Clay behind, and bring a choice of more suitable intimates within Miss Elliot's reach, was therefore an object of first-rate importance.

Mary Robinson, by or after Sir Joshua Reynolds (1723–1792), circa 1782. Robinson's novels, including *Angelina* (1796) and *Walsingham* (1797), are strongly feminist, as is her impassioned *Letter to the Women of England on the Injustice of Mental Subordina-tion* (1799).

A. Wallis Mills (1878–1940), Illustrations for *Persuasion,* 1908. Sir Walter speaks
haughtily to Mr. Shepherd about prospective tenants for Kellynch Hall.

3

1 Napoleon abdicated on April 11, 1814, and was sent into exile on Elba. With the wars apparently over, Britain demobilized many sailors.

2 The navies of warring countries routinely captured each other's ships as "prizes," and sailors—on the basis of rank—shared the value of the vessels they seized. "Under the rules of distribution, captains of ships might very easily amass a considerable fortune, while Commanders-in-Chief could hardly help doing so," writes Peter Kemp. In England the practice brought great wealth to naval men throughout the Napoleonic Wars. But not everyone approved of it. Many decried the division of prizes as unfair, while others regarded the entire system as little better than legalized piracy. In Maria Edgeworth's tale *Manoeuvring* (1809), the idealized Captain Walsingham captures a Spanish ship but is unconcerned with how much prize money it will bring him. "He is the right sort," declares Mr. Palmer. "Long may it be before our naval officers think more of prize-money than of glory! Long may it be before our honest tars turn into calculating pirates!" (Kemp, *Prize Money* [Aldershot: Gale and Polden, 1946], 19; see also "The Rewards of Success: Prize Money, Honours and Promotion," in Southam, 109–132; Edgeworth, *Works,* IV, 49–50).

3 By "liberal notions" Mr. Shepherd means "generous ideas about money."

"I MUST TAKE LEAVE TO OBSERVE, Sir Walter," said Mr. Shepherd one morning at Kellynch Hall, as he laid down the newspaper, "that the present juncture is much in our favour. This peace will be turning all our rich Navy Officers ashore.[1] They will be all wanting a home. Could not be a better time, Sir Walter, for having a choice of tenants, very responsible tenants. Many a noble fortune has been made during the war.[2] If a rich Admiral were to come in our way, Sir Walter—"

"He would be a very lucky man, Shepherd," replied Sir Walter, "that's all I have to remark. A prize indeed would Kellynch Hall be to him; rather the greatest prize of all, let him have taken ever so many before—hey, Shepherd?"

Mr. Shepherd laughed, as he knew he must, at this wit, and then added,

"I presume to observe, Sir Walter, that, in the way of business, gentlemen of the navy are well to deal with. I have had a little knowledge of their methods of doing business, and I am free to confess that they have very liberal notions,[3] and are as likely to make desirable tenants as any set of people one should meet with. Therefore, Sir Walter, what I would take leave to suggest is, that if in consequence of any rumours getting abroad of your intention—which must be contemplated as a possible thing, because we know how difficult it is to keep the actions and designs of one part of the world from the notice and curiosity of the other,—consequence has its tax—I, John Shepherd, might conceal any family-matters that I chose, for nobody would think it worth their while to observe me, but Sir

Walter Elliot has eyes upon him which it may be very difficult to elude—and therefore, thus much I venture upon, that it will not greatly surprise me if, with all our caution, some rumour of the truth should get abroad—in the supposition of which, as I was going to observe, since applications will unquestionably follow, I should think any from our wealthy naval commanders particularly worth attending to—and beg leave to add, that two hours will bring me over at any time, to save you the trouble of replying."

Sir Walter only nodded. But soon afterwards, rising and pacing the room, he observed sarcastically,

"There are few among the gentlemen of the navy, I imagine, who would not be surprised to find themselves in a house of this description."

"They would look around them, no doubt, and bless their good fortune," said Mrs. Clay, for Mrs. Clay was present; her father had driven her over, nothing being of so much use to Mrs. Clay's health as a drive to Kellynch: "but I quite agree with my father in thinking a sailor might be a very desirable tenant. I have known a good deal of the profession; and besides their liberality, they are so neat and careful in all their ways! These valuable pictures of yours, Sir Walter, if you chose to leave them, would be perfectly safe. Every thing in and about the house would be taken such excellent care of! the gardens and shrubberies would be kept in almost as high order as they are now. You need not be afraid, Miss Elliot, of your own sweet flower-garden's being neglected."

"As to all that," rejoined Sir Walter coolly, "supposing I were induced to let my house, I have by no means made up my mind as to the privileges to be annexed to it. I am not particularly disposed to favour a tenant. The park would be open to him of course, and few navy officers, or men of any other description, can have had such a range; but what restrictions I might impose on the use of the pleasure-grounds,[4] is another thing. I am not fond of the idea of my shrubberies being always approachable; and I should recommend Miss Elliot to be on her guard with respect to her flower-garden. I am very little disposed to grant a tenant of Kellynch Hall any extraordinary favour, I assure you, be he sailor or soldier."

4 The "park" or grounds of the estate were most often used for hunting and riding. The "pleasure-grounds" were landscaped areas used primarily for entertainment. In *Sense and Sensibility*, for example, the Palmers' home at Cleveland "had no park, but the pleasure-grounds were tolerably extensive" (III, 6).

Lord Nelson, by Sir William Beechey (1753–1839), 1800. Nelson arranged for Austen's sailor brother Francis to command the *Canopus*. "Captain Austen . . . is an excellent young man," wrote Nelson; "he cannot be better placed than in the *Canopus,* which was once a French Admiral's ship, and struck to me" (cited in David Nokes, *Jane Austen: A Life* [London: Fourth Estate, 1997], 291).

5 Mr. Shepherd has in mind treatises such as James Barry Bird's *Laws Respecting Landlords, Tenants, and Lodgers* (London: Clarke and Sons, 1805). In an appendix, Bird gives an example of a "*Lease of . . . Lands in the Country,*" which details how the lessee is obliged to maintain "the yard, barns, stables, buildings, outhouses, and appurtenances," as well as "all those several fields, closes, and parcels of arable, meadow, and pasture land" (89–90).

6 Led by Lord Nelson (1758–1805), the British navy scored victories over the French in decisive battles such as those of the Nile (1798) and of Trafalgar (1805). In 1806, Napoleon attempted a blockade to destroy British commerce, but the British navy mounted an effective counter-blockade that thwarted his plans.

7 A sailor's health and welfare were often severely undermined by the harsh circumstances of navy life, from disciplinary floggings, poor diet, and excessive physical labor to a wide-ranging number of diseases, including "Remittent fever," "Scurvy," "Rheumatism," "Dysentery," "Belly-ach," "Diarrhoea," "Inflammation," "Guinea worm," "Mortification," "Eruption," and "Excoriation" (Robert Robertson, *Observations on Diseases Incident to Seamen: A New Edition*, 4 vols. [London: Cadell and Davies, 1807], I, 343).

8 Austen's description of the rise of Lord St. Ives invokes the naval career of Lord Nelson, whose father was a village rector and whose genius as a commander led in 1801 to his elevation to a viscountcy, a title that ranks far above Sir Walter's baronetcy.

After a short pause, Mr. Shepherd presumed to say,

"In all these cases, there are established usages which make every thing plain and easy between landlord and tenant.[5] Your interest, Sir Walter, is in pretty safe hands. Depend upon me for taking care that no tenant has more than his just rights. I venture to hint, that Sir Walter Elliot cannot be half so jealous for his own, as John Shepherd will be for him."

Here Anne spoke,—

"The navy, I think, who have done so much for us,[6] have at least an equal claim with any other set of men, for all the comforts and all the privileges which any home can give. Sailors work hard enough for their comforts, we must all allow."

"Very true, very true. What Miss Anne says, is very true," was Mr. Shepherd's rejoinder, and "Oh! certainly," was his daughter's; but Sir Walter's remark was, soon afterwards—

"The profession has its utility, but I should be sorry to see any friend of mine belonging to it."

"Indeed!" was the reply, and with a look of surprise.

"Yes; it is in two points offensive to me; I have two strong grounds of objection to it. First, as being the means of bringing persons of obscure birth into undue distinction, and raising men to honours which their fathers and grandfathers never dreamt of; and secondly, as it cuts up a man's youth and vigour most horribly; a sailor grows old sooner than any other man;[7] I have observed it all my life. A man is in greater danger in the navy of being insulted by the rise of one whose father, his father might have disdained to speak to, and of becoming prematurely an object of disgust himself, than in any other line. One day last spring, in town, I was in company with two men, striking instances of what I am talking of, Lord St. Ives, whose father we all know to have been a country curate, without bread to eat; I was to give place to Lord St. Ives,[8] and a certain Admiral Baldwin, the most deplorable looking personage you can imagine, his face the colour of mahogany, rough and rugged to the last degree, all lines and wrinkles, nine grey hairs of a side, and nothing but a dab of powder at top.—'In the name of heaven, who is that old fellow?' said I, to a friend of mine who was standing near, (Sir Basil Morley.) 'Old fellow!'

A military flogging, by George Cruikshank (1792–1878), published 1825. All hands were assembled to witness the punishment. Marines were paraded on the poop deck to ensure that the seamen did not intervene. The culprit was secured to an upended grating and then lashed. In this picture, an innocent sailor is about to be flogged when the real offender steps forward to accept the punishment that will undoubtedly follow. Compare *Pride and Prejudice,* where Jane and Elizabeth return from Netherfield to learn that a Meryton "private had been flogged" (I, 12).

cried Sir Basil, 'it is Admiral Baldwin. What do you take his age to be?' 'Sixty,' said I, 'or perhaps sixty-two.' 'Forty,' replied Sir Basil, 'forty, and no more.' Picture to yourselves my amazement; I shall not easily forget Admiral Baldwin. I never saw quite so wretched an example of what a sea-faring life can do; but to a degree, I know it is the same with them all: they are all knocked about, and exposed to every climate, and every weather, till they are not fit to be seen. It is a pity they are not knocked on the head at once, before they reach Admiral Baldwin's age."

"Nay, Sir Walter," cried Mrs. Clay, "this is being severe indeed. Have a little mercy on the poor men. We are not all born to be handsome. The sea is no beautifier, certainly; sailors do grow old betimes; I have often observed it; they soon lose the look of youth. But then,

9 Mrs. Clay's response to Sir Walter's attack on the deplorable physical appearance of sailors is not simply a piece of well-judged sycophancy. Her arguments, writes June Sturrock, "like Sir Walter's scorn of the unfortunate Admiral Baldwin, represent the resistance of the Elliot circle to the normal effects on the body of an active and productive life. The deviations from the norm of regular beauty that result from time and experience are not to be tolerated. Like the dandies, the Elliots see appearances as a supreme value" (Sturrock, "Dandies, Beauties, and the Issue of Good Looks in *Persuasion*," in *Persuasions*, 26 [2004], 44).

10 "Quarter sessions" were sessions of a court held every three months by a justice of the peace to deal with criminal and civil proceedings. As the county town for Somersetshire, Taunton hosted the quarter sessions. In 1800, Austen's aunt, Jane Leigh-Perrot (1744–1836), was tried in Taunton for shoplifting.

is not it the same with many other professions, perhaps most other? Soldiers, in active service, are not at all better off: and even in the quieter professions, there is a toil and a labour of the mind, if not of the body, which seldom leaves a man's looks to the natural effect of time. The lawyer plods, quite care-worn; the physician is up at all hours, and travelling in all weather; and even the clergyman—" she stopt a moment to consider what might do for the clergyman;—"and even the clergyman, you know, is obliged to go into infected rooms, and expose his health and looks to all the injury of a poisonous atmosphere. In fact, as I have long been convinced, though every profession is necessary and honourable in its turn, it is only the lot of those who are not obliged to follow any, who can live in a regular way, in the country, choosing their own hours, following their own pursuits, and living on their own property, without the torment of trying for more; it is only *their* lot, I say, to hold the blessings of health and a good appearance to the utmost: I know no other set of men but what lose something of their personableness when they cease to be quite young."[9]

It seemed as if Mr. Shepherd, in this anxiety to bespeak Sir Walter's good-will towards a naval officer as tenant, had been gifted with foresight; for the very first application for the house was from an Admiral Croft, with whom he shortly afterwards fell into company in attending the quarter sessions at Taunton;[10] and indeed, he had received a hint of the admiral from a London correspondent. By the report which he hastened over to Kellynch to make, Admiral Croft was a native of Somersetshire, who having acquired a very handsome fortune, was wishing to settle in his own country, and had come down to Taunton in order to look at some advertised places in that immediate neighbourhood, which, however, had not suited him; that accidentally hearing—(it was just as he had foretold, Mr. Shepherd observed, Sir Walter's concerns could not be kept a secret,)—accidentally hearing of the possibility of Kellynch Hall being to let, and understanding his (Mr. Shepherd's) connection with the owner, he had introduced himself to him in order to make particular inquiries, and had, in the course of a pretty long conference, expressed as strong an inclination for the place as a man who knew it only by

So wretched an example of
what a sea-faring life can do.

Charles Edmund Brock (1870–1938), Illustrations for *Persuasion,* 1898. Sir Walter
deplores the physical appearance of Admiral Baldwin.

11 There were three ranks of admiral: in ascending or-der, they were the rear-admiral, the vice-admiral, and the admiral. Within each rank, there were three grades: from junior to senior, they were the blue, the white, and the red.

12 The Battle of Trafalgar was fought on October 21, 1805, off the southern coast of Spain. Under the com-mand of Lord Nelson, the British achieved a crucial victory over the French fleet. Lord Nelson was killed during the action, but not before he shattered Napo-leon's hopes of invading England.

13 "East Indies" was a broad geographical term that re-ferred to mainland southeast Asia and India, as well as to Indonesia and the Philippines.

14 The "deputation" is the right to shoot game. As lord of the manor, Sir Walter exclusively claims this right, but he can "deputize" others, including his tenants, if he so chooses.

description, could feel; and given Mr. Shepherd, in his explicit ac-count of himself, every proof of his being a most responsible, eligible tenant.

"And who is Admiral Croft?" was Sir Walter's cold suspicious in-quiry.

Mr. Shepherd answered for his being of a gentleman's family, and mentioned a place; and Anne, after the little pause which followed, added—

"He is rear admiral of the white.[11] He was in the Trafalgar action,[12] and has been in the East Indies[13] since; he has been stationed there, I believe, several years."

"Then I take it for granted," observed Sir Walter, "that his face is about as orange as the cuffs and capes of my livery."

Mr. Shepherd hastened to assure him, that Admiral Croft was a very hale, hearty, well-looking man, a little weather-beaten, to be sure, but not much; and quite the gentleman in all his notions and behaviour;—not likely to make the smallest difficulty about terms; —only wanted a comfortable home, and to get into it as soon as possible;—knew he must pay for his convenience;—knew what rent a ready-furnished house of that consequence might fetch;—should not have been surprised if Sir Walter had asked more;—had inquired about the manor;—would be glad of the deputation,[14] certainly, but made no great point of it;—said he sometimes took out a gun, but never killed;—quite the gentleman.

Mr. Shepherd was eloquent on the subject; pointing out all the circumstances of the admiral's family, which made him peculiarly de-sirable as a tenant. He was a married man, and without children; the very state to be wished for. A house was never taken good care of, Mr. Shepherd observed, without a lady: he did not know, whether furni-ture might not be in danger of suffering as much where there was no lady, as where there were many children. A lady, without a family, was the very best preserver of furniture in the world. He had seen Mrs. Croft, too; she was at Taunton with the admiral, and had been pres-ent almost all the time they were talking the matter over.

"And a very well-spoken, genteel, shrewd lady, she seemed to be," continued he; "asked more questions about the house, and terms, and taxes, than the admiral himself, and seemed more conversant with business. And moreover, Sir Walter, I found she was not quite unconnected in this country, any more than her husband; that is to say, she is sister to a gentleman who did live amongst us once; she told me so herself: sister to the gentleman who lived a few years back, at Monkford. Bless me! what was his name? At this moment I cannot recollect his name, though I have heard it so lately. Penelope, my dear, can you help me to the name of the gentleman who lived at Monkford—Mrs. Croft's brother?"

But Mrs. Clay was talking so eagerly with Miss Elliot, that she did not hear the appeal.

"I have no conception whom you can mean, Shepherd; I remember no gentleman resident at Monkford since the time of old Governor Trent."

"Bless me! how very odd! I shall forget my own name soon, I suppose. A name that I am so very well acquainted with; knew the gentleman so well by sight; seen him a hundred times; came to consult me once, I remember, about a trespass of one of his neighbours; farmer's man breaking into his orchard—wall torn down—apples stolen—caught in the fact;[15] and afterwards, contrary to my judgment, submitted to an amicable compromise. Very odd indeed!"

After waiting another moment—

"You mean Mr. Wentworth, I suppose," said Anne.

Mr. Shepherd was all gratitude.

"Wentworth was the very name! Mr. Wentworth was the very man. He had the curacy[16] of Monkford, you know, Sir Walter, some time back, for two or three years. Came there about the year ——5, I take it. You remember him, I am sure."

"Wentworth? Oh! ay,—Mr. Wentworth, the curate of Monkford. You misled me by the term *gentleman*. I thought you were speaking of some man of property: Mr. Wentworth was nobody, I remember; quite unconnected; nothing to do with the Strafford family.[17] One wonders how the names of many of our nobility become so common."

As Mr. Shepherd perceived that this connexion of the Crofts did them no service with Sir Walter, he mentioned it no more; returning,

15 "Fact" here means "an evil deed" or "a criminal act." Compare the poet and novelist Charlotte Smith (1749–1806) in *The Old Manor House* (1793), where "a wild and incorrigible boy" is "caught in the fact of hunting divers cats" (Smith, *Works,* VI, 5).

16 A curacy was a low-ranking position within the Church of England. A curate's role was to assist the rector in the duties of the parish.

17 The Straffords were an aristocratic family descended from Thomas Wentworth, first earl of Strafford (1593–1641) and the leading advisor of Charles I throughout the 1630s.

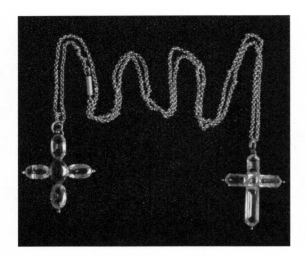

Charles Austen used his prize money to purchase these topaze crosses for his sisters Cassandra and Jane. "He has received 30£ for his share of the privateer & expects 10£ more," Jane wrote to Cassandra in May 1801. But "of what avail is it to take prizes if he lays out the produce in presents to his Sisters. He has been buying Gold chains & Topaze Crosses for us;—he must be well scolded" (Austen, *Letters,* 91). Compare *Mansfield Park,* where William Price gives his sister Fanny "a very pretty amber cross" (II, 8).

with all his zeal, to dwell on the circumstances more indisputably in their favour; their age, and number, and fortune; the high idea they had formed of Kellynch Hall, and extreme solicitude for the advantage of renting it; making it appear as if they ranked nothing beyond the happiness of being the tenants of Sir Walter Elliot: an extraordinary taste, certainly, could they have been supposed in the secret of Sir Walter's estimate of the dues of a tenant.

It succeeded, however; and though Sir Walter must ever look with an evil eye on any one intending to inhabit that house, and think them infinitely too well off in being permitted to rent it on the highest terms, he was talked into allowing Mr. Shepherd to proceed in the treaty, and authorising him to wait on Admiral Croft, who still remained at Taunton, and fix a day for the house being seen.

Sir Walter was not very wise; but still he had experience enough of the world to feel, that a more unobjectionable tenant, in all essentials, than Admiral Croft bid fair to be, could hardly offer. So far went his understanding; and his vanity supplied a little additional soothing, in the admiral's situation in life, which was just high enough, and not too high. "I have let my house to Admiral Croft," would sound extremely well; very much better than to any mere *Mr.* ——; a *Mr.* (save, perhaps, some half dozen in the nation,) always needs a note of explanation. An admiral speaks his own consequence, and, at the same time, can never make a baronet look small. In all their dealings and intercourse, Sir Walter Elliot must ever have the precedence.

Nothing could be done without a reference to Elizabeth; but her inclination was growing so strong for a removal, that she was happy to have it fixed and expedited by a tenant at hand; and not a word to suspend decision was uttered by her.

Mr. Shepherd was completely empowered to act; and no sooner had such an end been reached, than Anne, who had been a most attentive listener to the whole, left the room, to seek the comfort of cool air for her flushed cheeks; and as she walked along a favourite grove, said, with a gentle sigh, "a few months more, and *he,* perhaps, may be walking here."

4

He was not Mr. Wentworth, the former curate of Monkford, however suspicious appearances may be, but a captain Frederick Wentworth, his brother, who being made commander in consequence of the action off St. Domingo,[1] and not immediately employed,[2] had come into Somersetshire, in the summer of 1806; and having no parent living, found a home for half a year, at Monkford. He was, at that time, a remarkably fine young man, with a great deal of intelligence, spirit and brilliancy; and Anne an extremely pretty girl, with gentleness, modesty, taste, and feeling. —Half the sum of attraction, on either side, might have been enough, for he had nothing to do, and she had hardly any body to love; but the encounter of such lavish recommendations could not fail. They were gradually acquainted, and when acquainted, rapidly and deeply in love. It would be difficult to say which had seen highest perfection in the other, or which had been the happiest; she, in receiving his declarations and proposals, or he in having them accepted.

A short period of exquisite felicity followed, and but a short one. —Troubles soon arose. Sir Walter, on being applied to, without actually withholding his consent, or saying it should never be, gave it all the negative of great astonishment, great coldness, great silence, and a professed resolution of doing nothing for his daughter.[3] He thought it a very degrading alliance; and Lady Russell, though with more tempered and pardonable pride, received it as a most unfortunate one.

1 A commander ranked below a captain but above a first lieutenant and was in charge of a sloop, a small warship mounting about twenty guns. On February 6, 1806, Sir John Thomas Duckworth (1748–1817) led the British fleet in a rout of the French off St. Domingo in the Caribbean Sea. For his distinguished military services, Duckworth was made a baronet in 1813.

2 There were always more commanders than sloops, and so after his promotion Wentworth had to wait on half-pay (a reduced allowance that the navy paid to an officer who was not in actual service) until a vessel became available. Like Austen's sailor brother Francis Austen (1774–1865), Wentworth is lucky. He does not have to wait long. "Frank is made," Austen exulted in a December 28, 1798, letter to her beloved elder sister, Cassandra Austen (1773–1845). "—He was yesterday raised to the Rank of Commander, & appointed to the Petterel Sloop. . . . As soon as you have cried a little for Joy, you may go on" (Austen, *Letters,* 32). Just over seven years later, Frank, like Wentworth, fought at the Battle of St. Domingo.

3 Mr. William Elliot will inherit Kellynch, but Anne could still expect a dowry from her father, which apparently he had threatened to deny her if she married Wentworth.

A view of the south side of St. Domingo, by T. G. Dutton, after W. S. Andrews. In the autumn of 1795, Tom Fowle, the fiancé of Austen's sister, Cassandra, became chaplain to a regiment bound for the West Indies to fight the French. He was expected back in England eighteen months later, but instead Cassandra received the heartbreaking news that he had died of fever at St. Domingo on February 13, 1797.

Anne Elliot, with all her claims of birth, beauty, and mind, to throw herself away at nineteen; involve herself at nineteen in an engagement with a young man, who had nothing but himself to recommend him, and no hopes of attaining affluence, but in the chances of a most uncertain profession, and no connexions to secure even his farther rise in that profession;[4] would be, indeed, a throwing away, which she grieved to think of! Anne Elliot, so young; known to so few, to be snatched off by a stranger without alliance or fortune; or rather sunk by him into a state of most wearing, anxious, youth-killing dependance! It must not be, if by any fair interference of friendship, any representations from one who had almost a mother's love, and mother's rights, it would be prevented.

Captain Wentworth had no fortune. He had been lucky in his profession, but spending freely, what had come freely, had realized nothing. But, he was confident that he should soon be rich;—full of life and ardour, he knew that he should soon have a ship, and soon be on a station[5] that would lead to every thing he wanted. He had always been lucky; he knew he should be so still.—Such confidence, powerful in its own warmth, and bewitching in the wit which often expressed it, must have been enough for Anne; but Lady Russell saw it very differently.—His sanguine temper, and fearlessness of mind, operated very differently on her. She saw in it but an aggravation of the evil. It only added a dangerous character to himself. He was brilliant, he was headstrong.[6]—Lady Russell had little taste for wit; and of any thing approaching to imprudence a horror. She deprecated the connexion in every light.[7]

Such opposition, as these feelings produced, was more than Anne could combat. Young and gentle as she was, it might yet have been possible to withstand her father's ill-will, though unsoftened by one kind word or look on the part of her sister;—but Lady Russell, whom she had always loved and relied on, could not, with such steadiness of opinion, and such tenderness of manner, be continually advising her in vain. She was persuaded to believe the engagement a wrong thing—indiscreet, improper, hardly capable of success, and not deserving it.[8] But it was not a merely selfish caution, under which she acted, in putting an end to it. Had she not imagined herself consult-

4 Promotion through the naval ranks was very often a matter of having friends—or friends of friends—who were government ministers, powerful landowners, or high-ranking members of the admiralty. Wentworth, however, has "no connexions" and so must make his way on merit.

5 A "station" is an overseas base.

6 Austen's description of Wentworth as witty, "brilliant," and "headstrong" makes him sound "more like Elizabeth Bennet and Emma Woodhouse than Mr. Darcy and Mr. Knightley," Emily Auerbach remarks. "He seems the type of Austen man who often proves to be a rake—one seeking his own pleasure ('every thing he wanted') through luck and risk rather than through virtuous conduct and steady propriety." These qualities, Auerbach adds, make him "the most *romantic* hero in Austen—like a dashing John Willoughby but with integrity" (Auerbach, 239–240).

7 Lady Russell lists several reasons Anne should not marry Wentworth, but there is almost certainly an additional factor which is shaping her objections, and which she never fully articulates. Herself a widow, she is worried that if Anne marries Wentworth, the continuation of the war and the demands of his profession will lead to his death in the line of duty, leaving Anne a widow as well. Lady Russell's anxiety recalls the fate of Jane Fairfax's parents in *Emma:* "The marriage of Lieut. Fairfax, of the ———regiment of infantry, and Miss Jane Bates, had had its day of fame and pleasure, hope and interest; but nothing now remained of it, save the melancholy remembrance of him dying in action abroad—of his widow sinking under consumption and grief soon afterwards—and this girl" (II, 2).

8 As a young woman living in Regency England, Anne would have felt considerable social and moral pressure to conform to the wishes of her father and Lady Russell. In *Advice to Young Ladies, on the Improvement of the Mind* (1808), the Unitarian minister Thomas Broadhurst (circa 1767–1851) explains to young women that they are duty-bound to obey their parents, and that misery awaits them if they follow their own inclinations, especially when it comes to young men. "You can

find no advisers so truly open, sincere, and disinterested, as your parents, or those who stand in their place," Broadhurst insists; "and you will be highly blamable . . . if you take any step in life . . . without their perfect approbation and sanction. A thousand melancholy instances might be collected, from the private memoirs of the domestic circle, of families, whose peace and harmony have most unhappily been interrupted by . . . rash conduct and . . . perverse disobedience. . . . There is nothing, upon which your happiness really depends, which your parents, or guardians . . . will refuse to you: and even if they are rigid and uncomplying, it is better that you should implicitly acquiesce in their most unreasonable wishes, than be guilty of violating a maxim not only consecrated by the established usages and laws of civil society, but carrying in its face the solemn stamp also of divine authority" (Broadhurst, *Advice to Young Ladies* [Bath: Cruttwell, 1808], 125–126).

9 In *Persuasion,* Austen emphasizes the primacy of a woman's first love. But compare *Sense and Sensibility,* where Marianne "does not approve of second attachments" yet eventually renounces Willoughby and falls in love with Colonel Brandon (I, 11).

10 In this context, "nice" means "discriminating" or "refined."

ing his good, even more than her own, she could hardly have given him up.—The belief of being prudent, and self-denying principally for *his* advantage, was her chief consolation, under the misery of a parting—a final parting; and every consolation was required, for she had to encounter all the additional pain of opinions, on his side, totally unconvinced and unbending, and of his feeling himself ill-used by so forced a relinquishment.—He had left the country in consequence.

A few months had seen the beginning and the end of their acquaintance; but, not with a few months ended Anne's share of suffering from it. Her attachment and regrets had, for a long time, clouded every enjoyment of youth; and an early loss of bloom and spirits had been their lasting effect.

More than seven years were gone since this little history of sorrowful interest had reached its close; and time had softened down much, perhaps nearly all of peculiar attachment to him,—but she had been too dependant on time alone; no aid had been given in change of place, (except in one visit to Bath soon after the rupture,) or in any novelty or enlargement of society.—No one had ever come within the Kellynch circle, who could bear a comparison with Frederick Wentworth, as he stood in her memory. No second attachment,[9] the only thoroughly natural, happy, and sufficient cure, at her time of life, had been possible to the nice[10] tone of her mind, the fastidiousness of her taste, in the small limits of the society around them. She had been solicited, when about two-and-twenty, to change her name, by the young man, who not long afterwards found a more willing mind in her younger sister; and Lady Russell had lamented her refusal; for Charles Musgrove was the eldest son of a man, whose landed property and general importance, were second, in that country, only to Sir Walter's, and of good character and appearance; and however Lady Russell might have asked yet for something more, while Anne was nineteen, she would have rejoiced to see her at twenty-two, so respectably removed from the partialities and injustice of her father's house, and settled so permanently near herself. But in this case, Anne had left nothing for advice to do; and though Lady Russell, as satisfied as ever with her own discretion,

Sir J. T. Duckworth's Action off St. Domingo, February 6, 1806, engraved by Thomas Sutherland (1785–1838), after Thomas Whitcombe (circa 1760–1824). Captain Wentworth and Austen's brother Francis fought in the Battle of St. Domingo.

never wished the past undone, she began now to have the anxiety which borders on hopelessness for Anne's being tempted, by some man of talents and independence, to enter a state for which she held her to be peculiarly fitted by her warm affections and domestic habits.

They knew not each other's opinion, either its constancy or its change, on the one leading point of Anne's conduct, for the subject was never alluded to,—but Anne, at seven and twenty,[11] thought very differently from what she had been made to think at nineteen.—She did not blame Lady Russell, she did not blame herself for having been guided by her; but she felt that were any young person, in similar circumstances, to apply to her for counsel, they would never receive any of such certain immediate wretchedness, such uncertain future good.[12]—She was persuaded that under every disadvantage of disapprobation at home, and every anxiety attending his profession, all their probable fears, delays and disappointments, she should yet have been a happier woman in maintaining the engagement, than

11 Twenty-seven is a significant age for Austen. In *Sense and Sensibility,* Marianne laments that "a woman of seven and twenty . . . can never hope to feel or inspire affection again" (I, 8). Charlotte Lucas in *Pride and Prejudice* is "about twenty-seven" when she accepts the foolish Mr. Collins (I, 5). Indeed, Austen herself was "about twenty-seven" in early December 1802 when she accepted and then rejected a marriage proposal from Harris Bigg-Wither (1781–1833). Compare the novelist Frances Burney (1752–1840) in *Evelina* (1778), where the same point is made with much greater severity: "I don't know what the devil a woman lives for after thirty," snaps Lord Merton: "she is only in other folks way" (Burney, *Evelina,* ed. Edward A. Bloom, with an Introduction and Notes by Vivien Jones [Oxford: Oxford University Press, 2002], 275).

12 In the autumn of 1814, Austen found herself in a position similar to Lady Russell's when she was consulted by her beloved niece Fanny Knight (1793–1882) about a marriage proposal from John Plumtre (1791–1864). Austen felt profoundly ambivalent about Plumtre's proposal to Fanny and urged her niece to be cautious about entering into a long engagement: "I am perfectly convinced that your present feelings, supposing you were to marry *now,* would be sufficient for his happiness;—but when I think how very, very far it is from a *Now,* & take everything that *may be,* into consideration, I dare not say, 'determine to accept him.' The risk is too great for *you,* unless your own Sentiments prompt it." Austen then spelled out the anxiety that underwrote her response: "Nothing can be compared to the misery of being bound *without* Love, bound to one, & preferring another" (Austen, *Letters,* 285–286).

Frances d'Arblay, by her cousin Edward Francisco Burney (1760–1848),
circa 1784. Frances Burney, represented here under her married name,
d'Arblay, published novels of manners such as *Evelina* (1778), *Cecilia* (1782),
and *Camilla* (1796). Austen greatly admired these works, which often point
the way toward her own artistic achievements. Burney is also justly celebrated for her letters and journals.

she had been in the sacrifice of it; and this, she fully believed, had the usual share, had even more than a usual share of all such solicitudes and suspense been theirs, without reference to the actual results of their case, which, as it happened, would have bestowed earlier prosperity than could be reasonably calculated on. All his sanguine expectations, all his confidence had been justified. His genius and ardour had seemed to foresee and to command his prosperous path. He had, very soon after their engagement ceased, got employ; and all that he had told her would follow, had taken place. He had distinguished himself, and early gained the other step in rank—and must now, by successive captures, have made a handsome fortune.[13] She had only navy lists[14] and newspapers for her authority, but she could not doubt his being rich;—and, in favour of his constancy, she had no reason to believe him married.

How eloquent could Anne Elliot have been,—how eloquent, at least, were her wishes on the side of early warm attachment, and a cheerful confidence in futurity, against that over-anxious caution which seems to insult exertion and distrust Providence!—She had been forced into prudence in her youth, she learned romance as she grew older—the natural sequel of an unnatural beginning.[15]

With all these circumstances, recollections and feelings, she could not hear that Captain Wentworth's sister was likely to live at Kellynch, without a revival of former pain; and many a stroll and many a sigh were necessary to dispel the agitation of the idea. She often told herself it was folly, before she could harden her nerves sufficiently to feel the continual discussion of the Crofts and their business no evil. She was assisted, however, by that perfect indifference and apparent unconsciousness, among the only three of her own friends in the secret of the past, which seemed almost to deny any recollection of it. She could do justice to the superiority of Lady Russell's motives in this, over those of her father and Elizabeth; she could honour all the better feelings of her calmness—but the general air of oblivion among them was highly important, from whatever it sprung; and in the event of Admiral Croft's really taking Kellynch-hall, she rejoiced anew over the conviction which had always been most grateful[16] to

13 The "other step in rank" is from commander to captain. The promotion qualifies Wentworth for larger and better-equipped vessels and entitles him to a much greater share of the prize money.

14 The "Navy Lists" were up-to-date publications that recorded battles, ships in commission, serving and retired officers, admiralty judges, and so on. There were several of these publications, but the most popular was *Steel's Original and Correct List of the Royal Navy,* which was issued monthly. Compare *Mansfield Park,* where Fanny Price's father reads "only the newspaper and the navy-list" (III, 8).

15 In a copy of *Persuasion* that was once in the possession of the Austen family, someone has read of Anne's struggles against "the natural sequel of an unnatural beginning" and then written in the margin, "Dear dear Jane! This deserves to be written in letters of gold." Chapman believes the words belong to Austen's sister, Cassandra. "Who else, at any early date, would write 'Dear Jane'?" (Chapman, "Jane Austen's Text: Authoritative Manuscript Corrections," in *Times Literary Supplement* [February 13, 1937], 116).

16 "Grateful" here means "welcome" or "agreeable."

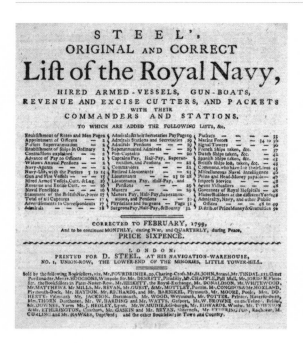

David Steel (d. circa 1810) published his *Original and Correct List of the Royal Navy* monthly during the war and quarterly during peacetime. In her desire to learn news of Captain Wentworth, Anne is as devoted to the *List of the Royal Navy* as her father is to his *Baronetage*.

her, of the past being known to those three only among her connexions, by whom no syllable, she believed, would ever be whispered, and in the trust that among his, the brother only with whom he had been residing, had received any information of their short-lived engagement.—That brother had been long removed from the country —and being a sensible man, and, moreover, a single man at the time, she had a fond dependance on no human creature's having heard of it from him.

The sister, Mrs. Croft, had then been out of England, accompanying her husband on a foreign station, and her own sister, Mary, had been at school while it all occurred—and never admitted by the pride of some, and the delicacy of others, to the smallest knowledge of it afterwards.

With these supports, she hoped that the acquaintance between herself and the Crofts, which, with Lady Russell, still resident in Kellynch, and Mary fixed only three miles off, must be anticipated, need not involve any particular awkwardness.

5

ON THE MORNING APPOINTED FOR Admiral and Mrs. Croft's seeing Kellynch-hall, Anne found it most natural to take her almost daily walk to Lady Russell's, and keep out of the way till all was over; when she found it most natural to be sorry that she had missed the opportunity of seeing them.

This meeting of the two parties proved highly satisfactory, and decided the whole business at once. Each lady was previously well disposed for an agreement, and saw nothing, therefore, but good manners in the other; and, with regard to the gentlemen, there was such an hearty good humour, such an open, trusting liberality on the Admiral's side, as could not but influence Sir Walter, who had besides been flattered into his very best and most polished behaviour by Mr. Shepherd's assurances of his being known, by report, to the Admiral, as a model of good breeding.

The house and grounds, and furniture, were approved, the Crofts were approved, terms, time, every thing, and every body, was right; and Mr. Shepherd's clerks were set to work, without there having been a single preliminary difference to modify of all that "This indenture sheweth."[1]

Sir Walter, without hesitation, declared the Admiral to be the best-looking sailor he had ever met with, and went so far as to say, that, if his own man might have had the arranging of his hair, he should not be ashamed of being seen with him any where; and the Admiral, with sympathetic cordiality, observed to his wife as they drove back through the Park, "I thought we should soon come to a

[1] "This indenture sheweth" is the customary preamble to a legal document.

2 "Never set the Thames on fire" is a proverbial expression used to describe someone who is dull, unre-
markable, or simple-minded.

3 Michaelmas was September 29, and the day on which
the feast of St. Michael was celebrated. It was also an
important business day, for it marked one of the four
times during the year when rents fell due and tenancies
began and ended.

4 Bath was largely constructed with local limestone.
When Austen visited the city in the spring of 1799, she
reported to Cassandra that when she arrived it was
raining and "all the Umbrellas were up, but now the
Pavements are getting very white again." The *Picturesque Guide to Bath* acknowledged that "the *whiteness* of
Bath is highly unfriendly to it, considered as a picturesque object" (Austen, *Letters,* 41; Harris, 169).

deal, my dear, in spite of what they told us at Taunton. The baronet
will never set the Thames on fire,[2] but there seems no harm in him:"
—reciprocal compliments, which would have been esteemed about
equal.

The Crofts were to have possession at Michaelmas,[3] and as Sir
Walter proposed removing to Bath in the course of the preceding
month, there was no time to be lost in making every dependant arrangement.

Lady Russell, convinced that Anne would not be allowed to be of
any use, or any importance, in the choice of the house which they
were going to secure, was very unwilling to have her hurried away so
soon, and wanted to make it possible for her to stay behind, till she
might convey her to Bath herself after Christmas; but having engagements of her own, which must take her from Kellynch for several
weeks, she was unable to give the full invitation she wished; and
Anne, though dreading the possible heats of September in all the
white glare of Bath,[4] and grieving to forego all the influence so sweet
and so sad of the autumnal months in the country, did not think that,
every thing considered, she wished to remain. It would be most right,
and most wise, and, therefore, must involve least suffering, to go
with the others.

Something occurred, however, to give her a different duty. Mary,
often a little unwell, and always thinking a great deal of her own complaints, and always in the habit of claiming Anne when any thing was
the matter, was indisposed; and foreseeing that she should not have a
day's health all the autumn, entreated, or rather required her, for it
was hardly entreaty, to come to Uppercross Cottage, and bear her
company as long as she should want her, instead of going to Bath.

"I cannot possibly do without Anne," was Mary's reasoning; and
Elizabeth's reply was, "Then I am sure Anne had better stay, for nobody will want her in Bath."

To be claimed as a good, though in an improper style, is at least
better than being rejected as no good at all; and Anne, glad to be
thought of some use, glad to have any thing marked out as a duty, and
certainly not sorry to have the scene of it in the country, and her own
dear country, readily agreed to stay.

This invitation of Mary's removed all Lady Russell's difficulties, and it was consequently soon settled that Anne should not go to Bath till Lady Russell took her, and that all the intervening time should be divided between Uppercross Cottage and Kellynch-lodge.

So far all was perfectly right; but Lady Russell was almost startled by the wrong of one part of the Kellynch-hall plan, when it burst on her, which was, Mrs. Clay's being engaged to go to Bath with Sir Walter and Elizabeth, as a most important and valuable assistant to the latter in all the business before her. Lady Russell was extremely sorry that such a measure should have been resorted to at all—wondered, grieved, and feared—and the affront it contained to Anne, in Mrs. Clay's being of so much use, while Anne could be of none, was a very sore aggravation.

Anne herself was become hardened to such affronts; but she felt the imprudence of the arrangement quite as keenly as Lady Russell. With a great deal of quiet observation, and a knowledge, which she often wished less, of her father's character, she was sensible[5] that results the most serious to his family from the intimacy, were more than possible. She did not imagine that her father had at present an idea of the kind. Mrs. Clay had freckles; and a projecting tooth, and a clumsy wrist, which he was continually making severe remarks upon, in her absence; but she was young, and certainly altogether well-looking, and possessed, in an acute mind and assiduous pleasing manners, infinitely more dangerous attractions than any merely personal might have been. Anne was so impressed by the degree of their danger, that she could not excuse herself from trying to make it perceptible to her sister. She had little hope of success; but Elizabeth, who in the event of such a reverse would be so much more to be pitied than herself, should never, she thought, have reason to reproach her for giving no warning.

She spoke, and seemed only to offend. Elizabeth could not conceive how such an absurd suspicion should occur to her; and indignantly answered for each party's perfectly knowing their situation.

"Mrs. Clay," said she warmly, "never forgets who she is; and as I am rather better acquainted with her sentiments than you can be, I can assure you, that upon the subject of marriage they are particularly

5 "Sensible" is "cognizant, conscious, aware of something" *(OED)*. Compare Walter Scott in *The Betrothed* (1825), where Guenwyn is "sensible that the alliance which he meditated might indeed be tolerated, but could not be approved, by his subjects and followers" (Scott, *The Betrothed,* ed. J. B. Ellis [Edinburgh: Edinburgh University Press, 2009], 18).

6 "Office" means "the customary or intended action of something."

7 Sir Walter has clearly been persuaded to accept some measures of economy, for he is giving up his carriage.

8 Sir Walter's tenants are so disillusioned with him that the traditional send-off given to the landlord is attended only by those "who might have had a hint to shew themselves."

nice; and that she reprobates all inequality of condition and rank more strongly than most people. And as to my father, I really should not have thought that he, who has kept himself single so long for our sakes, need be suspected now. If Mrs. Clay were a very beautiful woman, I grant you, it might be wrong to have her so much with me; not that any thing in the world, I am sure, would induce my father to make a degrading match; but he might be rendered unhappy. But poor Mrs. Clay, who, with all her merits, can never have been reckoned tolerably pretty! I really think poor Mrs. Clay may be staying here in perfect safety. One would imagine you had never heard my father speak of her personal misfortunes, though I know you must fifty times. That tooth of her's! and those freckles! Freckles do not disgust me so very much as they do him: I have known a face not materially disfigured by a few, but he abominates them. You must have heard him notice Mrs. Clay's freckles."

"There is hardly any personal defect," replied Anne, "which an agreeable manner might not gradually reconcile one to."

"I think very differently," answered Elizabeth, shortly; "an agreeable manner may set off handsome features, but can never alter plain ones. However, at any rate, as I have a great deal more at stake on this point than any body else can have, I think it rather unnecessary in you to be advising me."

Anne had done—glad that it was over, and not absolutely hopeless of doing good. Elizabeth, though resenting the suspicion, might yet be made observant by it.

The last office[6] of the four carriage-horses[7] was to draw Sir Walter, Miss Elliot, and Mrs. Clay to Bath. The party drove off in very good spirits; Sir Walter prepared with condescending bows for all the afflicted tenantry and cottagers who might have had a hint to shew themselves:[8] and Anne walked up at the same time, in a sort of desolate tranquillity, to the Lodge, where she was to spend the first week.

Her friend was not in better spirits than herself. Lady Russell felt this break-up of the family exceedingly. Their respectability was as dear to her as her own; and a daily intercourse had become precious by habit. It was painful to look upon their deserted grounds, and still worse to anticipate the new hands they were to fall into; and to es-

William Buchan, by an unknown artist, published in 1821. Buchan's *Domestic Medicine* remained phenomenally popular for the next fifty years. Between its first publication in 1769 and its last issue in 1871, there were at least 142 separate English-language editions.

9 "Viranda" was a common eighteenth-century spelling of "veranda."

10 Mary's hypochondria was a condition closely associated with her social status. According to the physician and immensely popular author William Buchan (1729–1805) in his book *Domestic Medicine* (1769), "hypochondriasis" was "the disease of the wealthy and luxurious alone; and in point of *respectability,* may certainly, next to gout, claim the precedence of all others" (Buchan, 83).

cape the solitariness and the melancholy of so altered a village, and be out of the way when Admiral and Mrs. Croft first arrived, she had determined to make her own absence from home begin when she must give up Anne. Accordingly their removal was made together, and Anne was set down at Uppercross Cottage, in the first stage of Lady Russell's journey.

Uppercross was a moderate-sized village, which a few years back had been completely in the old English style; containing only two houses superior in appearance to those of the yeomen and labourers,—the mansion of the 'squire, with its high walls, great gates, and old trees, substantial and unmodernized—and the compact, tight parsonage, enclosed in its own neat garden, with a vine and a pear-tree trained round its casements; but upon the marriage of the young 'squire, it had received the improvement of a farm-house elevated into a cottage for his residence; and Uppercross Cottage, with its viranda,[9] French windows, and other prettinesses, was quite as likely to catch the traveller's eye, as the more consistent and considerable aspect and premises of the Great House, about a quarter of a mile farther on.

Here Anne had often been staying. She knew the ways of Uppercross as well as those of Kellynch. The two families were so continually meeting, so much in the habit of running in and out of each other's house at all hours, that it was rather a surprise to her to find Mary alone; but being alone, her being unwell and out of spirits, was almost a matter of course. Though better endowed than the elder sister, Mary had not Anne's understanding or temper. While well, and happy, and properly attended to, she had great good humour and excellent spirits; but any indisposition sunk her completely; she had no resources for solitude; and inheriting a considerable share of the Elliot self-importance, was very prone to add to every other distress that of fancying herself neglected and ill-used.[10] In person, she was inferior to both sisters, and had, even in her bloom, only reached the dignity of being "a fine girl." She was now lying on the faded sofa of the pretty little drawing-room, the once elegant furniture of which had been gradually growing shabby, under the influence of four summers and two children; and, on Anne's appearing, greeted her with,

"So, you are come at last! I began to think I should never see you. I am so ill I can hardly speak. I have not seen a creature the whole morning!"[11]

"I am sorry to find you unwell," replied Anne. "You sent me such a good account of yourself on Thursday!"

"Yes, I made the best of it; I always do; but I was very far from well at the time; and I do not think I ever was so ill in my life as I have been all this morning—very unfit to be left alone, I am sure. Suppose I were to be seized of a sudden in some dreadful way, and not able to ring the bell! So, Lady Russell would not get out.[12] I do not think she has been in this house three times this summer."

Anne said what was proper, and enquired after her husband. "Oh! Charles is out shooting. I have not seen him since seven o'clock. He would go, though I told him how ill I was. He said he should not stay out long; but he has never come back, and now it is almost one. I assure you, I have not seen a soul this whole long morning."

"You have had your little boys with you?"

"Yes, as long as I could bear their noise; but they are so unmanageable that they do me more harm than good. Little Charles does not mind a word I say, and Walter is growing quite as bad."

"Well, you will soon be better now," replied Anne, cheerfully. "You know I always cure you when I come. How are your neighbours at the Great House?"

"I can give you no account of them. I have not seen one of them to-day, except Mr. Musgrove, who just stopped and spoke through the window, but without getting off his horse; and though I told him how ill I was, not one of them have been near me. It did not happen to suit the Miss Musgroves, I suppose, and they never put themselves out of their way."

"You will see them yet, perhaps, before the morning is gone. It is early."

"I never want them, I assure you. They talk and laugh a great deal too much for me. Oh! Anne, I am so very unwell! It was quite unkind of you not to come on Thursday."

"My dear Mary, recollect what a comfortable account you sent me of yourself! You wrote in the cheerfullest manner, and said you were

11 In Austen's day, "morning" extended from breakfast through to the hour of the evening meal, which could be served at any time from four to six thirty. "We breakfasted before 9 & do not dine till ½ past 6 on the occasion, so I hope we three shall have a long Morning enough," Austen wrote to Cassandra in October 1813 (Austen, *Letters,* 244).

12 Lady Russell stopped her carriage at Uppercross Cottage to deliver Anne but did not herself "get out" to pay a visit to Mary.

13 In discussing her "ailments" with Anne, Mary "covers the primitive and manipulative possibilities of whining with amazing efficiency," remarks Jan Fergus. "She vents her misery at being left alone with the repetitiveness characteristic of an inveterate whiner, and she openly and tacitly blames Anne and others for not paying attention to her." The conversation establishes a stark contrast between the two women: Mary whines to vent her unhappiness, while Anne puts on a brave face and suppresses hers. Fergus has some sympathy for Mary, who was "evidently a neglected child. Elizabeth was her father's favorite, and we can infer that Anne was her mother's as she is now Lady Russell's. . . . Mary is less attractive than either of her sisters, and less secure" (Fergus, " 'My Sore Throats, You Know, Are Always Worse Than Anybody's': Mary Musgrove and Jane Austen's Art of Whining," in *Persuasions*, 15 [1993], 140, 144–145).

perfectly well, and in no hurry for me; and that being the case, you must be aware that my wish would be to remain with Lady Russell to the last: and besides what I felt on her account, I have really been so busy, have had so much to do, that I could not very conveniently have left Kellynch sooner."

"Dear me! what can *you* possibly have to do?"

"A great many things, I assure you. More than I can recollect in a moment: but I can tell you some. I have been making a duplicate of the catalogue of my father's books and pictures. I have been several times in the garden with Mackenzie, trying to understand, and make him understand, which of Elizabeth's plants are for Lady Russell. I have had all my own little concerns to arrange—books and music to divide, and all my trunks to repack, from not having understood in time what was intended as to the waggons. And one thing I have had to do, Mary, of a more trying nature; going to almost every house in the parish, as a sort of take-leave. I was told that they wished it. But all these things took up a great deal of time."

"Oh! well;"—and after a moment's pause, "But you have never asked me one word about our dinner at the Pooles yesterday."

"Did you go then? I have made no enquiries, because I concluded you must have been obliged to give up the party."

"Oh! yes, I went. I was very well yesterday; nothing at all the matter with me till this morning. It would have been strange if I had not gone."

"I am very glad you were well enough, and I hope you had a pleasant party."

"Nothing remarkable. One always knows beforehand what the dinner will be, and who will be there. And it is so very uncomfortable, not having a carriage of one's own. Mr. and Mrs. Musgrove took me, and we were so crowded! They are both so very large, and take up so much room! And Mr. Musgrove always sits forward. So, there was I, crowded into the back seat with Henrietta and Louisa. And I think it very likely that my illness to-day may be owing to it."[13]

A little farther perseverance in patience, and forced cheerfulness on Anne's side, produced nearly a cure on Mary's. She could soon sit upright on the sofa, and began to hope she might be able to leave it by dinner-time. Then, forgetting to think of it, she was at the other end of the room, beautifying a nosegay; then, she ate her cold meat; and then she was well enough to propose a little walk.

"Where shall we go?" said she, when they were ready. "I suppose you will not like to call at the Great House before they have been to see you?"

"I have not the smallest objection on that account," replied Anne.[14] "I should never think of standing on such ceremony with people I know so well as Mrs. and the Miss Musgroves."

"Oh! but they ought to call upon you as soon as possible. They ought to feel what is due to you as *my* sister. However, we may as well go and sit with them a little while, and when we have got that over, we can enjoy our walk."

Anne had always thought such a style of intercourse highly imprudent; but she had ceased to endeavour to check it, from believing that, though there were on each side continual subjects of offence, neither family could now do without it. To the Great House accordingly they went, to sit the full half hour[15] in the old-fashioned square parlour, with a small carpet and shining floor, to which the present

14 Technically speaking, the Musgroves should visit Anne first because her social rank is much higher than theirs. But Anne does not share Mary's fixation with status and precedence.

15 Thirty minutes was the maximum amount of time for a formal morning visit. "On paying visits of ceremony, care should be taken not to make them too long, nor too frequent," cautioned John Trusler (1735–1820), a Church of England clergyman and prolific author; "a quarter of an hour, or twenty minutes, is sufficient time to exchange compliments, or run over the topics of the day" (Trusler, 31).

Drawing Room Scene, engraved by Anker Smith (1759–1819), after Henry Singleton (1766–1839). The picture depicts a scene from *The Social Day* (1822), a poem by Peter Coxe (circa 1753–1844). The Musgrove drawing room at Uppercross—with its "proper air of confusion"—must often have resembled this one.

16 Exeter is the county town of Devon and lies on the River Exe about ten miles above the river's entry into the English Channel.

17 For young women such as Henrietta and Louisa, the "usual stock of accomplishments" meant proficiency in dancing and singing, in playing the harp or piano, in drawing and screen-painting, and in languages such as French and Italian. These "graces" were acquired, not primarily for their educational value, but because they markedly improved a woman's chances in the highly competitive marriage market, where they enabled her to demonstrate that she would be an interesting and genteel companion to any prospective husband.

Austen's dismissive attitude toward female accomplishments is clear as early as *Catharine*, the most accomplished piece of her *Juvenilia*, where she describes Camilla Stanley as devoting twelve years "to the acquirement of Accomplishments which were now to be displayed and in a few Years entirely neglected. She was elegant in her appearance, rather handsome, and naturally not deficient in Abilities; but those Years which ought to have been spent in the attainment of useful knowledge and Mental Improvement, had been all bestowed in learning Drawing, Italian and Music, more especially the latter, and she now united to these Accomplishments, an Understanding unimproved by reading and a Mind totally devoid either of Taste or Judgement."

Austen's views on female education were shared by Mary Wollstonecraft (1759–1797), who wrote her groundbreaking work of feminist criticism, *A Vindication of the Rights of Woman* (1792), at almost the same moment that Austen produced *Catharine*. For Wollstonecraft, "accomplishments" are another name for "weaknesses," and in the *Rights of Woman* she argues passionately that the traditional education of women enslaves them by turning them into dolls who must simper and scheme in order to attract a man, whereas a system of education that recognized that women—like men—were possessed of reason and virtue would render them multidimensional human beings who were fully capable of carrying out their duties as mothers,

A young woman plays the harp at an evening party; artist unknown. Her "musical accomplishments" draw the attention of a young man, as Louisa and Henrietta hope their charms will attract Captain Wentworth.

daughters of the house were gradually giving the proper air of confusion by a grand piano forte and a harp, flower-stands and little tables placed in every direction. Oh! could the originals of the portraits against the wainscot, could the gentlemen in brown velvet and the ladies in blue satin have seen what was going on, have been conscious of such an overthrow of all order and neatness! The portraits themselves seemed to be staring in astonishment.

The Musgroves, like their houses, were in a state of alteration, perhaps of improvement. The father and mother were in the old English style, and the young people in the new. Mr. and Mrs. Musgrove were a very good sort of people; friendly and hospitable, not much educated, and not at all elegant. Their children had more modern minds and manners. There was a numerous family; but the only two grown up, excepting Charles, were Henrietta and Louisa, young ladies of nineteen and twenty, who had brought from a school at Exeter[16] all the usual stock of accomplishments,[17] and were now, like thousands of other young ladies, living to be fashionable, happy, and merry. Their dress had every advantage, their faces were rather pretty, their spirits extremely good, their manner unembarrassed and pleasant; they were of consequence at home, and favourites abroad. Anne always contemplated them as some of the happiest creatures of her acquaintance; but still, saved as we all are by some comfortable feeling of superiority from wishing for the possibility of exchange, she would not have given up her own more elegant and cultivated mind for all their enjoyments; and envied them nothing but that seemingly perfect good understanding and agreement together, that good-humoured mutual affection, of which she had known so little herself with either of her sisters.

They were received with great cordiality. Nothing seemed amiss on the side of the Great House family, which was generally, as Anne very well knew, the least to blame. The half hour was chatted away pleasantly enough; and she was not at all surprised, at the end of it, to have their walking party joined by both the Miss Musgroves, at Mary's particular invitation.

wives, and citizens. Under the present system of female education, Wollstonecraft declares, "gentleness, docility, and a spaniel-like affection are . . . consistently recommended as the cardinal virtues of the sex. . . . One writer has declared that it is masculine for a woman to be melancholy. She was created to be the toy of man, his rattle, and it must jingle in his ears whenever, dismissing reason, he chooses to be amused." Such an account of women appears "abject," acknowledges Wollstonecraft, but this is an accurate portrait of what it means to be "accomplished" (Wollstonecraft, *Works,* V, 102).

Mary Wollstonecraft, by John Opie (1761–1807), circa 1797. In addition to her famous *Vindication of the Rights of Woman,* Wollstonecraft published *Thoughts on the Education of Daughters* (1787), *An Historical and Moral View of the Origin and Progress of the French Revolution* (1794), and *Letters Written during a Short Residence in Sweden, Norway, and Denmark* (1796). In *Persuasion,* Austen's indictment of sentimentality, patriarchy, and the deficiencies of female education roots her firmly in the Enlightenment feminism espoused by Wollstonecraft.

6

1 "Had not wanted" here means "did not need."

2 The renowned architect John Wood the Elder (1704–1754) completed the construction of Queen Square in 1736. By 1814 it was not fashionable enough for Henrietta and Louisa, but fifteen years earlier Austen herself had enjoyed her stay there when she, her mother, Cassandra Leigh Austen (1739–1827), and her brother Edward Austen (1767–1852) briefly took up lodgings at Number Thirteen. "I like our situation very much," Austen informed her sister Cassandra; ". . . the prospect from the Drawingroom window at which I now write, is rather picturesque." In 1801, Austen returned with her family to Bath to hunt for a permanent home. She reported to Cassandra that their mother "hankers . . . dreadfully" after a house in Queen Square (Austen, *Letters,* 41, 76).

ANNE HAD NOT WANTED[1] THIS VISIT to Uppercross, to learn that a removal from one set of people to another, though at a distance of only three miles, will often include a total change of conversation, opinion, and idea. She had never been staying there before, without being struck by it, or without wishing that other Elliots could have her advantage in seeing how unknown, or unconsidered there, were the affairs which at Kellynch-hall were treated as of such general publicity and pervading interest; yet, with all this experience, she believed she must now submit to feel that another lesson, in the art of knowing our own nothingness beyond our own circle, was become necessary for her;—for certainly, coming as she did, with a heart full of the subject which had been completely occupying both houses in Kellynch for many weeks, she had expected rather more curiosity and sympathy than she found in the separate, but very similar remark of Mr. and Mrs. Musgrove—"So, Miss Anne, Sir Walter and your sister are gone; and what part of Bath do you think they will settle in?" and this, without much waiting for an answer;—or in the young ladies addition of, "I hope *we* shall be in Bath in the winter; but remember, papa, if we do go, we must be in a good situation—none of your Queen-squares for us!"[2] or in the anxious supplement from Mary, of "Upon my word, I shall be pretty well off, when you are all gone away to be happy at Bath!"

She could only resolve to avoid such self-delusion in future, and think with heightened gratitude of the extraordinary blessing of having one such truly sympathising friend as Lady Russell.

The Mr. Musgroves had their own game to guard, and to destroy; their own horses, dogs, and newspapers to engage them; and the females were fully occupied in all the other common subjects of housekeeping, neighbours, dress, dancing, and music. She acknowledged it to be very fitting, that every little social commonwealth should dictate its own matters of discourse; and hoped, ere long, to become a not unworthy member of the one she was now transplanted into. — With the prospect of spending at least two months at Uppercross, it was highly incumbent on her to clothe her imagination, her memory, and all her ideas in as much of Uppercross as possible.

She had no dread of these two months. Mary was not so repulsive[3] and unsisterly as Elizabeth, nor so inaccessible to all influence of hers; neither was there any thing among the other component parts of the cottage inimical to comfort. — She was always on friendly terms with her brother-in-law; and in the children, who loved her nearly as well, and respected her a great deal more than their mother, she had an object of interest, amusement, and wholesome exertion.

Charles Musgrove was civil and agreeable; in sense and temper he was undoubtedly superior to his wife; but not of powers, or conversation, or grace, to make the past, as they were connected together,

3 By "repulsive" Austen means "cold" or "forbidding."

A British sportsman shooting ducks, by H. Merke, after Samuel Howitt (1756–1822), circa 1809. Hunting is Charles Musgrove's favorite pastime.

Evening Dresses for August 1808, an illustration from *Le Beau Monde, or Literary and Fashionable Magazine.* Like Captain Wentworth, this gentleman enjoys the attention of two young women.

at all a dangerous contemplation; though, at the same time, Anne could believe, with Lady Russell, that a more equal match might have greatly improved him; and that a woman of real understanding might have given more consequence to his character, and more usefulness, rationality, and elegance to his habits and pursuits. As it was, he did nothing with much zeal, but sport; and his time was otherwise trifled away, without benefit from books, or any thing else. He had very good spirits, which never seemed much affected by his wife's occasional lowness; bore with her unreasonableness sometimes to Anne's admiration; and, upon the whole, though there was very often a little disagreement, (in which she had sometimes more share than she wished, being appealed to by both parties) they might pass for a happy couple. They were always perfectly agreed in the want of more money, and a strong inclination for a handsome present from his father; but here, as on most topics, he had the superiority, for while Mary thought it a great shame that such a present was not made, he always contended for his father's having many other uses for his money, and a right to spend it as he liked.

As to the management of their children, his theory was much better than his wife's, and his practice not so bad.—"I could manage them very well, if it were not for Mary's interference,"—was what Anne often heard him say, and had a good deal of faith in; but when listening in turn to Mary's reproach of "Charles spoils the children so that I cannot get them into any order,"—she never had the smallest temptation to say, "Very true."

One of the least agreeable circumstances of her residence there, was her being treated with too much confidence by all parties, and being too much in the secret of the complaints of each house. Known to have some influence with her sister, she was continually requested, or at least receiving hints to exert it, beyond what was practicable. "I wish you could persuade Mary not to be always fancying herself ill," was Charles's language; and, in an unhappy mood, thus spoke Mary;—"I do believe if Charles were to see me dying, he would not think there was any thing the matter with me. I am sure, Anne, if you would, you might persuade him that I really am very ill—a great deal worse than I ever own."

Mary's declaration was, "I hate sending the children to the Great House, though their grandmamma is always wanting to see them, for she humours and indulges them to such a degree, and gives them so much trash and sweet things, that they are sure to come back sick and cross for the rest of the day."—And Mrs. Musgrove took the first opportunity of being alone with Anne, to say, "Oh! Miss Anne, I cannot help wishing Mrs. Charles had a little of your method with those children. They are quite different creatures with you! But to be sure, in general they are so spoilt! It is a pity you cannot put your sister in the way of managing them. They are as fine healthy children as ever were seen, poor little dears, without partiality; but Mrs. Charles knows no more how they should be treated!—Bless me, how troublesome they are sometimes!—I assure you, Miss Anne, it prevents my wishing to see them at our house so often as I otherwise should. I believe Mrs. Charles is not quite pleased with my not inviting them oftener; but you know it is very bad to have children with one, that one is obliged to be checking every moment; 'don't do this, and don't do that;'—or that one can only keep in tolerable order by more cake than is good for them."

She had this communication, moreover, from Mary. "Mrs. Musgrove thinks all her servants so steady, that it would be high treason to call it in question; but I am sure, without exaggeration, that her upper house-maid and laundry-maid, instead of being in their business, are gadding about the village, all day long. I meet them wherever I go; and I declare, I never go twice into my nursery without seeing something of them. If Jemima were not the trustiest, steadiest creature in the world, it would be enough to spoil her; for she tells me, they are always tempting her to take a walk with them." And on Mrs. Musgrove's side, it was,—"I make a rule of never interfering in any of my daughter-in-law's concerns, for I know it would not do; but I shall tell *you,* Miss Anne, because you may be able to set things to rights, that I have no very good opinion of Mrs. Charles's nursery-maid: I hear strange stories of her; she is always upon the gad:[4] and from my own knowledge, I can declare, she is such a fine-dressing lady, that she is enough to ruin any servants she comes near. Mrs. Charles quite swears by her, I know; but I just give you this hint, that

4 "Upon the gad" is "on the move" or "going about" (*OED*). Compare Tobias Smollett (1721–1771) in his epistolary novel *Humphry Clinker* (1771): "Here is such dressing, and fidling, and dancing, and gadding, and courting, and plotting" (Smollett, *Humphry Clinker,* 41).

5 If all things were equal, Mary—as the younger woman—would give place to Mrs. Musgrove. But all things are not equal. Mary is the daughter of a baronet, and so, as rank counts for more than age, she should lead into and out of the dining room, even when they are in Mrs. Musgrove's home. The fact that she so often insists on these strict rules of etiquette is of course a source of considerable irritation to the Musgroves.

you may be upon the watch; because, if you see any thing amiss, you need not be afraid of mentioning it."

Again; it was Mary's complaint, that Mrs. Musgrove was very apt not to give her the precedence that was her due,[5] when they dined at the Great House with other families; and she did not see any reason why she was to be considered so much at home as to lose her place. And one day, when Anne was walking with only the Miss Musgroves, one of them, after talking of rank, people of rank, and jealousy of rank, said, "I have no scruple of observing to *you,* how nonsensical some persons are about their place, because, all the world knows how easy and indifferent you are about it: but I wish any body could give Mary a hint that it would be a great deal better if she were not so very tenacious; especially, if she would not be always putting herself forward to take place of mamma. Nobody doubts her right to have precedence of mamma, but it would be more becoming in her not to be always insisting on it. It is not that mamma cares about it the least in the world, but I know it is taken notice of by many persons."

How was Anne to set all these matters to rights? She could do little more than listen patiently, soften every grievance, and excuse each to the other; give them all hints of the forbearance necessary between such near neighbours, and make those hints broadest which were meant for her sister's benefit.

In all other respects, her visit began and proceeded very well. Her own spirits improved by change of place and subject, by being removed three miles from Kellynch: Mary's ailments lessened by having a constant companion; and their daily intercourse with the other family, since there was neither superior affection, confidence, nor employment in the cottage, to be interrupted by it, was rather an advantage. It was certainly carried nearly as far as possible, for they met every morning, and hardly ever spent an evening asunder; but she believed they should not have done so well without the sight of Mr. and Mrs. Musgrove's respectable forms in the usual places, or without the talking, laughing, and singing of their daughters.

She played a great deal better than either of the Miss Musgroves; but having no voice, no knowledge of the harp, and no fond parents to sit by and fancy themselves delighted, her performance was little thought of, only out of civility, or to refresh the others, as she was well aware. She knew that when she played she was giving pleasure only to herself; but this was no new sensation: excepting one short period of her life, she had never, since the age of fourteen, never since the loss of her dear mother, known the happiness of being listened to, or encouraged by any just appreciation or real taste. In music she had been always used to feel alone in the world; and Mr. and Mrs. Musgrove's fond partiality for their own daughters' performance, and total indifference to any other person's, gave her much more pleasure for their sakes, than mortification for her own.

The party at the Great House was sometimes increased by other company. The neighbourhood was not large, but the Musgroves were visited by every body, and had more dinner parties, and more callers, more visitors by invitation and by chance, than any other family. There were more completely popular.

The girls were wild for dancing; and the evenings ended, occasionally, in an unpremeditated little ball. There was a family of cousins within a walk of Uppercross, in less affluent circumstances, who depended on the Musgroves for all their pleasures: they would come at any time, and help play at any thing, or dance any where; and Anne, very much preferring the office of musician to a more active post, played country dances[6] to them by the hour together; a kindness which always recommended her musical powers to the notice of Mr. and Mrs. Musgrove more than any thing else, and often drew this compliment;—"Well done, Miss Anne! very well done indeed! Lord bless me! how those little fingers of yours fly about!"

So passed the first three weeks. Michaelmas came; and now Anne's heart must be in Kellynch again. A beloved home made over to others; all the precious rooms and furniture, groves, and prospects, beginning to own[7] other eyes and other limbs! She could not think of much else on the 29th of September; and she had this sympathetic touch in the evening, from Mary, who, on having occasion to note down the day of the month, exclaimed, "Dear me! is not this the day the Crofts were to come to Kellynch? I am glad I did not think of it before. How low it makes me!"

6 Anne's decision on these occasions to play the music rather than to dance and socialize indicates that she has removed herself from the marriage market.

7 By "own," Austen means "to recognize as familiar" (*OED*).

8 Presumably Anne could not go to visit the Crofts because, as we later learn, Charles drives a curricle, which holds only two people. Compare *Mansfield Park,* where Mr. Rushworth mentions his curricle, and Mr. Crawford suggests "the greater desirableness of some carriage which might convey more than two" (I, 9).

9 The metaphorical usage of "electrified" was common in the period. Compare the novelist and poet Charlotte Dacre (circa 1782–1825) in *Zofloya* (1806), where the evil Victoria hears the name of "a dire foe" and is "in a moment electrified." In Walter Scott's *Ivanhoe* (1820), the loyal swineherd Gurth starts up "as if electrified" after the mysterious Pilgrim whispers something in his ear (Dacre, *Zofloya,* ed. Kim Ian Michasiw [Oxford: Oxford University Press, 1997], 263; Scott, *Ivanhoe,* ed. Graham Tulloch [Edinburgh: Edinburgh University Press, 1998], 60).

The Crofts took possession with true naval alertness, and were to be visited. Mary deplored the necessity for herself. "Nobody knew how much she should suffer. She should put it off as long as she could." But was not easy till she had talked Charles into driving her over on an early day; and was in a very animated, comfortable state of imaginary agitation, when she came back. Anne had very sincerely rejoiced in there being no means of her going.[8] She wished, however, to see the Crofts, and was glad to be within when the visit was returned. They came; the master of the house was not at home, but the two sisters were together; and as it chanced that Mrs. Croft fell to the share of Anne, while the admiral sat by Mary, and made himself very agreeable by his good-humoured notice of her little boys, she was well able to watch for a likeness, and if it failed her in the features, to catch it in the voice, or the turn of sentiment and expression.

Mrs. Croft, though neither tall nor fat, had a squareness, uprightness, and vigour of form, which gave importance to her person. She had bright dark eyes, good teeth, and altogether an agreeable face; though her reddened and weather-beaten complexion, the consequence of her having been almost as much at sea as her husband, made her seem to have lived some years longer in the world than her real eight and thirty. Her manners were open, easy, and decided, like one who had no distrust of herself, and no doubts of what to do; without any approach to coarseness, however, or any want of good humour. Anne gave her credit, indeed, for feelings of great consideration towards herself, in all that related to Kellynch; and it pleased her: especially, as she had satisfied herself in the very first half minute, in the instant even of introduction, that there was not the smallest symptom of any knowledge or suspicion on Mrs. Croft's side, to give a bias of any sort. She was quite easy on that head, and consequently full of strength and courage, till for a moment electrified[9] by Mrs. Croft's suddenly saying,—

"It was you, and not your sister, I find, that my brother had the pleasure of being acquainted with, when he was in this country."

Anne hoped she had outlived the age of blushing; but the age of emotion she certainly had not.

"Perhaps you may not have heard that he is married," added Mrs. Croft.

She could now answer as she ought; and was happy to feel, when Mrs. Croft's next words explained it to be Mr. Wentworth[10] of whom she spoke, that she had said nothing which might not do for either brother. She immediately felt how reasonable it was, that Mrs. Croft should be thinking and speaking of Edward, and not of Frederick; and with shame at her own forgetfulness, applied herself to the knowledge of their former neighbour's present state, with proper interest.

The rest was all tranquillity; till just as they were moving, she heard the admiral say to Mary,

"We are expecting a brother of Mrs. Croft's here soon; I dare say you know him by name."

He was cut short by the eager attacks of the little boys, clinging to him like an old friend, and declaring he should not go; and being too much engrossed by proposals of carrying them away in his coat pocket, &c. to have another moment for finishing or recollecting what he had begun, Anne was left to persuade herself, as well as she could, that the same brother must still be in question. She could not, however, reach such a degree of certainty, as not to be anxious to hear whether any thing had been said on the subject at the other house, where the Crofts had previously been calling.

The folks of Great House were to spend the evening of this day at the Cottage; and it being now too late in the year for such visits to be made on foot, the coach was beginning to be listened for, when the youngest Miss Musgrove walked in. That she was coming to apologize, and that they should have to spend the evening by themselves, was the first black idea; and Mary was quite ready to be affronted, when Louisa made all right by saying, that she only came on foot, to leave more room for the harp, which was bringing[11] in the carriage.

"And I will tell you our reason," she added, "and all about it. I am come on to give you notice, that papa and mamma are out of spirits this evening, especially mamma; she is thinking so much of poor Richard! And we agreed it would be best to have the harp, for it seems to amuse her more than the piano-forte. I will tell you why

10 "Mr. Wentworth" indicates that Edward is the eldest son, as "Miss Elliot" designates Elizabeth as the eldest daughter.

11 "Bringing" here means "being brought."

Declaring he should not go.

Hugh Thomson (1860–1920), Illustrations for *Persuasion,* 1897. Admiral Croft is restrained by the rambunctious young Musgrove boys.

12 With his ship presumably decommissioned after the 1814 abdication of Napoleon, Wentworth has returned to England and is now on half-pay.

13 "Intelligence" is "news" or "information."

14 Austen's severe treatment of Dick Musgrove has been much discussed. According to Julia Prewitt Brown, the passage "is one of the few instances in Jane Austen in which we sense a loss of control, perhaps because the exact source of the statement is confused. The sentiment of the passage comes both from a narrator (in some ways the old Jane Austen narrator appearing suddenly) and from the central consciousness of Anne. Like Sir Walter in the opening scene, Dick Musgrove is seen as the frustrated Anne might see him." Brown concludes that the "animus behind the statement ('and the good fortune to lose him') is as anarchic as a modern conception of truth usually is. The narrator is saying that some lives really are worthless. This is the dark, unfamiliar side of the narrator's characteristically didactic insistence that some lives really are worth something" (Brown, 133–134).

15 Midshipmen were noncommissioned (and often very young) officers ranking immediately below the most junior commissioned officers. Dick Musgrove's ineptitude would have been a real liability to Wentworth, for midshipmen "kept watches at sea and in harbour, learning how to take sights, how to handle parties of men, how to deal with various events and emergencies of shipboard life. They also ran the ship's boats" (John Winton, "Life and Education in a Technically Evolving Navy, 1815–1925," in *The Oxford Illustrated History of the Royal Navy* [Oxford: Oxford University Press, 1995], 268).

16 A frigate was "the most glamorous type of ship in the navy. It was big enough to carry a significant gun power, but fast enough to evade larger enemies. . . . It often fought single-ship actions against enemy frigates, and these were followed avidly by the press and public. Successful frigate captains . . . achieved great fame, and some became extremely rich on prize

she is out of spirits. When the Crofts called this morning, (they called here afterwards, did not they?) they happened to say, that her brother, Captain Wentworth, is just returned to England, or paid off, or something,[12] and is coming to see them almost directly; and most unluckily it came into mamma's head, when they were gone, that Wentworth, or something very like it, was the name of poor Richard's captain, at one time, I do not know when or where, but a great while before he died, poor fellow! And upon looking over his letters and things, she found it was so; and is perfectly sure that this must be the very man, and her head is quite full of it, and of poor Richard! So we must all be as merry as we can, that she may not be dwelling upon such gloomy things."

The real circumstances of this pathetic piece of family history were, that the Musgroves had had the ill fortune of a very troublesome, hopeless son; and the good fortune to lose him before he reached his twentieth year; that he had been sent to sea, because he was stupid and unmanageable on shore; that he had been very little cared for at any time by his family, though quite as much as he deserved; seldom heard of, and scarcely at all regretted, when the intelligence[13] of his death abroad had worked its way to Uppercross, two years before.

He had, in fact, though his sisters were now doing all they could for him, by calling him "poor Richard," been nothing better than a thick-headed, unfeeling, unprofitable Dick Musgrove, who had never done any thing to entitle himself to more than the abbreviation of his name, living or dead.[14]

He had been several years at sea, and had, in the course of those removals to which all midshipmen[15] are liable, and especially such midshipmen as every captain wishes to get rid of, been six months on board Captain Frederick Wentworth's frigate,[16] the Laconia; and from the Laconia he had, under the influence of his captain, written the only two letters which his father and mother had ever received from him during the whole of his absence; that is to say, the only two disinterested letters; all the rest had been mere applications for money.

The English frigate *Unicorn* in action against the French frigate *La Tribune* off the Scilly Isles on June 8, 1796. The picture is believed to be the work of one of the officers of the *Unicorn.*

money. . . . The frigate was used for convoy escort, commerce raiding, and patrols. It also provided the main reconnaissance force for the battlefleet." A large frigate was allowed twenty-four midshipmen, a small to medium-sized one only six (Lavery, 49, 90).

17 "Incurious," meaning "uncritical" or "not precise" *(OED),* is now obsolete, but it was common in Austen's era. See, for example, Matthew Lewis (1775–1818) in *The Monk* (1796), where the nobleman Don Raymond encounters an old innkeeper who is "credulous and incurious" (Lewis, *The Monk,* ed. Howard Anderson [Oxford: Oxford University Press, 1998], 146).

In each letter he had spoken well of his captain; but yet, so little were they in the habit of attending to such matters, so unobservant and incurious[17] were they as to the names of men or ships, that it had made scarcely any impression at the time; and that Mrs. Musgrove should have been suddenly struck, this very day, with a recollection of the name of Wentworth, as connected with her son, seemed one of those extraordinary bursts of mind which do sometimes occur.

She had gone to her letters, and found it all as she supposed; and the reperusal of these letters, after so long an interval, her poor son gone for ever, and all the strength of his faults forgotten, had affected her spirits exceedingly, and thrown her into greater grief for him than she had known on first hearing of his death. Mr. Musgrove was, in a lesser degree, affected likewise; and when they reached the cottage, they were evidently in want, first, of being listened to anew on this subject, and afterwards, of all the relief which cheerful companions could give.

18 Clifton was a fashionable spa resort situated on the hill just west of Bristol. By the early nineteenth century, its popularity was in decline.

19 "Enure" is an obsolete form of "inure," meaning to accept or become hardened to.

20 By "insensible," Austen means "not sensitive."

21 It was the captain's duty to see that the boys under his command were taught writing, grammar, mathematics, and navigation. On the larger ships, these responsibilities usually fell to a schoolmaster, but many of them were ill qualified for the position, as Dick Musgrove's shoddy spelling and improper usage make plain. In alluding to Wentworth's conscientiousness about the education of his men, Austen may be recalling Lord Nelson, who "every day . . . went into the school-room" to see that his midshipmen were "pursuing their nautical studies" (Margarette Lincoln, *Representing the Royal Navy: British Sea Power, 1750–1815* [Aldershot: Ashgate, 2002], 23; Robert Southey, *The Life of Nelson,* 2 vols. [London: John Murray, 1813], I, 52–53).

To hear them talking so much of Captain Wentworth, repeating his name so often, puzzling over past years, and at last ascertaining that it *might,* that it probably *would,* turn out to be the very same Captain Wentworth whom they recollected meeting, once or twice, after their coming back from Clifton;[18]—a very fine young man; but they could not say whether it was seven or eight years ago,—was a new sort of trial to Anne's nerves. She found, however, that it was one to which she must enure[19] herself. Since he actually was expected in the country, she must teach herself to be insensible[20] on such points. And not only did it appear that he was expected, and speedily, but the Musgroves, in their warm gratitude for the kindness he had shewn poor Dick, and very high respect for his character, stamped as it was by poor Dick's having been six months under his care, and mentioning him in strong, though not perfectly well spelt praise, as "a fine dashing felow, only two perticular about the schoolmaster,"[21] were bent on introducing themselves, and seeking his acquaintance, as soon as they could hear of his arrival.

The resolution of doing so helped to form the comfort of their evening.

7

A VERY FEW DAYS MORE, and Captain Wentworth was known to be at Kellynch, and Mr. Musgrove had called on him, and come back warm in his praise, and he was engaged with the Crofts to dine at Uppercross, by the end of another week. It had been a great disappointment to Mr. Musgrove, to find that no earlier day could be fixed, so impatient was he to shew his gratitude, by seeing Captain Wentworth under his own roof, and welcoming him to all that was strongest and best in his cellars.[1] But a week must pass; only a week, in Anne's reckoning, and then, she supposed, they must meet; and soon she began to wish that she could feel secure even for a week.

Captain Wentworth made a very early return to Mr. Musgrove's civility, and she was all but calling there in the same half hour!—She and Mary were actually setting forward for the great house, where, as she afterwards learnt, they must inevitably have found him, when they were stopped by the eldest boy's being at that moment brought home in consequence of a bad fall. The child's situation put the visit entirely aside, but she could not hear of her escape with indifference, even in the midst of the serious anxiety which they afterwards felt on his account.

His collar-bone was found to be dislocated, and such injury received in the back, as roused the most alarming ideas. It was an afternoon of distress, and Anne had every thing to do at once—the apothecary[2] to send for—the father to have pursued and informed—the mother to support and keep from hysterics[3]—the servants to control—the youngest child to banish, and the poor suffering one to

1 The "cellars" are of course Mr. Musgrove's wine cellars.

2 Apothecaries were pharmacists, but (especially in the country) they routinely acted as general medical practitioners. See the great poet and satirist Alexander Pope (1688–1744) in *An Essay on Criticism* (1711): "So modern *Pothecaries,* taught the Art / By *Doctor's Bills* to play the *Doctor's Part*" (Pope, I, 251).

3 The "hysteric fit," advised the physician and author William Buchan, sometimes "resembles a swoon," while on other occasions "the patient is affected with catchings and strong convulsions." Women of a "delicate habit," he added, are most subject to these fits, which are brought on "by violent passions or affections of the mind, as fear, grief, anger, or great disappointments" (Buchan, 308–309).

Brought home in consequence of a bad fall.

Charles Edmund Brock, Illustrations for *Persuasion,* 1898. Young Charles Musgrove
is carried home after hurting his collarbone.

attend and soothe;—besides sending, as soon as she recollected it, proper notice to the other house, which brought her an accession rather of frightened, enquiring companions, than of very useful assistants.[4]

Her brother's return[5] was the first comfort; he could take best care of his wife, and the second blessing was the arrival of the apothecary. Till he came and had examined the child, their apprehensions were the worse for being vague;—they suspected great injury, but knew not where; but now the collar-bone was soon replaced, and though Mr. Robinson felt and felt, and rubbed, and looked grave, and spoke low words both to the father and the aunt, still they were all to hope the best, and to be able to part and eat their dinner in tolerable ease of mind; and then it was just before they parted, that the two young aunts were able so far to digress from their nephew's state, as to give the information of Captain Wentworth's visit;—staying five minutes behind their father and mother, to endeavour to express how perfectly delighted they were with him, how much handsomer, how infinitely more agreeable they thought him than any individual among their male acquaintance, who had been at all a favourite before—how glad they had been to hear papa invite him to stay dinner—how sorry when he said it was quite out of his power—and how glad again, when he had promised in reply[6] to papa and mamma's farther pressing invitations, to come and dine with them on the morrow, actually on the morrow!—And he had promised it in so pleasant a manner, as if he felt all the motive of their attention just as he ought!—And, in short, he had looked and said every thing with such exquisite grace, that they could assure them all, their heads were both turned by him!—And off they ran, quite as full of glee as of love, and apparently more full of Captain Wentworth than of little Charles.

The same story and the same raptures were repeated, when the two girls came with their father, through the gloom of the evening, to make enquiries; and Mr. Musgrove, no longer under the first uneasiness about his heir, could add his confirmation and praise, and hope there would be now no occasion for putting Captain Wentworth off, and only be sorry to think that the cottage party, probably, would not like to leave the little boy, to give him the meeting.—"Oh,

4 Anne's role in dealing with the young boy's mishap recalls Maria Edgeworth's assertion in *Madame de Fleury* (1809) that "in most sudden accidents, and in all domestic misfortunes, female resolution and presence of mind are indispensably requisite: safety, health, and life, often depend upon the fortitude of women. Happy they, who . . . possess strength of mind united with the utmost gentleness of manner and tenderness of disposition!" (Edgeworth, *Works*, V, 211).

5 "Brother," as Austen employs the term, can mean—as here—"brother-in-law." The same applies later in the novel to her use of "sister" for "sister-in-law."

6 The text has been amended here from "to reply" to "in reply."

no! as to leaving the little boy!"—both father and mother were in much too strong and recent alarm to bear the thought; and Anne, in the joy of the escape, could not help adding her warm protestations to theirs.

Charles Musgrove, indeed, afterwards shewed more of inclination; "the child was going on so well—and he wished so much to be introduced to Captain Wentworth, that, perhaps, he might join them in the evening; he would not dine from home, but he might walk in for half an hour." But in this he was eagerly opposed by his wife, with "Oh, no! indeed, Charles, I cannot bear to have you go away. Only think, if any thing should happen!"

The child had a good night, and was going on well the next day. It must be a work of time to ascertain that no injury had been done to the spine, but Mr. Robinson found nothing to increase alarm, and Charles Musgrove began consequently to feel no necessity for longer confinement. The child was to be kept in bed, and amused as quietly as possible; but what was there for a father to do? This was quite a female case, and it would be highly absurd in him, who could be of no use at home, to shut himself up. His father very much wished him to meet Captain Wentworth, and there being no sufficient reason against it, he ought to go; and it ended in his making a bold public declaration, when he came in from shooting, of his meaning to dress directly, and dine at the other house.

"Nothing can be going on better than the child," said he, "so I told my father just now that I would come, and he thought me quite right. Your sister being with you, my love, I have no scruple at all. You would not like to leave him yourself, but you see I can be of no use. Anne will send for me if any thing is the matter."

Husbands and wives generally understand when opposition will be vain. Mary knew, from Charles's manner of speaking, that he was quite determined on going, and that it would be of no use to teaze him. She said nothing, therefore, till he was out of the room, but as soon as there was only Anne to hear,

"So! You and I are to be left to shift by ourselves, with this poor sick child—and not a creature coming near us all the evening! I knew how it would be. This is always my luck! If there is any thing disagreeable going on, men are always sure to get out of it, and Charles is as bad as any of them. Very unfeeling! I must say it is very unfeeling of him, to be running away from his poor little boy; talks of his being going on so well! How does he know that he is going on well, or that there may not be a sudden change half an hour hence? I did not think Charles would have been so unfeeling. So, here he is to go away and enjoy himself, and because I am the poor mother, I am not to be allowed to stir;—and yet, I am sure, I am more unfit than any body else to be about the child. My being the mother is the very reason why my feelings should not be tried. I am not at all equal to it. You saw how hysterical I was yesterday."

"But that was only the effect of the suddenness of your alarm—of the shock. You will not be hysterical again. I dare say we shall have nothing to distress us. I perfectly understand Mr. Robinson's directions, and have no fears; and indeed, Mary, I cannot wonder at your husband. Nursing does not belong to a man, it is not his province. A sick child is always the mother's property, her own feelings generally make it so."

"I hope I am as fond of my child as any mother—but I do not know that I am of any more use in the sick-room than Charles, for I cannot be always scolding and teazing a poor child when it is ill; and you saw, this morning, that if I told him to keep quiet, he was sure to begin kicking about. I have not nerves for the sort of thing."

"But, could you be comfortable yourself, to be spending the whole evening away from the poor boy?"

"Yes; you see his papa can, and why should not I?—Jemima is so careful! And she could send us word every hour how he was. I really think Charles might as well have told his father we would all come. I am not more alarmed about little Charles now than he is. I was dreadfully alarmed yesterday, but the case is very different to-day."

"Well—if you do not think it too late to give notice for yourself, suppose you were to go, as well as your husband. Leave little Charles to my care. Mr. and Mrs. Musgrove cannot think it wrong, while I remain with him."

"Are you serious?" cried Mary, her eyes brightening. "Dear me! that's a very good thought, very good indeed. To be sure I may just as well go as not, for I am of no use at home—am I? and it only harasses me. You, who have not a mother's feelings, are a great deal the properest person. You can make little Charles do any thing; he always minds you at a word. It will be a great deal better than leaving him with only Jemima. Oh! I will certainly go; I am sure I ought if I can, quite as much as Charles, for they want me excessively to be acquainted with Captain Wentworth, and I know you do not mind being left alone. An excellent thought of yours, indeed, Anne! I will go and tell Charles, and get ready directly. You can send for us, you know, at a moment's notice, if any thing is the matter; but I dare say there will be nothing to alarm you. I should not go, you may be sure, if I did not feel quite at ease about my dear child."

The next moment she was tapping at her husband's dressing-room door, and as Anne followed her up stairs, she was in time for the whole conversation, which began with Mary's saying, in a tone of great exultation,

"I mean to go with you, Charles, for I am of no more use at home than you are. If I were to shut myself up for ever with the child, I should not be able to persuade him to do any thing he did not like. Anne will stay; Anne undertakes to stay at home and take care of him. It is Anne's own proposal, and so I shall go with you, which will be a great deal better, for I have not dined at the other house since Tuesday."

"This is very kind of Anne," was her husband's answer, "and I should be very glad to have you go; but it seems rather hard that she should be left at home by herself, to nurse our sick child."

Anne was now at hand to take up her own cause, and the sincerity of her manner being soon sufficient to convince him, where conviction was at least very agreeable, he had no farther scruples as to her being left to dine alone, though he still wanted her to join them in the evening, when the child might be at rest for the night, and kindly urged her to let him come and fetch her; but she was quite unpersuadable; and this being the case, she had ere long the pleasure of seeing them set off together in high spirits. They were gone, she hoped, to be happy, however oddly constructed such happiness might seem; as for herself, she was left with as many sensations of comfort, as were, perhaps, ever likely to be hers. She knew herself to be of the first utility to the child; and what was it to her, if Frederick Wentworth were only half a mile distant, making himself agreeable to others!

She would have liked to know how he felt as to a meeting. Perhaps indifferent, if indifference could exist under such circumstances. He must be either indifferent or unwilling. Had he wished ever to see her again, he need not have waited till this time; he would have done what she could not but believe that in his place she should have done long ago, when events had been early giving him the independence which alone had been wanting.

Her brother and sister came back delighted with their new acquaintance, and their visit in general. There had been music, singing, talking, laughing, all that was most agreeable; charming manners in Captain Wentworth, no shyness or reserve; they seemed all to know each other perfectly, and he was coming the very next morning to shoot with Charles. He was to come to breakfast, but not at the Cottage, though that had been proposed at first; but then he had been pressed to come to the Great House instead, and he seemed afraid of being in Mrs. Charles Musgrove's way, on account of the child; and therefore, somehow, they hardly knew how, it ended in Charles's being to meet him to breakfast at his father's.

Anne understood it. He wished to avoid seeing her. He had enquired after her, she found, slightly, as might suit a former slight acquaintance, seeming to acknowledge such as she had acknowledged, actuated, perhaps, by the same view of escaping introduction when they were to meet.

The morning hours of the Cottage were always later than those of the other house; and on the morrow the difference was so great, that Mary and Anne were not more than beginning breakfast when Charles came in to say that they were just setting off, that he was come for his dogs, that his sisters were following with Captain Wentworth, his sisters meaning to visit Mary and the child, and Captain Wentworth proposing also to wait on her for a few minutes, if not

Samuel Johnson, portrait in oils, by Sir Joshua Reynolds, 1756–1757. Johnson's writings left a deep and indelible mark on Austen's novels. According to Henry Austen in his "Biographical Notice" of his sister, Johnson was her favorite moral writer in prose (see Appendix B of this edition).

7 David Cecil remarks that "one of the most important facts" about Austen is that she was "born in the
eighteenth century; and, spiritually speaking, she
stayed there. A contemporary of Coleridge and Wordsworth, her view of things had much more in common"
with that of Samuel Johnson (1709–1784), the great
eighteenth-century critic and man of letters. Yet as
Norman Page observes, when Austen describes the
"thousand feelings" that rush on Anne, she is testing a
style that breaks decisively from the kind of prose she
has written in the past, a style that looks forward to
the twentieth-century novels of Virginia Woolf (1882–
1941), such as *Mrs. Dalloway* (1925) and *To The Light-
house* (1927), rather than backward to the elaborate
cadences and balanced precision of Johnson in essay
collections such as *The Rambler* (1750–1752). "The
abrupt phrases and the absence of coordination make
this as far from the Johnsonian model as it could well
be," Page asserts: "it is in fact much closer to *Mrs. Dalloway* than to *The Rambler* in style and sensibility. Partly
because so much of the heroine's emotional life is lived
secretly, Jane Austen's last novel is especially rich in
what amounted to an experimental prose." Marilyn
Butler concludes that "there is nothing in subjective
writing in any earlier English novel to compare in sub-
tlety of insight or depth of feeling with the sequence of
nervous scenes between the hero and the heroine in
Persuasion" (Cecil, 12–13; Page, "Jane Austen's Language," in Grey, 263; Butler, 278).

8 Anne's remembrance of things past locks her vividly
within history. Eight and a half years have elapsed since
her break with Wentworth, and she has worked hard
during that time to give him up and move on. But when
he returns she finds that her emotional connection
to him is far stronger than her chronological distance
from him. "Try as she might," Mary Favret asserts,
"Anne Elliot cannot find peace in peacetime; the peace
she thinks she has achieved during her nearly eight
years of limbo is too fragile, too easily broken. . . . Like
Anne's sense of peace, the clock time of historicism,
with its clear divisions and oblivions, falls apart
through the uncertain chronology of affect: 'Alas! with

inconvenient; and though Charles had answered for the child's being
in no such state as could make it inconvenient, Captain Wentworth
would not be satisfied without his running on to give notice.

Mary, very much gratified by this attention, was delighted to receive him; while a thousand feelings rushed on Anne, of which this
was the most consoling, that it would soon be over. And it was soon
over. In two minutes after Charles's preparation, the others appeared; they were in the drawing-room. Her eye half met Captain
Wentworth's; a bow, a curtsey passed; she heard his voice—he talked
to Mary; said all that was right; said something to the Miss Musgroves, enough to mark an easy footing: the room seemed full—full
of persons and voices—but a few minutes ended it. Charles shewed
himself at the window, all was ready, their visitor had bowed and was
gone; the Miss Musgroves were gone too, suddenly resolving to walk
to the end of the village with the sportsmen: the room was cleared,
and Anne might finish her breakfast as she could.[7]

"It is over! it is over!" she repeated to herself again, and again, in
nervous gratitude. "The worst is over!"

Mary talked, but she could not attend. She had seen him. They
had met. They had been once more in the same room!

Soon, however, she began to reason with herself, and try to be feeling less. Eight years, almost eight years had passed, since all had been
given up. How absurd to be resuming the agitation which such an
interval had banished into distance and indistinctness! What might
not eight years do? Events of every description, changes, alienations,
removals,—all, all must be comprised in it; and oblivion of the past—
how natural, how certain too! It included nearly a third part of her
own life.

Alas! with all her reasonings, she found, that to retentive feelings
eight years may be little more than nothing.[8]

Now, how were his sentiments to be read? Was this like wishing to
avoid her? And the next moment she was hating herself for the folly
which asked the question.

On one other question, which perhaps her utmost wisdom might
not have prevented, she was soon spared all suspense; for after the

Miss Musgroves had returned and finished their visit at the Cottage, she had this spontaneous information from Mary:

"Captain Wentworth is not very gallant by you, Anne, though he was so attentive to me. Henrietta asked him what he thought of you, when they went away; and he said, 'You were so altered he should not have known you again.'"

Mary had no feelings to make her respect her sister's[9] in a common way; but she was perfectly unsuspicious of inflicting[10] any peculiar wound.

"Altered beyond his knowledge!" Anne fully submitted, in silent, deep mortification. Doubtless it was so; and she could take no revenge, for he was not altered, or not for the worse. She had already acknowledged it to herself, and she could not think differently, let him think of her as he would. No; the years which had destroyed her youth and bloom had only given him a more glowing, manly, open look, in no respect lessening his personal advantages. She had seen the same Frederick Wentworth.

"So altered that he should not have known her again!" These were words which could not but dwell with her. Yet she soon began to rejoice that she had heard them. They were of sobering tendency; they allayed agitation; they composed, and consequently must make her happier.

Frederick Wentworth had used such words, or something like them, but without an idea that they would be carried round to her. He had thought her wretchedly altered, and, in the first moment of appeal, had spoken as he felt.[11] He had not forgiven Anne Elliot. She had used him ill; deserted and disappointed him; and worse, she had shewn a feebleness of character in doing so, which his own decided, confident temper could not endure. She had given him up to oblige others. It had been the effect of over-persuasion. It had been weakness and timidity.

He had been most warmly attached to her, and had never seen a woman since whom he thought her equal; but, except from some natural sensation of curiosity, he had no desire of meeting her again. Her power with him was gone for ever.

all her reasonings, she found, that to retentive feelings eight years may be little more than nothing.' Anne's love for Wentworth, in fact, has to break through such false peace and tidy chronology into the stir and roar of a messier, potentially traumatic history" (Favret, *War at a Distance: Romanticism and the Making of Modern Wartime* [Princeton: Princeton University Press, 2010], 162).

9 The text has been amended here from "sisters" to "sister's."

10 The text has been amended here from "of being inflicting" to "of inflicting."

11 Austen concentrates much of her attention on Anne's inner life, but this passage marks one of the rare instances when she leaves her to enter into the thoughts of another character, on this occasion, Wentworth.

12 Wentworth's deep confusion about love and relationships is especially clear when he states that "the
woman he should wish to meet with" must possess "a
strong mind, with sweetness of manner." Mary Waldron tersely observes that "he seems little interested in
how that sweetness can be maintained while she defies
the counsels of her family." Judith Terry pursues the
same point from a different angle. Wentworth's speech
dismissing Anne is "a wonderful piece of tangled logic
. . . and so exactly the way in which other people contradict themselves completely within the space of ten
minutes." Moreover, "if we are already lukewarm towards Anne . . . when Wentworth charges [her] here
with feebleness, weakness and timidity, it authorises
us to acknowledge, perhaps even justify, what we may
have been trying to suppress: our irritation with Anne
for being so stupid as to listen to that old bat Lady Russell instead of the urgings of her own true love. So what
we do as readers outside the text is not unlike what
Wentworth does within it: misread Anne. That unacknowledged conflict within him is ours also" (Waldron,
141; Terry, "The Slow Process of *Persuasion*," in *Jane
Austen's Business,* ed. Juliet McMaster and Bruce Stovel
[London: Macmillan, 1996], 130).

It was now his object to marry. He was rich, and being turned
on shore, fully intended to settle as soon as he could be properly
tempted; actually looking round, ready to fall in love with all the
speed which a clear head and quick taste could allow. He had a heart
for either of the Miss Musgroves, if they could catch it; a heart, in
short, for any pleasing young woman who came in his way, excepting
Anne Elliot. This was his only secret exception, when he said to his
sister, in answer to her suppositions,

"Yes, here I am, Sophia, quite ready to make a foolish match. Any
body between fifteen and thirty may have me for asking. A little
beauty, and a few smiles, and a few compliments to the navy, and I am
a lost man. Should not this be enough for a sailor, who has had no
society among women to make him nice?"

He said it, she knew, to be contradicted. His bright, proud eye
spoke the happy conviction that he was nice; and Anne Elliot was
not out of his thoughts, when he more seriously described the woman
he should wish to meet with. "A strong mind, with sweetness of manner," made the first and the last of the description.[12]

"That is the woman I want," said he. "Something a little inferior I
shall of course put up with, but it must not be much. If I am a fool, I
shall be a fool indeed, for I have thought on the subject more than
most men."

8

FROM THIS TIME CAPTAIN WENTWORTH and Anne Elliot were repeatedly in the same circle. They were soon dining in company together at Mr. Musgrove's, for the little boy's state could no longer supply his aunt with a pretence for absenting herself; and this was but the beginning of other dinings and other meetings.

Whether former feelings were to be renewed, must be brought to the proof; former times must undoubtedly be brought to the recollection of each; *they* could not but be reverted to; the year of their engagement could not but be named by him, in the little narratives or descriptions which conversation called forth. His profession qualified him, his disposition led him, to talk; and "*That* was in the year six;" "*That* happened before I went to sea in the year six," occurred in the course of the first evening they spent together: and though his voice did not falter, and though she had no reason to suppose his eye wandering towards her while he spoke, Anne felt the utter impossibility, from her knowledge of his mind, that he could be unvisited by remembrance any more than herself. There must be the same immediate association of thought, though she was very far from conceiving it to be of equal pain.

They had no conversation together, no intercourse but what the commonest civility required. Once so much to each other! Now nothing! There *had* been a time, when of all the large party now filling the drawing-room at Uppercross, they would have found it most difficult to cease to speak to one another. With the exception, perhaps, of Admiral and Mrs. Croft, who seemed particularly attached

1 Conditions in the Royal Navy improved dramatically over the course of the eighteenth century. In Austen's age, "captains furnished their own cabins according to personal taste. They could live in solitary splendour, or they could surround themselves with their own servants and followers, or they could dine frequently with their officers; the latter was probably the most common." One chaplain reported that when he boarded a ship, he brought with him "an assortment of shirts, neckcloths, stockings, black silk handkerchiefs, bed and bedding, two silver spoons and a silver fork for the mess" (Lavery, 109, 112).

2 Wentworth's deep attachment to the navy does not prevent him from indulging a dry wit. The *Asp* was not fit for long journeys, and so the admiralty dispatched it all the way to the West Indies, the group of islands that extends from the tip of the Florida Peninsula to the northern coast of South America. The islands constituted Britain's most important colony, and throughout the Napoleonic Wars the navy was charged with ensuring that their enormous riches continued to flow back to Britain. Austen's references to—and attitudes toward—the West Indies have in recent years been vigorously investigated. "Just because Austen referred to Antigua in *Mansfield Park* or to realms visited by the British navy in *Persuasion* without any thought of possible responses by the Caribbean or Indian natives resident there is no reason for us to do the same," writes Edward Said. "We now know that these non-European peoples did not accept with indifference the authority projected over them, or the general silence on which their presence in variously attenuated forms is predicated" (Said, *Culture and Imperialism* [New York: Alfred A. Knopf, 1993], 66).

and happy, (Anne could allow no other exception even among the married couples) there could have been no two hearts so open, no tastes so similar, no feelings so in unison, no countenances so beloved. Now they were as strangers; nay, worse than strangers, for they could never become acquainted. It was a perpetual estrangement.

When he talked, she heard the same voice, and discerned the same mind. There was a very general ignorance of all naval matters throughout the party; and he was very much questioned, and especially by the two Miss Musgroves, who seemed hardly to have any eyes but for him, as to the manner of living on board, daily regulations, food, hours, &c.; and their surprise at his accounts, at learning the degree of accommodation and arrangement which was practicable, drew from him some pleasant ridicule, which reminded Anne of the early days when she too had been ignorant, and she too had been accused of supposing sailors to be living on board without any thing to eat, or any cook to dress it if there were, or any servant to wait, or any knife and fork to use.[1]

From thus listening and thinking, she was roused by a whisper of Mrs. Musgrove's, who, overcome by fond regrets, could not help saying,

"Ah! Miss Anne, if it had pleased Heaven to spare my poor son, I dare say he would have been just such another by this time."

Anne suppressed a smile, and listened kindly, while Mrs. Musgrove relieved her heart a little more; and for a few minutes, therefore, could not keep pace with the conversation of the others.—When she could let her attention take its natural course again, she found the Miss Musgroves just fetching the navy-list,—(their own navy list, the first that had ever been at Uppercross); and sitting down together to pore over it, with the professed view of finding out the ships which Captain Wentworth had commanded.

"Your first was the Asp, I remember; we will look for the Asp."

"You will not find her there.—Quite worn out and broken up. I was the last man who commanded her.—Hardly fit for service then. —Reported fit for home service for a year or two,—and so I was sent off to the West Indies."[2]

The girls looked all amazement.

"The admiralty," he continued, "entertain themselves now and then, with sending a few hundred men to sea, in a ship not fit to be employed. But they have a great many to provide for; and among the thousands that may just as well go to the bottom as not, it is impossible for them to distinguish the very set who may be least missed."

"Phoo! phoo!" cried the admiral, "what stuff these young fellows talk! Never was a better sloop than the Asp in her day.—For an old built sloop, you would not see her equal. Lucky fellow to get her!—He knows there must have been twenty better men than himself applying for her at the same time. Lucky fellow to get any thing so soon, with no more interest[3] than his."

"I felt my luck, admiral, I assure you;" replied Captain Wentworth, seriously.—"I was as well satisfied with my appointment as you can desire. It was a great object with me, at that time, to be at sea,—a very great object. I wanted to be doing something."[4]

"To be sure you did.—What should a young fellow, like you, do ashore, for half a year together?—If a man has not a wife, he soon wants to be afloat again."

3 Admiral Croft means that Wentworth lacked friends in high places who had an "interest" in advancing his career.

4 Wentworth is addressing these words to the general company, but of course they have a special meaning for Anne. He was appointed to the *Asp* in the months immediately following the collapse of his engagement to her in the summer of 1806, and he was desperate "to be doing something" to take his mind off the pain of their separation. Juliet McMaster contends that Wentworth was almost suicidal when he "went to sea in a leaky ship, and would as soon have gone to the bottom as not" (*Jane Austen on Love, English Literary Studies,* 13 [Victoria, BC: University of Victoria Press, 1978], 40).

The Fall of Nelson, Battle of Trafalgar, 21 October 1805, by Denis Dighton (1791–1827). Nelson is on the right and is seen at the moment he falls. Most of the crew appear unaware that he has been hit, but in the center foreground a midshipman aims his musket at the French marksman who fired the fatal shot.

5 A "pelisse" is a long cloak or coat, trimmed or lined with fur.

6 "Privateers" were armed private ships commissioned by the government to attack enemy vessels.

7 Wentworth "wanted" this French frigate for the prize money it would bring him and his crew, but also because capturing it with a sloop—a much less powerful and well-equipped vessel—gave him a prime opportunity to demonstrate his skill and courage as a naval officer.

8 Plymouth is a seaport on the coast of Devon, a county bounded on the west by Cornwall and on the east by Dorset and Somerset. The Sound is the inlet that leads from the English Channel into Plymouth Harbour.

9 The "Great Nation" is an ironic reference to France, which had been at war with Britain since 1793.

10 Anne of course reads every corner of the newspapers and the navy lists in the hope of learning anything at all about Wentworth. She would certainly have seen a notice of his death. William Deresiewicz observes that her "state of wan hopelessness and perpetual regret" is "enlivened only by a self-tormenting addiction to the navy lists" (Deresiewicz, 130).

11 The "Rock of Gibraltar" is a British overseas territory located on Spain's southern Mediterranean coast. It guards the Strait of Gibraltar, which is the only way to pass from the Mediterranean Sea to the Atlantic Ocean, and was a crucial base for the Royal Navy throughout the Napoleonic Wars.

"But, Captain Wentworth," cried Louisa, "how vexed you must have been when you came to the Asp, to see what an old thing they had given you."

"I knew pretty well what she was, before that day;" said he, smiling. "I had no more discoveries to make, than you would have as to the fashion and strength of any old pelisse,[5] which you had seen lent about among half your acquaintance, ever since you could remember, and which at last, on some very wet day, is lent to yourself.—Ah! she was a dear old Asp to me. She did all that I wanted. I knew she would.—I knew that we should either go to the bottom together, or that she would be the making of me; and I never had two days of foul weather all the time I was at sea in her; and after taking privateers[6] enough to be very entertaining, I had the good luck, in my passage home the next autumn, to fall in with the very French frigate I wanted.[7]—I brought her into Plymouth; and here was another instance of luck. We had not been six hours in the Sound,[8] when a gale came on, which lasted four days and nights, and which would have done for poor old Asp, in half the time; our touch with the Great Nation[9] not having much improved our condition. Four-and-twenty hours later, and I should only have been a gallant Captain Wentworth, in a small paragraph at one corner of the newspapers; and being lost in only a sloop, nobody would have thought about me."

Anne's shudderings were to herself, alone:[10] but the Miss Musgroves could be as open as they were sincere, in their exclamations of pity and horror.

"And so then, I suppose," said Mrs. Musgrove, in a low voice, as if thinking aloud, "so then he went away to the Laconia, and there he met with our poor boy.—Charles, my dear," (beckoning him to her), "do ask Captain Wentworth where it was he first met with your poor brother. I always forget."

"It was at Gibraltar,[11] mother, I know. Dick had been left ill at Gibraltar, with a recommendation from his former captain to Captain Wentworth."

"Oh!—but, Charles, tell Captain Wentworth, he need not be afraid of mentioning poor Dick before me, for it would be rather a pleasure to hear him talked of, by such a good friend."

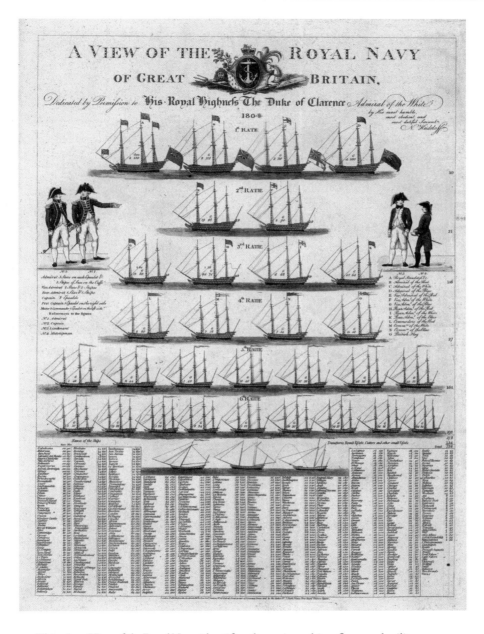

This 1804 *View of the Royal Navy* identifies the various ships, flags, and military uniforms of the British navy. It also lists the names of the ships, together with the number of guns and men aboard each one. Austen's brother Francis was in command of the *Canopus,* which is listed here in the first column. Compare *Mansfield Park,* where the *Canopus* is anchored in Portsmouth Harbor (III, 7).

12 In this scene, Austen subtly juxtaposes Captain Wentworth's pleasure in the navy lists with Sir Walter's in the *Baronetage*.

13 There were six classes of navy ships, and they were rated according to the number of guns they carried. First rates were three-deckers of one hundred guns or more. Fifth or six rates included frigates such as the *Laconia,* which Wentworth commanded when Dick Musgrove was one of his midshipmen. Unrated ships, such as Wentworth's sloop the *Asp,* carried about twenty guns. A "non-commissioned vessel" was one that had been taken out of service (Lavery, 40).

14 A "cruise" was a raiding expedition in pursuit of plunder, and Wentworth's was "lovely" because it was so lucrative. The "Western Islands" refers to the Azores, an archipelago composed of nine major islands in the North Atlantic, roughly 1,000 miles west of Portugal. Austen's brother Francis cruised there in the closing months of 1812, when his ship the *Elephant* captured the *Swordfish,* an American privateer. Wentworth's tales of the high seas are compelling and certainly impress his audience at Uppercross. But they "ignore some of the harsher realities of naval service and therefore offer a romanticised view of it," Roger Sales points out. "They do not deal with the widespread anxieties over homosexual practices." What is more, "sailors were about four times as likely to die either of disease, or in an accident, than they were to be killed in action. Naval surgeons usually had fewer paper qualifications than those who practised on land.... Nelson, himself a walking testimonial to the skill of the surgeons, was worried that the best ones were always in danger of leaving. Elaborate precautions were taken to prevent sailors from deserting" (Sales, 184).

15 In his recollection of "those pleasant days" Wentworth reveals both his genuine concern for the Harvilles and his own inability to forget about Anne. "To most of his hearers this sounds merely like an expression of the Captain's sympathy for his friend," Howard S. Babb remarks. "But the association of money with marriage, especially in company with the phrase 'worse

Nelson Boarding the San Nicolas *in the Victory off Cape St. Vincent . . . 14 February 1797,* by A. W. Reeve, after W. R. Thomas. Nelson captured the *San Nicolas* and then, from its deck, boarded and took a second ship, the *San Josef.* He received a knighthood for his actions.

Charles, being somewhat more mindful of the probabilities of the case, only nodded in reply, and walked away.

The girls were now hunting for the Laconia; and Captain Wentworth could not deny himself the pleasure of taking the precious volume into his own hands to save them the trouble,[12] and once more read aloud the little statement of her name and rate, and present non-commissioned class,[13] observing over it, that she too had been one of the best friends man ever had.

"Ah! those were pleasant days when I had the Laconia! How fast I made money in her.—A friend of mine, and I, had such a lovely cruise together off the Western Islands.[14]—Poor Harville, sister! You know how much he wanted money—worse than myself. He had a wife.[15]— Excellent fellow! I shall never forget his happiness. He felt it all, so much for her sake.—I wished for him again the next summer, when I had still the same luck in the Mediterranean."

"And I am sure, Sir," said Mrs. Musgrove, "it was a lucky day for *us*, when you were put captain into that ship. *We* shall never forget what you did."

Her feelings made her speak low; and Captain Wentworth, hearing only in part, and probably not having Dick Musgrove at all near his thoughts, looked rather in suspense, and as if waiting for more.

"My brother," whispered one of the girls; "mamma is thinking of poor Richard."

"Poor dear fellow!" continued Mrs. Musgrove; "he was grown so steady, and such an excellent correspondent, while he was under your care! Ah! it would have been a happy thing, if he had never left you. I assure you, Captain Wentworth, we are very sorry he ever left you."

There was a momentary expression in Captain Wentworth's face at this speech, a certain glance of his bright eye, and curl of his handsome mouth, which convinced Anne, that instead of sharing in Mrs. Musgrove's kind wishes, as to her son, he had probably been at some pains to get rid of him; but it was too transient an indulgence of self-amusement to be detected by any who understood him less than herself; in another moment he was perfectly collected and serious; and almost instantly afterwards coming up to the sofa, on which she and Mrs. Musgrove were sitting, took a place by the latter, and entered into conversation with her, in a low voice, about her son, doing it with so much sympathy and natural grace, as shewed the kindest consideration for all that was real and unabsurd in the parent's feelings.[16]

They were actually on the same sofa, for Mrs. Musgrove had most readily made room for him;—they were divided only by Mrs. Musgrove. It was no insignificant barrier indeed. Mrs. Musgrove was of a comfortable substantial size, infinitely more fitted by nature to express good cheer and good humour, than tenderness and sentiment; and while the agitations of Anne's slender form, and pensive face, may be considered as very completely screened, Captain Wentworth should be allowed some credit for the self-command with which he

than myself,' proves his lingering sensitivity to what Anne has deprived him of" (Babb, *Jane Austen's Novels: The Fabric of Dialogue* [Columbus: Ohio State University Press, 1962], 222).

16 Stuart Tave notes that Wentworth's ability to make "the important distinctions between what is absurd in Mrs. Musgrove and what is real" is crucial because it enables us to "understand better why a woman like Anne Elliot can love him, and it is necessary that we think well of him, think him worthy of Anne, if her feelings are to be important to us and if we are to desire their union" (Tave, 261).

He attended to her large, fat sighings.

Hugh Thomson, Illustrations for *Persuasion*, 1897. Anne and Captain Wentworth sit on the same couch, divided by Mrs. Musgrove, to whom Captain Wentworth listens respectfully.

17 Mrs. Musgrove's "large fat sighings" have been examined at great length. "Some critics used to say that this harshness was clearly an error and would have been removed had *Persuasion* been thoroughly revised," Janet Todd asserts. "But why should Austen not stand by these observations, which are common-sensical though not compassionate?" For Nina Auerbach, Mrs. Musgrove's sighs contain "all the potential insincerity and ludicrousness of Anne's protracted mourning over the death of feeling. These flat, comic characters siphon off our subversive impulses toward the romantic heroine and probably . . . Austen's subversive impulses as well. They allow a full acceptance of Anne's emotional world." Perhaps most compellingly, Adela Pinch finds that "Austen applies the language of neo-classical aesthetic judgement ('unbecoming conjunctions . . . taste cannot tolerate') to Mrs. Musgrove's expressive body, as if she were a bad poem or book. The result is not far from the physical snobbery of Sir Walter Elliot." But, Pinch observes, "if extreme physical snobbery has already been represented and ridiculed *within* the novel in the characters of Sir Walter and Elizabeth Elliot, finding the narrator raising similar questions suggests that a serious inquiry of some kind about the relationship between personal form and mental life is taking place here" (Todd, "Jane Austen, Politics and Sensibility," in *Feminist Criticism: Theory and Practice,* ed. Susan Sellers [New York: Harvester Wheatsheaf, 1991], 72; Auerbach, "O Brave New World: Evolution and Revolution in *Persuasion,*" in *ELH,* 39 [1972], 115; Adela Pinch, "Lost in a Book: Jane Austen's *Persuasion,*" in *Studies in Romanticism,* 32 [1993], 101–102).

Gosport: The Entrance to Portsmouth Harbor, by J. M.W. Turner (1775–1851). Austen's two sailor brothers, Francis and Charles, were educated at the Royal Navy Academy in Portsmouth.

attended to her large fat sighings over the destiny of a son, whom alive nobody had cared for.

Personal size and mental sorrow have certainly no necessary proportions. A large bulky figure has as good a right to be in deep affliction, as the most graceful set of limbs in the world. But, fair or not fair, there are unbecoming conjunctions, which reason will patronize in vain,—which taste cannot tolerate,—which ridicule will seize.[17]

The admiral, after taking two or three refreshing turns about the room with his hands behind him, being called to order by his wife, now came up to Captain Wentworth, and without any observation of what he might be interrupting, thinking only of his own thoughts, began with,

"If you had been a week later at Lisbon, last spring, Frederick, you would have been asked to give a passage to Lady Mary Grierson and her daughters."

"Should I? I am glad I was not a week later then."

The admiral abused him for his want of gallantry. He defended himself; though professing that he would never willingly admit any

ladies on board a ship of his,[18] excepting for a ball, or a visit, which a few hours might comprehend.

"But, if I know myself," said he, "this is from no want of gallantry towards them. It is rather from feeling how impossible it is, with all one's efforts, and all one's sacrifices, to make the accommodations on board, such as women ought to have. There can be no want of gallantry, admiral, in rating the claims of women to every personal comfort *high*—and this is what I do. I hate to hear of women on board, or to see them on board; and no ship, under my command, shall ever convey a family of ladies any where, if I can help it."

This brought his sister upon him.

"Oh Frederick!—But I cannot believe it of you.—All idle refinement!—Women may be as comfortable on board, as in the best house in England. I believe I have lived as much on board as most women, and I know nothing superior to the accommodations of a man of war.[19] I declare I have not a comfort or an indulgence about me, even at Kellynch-hall," (with a kind bow to Anne) "beyond what I always had in most of the ships I have lived in; and they have been five altogether."

"Nothing to the purpose," replied her brother. "You were living with your husband; and were the only woman on board."

"But you, yourself, brought Mrs. Harville, her sister, her cousin, and the three children, round from Portsmouth[20] to Plymouth. Where was this superfine, extraordinary sort of gallantry[21] of yours, then?"

"All merged in my friendship, Sophia. I would assist any brother officer's wife that I could, and I would bring any thing of Harville's from the world's end, if he wanted it. But do not imagine that I did not feel it an evil in itself."

"Depend upon it they were all perfectly comfortable."

"I might not like them the better for that, perhaps. Such a number of women and children have no *right* to be comfortable on board."

"My dear Frederick, you are talking quite idly. Pray, what would become of us poor sailors' wives, who often want to be conveyed to one port or another, after our husbands, if every body had your feelings?"

18 Wentworth is following the rules when he declares that "he would never willingly admit any ladies on board a ship of his," for the *Regulations and Instructions Relating to His Majesty's Service at Sea* (1790) state that the captain or commander was not to "carry any Woman to Sea . . . without Orders from the Admiralty." In practice, however, the observance of these rules varied a great deal from ship to ship, and much depended on individual captains, with the result that the wives of officers and petty officers often accompanied their husbands to sea (Southam, 276–277).

19 Strictly speaking, a "man of war" was the term used for a ship of any size that was ready for combat. But presumably Mrs. Croft refers to a three-decker, where the captain's cabin was the full width of the ship and divided into several compartments, including a day cabin, a dining cabin, and a state room (Lavery, 108–109). There is also perhaps an amorous pun here in Mrs. Croft's declaration that she knows "nothing superior to the accommodations of a man of war."

20 Portsmouth is a seaport on the Hampshire coast, and home to a major Royal Navy base. It lies approximately 170 miles to the east of Plymouth.

21 As Claudia Johnson points out, in this debate with his sister about "gallantry," Wentworth takes a position which is "very different from what Lady Russell would expect," and which betrays a fundamental confusion in his character that makes it very difficult for him to see Anne clearly. "Since Wentworth has no place in, and indeed is actually hostile to, the patriarchal world of family and neighbourhood which Sir Walter represents, though none too well, his 'superfine' gallantry has no rationale and operates at political cross-purposes with his own designs and energies" (Johnson, 151, 154).

22 Mrs. Croft's description of women as "rational creatures" parallels Elizabeth Bennet's assertion in *Pride and Prejudice* when she rejects Mr. Collins's marriage proposal: "Do not consider me now as an elegant female intending to plague you, but as a rational creature speaking the truth from her heart" (I, 19). More pressingly, the use of the phrase by Elizabeth and Mrs. Croft recalls Wollstonecraft in her *Vindication of the Rights of Woman.* "My own sex, I hope, will excuse me, if I treat them like rational creatures, instead of flattering their *fascinating* graces, and viewing them as if they were in a state of perpetual childhood," Wollstonecraft asserts. ". . . . I wish to persuade women to endeavour to acquire strength, both of mind and body, and to convince them that the soft phrases, susceptibility of heart, delicacy of sentiment, and refinement of taste, are almost synonymous with epithets of weakness" (Wollstonecraft, *Works,* V, 75).

Fourteen years after *Persuasion* was published, the writer and literary reviewer Maria Jane Jewsbury (1800–1833) also used the phrase "rational creatures," and in a way that would undoubtedly have pleased both Wollstonecraft and Austen. "Poets and novelists," Jewsbury observes, habitually present women, not as "rational creatures," but as "angels" who are "such personifications of tears, love, death, poetry, and helplessness, that an honest man, linked to such in real life, would surely be at his wits' ends before the end of the honey-moon" (Jewsbury, "On Modern Female Cultivation, Number Two," in *The Athenaeum,* 224 [February 11, 1832], 95–96).

23 Cork, on the southwestern side of Ireland, was the home station for the Irish Squadron. Lisbon, the capital of Portugal, stands on the westernmost point of land in continental Europe and was home to the Royal Navy's Mediterranean Fleet.

24 The "Streights" are not, as is often thought, "the Straits of Gibraltar," but rather the "Straits of Florida," which extend from the Florida Keys in the north to Cuba in the south, and connect the Gulf of Mexico with the Atlantic Ocean (Harris, 79).

"My feelings, you see, did not prevent my taking Mrs. Harville, and all her family, to Plymouth."

"But I hate to hear you talking so, like a fine gentleman, and as if women were all fine ladies, instead of rational creatures.[22] We none of us expect to be in smooth water all our days."

"Ah! my dear," said the admiral, "when he has got a wife, he will sing a different tune. When he is married, if we have the good luck to live to another war, we shall see him do as you and I, and a great many others, have done. We shall have him very thankful to any body that will bring him his wife."

"Ay, that we shall."

"Now I have done," cried Captain Wentworth—"When once married people begin to attack me with, 'Oh! you will think very differently, when you are married.' I can only say, 'No, I shall not;' and then they say again, 'Yes, you will,' and there is an end of it."

He got up and moved away.

"What a great traveller you must have been, ma'am!" said Mrs. Musgrove to Mrs. Croft.

"Pretty well, ma'am, in the fifteen years of my marriage; though many women have done more. I have crossed the Atlantic four times, and have been once to the East Indies, and back again; and only once, besides being in different places about home—Cork, and Lisbon,[23] and Gibraltar. But I never went beyond the Streights[24]—and never was in the West Indies. We do not call Bermuda or Bahama,[25] you know, the West Indies."

Mrs. Musgrove had not a word to say in dissent; she could not accuse herself of having ever called them any thing in the whole course of her life.

"And I do assure you, ma'am," pursued Mrs. Croft, "that nothing can exceed the accommodations of a man of war; I speak, you know, of the higher rates. When you come to a frigate, of course, you are more confined—though any reasonable woman may be perfectly happy in one of them; and I can safely say, that the happiest part of my life has been spent on board a ship. While we were together, you know, there was nothing to be feared. Thank God! I have always been blessed with excellent health, and no climate disagrees with me. A little disordered always the first twenty-four hours of going to sea, but never knew what sickness was afterwards. The only time that I ever really suffered in body or mind, the only time that I ever fancied myself unwell, or had any ideas of danger, was the winter that I passed by myself at Deal,[26] when the Admiral (*Captain* Croft then) was in the North Seas.[27] I lived in perpetual fright at that time, and had all manner of imaginary complaints from not knowing what to do with myself, or when I should hear from him next; but as long as we could be together, nothing ever ailed me, and I never met with the smallest inconvenience."

"Ay, to be sure.—Yes, indeed, oh yes, I am quite of your opinion, Mrs. Croft," was Mrs. Musgrove's hearty answer. "There is nothing so bad as a separation. I am quite of your opinion. *I* know what it is, for Mr. Musgrove always attends the assizes,[28] and I am so glad when they are over, and he is safe back again."

The evening ended with dancing. On its being proposed, Anne offered her services, as usual, and though her eyes would sometimes fill with tears as she sat at the instrument, she was extremely glad to be employed, and desired nothing in return but to be unobserved.

It was a merry, joyous party, and no one seemed in higher spirits than Captain Wentworth. She felt that he had every thing to elevate him, which general attention and deference, and especially the attention of all the young women could do. The Miss Hayters, the females of the family of cousins already mentioned, were apparently admitted to the honour of being in love with him; and as for Henrietta and Louisa, they both seemed so entirely occupied by him, that nothing but the continued appearance of the most perfect good-will between themselves, could have made it credible that they were not decided rivals. If he were a little spoilt by such universal, such eager admiration, who could wonder?

These were some of the thoughts which occupied Anne, while her fingers were mechanically at work, proceeding for half an hour together, equally without error, and without consciousness. *Once* she felt that he was looking at herself—observing her altered features, perhaps, trying to trace in them the ruins of the face which had once charmed him; and *once* she knew that he must have spoken of her;—

25 Bermuda is an archipelago of seven main islands located in the western North Atlantic Ocean, about 650 miles east of North Carolina. The Commonwealth of the Bahamas is an archipelago that stretches from about 60 miles off the southeastern coast of Florida to some 50 miles from the eastern tip of Cuba.

26 Deal is a seaport on the coast of Kent, a county lying along the English Channel at the southeastern extremity of England.

27 The North Sea is located between the British Isles and the mainland of northwestern Europe.

28 The assizes were sessions of the superior courts held periodically in each county of England for the purpose of administering criminal and civil justice.

Maria Jane Jewsbury, engraved by John Cochran, after a painting by G. Freeman. Jewsbury published a collection of poetry and prose entitled *Phantasmagoria* (1825), as well as numerous articles and reviews in *The Athenaeum*, including an insightful 1831 essay on Austen. It is the first identifiable publication on Austen written by a woman.

she was hardly aware of it, till she heard the answer; but then she was sure of his having asked his partner whether Miss Elliot never danced? The answer was, "Oh! no, never; she has quite given up dancing. She had rather play. She is never tired of playing." Once, too, he spoke to her. She had left the instrument on the dancing being over, and he had sat down to try to make out an air which he wished to give the Miss Musgroves an idea of. Unintentionally she returned to that part of the room; he saw her, and, instantly rising, said, with studied politeness,

"I beg your pardon, madam, this is your seat;" and though she immediately drew back with a decided negative, he was not to be induced to sit down again.

Anne did not wish for more of such looks and speeches. His cold politeness, his ceremonious grace, were worse than any thing.

An 1821 map of the West Indies by James V. Seaman showing various areas mentioned in *Persuasion*, including St. Domingo, the Bahamas, and the Straits of Florida.

9

CAPTAIN WENTWORTH WAS COME TO KELLYNCH as to a home, to stay as long as he liked, being as thoroughly the object of the Admiral's fraternal kindness as of his wife's. He had intended, on first arriving, to proceed very soon into Shropshire,[1] and visit the brother settled in that county, but the attractions of Uppercross induced him to put this off. There was so much of friendliness, and of flattery, and of every thing most bewitching in his reception there; the old were so hospitable, the young so agreeable, that he could not but resolve to remain where he was, and take all the charms and perfections of Edward's wife upon credit a little longer.

It was soon Uppercross with him almost every day. The Musgroves could hardly be more ready to invite than he to come, particularly in the morning, when he had no companion at home, for the Admiral and Mrs. Croft were generally out of doors together, interesting themselves in their new possessions, their grass, and their sheep, and dawdling about in a way not endurable to a third person, or driving out in a gig,[2] lately added to their establishment.

Hitherto there had been but one opinion of Captain Wentworth, among the Musgroves and their dependencies. It was unvarying, warm admiration every where. But this intimate footing was not more than established, when a certain Charles Hayter returned among them, to be a good deal disturbed by it, and to think Captain Wentworth very much in the way.

Charles Hayter was the eldest of all the cousins, and a very amiable, pleasing young man, between whom and Henrietta there had

1 Shropshire is a county in western England bordering on Wales.

2 A gig is a two-wheeled carriage drawn by one horse and suitable for two people. In *A Treatise on Carriages* (1794), the coachmaker William Felton described it as "a one-horse chaise of the most fashionable make" that was "built as light and easy as possible" (Felton, II, 128).

3 "In orders" means "to enter the ministry of the Church, to be ordained" *(OED)*. Compare Austen in *Mansfield Park,* where Julia cries, "My dear Edmund, if you were but in orders now, you might perform the ceremony directly. How unlucky that you are not ordained, Mr. Rushworth and Maria are quite ready" (I, 9).

4 Charles Hayter has "chosen to be a scholar and a gentleman," which means that he has been to university at either Oxford or Cambridge (England's only two universities at the time), for in the early nineteenth century "it was virtually impossible to become ordained in the Church of England" without a university degree (Collins, 19).

been a considerable appearance of attachment previous to Captain Wentworth's introduction. He was in orders,[3] and having a curacy in the neighbourhood where residence was not required, lived at his father's house, only two miles from Uppercross. A short absence from home had left his fair one unguarded by his attentions at this critical period, and when he came back he had the pain of finding very altered manners, and of seeing Captain Wentworth.

Mrs. Musgrove and Mrs. Hayter were sisters. They had each had money, but their marriages had made a material difference in their degree of consequence. Mr. Hayter had some property of his own, but it was insignificant compared with Mr. Musgrove's; and while the Musgroves were in the first class of society in the country, the young Hayters would, from their parents' inferior, retired, and unpolished way of living, and their own defective education, have been hardly in any class at all, but for their connexion with Uppercross; this eldest son of course excepted, who had chosen to be a scholar and a gentleman,[4] and who was very superior in cultivation and manners to all the rest.

The two families had always been on excellent terms, there being no pride on one side, and no envy on the other, and only such a consciousness of superiority in the Miss Musgroves, as made them pleased to improve their cousins. — Charles's attentions to Henrietta had been observed by her father and mother without any disapprobation. "It would not be a great match for her; but if Henrietta liked him, — and Henrietta *did* seem to like him."

Henrietta fully thought so herself, before Captain Wentworth came; but from that time Cousin Charles had been very much forgotten.

Which of the two sisters was preferred by Captain Wentworth was as yet quite doubtful, as far as Anne's observation reached. Henrietta was perhaps the prettiest, Louisa had the higher spirits; and she knew not *now,* whether the more gentle or the more lively character were most likely to attract him.

Mr. and Mrs. Musgrove, either from seeing little, or from an entire confidence in the discretion of both their daughters, and of all the young men who came near them, seemed to leave every thing to take its chance. There was not the smallest appearance of solicitude or remark about them, in the Mansion-house;[5] but it was different at the Cottage: the young couple there were more disposed to speculate and wonder; and Captain Wentworth had not been above four or five times in the Miss Musgroves' company, and Charles Hayter had but just reappeared, when Anne had to listen to the opinions of her brother and sister, as to *which* was the one liked best. Charles gave it for Louisa, Mary for Henrietta, but quite agreeing that to have him marry either would be extremely delightful.

Charles "had never seen a pleasanter man in his life; and from what he had once heard Captain Wentworth himself say, was very sure that he had not made less than twenty thousand pounds by the war.[6] Here was a fortune at once; besides which, there would be the chance of what might be done in any future war; and he was sure Captain Wentworth was as likely a man to distinguish himself as any officer in the navy. Oh! it would be a capital match for either of his sisters."

"Upon my word it would," replied Mary. "Dear me! If he should rise to any very great honours! If he should ever be made a Baronet! 'Lady Wentworth' sounds very well. That would be a noble thing, indeed, for Henrietta! She would take place of me then,[7] and Henrietta would not dislike that. Sir Frederick and Lady Wentworth! It would be but a new creation, however, and I never think much of your new creations."[8]

It suited Mary best to think Henrietta the one preferred, on the very account of Charles Hayter, whose pretensions she wished to see put an end to. She looked down very decidedly upon the Hayters, and thought it would be quite a misfortune to have the existing connection between the families renewed—very sad for herself and her children.

"You know," said she, "I cannot think him at all a fit match for Henrietta; and considering the alliances which the Musgroves have made, she has no right to throw herself away. I do not think any young woman has a right to make a choice that may be disagreeable and inconvenient to the *principal* part of her family, and be giving bad

5 More commonly, Austen calls the "Mansion-house" the "Great House."

6 The fortune of £20,000 has of course come primarily, not from Wentworth's wage, but from prize money. Later in the novel, it is revealed that Wentworth's fortune is actually £25,000, which means that—invested in 5 percent government funds—his yearly income would be approximately £1,250, a substantial sum at the time, though far below what Darcy (£10,000 a year) and Bingley (£4,000 or £5,000 a year) make in *Pride and Prejudice,* and indeed even a good measure below Mr. Bennet's income (£2,000 a year). Measuring what these sums would be in today's terms is notoriously difficult, as there are at least five different ways of computing the relative value of the British pound. According to the retail price index, which measures what goods and services would have cost in any given year, £1 in 1814 was worth £55.39 in 2008. Calculated in terms of average earnings, £1 in 1814 was worth £664.78 in 2008. For full details, see the Economic Services website: www.eh.net.

7 As Mary recognizes with some unease, a baronet's wife takes precedence over a baronet's daughter.

8 A "new creation" was a title that had been awarded in the recent past, though what constituted "recent" was a matter of considerable debate. "I cannot call any one an old peer whose creation was subsequent to the death of Charles II," Sir Egerton Brydges observed snootily in 1834. "In truth I think we ought not to include any in this class subsequent to the first ten years of James I." Mary—to say nothing of Sir Walter— would have been deeply distressed by such a calculation, for it meant that the Elliot baronetcy was a "new creation," as the first ten years of James I's reign ended in 1613, while the Elliots were not given their title until Charles II became king in 1660 (Brydges, *Autobiography,* II, 49).

9 As William Elliot will eventually acquire Kellynch, so both Charles Musgrove and Charles Hayter will inherit their fathers' estates, for all three men are the beneficiaries of the law of primogeniture, which stated that the eldest son, or nearest male relative, was the sole heir.

10 In the Church of England, the person who owned the clerical living for a parish appointed its rector or vicar. Local squires controlled many such livings, and they often used them to provide employment for younger sons or relatives. Bishops, the Crown, and the universities of Oxford and Cambridge also had it in their gift to dispose of livings, and they commonly did so through patronage.

11 Freehold property was property held for life, as opposed to property that was held through a lease.

connections to those who have not been used to them. And, pray, who is Charles Hayter? Nothing but a country curate. A most improper match for Miss Musgrove, of Uppercross."

Her husband, however, would not agree with her here; for besides having a regard for his cousin, Charles Hayter was an eldest son,[9] and he saw things as an eldest son himself.

"Now you are talking nonsense, Mary," was therefore his answer. "It would not be a *great* match for Henrietta, but Charles has a very fair chance, through the Spicers, of getting something from the Bishop[10] in the course of a year or two; and you will please to remember, that he is the eldest son; whenever my uncle dies, he steps into very pretty property. The estate at Winthrop is not less than two hundred and fifty acres, besides the farm near Taunton, which is some of the best land in the country. I grant you, that any of them but Charles would be a very shocking match for Henrietta, and indeed it could not be; he is the only one that could be possible; but he is a very good-natured, good sort of a fellow; and whenever Winthrop comes into his hands, he will make a different sort of place of it, and live in a very different sort of way; and with that property, he will never be a contemptible man. Good, freehold property.[11] No, no; Henrietta might do worse than marry Charles Hayter; and if she has him, and Louisa can get Captain Wentworth, I shall be very well satisfied."

"Charles may say what he pleases," cried Mary to Anne, as soon as he was out of the room, "but it would be shocking to have Henrietta marry Charles Hayter; a very bad thing for *her,* and still worse for *me;* and therefore it is very much to be wished that Captain Wentworth may soon put him quite out of her head, and I have very little doubt that he has. She took hardly any notice of Charles Hayter yesterday. I wish you had been there to see her behaviour. And as to Captain Wentworth's liking Louisa as well as Henrietta, it is nonsense to say so; for he certainly *does* like Henrietta a great deal the best. But Charles is so positive! I wish you had been with us yesterday, for then you might have decided between us; and I am sure you would have thought as I did, unless you had been determined to give it against me."

A dinner at Mr. Musgrove's had been the occasion, when all these things should have been seen by Anne; but she had staid[12] at home, under the mixed plea of a head-ache of her own, and some return of indisposition in little Charles. She had thought only of avoiding Captain Wentworth; but an escape from being appealed to as umpire, was now added to the advantages of a quiet evening.

As to Captain Wentworth's views, she deemed it of more consequence that he should know his own mind, early enough not to be endangering the happiness of either sister, or impeaching his own honour, than that he should prefer Henrietta to Louisa, or Louisa to Henrietta.[13] Either of them would, in all probability, make him an affectionate, good-humoured wife. With regard to Charles Hayter, she had delicacy which must be pained by any lightness of conduct in a well-meaning young woman, and a heart to sympathize in any of the sufferings it occasioned; but if Henrietta found herself mistaken in the nature of her feelings, the alteration could not be understood too soon.

Charles Hayter had met with much to disquiet and mortify him in his cousin's behaviour. She had too old a regard for him to be so wholly estranged, as might in two meetings extinguish every past hope, and leave him nothing to do but to keep away from Uppercross; but there was such a change as became very alarming, when such a man as Captain Wentworth was to be regarded as the probable cause. He had been absent only two Sundays; and when they parted, had left her interested even to the height of his wishes, in his prospect of soon quitting his present curacy, and obtaining that of Uppercross instead. It had then seemed the object nearest her heart, that Dr. Shirley, the rector, who for more than forty years had been zealously discharging all the duties of his office, but was now growing too infirm for many of them, should be quite fixed on engaging a curate; should make his curacy quite as good as he could afford, and should give Charles Hayter the promise of it. The advantage of his having to come only to Uppercross, instead of going six miles another way; of his having, in every respect, a better curacy; of his belonging to their dear Dr. Shirley, and of dear, good Dr. Shirley's being relieved from the duty which he could no longer get through without

12 "Staid" is an older spelling of "stayed."

13 Anne stands firm in her devotion to Wentworth despite his willingness to indulge in behavior that seems almost consciously intended to hurt her. "The strength of her feeling overcomes what is clearly seen both by herself and by the reader as unscrupulousness and arrogant petulance in [Wentworth's] flirtation with the Musgrove daughters," Mary Waldron asserts. "By all contemporary fictional standards Anne ought to disapprove enough to resolve to have nothing more to do with him. But it never crosses her mind. What we are

An engraving of Maria Edgeworth published by Evert Augustus Duyckinck (1816–1878) in his *Portrait Gallery of Eminent Women* (1813). Austen praised Edgeworth's novel *Belinda* in *Northanger Abbey,* and in 1814 she told her niece Anna that she had made up her mind "to like no Novels really, but Miss Edgeworth's, Yours & my own" (Austen, *Letters,* 278).

seeing here is not the anxious internal debate about what is *right* which so often dominates the proceedings in Burney and Edgeworth, for instance, but the unstructured reactions of strong emotion" (Waldron, 142–143).

To some extent, Anne is willing to forgive Wentworth because she understands what he does not: that men had a fine line to walk in their courtship of women. It was a subject discussed at considerable length in contemporary conduct books and etiquette manuals. "If gallantry to the ladies, be considered as part of the accomplishments of a gentleman, it is that only which consists in a respectful and lively attention, perhaps addressed to their vanity, their beauty, or their good sense," explained the clergyman and author John Trusler. "If you do not make yourself agreeable to the woman, you will assuredly lose ground among the men; but as a man of sense, I would never compliment a lady at the expence of truth." In paying attention to both Louisa and Henrietta, and in enjoying their shared interest in him, Wentworth is "endangering the happiness" of the two sisters while running the risk of "impeaching his own honour." Anne wishes him to "know his own mind" before he proceeds much further. Trusler similarly urges both clearheadedness and caution: "I . . . advise you to steer clear of giving any particular lady to understand, that you are more attached to her than others; unless the case be really so, and you mean to pursue it up with honor. Such misrepresentations on your part, and misconceptions on hers, may lead to entanglements, attended with ruinous consequences. Let your attention to the women be general, and general only; and if you find among your female acquaintance, one more partial and attentive to you than ordinary, after consulting your own heart, and perhaps advising with your best friends, if you discover that a matrimonial alliance with that lady, would be imprudent, and not what you like; withdraw your attention immediately, and not suffer any attachment either on her side or yours, to take place" (Trusler, 53–54).

most injurious fatigue, had been a great deal, even to Louisa, but had been almost every thing to Henrietta. When he came back, alas! the zeal of the business was gone by. Louisa could not listen at all to his account of a conversation which he had just held with Dr. Shirley: she was at window, looking out for Captain Wentworth; and even Henrietta had at best only a divided attention to give, and seemed to have forgotten all the former doubt and solicitude of the negotiation.

"Well, I am very glad indeed, but I always thought you would have it; I always thought you sure. It did not appear to me that— In short, you know, Dr. Shirley *must* have a curate, and you had secured his promise. Is he coming, Louisa?"

One morning, very soon after the dinner at the Musgroves, at which Anne had not been present, Captain Wentworth walked into the drawing-room at the Cottage, where were only herself and the little invalid Charles, who was lying on the sofa.

The surprise of finding himself almost alone with Anne Elliot, deprived his manners of their usual composure: he started, and could only say, "I thought the Miss Musgroves had been here—Mrs. Musgrove told me I should find them here," before he walked to the window to recollect himself, and feel how he ought to behave.

"They are up stairs with my sister—they will be down in a few moments, I dare say,"—had been Anne's reply, in all the confusion that was natural; and if the child had not called her to come and do something for him, she would have been out of the room the next moment, and released Captain Wentworth as well as herself.

He continued at the window; and after calmly and politely saying, "I hope the little boy is better," was silent.

She was obliged to kneel down by the sofa, and remain there to satisfy her patient; and thus they continued a few minutes, when, to her very great satisfaction, she heard some other person crossing the little vestibule. She hoped, on turning her head, to see the master of the house; but it proved to be one much less calculated for making matters easy—Charles Hayter, probably not at all better pleased by the sight of Captain Wentworth, than Captain Wentworth had been by the sight of Anne.

In another moment...... someone was taking him from her.

Charles Edmund Brock, Illustrations for *Persuasion,* 1898. Captain Wentworth removes young Walter from Anne's back.

14 Wentworth's removal of the boy from Anne's back was famously commented upon by Austen's fellow novelist Maria Edgeworth. In a letter to her aunt written just shortly after *Persuasion* appeared, Edgeworth declared, "The love and the lover admirably well drawn; don't you see Captain Wentworth, or rather don't you in her place feel him, taking the boisterous child off her back as she kneels by the sick boy on the sofa?" More recently, Penny Gay points to the ways in which this scene draws on the conventions and improprieties of melodrama, for in it Wentworth and Anne are involved in "taboo-breaking physical contact—such as audiences might see at any point in theatre history from a daring actor who wanted to stretch the boundaries of dramatic representation. But as readers we are privileged to see these moments empathetically rather than as simple voyeurs: it is as though 'Anne Elliot' is being performed by a great actress, who allows us to see and share her succession of feelings. . . . The sexual connotations of 'done' in the context of Anne's febrile responses cannot be ignored. His body has been in close contact with hers" (*The Life and Letters of Maria Edgeworth,* ed. Augustus J. C. Hare, 2 vols. [Boston: Houghton, Mifflin and Company, 1895], I, 260; Gay, *Jane Austen and the Theatre* [Cambridge: Cambridge University Press, 2002], 158–159).

She only attempted to say, "How do you do? Will not you sit down? The others will be here presently."

Captain Wentworth, however, came from his window, apparently not ill-disposed for conversation; but Charles Hayter soon put an end to his attempts, by seating himself near the table, and taking up the newspaper; and Captain Wentworth returned to his window.

Another minute brought another addition. The younger boy, a remarkable stout, forward child, of two years old, having got the door opened for him by some one without, made his determined appearance among them, and went straight to the sofa to see what was going on, and put in his claim to any thing good that might be giving away.

There being nothing to be eat, he could only have some play; and as his aunt would not let him teaze his sick brother, he began to fasten himself upon her, as she knelt, in such a way that, busy as she was about Charles, she could not shake him off. She spoke to him—ordered, intreated, and insisted in vain. Once she did contrive to push him away, but the boy had the greater pleasure in getting upon her back again directly.

"Walter," said she, "get down this moment. You are extremely troublesome. I am very angry with you."

"Walter," cried Charles Hayter, "why do you not do as you are bid? Do not you hear your aunt speak? Come to me, Walter, come to cousin Charles."

But not a bit did Walter stir.

In another moment, however, she found herself in the state of being released from him; some one was taking him from her, though he had bent down her head so much, that his little sturdy hands were unfastened from around her neck, and he was resolutely borne away, before she knew that Captain Wentworth had done it.[14]

Her sensations on the discovery made her perfectly speechless. She could not even thank him. She could only hang over little Charles, with most disordered feelings. His kindness in stepping forward to her relief—the manner—the silence in which it had passed—the little particulars of the circumstance—with the conviction soon forced on her by the noise he was studiously making with the child, that he meant to avoid hearing her thanks, and rather sought to testify that her conversation was the last of his wants, produced such a confusion of varying, but very painful agitation, as she could not recover from, till enabled by the entrance of Mary and the Miss Musgroves to make over her little patient to their cares, and leave the room. She could not stay. It might have been an opportunity of watching the loves and jealousies of the four; they were now all together, but she could stay for none of it. It was evident that Charles Hayter was not well inclined towards Captain Wentworth. She had a strong impression of his having said, in a vext tone of voice, after Captain Wentworth's interference, "You ought to have minded *me,* Walter; I told you not to teaze your aunt;" and could comprehend his regretting that Captain Wentworth should do what he ought to have done himself. But neither Charles Hayter's feelings, nor any body's feelings, could interest her, till she had a little better arranged her own. She was ashamed of herself, quite ashamed of being so nervous, so overcome by such a trifle; but so it was; and it required a long application of solitude and reflection to recover her.

IO

OTHER OPPORTUNITIES OF MAKING HER OBSERVATIONS could not fail to occur. Anne had soon been in company with all the four together often enough to have an opinion, though too wise to acknowledge as much at home, where she knew it would have satisfied neither husband nor wife; for while she considered Louisa to be rather the favourite, she could not but think, as far as she might dare to judge from memory and experience, that Captain Wentworth was not in love with either. They were more in love with him; yet there it was not love. It was a little fever of admiration; but it might, probably must, end in love with some. Charles Hayter seemed aware of being slighted, and yet Henrietta had sometimes the air of being divided between them. Anne longed for the power of representing to them all what they were about, and of pointing out some of the evils they were exposing themselves to. She did not attribute guile to any. It was the highest satisfaction to her, to believe Captain Wentworth not in the least aware of the pain he was occasioning. There was no triumph, no pitiful triumph in his manner. He had, probably, never heard, and never thought of any claims of Charles Hayter. He was only wrong in accepting the attentions—(for accepting must be the word) of two young women at once.

After a short struggle, however, Charles Hayter seemed to quit the field. Three days had passed without his coming once to Uppercross; a most decided change. He had even refused one regular invitation to dinner; and having been found on the occasion by Mr. Musgrove with some large books before him, Mr. and Mrs. Musgrove

An 1815 print of a young woman in an autumnal walking dress taken from *La Belle Assemblée,* a magazine "Addressed Particularly to the Ladies." The outfit is a "jacconet muslin high dress" with a "long sleeve, prettily and tastefully ornamented at top with letting-in lace, in such a manner as to form a very novel half sleeve. The bottom of the dress is finished by a triple flounce of worked muslin or lace. . . . The bottom of the sleeve is ornamented in a similar style, but the collar is trimmed only with a single fall of lace or work." The dress undoubtedly resembles the kind of clothing worn by the Musgrove and Elliot sisters on their November 1814 walk from Uppercross to Winthrop (*La Belle Assemblée,* 12.75, October 1815, p. 129).

A miniature of Austen's oldest brother, James, dating from about 1790, when he was twenty-five years old and serving as a curate at Overton. James had a passion for hunting, as well as for poetry.

were sure all could not be right, and talked, with grave faces, of his studying himself to death. It was Mary's hope and belief, that he had received a positive dismissal from Henrietta, and her husband lived under the constant dependance of seeing him to-morrow. Anne could only feel that Charles Hayter was wise.

One morning, about this time, Charles Musgrove and Captain Wentworth being gone a shooting together, as the sisters in the cottage were sitting quietly at work, they were visited at the window by the sisters from the mansion-house.

It was a very fine November day, and the Miss Musgroves came through the little grounds, and stopped for no other purpose than to say, that they were going to take a *long* walk, and, therefore, concluded Mary could not like to go with them; and when Mary immediately replied, with some jealousy, at not being supposed a good walker, "Oh, yes, I should like to join you very much, I am very fond of a long walk," Anne felt persuaded, by the looks of the two girls, that it was precisely what they did not wish, and admired again the sort of necessity which the family-habits seemed to produce, of every thing being to be communicated, and every thing being to be done together, however undesired and inconvenient. She tried to dissuade Mary from going, but in vain; and that being the case, thought it best to accept the Miss Musgroves' much more cordial invitation to herself to go likewise, as she might be useful in turning back with her sister, and lessening the interference in any plan of their own.

"I cannot imagine why they should suppose I should not like a long walk!" said Mary, as she went up stairs. "Every body is always supposing that I am not a good walker! And yet they would not have been pleased, if we had refused to join them. When people come in this manner on purpose to ask us, how can one say no?"

Just as they were setting off, the gentlemen returned. They had taken out a young dog, who had spoilt their sport, and sent them back early. Their time and strength, and spirits, were, therefore, exactly ready for this walk, and they entered into it with pleasure. Could Anne have foreseen such a junction, she would have staid at home; but, from some feelings of interest and curiosity, she fancied now that it was too late to retract, and the whole six set forward together in the direction chosen by the Miss Musgroves, who evidently considered the walk as under their guidance.

Anne's object was, not to be in the way of any body, and where the narrow paths across the fields made many separations necessary, to keep with her brother and sister. Her *pleasure* in the walk must arise from the exercise and the day, from the view of the last smiles of the year upon the tawny leaves and withered hedges, and from repeating to herself some few of the thousand poetical descriptions extant of autumn, that season of peculiar and inexhaustible influence on the mind of taste and tenderness, that season which has drawn from every poet, worthy of being read, some attempt at description, or some lines of feeling.[1] She occupied her mind as much as possible in such like musings and quotations; but it was not possible, that when within reach of Captain Wentworth's conversation with either of the Miss Musgroves, she should not try to hear it; yet she caught little very remarkable. It was mere lively chat,—such as any young persons, on an intimate footing, might fall into. He was more engaged with Louisa than with Henrietta. Louisa certainly put more forward for his notice than her sister. This distinction appeared to increase, and there was one speech of Louisa's which struck her. After one of the many praises of the day, which were continually bursting forth, Captain Wentworth added,

"What glorious weather for the Admiral and my sister! They meant to take a long drive this morning; perhaps we may hail them from some of these hills. They talked of coming into this side of the country. I wonder whereabouts they will upset to-day.[2] Oh! it does happen very often, I assure you—but my sister makes nothing of it—she would as lieve[3] be tossed out as not."

"Ah! You make the most of it, I know," cried Louisa, "but if it were really so, I should do just the same in her place. If I loved a man, as she loves the Admiral, I would be always with him, nothing should ever separate us, and I would rather be overturned by him, than driven safely by anybody else."

[1] In observing that autumn "has drawn from every poet, worthy of being read, some attempt at description, or some lines of feeling," Austen recollects Samuel Johnson's assertion that there is "scarce any poet of eminence, who has not left some testimony of his fondness for the flowers, the zephyrs, and the warblers of the spring." Austen does not name specific poets, but she almost certainly has in mind James Thomson (1700–1748). His *Seasons*, published between 1726 and 1730, was divided into sections on "Winter," "Summer," "Spring," and "Autumn" and became one of the most popular poems of the eighteenth century. "The pale descending year, yet pleasing still, / A gentler mood inspires," Thomson writes in "Autumn";

> for now the leaf
> Incessant rustles from the mournful grove,
> Oft startling such as studious walk below,
> And slowly circles through the waving air.

Austen is also undoubtedly recalling the poetry of her eldest brother, James Austen (1765–1819). "Autumn," he observes,

> speaks in graver tone;
> Reminds us, that as woodlands pour
> A thick & never ceasing shower,
> So every minute tolls the bell
> For man's frail race the parting knell:
> So generations pass away,
> And life is one autumnal day.

(Harris, 217; Johnson, *Rambler*, III, 26; *James Thomson: Poetical Works*, ed. J. Logie Robertson [London: Oxford University Press, 1965], 168; *The Complete Poems of James Austen*, ed. David Selwyn [Chawton: Jane Austen Society, 2003], 81).

[2] In wondering "whereabouts they will upset to-day," Wentworth speaks like the sailor he is, for the word "upset" was closely associated with "naval language," where it meant to "capsize" or "turn over anything" (*OED*).

[3] "Lieve" is the archaic spelling of "lief," which means "gladly" or "willingly."

4 William Shakespeare (1564–1616) writes poignantly of autumn in "Sonnet Seventy-Three," and this may well be the "tender sonnet" Anne has in mind. "That time of year thou mayst in me behold," Shakespeare asserts,

When yellow leaves, or none, or few, do hang
Upon those boughs which shake against the cold,
Bare [ruin'd] choirs, where late the sweet birds sang.
In me thou seest the twilight of such day
As after sunset fadeth in the west,
Which by and by black night doth take away,
Death's second self, that seals up all in rest.
In me thou seest the glowing of such fire
That on the ashes of his youth doth lie,
As the death-bed whereon it must expire,
Consum'd with that which it was nourish'd by.
This thou perceiv'st, which makes thy love more
    strong,
To love that well, which thou must leave ere long.

Anne may also be thinking of Charlotte Smith's *Elegiac Sonnets,* which were first published in a slim volume in 1784, but which had reached two volumes and a ninth edition by 1800. Smith composed Sonnet Forty-Two "during a walk on the Downs, in November 1787," the same month (though not the same year) that Anne and the rest of the party walk through the Somerset countryside. Writes Smith:

The dark and pillowy cloud, the sallow trees,
    Seem o'er the ruins of the year to mourn;
And, cold and hollow, the inconstant breeze
    Sobs thro' the falling leaves and wither'd fern.
O'er the tall brow of yonder chalky bourn,
    The evening shades their gather'd darkness fling,
While, by the lingering light, I scarce discern
    The shrieking night-jar sail on heavy wing.
Ah! yet a little—and propitious Spring
    Crown'd with fresh flowers shall wake the
    woodland strain;
But no gay change revolving seasons bring
    To call forth pleasure from the soul of pain!
Bid Syren Hope resume her long-lost part,
    And chase the vulture Care—that feeds upon the
    heart!

(Smith, *Works,* XIV, 42).

It was spoken with enthusiasm.

"Had you?" cried he, catching the same tone; "I honour you!" And there was silence between them for a little while.

Anne could not immediately fall into a quotation again. The sweet scenes of autumn were for a while put by—unless some tender sonnet, fraught with the apt analogy of the declining year, with declining happiness, and the images of youth and hope, and spring, all gone together, blessed her memory.[4] She roused herself to say, as they struck by order into another path, "Is not this one of the ways to Winthrop?" But nobody heard, or, at least, nobody answered her.

Winthrop, however, or its environs—for young men are, sometimes, to be met with, strolling about near home, was their destination; and after another half mile of gradual ascent through large enclosures,[5] where the ploughs at work, and the fresh-made path spoke the farmer, counteracting the sweets of poetical despondence, and meaning to have spring again, they gained the summit of the most considerable hill, which parted Uppercross and Winthrop, and soon commanded a full view of the latter, at the foot of the hill on the other side.[6]

Winthrop, without beauty and without dignity, was stretched before them; an indifferent house, standing low, and hemmed in by the barns and buildings of a farm-yard.

Mary exclaimed, "Bless me! here is Winthrop—I declare I had no idea! ——well, now I think we had better turn back; I am excessively tired."

Henrietta, conscious[7] and ashamed, and seeing no cousin Charles walking along any path, or leaning against any gate, was ready to do as Mary wished; but "No," said Charles Musgrove, and "No, no," cried Louisa more eagerly, and taking her sister aside, seemed to be arguing the matter warmly.

Charles, in the meanwhile, was very decidedly declaring his resolution of calling on his aunt, now that he was so near; and very evidently, though more fearfully, trying to induce his wife to go too. But this was one of the points on which the lady shewed her strength, and when he recommended the advantage of resting herself a quarter of an hour at Winthrop, as she felt so tired, she resolutely an-

Engraved by Freeman, from an Original Painting.

Mrs Charlotte Smith.

Publish'd by Vernor, Hood & Sharpe, Poultry, April 1 1808.

Charlotte Smith, by Samuel Freeman (1773–1857), after John Opie, published 1808. In addition to her poetry, Smith wrote novels such as *Emmeline* (1788), *The Old Manor House* (1793), and *Marchmont* (1796). Smith may also have shaped Austen's portrait of her namesake Mrs. Smith in *Persuasion,* for she too was plagued by ill health, penury, and an extravagant husband.

5 "Enclosures" were carefully delineated and individually owned farm plots that had been created by fencing off once communal pastures and meadows.

6 Virginia Woolf contends that in *Persuasion* Austen begins "to discover that the world is larger, more mysterious, and more romantic than she had supposed." Anne's walk to Winthrop is often cited as an example of Austen's new commitment to a darker and more passionate world in which she values feeling over prudence, and in which she explores her own deep sense of personal sorrow through techniques and natural settings that are more commonly associated with her major poetic contemporaries such as William Wordsworth (1770–1850), Samuel Taylor Coleridge (1772–1834), Percy Bysshe Shelley (1792–1822), and John Keats (1795–1821). The effects of this autumn walk "are new to Jane Austen's art," declares A. Walton Litz. "Anne's consciousness is the focus of the scene, and our interest is in her reactions, but these reactions are expressed more through descriptive details than through exposition. The tone of the landscape controls the passage: Anne's regret is imaged in the autumn scene, while the reminder of spring—in immediate context a sad reminder—may also be read as a hint of future happiness. . . . In their quiet and restrained fashion . . . Austen's last works are part of the new movement in English literature. She has learned that the natural setting can convey, more surely than any abstract vocabulary, the movements of an individual imagination" (*The Essays of Virginia Woolf,* ed. Andrew McNeillie and Stuart N. Clarke, 5 vols. [London: The Hogarth Press, 1986–], IV, 154; Litz, *Jane Austen: A Study of Her Artistic Development* [New York: Oxford University Press, 1965], 152–153).

7 Austen uses "conscious" here in an older sense, closer to its Latin etymology of "knowing something with others, knowing in oneself." It means "embarrassed," "guilty," "inwardly sensible of wrong-doing" (*OED).*

8 In this context, "connexions" means "relatives."

9 A "stile" is a stepladder for climbing over a fence or gate.

10 Austen's description of this hedgerow—with its channel "down the centre"—is undoubtedly drawn from childhood recollections of the hedgerows around the Hampshire village of Steventon, where she grew up. According to her nephew James Edward Austen-Leigh (1798–1874), "the chief beauty of Steventon consisted in its hedgerows. A hedgerow, in that country, does not mean a thin formal line of quickset, but an irregular border of copse-wood and timber, often wide enough to contain within it a winding footpath, or a rough cart track. Under its shelter the earliest primroses, anemones, and wild hyacinths were to be found; sometimes, the first bird's-nest; and, now and then, the unwelcome adder." In January 1813, as she worked on *Mansfield Park,* Austen wrote to Cassandra to ask if she could "discover whether Northamptonshire is a Country of Hedgerows," leading several critics to speculate that the device in *Persuasion* of the heroine's overhearing a conversation might have originally been intended for *Mansfield Park,* where (presumably) Fanny would overhear a conversation between Edmund and Mary (Austen-Leigh, *Memoir,* 23; Austen, *Letters,* 202).

swered, "Oh! no, indeed!—walking up that hill again would do her more harm than any sitting down could do her good;"—and, in short, her look and manner declared, that go she would not.

After a little succession of these sort of debates and consultations, it was settled between Charles and his two sisters, that he, and Henrietta, should just run down for a few minutes, to see their aunt and cousins, while the rest of the party waited for them at the top of the hill. Louisa seemed the principal arranger of the plan; and, as she went a little way with them, down the hill, still talking to Henrietta, Mary took the opportunity of looking scornfully around her, and saying to Captain Wentworth,

"It is very unpleasant, having such connexions![8] But I assure you, I have never been in the house above twice in my life."

She received no other answer, than an artificial, assenting smile, followed by a contemptuous glance, as he turned away, which Anne perfectly knew the meaning of.

The brow of the hill, where they remained, was a cheerful spot; Louisa returned, and Mary finding a comfortable seat for herself, on the step of a stile,[9] was very well satisfied so long as the others all stood about her; but when Louisa drew Captain Wentworth away, to try for a gleaning of nuts in an adjoining hedge-row, and they were gone by degrees quite out of sight and sound, Mary was happy no longer; she quarrelled with her own seat,—was sure Louisa had got a much better somewhere,—and nothing could prevent her from going to look for a better also. She turned through the same gate,—but could not see them.—Anne found a nice seat for her, on a dry sunny bank, under the hedge-row, in which she had no doubt of their still being—in some spot or other. Mary sat down for a moment, but it would not do; she was sure Louisa had found a better seat somewhere else, and she would go on, till she overtook her.

Anne, really tired herself, was glad to sit down; and she very soon heard Captain Wentworth and Louisa in the hedge-row, behind her, as if making their way back, along the rough, wild sort of channel, down the centre.[10] They were speaking as they drew near. Louisa's voice was the first distinguished. She seemed to be in the middle of some eager speech. What Anne first heard was,

Charles Edmund Brock, Illustrations for *Persuasion*, 1898. Captain Wentworth
speaks to Louisa, unaware that Anne is near.

11 Wentworth's use of the hazelnut is "one of the rare emblematic aids to discourse in Jane Austen," observes Tony Tanner. Wittily, he adds that "praising its exemplary enduring strength and hardness, and asserting, rather foolishly, that its 'happiness' is a function of its unpunctured 'firmness'" is "a 'nutty' happiness indeed, but not perhaps a very helpful model for a young—and virgin—woman!" (Tanner, 233).

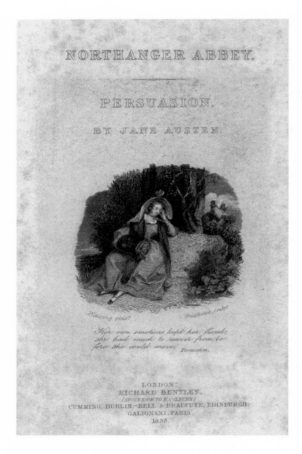

The frontispiece from the 1833 *Standard Novels* edition of *Persuasion,* published by Richard Bentley (1794–1871). After overhearing the conversation between Captain Wentworth and Louisa, Anne is unable to move.

"And so, I made her go. I could not bear that she should be frightened from the visit by such nonsense. What!—would I be turned back from doing a thing that I had determined to do, and that I knew to be right, by the airs and interference of such a person?—or, of any person I may say. No,—I have no idea of being so easily persuaded. When I have made up my mind, I have made it. And Henrietta seemed entirely to have made up hers to call at Winthrop to-day—and yet, she was as near giving it up, out of nonsensical complaisance!"

"She would have turned back then, but for you?"

"She would indeed. I am almost ashamed to say it."

"Happy for her, to have such a mind as yours at hand!—After the hints you gave just now, which did but confirm my own observations, the last time I was in company with him, I need not affect to have no comprehension of what is going on. I see that more than a mere dutiful morning-visit to your aunt was in question;—and woe betide him, and her too, when it comes to things of consequence, when they are placed in circumstances, requiring fortitude and strength of mind, if she have not resolution enough to resist idle interference in such a trifle as this. Your sister is an amiable creature; but *yours* is the character of decision and firmness, I see. If you value her conduct or happiness, infuse as much of your own spirit into her, as you can. But this, no doubt, you have been always doing. It is the worst evil of too yielding and indecisive a character, that no influence over it can be depended on.—You are never sure of a good impression being durable. Every body may sway it; let those who would be happy be firm.—Here is a nut," said he, catching one down from an upper bough. "To exemplify,—a beautiful glossy nut, which, blessed with original strength, has outlived all the storms of autumn. Not a puncture, not a weak spot any where.—This nut," he continued, with playful solemnity,—"while so many of its brethren have fallen and been trodden under foot, is still in possession of all the happiness that a hazelnut can be supposed capable of."[11] Then, returning to his former earnest tone: "My first wish for all, whom I am interested in, is that they should be firm. If Louisa Musgrove would be beautiful and happy in her November of life, she will cherish all her present powers of mind."[12]

He had done,—and was unanswered. It would have surprised Anne, if Louisa could have readily answered such a speech—words of such interest, spoken with such serious warmth!—she could imagine what Louisa was feeling. For herself—she feared to move, lest she should be seen. While she remained, a bush of low rambling holly protected her, and they were moving on. Before they were beyond her hearing, however, Louisa spoke again.

"Mary is good-natured enough in many respects," said she; "but she does sometimes provoke me excessively, by her nonsense and her pride; the Elliot pride. She has a great deal too much of the Elliot pride.—We do so wish that Charles had married Anne instead.—I suppose you know he wanted to marry Anne?"

After a moment's pause, Captain Wentworth said,

"Do you mean that she refused him?"

"Oh! yes, certainly."

"When did that happen?"

"I do not exactly know, for Henrietta and I were at school at the time; but I believe about a year before he married Mary. I wish

The Midshipmans' Berth, by Charles Random Deberenger, circa 1820. The atmosphere in the midshipmen's berth was often lighthearted, but "many of the pranks were cruel and dangerous" and there was "much bullying of younger or unpopular members of the mess" (Lavery, 90).

12 In this scene, Louisa and Wentworth are, in effect, examining the crucial role that "persuasion" plays in human relationships. For Samuel Johnson in his famous *Dictionary of the English Language* (1755), "persuasion" is first "the act of persuading," then "the act of influencing by expostulation," and finally "the act of gaining or attempting the passions." Johnson's definition, then, moves from the rational in the first clause, to the rhetorical in the second, to the seductive in the third, and it highlights the ways in which "persuasion" is both fundamental to the art of communication and bristling with moral danger. At the time of her death, Austen seems not to have decided on *Persuasion* as the title for her novel, and indeed Cassandra later reported that "among several possible titles, the one that seemed most likely to be chosen was 'The Elliots.'" In the event, it was probably Austen's brother Henry Austen (1771–1850) who called the novel *Persuasion,* in recognition of the numerous and shifting contexts in which Austen uses the word and its variants (including "persuade," "persuadable," and "unpersuadable") (William Austen-Leigh and Richard Arthur Austen-Leigh, *Jane Austen: A Family Record,* revised and enlarged by Deirdre le Faye [London: British Library, 1989], 214).

Louisa's and Wentworth's respective opinions on the subject of "persuasion" reveal the shortcomings in their characters that will so thoroughly shape the action to come. Louisa's speech, and "Wentworth's enthusiastic response to it, are not the simple assertions of principled self-determination they appear to be," Claudia Johnson states. "Louisa, after all, did not disinterestedly supplement her sister's faltering powers of mind with the strength of her own. Instead, she took advantage of her sister's persuadability in order to clear the field for Wentworth and herself. Further, Louisa recommends independence even as she congratulates herself for her own interference: 'I made her go.' Finally, Wentworth disdains the feeble malleability of 'too yielding and indecisive a character' when it defies him as Anne's did, but he does not seem to mind or even to notice the same qualities when they malleably conform to his own influence. Louisa has really done no more than give Wentworth what he wants to hear, and unaware that Louisa's strength of mind is really only persuadability to him in disguise, he rewards her with his praise: 'Happy for [Henrietta], to have such a mind as yours at hand'. . . . Clearly, Wentworth's preference for singlemindedness is as indiscriminating and self-serving in its own way as Lady Russell's prejudice in favor of wealth and family is in its" (Johnson, 156).

13 Austen refers to the proverb "Listeners hear no . . . good of themselves." Compare Charles Dickens (1812–1870) in *Nicholas Nickleby* (1838–1839), where Mrs. Browdie notes that "if it's fated that listeners are never to hear any good of themselves . . . I can't help it, and I am very sorry for it" (*The Oxford Dictionary of English Proverbs,* 3rd ed., revised by F. P. Wilson [Oxford: Clarendon Press, 1970], 468; Dickens, *Nicholas Nickleby,* ed. Paul Schlicke [Oxford: Oxford University Press, 1998], 549).

14 "They were devoted to each other" means that they paid attention only to each other.

she had accepted him. We should all have liked her a great deal better; and papa and mamma always think it was her great friend Lady Russell's doing, that she did not.—They think Charles might not be learned and bookish enough to please Lady Russell, and that therefore, she persuaded Anne to refuse him."

The sounds were retreating, and Anne distinguished no more. Her own emotions still kept her fixed. She had much to recover from, before she could move. The listener's proverbial fate was not absolutely hers; she had heard no evil of herself,[13]—but she had heard a great deal of very painful import. She saw how her own character was considered by Captain Wentworth; and there had been just that degree of feeling and curiosity about her in his manner, which must give her extreme agitation.

As soon as she could, she went after Mary, and having found, and walked back with her to their former station, by the stile, felt some comfort in their whole party being immediately afterwards collected, and once more in motion together. Her spirits wanted the solitude and silence which only numbers could give.

Charles and Henrietta returned, bringing, as may be conjectured, Charles Hayter with them. The minutiæ of the business Anne could not attempt to understand; even Captain Wentworth did not seem admitted to perfect confidence here; but that there had been a withdrawing on the gentleman's side, and a relenting on the lady's, and that they were now very glad to be together again, did not admit a doubt. Henrietta looked a little ashamed, but very well pleased;—Charles Hayter exceedingly happy, and they were devoted to each other[14] almost from the first instant of their all setting forward for Uppercross.

Every thing now marked out Louisa for Captain Wentworth; nothing could be plainer; and where many divisions were necessary, or even where they were not, they walked side by side, nearly as much as the other two. In a long strip of meadow-land, where there was ample space for all, they were thus divided—forming three distinct parties; and to that party of the three which boasted least animation, and least complaisance, Anne necessarily belonged. She joined Charles and Mary, and was tired enough to be very glad of Charles's other arm;—but Charles, though in very good humour with her, was out of temper with his wife. Mary had shewn herself disobliging to him, and was now to reap the consequence, which consequence was his dropping her arm almost every moment, to cut off the heads of some nettles in the hedge with his switch;[15] and when Mary began to complain of it, and lament her being ill-used, according to custom, in being on the hedge side, while Anne was never incommoded[16] on the other, he dropped the arms of both to hunt after a weasel which he had a momentary glance of; and they could hardly get him along at all.

This long meadow bordered a lane, which their footpath, at the end of it, was to cross; and when the party had all reached the gate of exit, the carriage advancing in the same direction, which had been some time heard, was just coming up, and proved to be Admiral Croft's gig.—He and his wife had taken their intended drive, and were returning home. Upon hearing how long a walk the young people had engaged in, they kindly offered a seat to any lady who might be particularly tired; it would save her full a mile, and they were going through Uppercross. The invitation was general, and generally declined. The Miss Musgroves were not at all tired, and Mary was either offended, by not being asked before any of the others, or what Louisa called the Elliot pride could not endure to make a third in a one horse chaise.[17]

The walking-party had crossed the lane, and were surmounting an opposite stile; and the admiral was putting his horse into motion again, when Captain Wentworth cleared the hedge in a moment to say something to his sister.—The something might be guessed by its effects.

"Miss Elliot, I am sure *you* are tired," cried Mrs. Croft. "Do let us have the pleasure of taking you home. Here is excellent room for three, I assure you. If we were all like you, I believe we might sit four.—You must, indeed, you must."

Anne was still in the lane; and though instinctively beginning to decline, she was not allowed to proceed. The admiral's kind urgency came in support of his wife's; they would not be refused; they compressed themselves into the smallest possible space to leave her a

15 A "switch" is a slender, flexible riding whip.

16 "Incommoded" is "inconvenienced."

17 A "one horse chaise" sat two people comfortably. Three would have to squeeze in. In mentioning the Crofts' modest form of transportation, Austen is making an important financial point. When Sir Walter lived at Kellynch, he paraded about the countryside in a four-horse carriage that he could not afford. The Crofts, who have supplanted him in his ancestral home, do have the money for such extravagance, but they choose instead to drive an economical one-horse gig, which costs them far less in terms of everything from grain to horseshoes to the annual tax on carriages. Sir Walter blithely lives beyond his means. The Crofts are happy and determined to live well within theirs.

18 During their brief engagement in the summer of 1806, Anne and Wentworth probably enjoyed a degree of physical intimacy. They touch again in Uppercross Cottage when Wentworth removes the boisterous child from Anne's back, as they do here when he thoughtfully takes her hand and guides her into the chaise. In his speech about firmness and determination earlier in the afternoon, Wentworth addressed Louisa but clearly spoke with Anne in mind as well. On the walk back through the fields, though again engaged in conversation with Louisa, he noticed that Anne was fatigued. Now he takes the steps necessary to ensure that her discomfort is relieved and she is returned to Uppercross in the chaise. Anne may convince herself that the incident shows him to be kind but "careless of her"—that is, "indifferent to her." His own confusion of purpose, however, runs much deeper, for the erotically charged episode demonstrates that he has Anne in his eye even as he deepens his pursuit of Louisa. *Persuasion* is Austen's "most unreservedly physical novel," remarks Judy Van Sickle Johnson. Its power "resides in Austen's success in sustaining the credibility of a renewed emotional attachment through physical signs. Although they are seemingly distant, Anne and Wentworth become increasingly more intimate through seductive half-glances, conscious gazes, and slight bodily contact" (Van Sickle Johnson, "The Bodily Frame: Learning Romance in *Persuasion*," in *Nineteenth-Century Fiction*, 38 [1983], 60–61).

19 "North Yarmouth" is almost certainly "Great Yarmouth," a minor naval station on the coast of Norfolk, a county of eastern England bounded on the north and east by the North Sea.

corner, and Captain Wentworth, without saying a word, turned to her, and quietly obliged her to be assisted into the carriage.

Yes,—he had done it. She was in the carriage, and felt that he had placed her there, that his will and his hands had done it, that she owed it to his perception of her fatigue, and his resolution to give her rest. She was very much affected by the view of his disposition towards her which all these things made apparent. This little circumstance seemed the completion of all that had gone before. She understood him. He could not forgive her,—but he could not be unfeeling. Though condemning her for the past, and considering it with high and unjust resentment, though perfectly careless of her, and though becoming attached to another, still he could not see her suffer, without the desire of giving her relief.[18] It was a remainder of former sentiment; it was an impulse of pure, though unacknowledged friendship; it was a proof of his own warm and amiable heart, which she could not contemplate without emotions so compounded of pleasure and pain, that she knew not which prevailed.

Her answers to the kindness and the remarks of her companions were at first unconsciously given. They had travelled half their way along the rough lane, before she was quite awake to what they said. She then found them talking of "Frederick."

"He certainly means to have one or other of those two girls, Sophy," said the admiral;—"but there is no saying which. He has been running after them, too, long enough, one would think, to make up his mind. Ay, this comes of the peace. If it were war, now, he would have settled it long ago.—We sailors, Miss Elliot, cannot afford to make long courtships in time of war. How many days was it, my dear, between the first time of my seeing you, and our sitting down together in our lodgings at North Yarmouth?"[19]

"We had better not talk about it, my dear," replied Mrs. Croft, pleasantly; "for if Miss Elliot were to hear how soon we came to an understanding, she would never be persuaded that we could be happy together. I had known you by character, however, long before."

"Well, and I had heard of you as a very pretty girl; and what were we to wait for besides?—I do not like having such things so long in hand. I wish Frederick would spread a little more canvas,[20] and bring us home one of these young ladies to Kellynch. Then, there would always be company for us.[21]—And very nice young ladies they both are; I hardly know one from the other."

"Very good humoured, unaffected girls, indeed," said Mrs. Croft, in a tone of calmer praise, such as made Anne suspect that her keener powers might not consider either of them as quite worthy of her brother; "and a very respectable family. One could not be connected with better people.—My dear admiral, that post!—we shall certainly take that post."

But by coolly giving the reins a better direction herself, they happily passed the danger; and by once afterwards judiciously putting out her hand, they neither fell into a rut, nor ran foul of a dung-cart; and Anne, with some amusement at their style of driving, which she imagined no bad representation of the general guidance of their affairs, found herself safely deposited by them at the cottage.[22]

20 To "spread a little more canvas" is a nautical expression that means "to unfurl additional or bigger sails in order to catch more wind and gain more speed."

21 The text has been amended here from "for them" to "for us."

22 The Crofts barely avoid accidents on the road, but theirs is a very successful partnership. Why? The answer, Emily Auerbach believes, is "their freedom from restrictive roles for men and women." Mrs. Croft is "an unusually self-assured, outspoken woman" who "rejects traditional notions of feminine refinement," and who enjoys walking and riding and traveling with her husband, all of which he welcomes. "Unlike many a contemporary husband resenting his wife for reading a map and implying that he might be lost," Auerbach contends, "the Admiral happily shares the reins with his cool-headed wife and thus arrives safely at the right destination. . . . This unconventional marriage succeeds both because Mrs. Croft has spunk and because Admiral Croft has a solid, secure sense of identity. Austen emphasizes Admiral Croft's traditional manly qualities . . . but then shows that this macho admiral has no need to dominate his wife. . . . A true man can share the power and form a genuine partnership with a woman without feeling his manhood threatened" (Auerbach, 242–244).

II

THE TIME NOW APPROACHED FOR Lady Russell's return; the day was even fixed, and Anne, being engaged to join her as soon as she was resettled, was looking forward to an early removal to Kellynch, and beginning to think how her own comfort was likely to be affected by it.

It would place her in the same village with Captain Wentworth, within half a mile of him; they would have to frequent the same church, and there must be intercourse between the two families. This was against her; but, on the other hand, he spent so much of his time at Uppercross, that in removing thence she might be considered rather as leaving him behind, than as going towards him; and, upon the whole, she believed she must, on this interesting question, be the gainer, almost as certainly as in her change of domestic society, in leaving poor Mary for Lady Russell.

She wished it might be possible for her to avoid ever seeing Captain Wentworth at the hall;—those rooms had witnessed former meetings which would be brought too painfully before her; but she was yet more anxious for the possibility of Lady Russell and Captain Wentworth never meeting any where. They did not like each other, and no renewal of acquaintance now could do any good; and were Lady Russell to see them together, she might think that he had too much self-possession, and she too little.

These points formed her chief solicitude in anticipating her removal from Uppercross, where she felt she had been stationed quite long enough. Her usefulness to little Charles would always give some

A View of Lyme Regis, by Charles Dibdin (1745–1814), circa 1760–1814. The picture shows the view from the Cobb looking east, with two fishermen in the foreground, the cottages of Lyme Regis coming down to the shore, and the hills about Charmouth in the background.

1 Lyme Regis is a small town on the coast of Dorset, a county in southwestern England. For centuries it was an important port, but by the early nineteenth century trade had sharply declined, and the town had been transformed into a popular seaside resort. In 1803 and again in 1804, Austen herself spent family holidays there, walking, dancing, bathing, and keenly observing both the landscape and the people.

2 Sir Walter seems to think the weather inflicts the most severe damage on the constitution of British sailors. But as Harville's "severe wound" reminds us, sailors faced threats far graver than the weather. *Persuasion,* asserts Joseph Duffy, is pervaded by "symbols of decay" and by "reports of death and illness (the book's toll of dead and of victims of illness and accident would provide a mournful set of statistics on human mortality)." John Wiltshire declares that "*Persuasion* is a novel of trauma: of broken bones, broken heads and broken hearts" (Duffy, 274; Wiltshire, 165).

sweetness to the memory of her two months visit there, but he was gaining strength apace, and she had nothing else to stay for.

The conclusion of her visit, however, was diversified in a way which she had not at all imagined. Captain Wentworth, after being unseen and unheard of at Uppercross for two whole days, appeared again among them to justify himself by a relation of what had kept him away.

A letter from his friend, Captain Harville, having found him out at last, had brought intelligence of Captain Harville's being settled with his family at Lyme[1] for the winter; of their being, therefore, quite unknowingly, within twenty miles of each other. Captain Harville had never been in good health since a severe wound which he received two years before,[2] and Captain Wentworth's anxiety to see him had determined him to go immediately to Lyme. He had been there for four-and-twenty hours. His acquittal was complete, his friendship warmly honoured, a lively interest excited for his friend,

3 It is only seventeen miles from Uppercross to Lyme, but it takes three-and-a-half hours each way because the journey is across a series of steep hills.

4 A coach was "convenient for large families" and was "capable of holding six persons," though in this instance it had to carry only the two Musgrove and the two Elliot sisters. Charles and Wentworth travel in a curricle, a two-wheeled, open carriage that held two people and took two horses, so that it was faster than other carriages. William Felton noted that curricles were "built much stronger and heavier than what is necessary for one horse chaises, and the larger they are the better they look, if not to an extreme" (Felton, I, 36; II, 115).

5 In *A Guide to all the Watering and Sea-Bathing Places* (circa 1803), John Feltham (fl. 1797–1821) describes how Lyme is "built on the declivity of a craggy hill, at the head of a little inlet of the sea, and contains many respectable looking houses, with pleasant gardens, particularly in the upper part of the town; but the streets are steep, rugged, and unpleasant" (Feltham, 355).

6 The party would have had a choice between the two principal inns that operated in Lyme in Austen's day: the Golden Lion and the Three Cups. They probably decided on the latter, as it was the more fashionable of the two. "The Three-cups-Inn, and Hotel, kept by Mr. Manning," remarked "M. Phillips" in his *Picture of Lyme-Regis* (1817), "is an excellent house, pleasantly situated opposite the bay, commanding an extensive view of the

and his description of the fine country about Lyme so feelingly attended to by the party, that an earnest desire to see Lyme themselves, and a project for going thither was the consequence.

The young people were all wild to see Lyme. Captain Wentworth talked of going there again himself; it was only seventeen miles from Uppercross; though November, the weather was by no means bad; and, in short, Louisa, who was the most eager of the eager, having formed the resolution to go, and besides the pleasure of doing as she liked, being now armed with the idea of merit in maintaining her own way, bore down all the wishes of her father and mother for putting it off till summer; and to Lyme they were to go—Charles, Mary, Anne, Henrietta, Louisa, and Captain Wentworth.

The first heedless scheme had been to go in the morning and return at night, but to this Mr. Musgrove, for the sake of his horses, would not consent; and when it came to be rationally considered, a day in the middle of November would not leave much time for seeing a new place, after deducting seven hours, as the nature of the country required, for going and returning.[3] They were consequently to stay the night there, and not to be expected back till the next day's dinner. This was felt to be a considerable amendment; and though they all met at the Great House at rather an early breakfast hour, and set off very punctually, it was so much past noon before the two carriages, Mr. Musgrove's coach containing the four ladies, and Charles's curricle,[4] in which he drove Captain Wentworth, were descending the long hill into Lyme, and entering upon the still steeper

The prince regent in a curricle, by Thomas Rowlandson. The curricle was the Regency equivalent of a sports car. Compare *Sense and Sensibility,* where Willoughby and Marianne drive "through the park very fast" and are "soon out of sight." "Did not you know," Willoughby says on their return, "that we had been out in my curricle?" (I, 13).

The Assembly Rooms at Cobb Gate, Lyme Regis, attributed to Reed. In September 1804, during one of her two stays at Lyme, Austen wrote to Cassandra that "we all of us" attend "the Rooms" (Austen, *Letters,* 93).

street of the town itself,[5] that it was very evident they would not have more than time for looking about them, before the light and warmth of the day were gone.

After securing accommodations, and ordering a dinner at one of the inns,[6] the next thing to be done was unquestionably to walk directly down to the sea. They were come too late in the year for any amusement or variety which Lyme, as a public place, might offer; the rooms[7] were shut up, the lodgers almost all gone, scarcely any family but of the residents left—and, as there is nothing to admire in the buildings themselves, the remarkable situation of the town, the principal street almost hurrying into the water, the walk to the Cobb,[8] skirting round the pleasant little bay, which in the season is animated with bathing machines[9] and company, the Cobb itself, its old wonders and new improvements, with the very beautiful line of cliffs stretching out to the east of the town, are what the stranger's eye will seek; and a very strange stranger it must be, who does not see charms

Ocean, and of the picturesque ridge of the Hills to the east.—Here Families, Parties, or single Gentlemen, are accommodated in every way agreeably to the wish of the visitant" (Feltham, 356; Phillips, 12–13; Maggie Lane, *Jane Austen and Lyme Regis* [Chawton: Jane Austen Society, 2007], 41).

7 The "rooms" were the "Assembly Rooms," where people gathered to dance and enjoy concerts. By November, when Anne visits, the social season has passed, and only the residents of Lyme remain. Austen herself went to a ball in the Lyme Assembly Rooms in September 1804: "Nobody asked me the two first dances," she reported to Cassandra, "—the two next I danced with Mr. Crawford—& had I chosen to stay longer might have danced with Mr. Granville" (Austen, *Letters,* 94).

8 The Cobb is a giant, two-level, semicircular stone breakwater. Constructed in medieval times to create a harbor for Lyme, it has been rebuilt many times since then. In Austen's day it was made of "vast stones, weighed out of the sea, and arranged in such a manner as to break the violence of the tide, which has made great encroachments, the cliffs being composed of a kind of marl and blue clay incorporated with lime, that easily give way." There were a number of rough-hewn stone steps jutting out from the wall leading from the Upper Cobb down to the Lower Cobb. It was an ideal place from which to view the sea (Feltham, 356).

9 Bathing machines were mobile cabins that could be moved from the beach out into the sea. They allowed people to dip themselves into the salt water to receive its medicinal benefits while keeping their modesty intact. "The Invalid," declared Phillips, "from the fine sea bathing and sea air, for such it may be truly expressed, rarely visits Lyme without great benefit." Later Phillips added that the "Bathing-Rooms" in Lyme "afford another superior attraction, and accommodation, and are situated at the eastern part of the town; and another equally commodious, at the Cobb, where hot and cold baths, together with shower baths, are as complete as can be desired. It is but just to observe, that an eminent Physician, Dr. Baker, in analysing the sea waters, at different places, found sea water

at Lyme to be more saline and heavier than the sea water at any other part of the coast" (Phillips, 6, 14).

10 Traveling through the south of England in August 1791, Frances Burney was as captivated by Lyme as was Austen herself: "We set out, after Dinner, for Lime, & the Road through which we travelled is the very most beautiful to which my wandering destinies have yet sent me. It is diversified with all that can compose luxuriant scenery, & with just as much of the approach to sublime, as is in the province of unterrific beauty. The Hills are the highest, I fancy, in the South of this country, the boldest, & noblest;—the vales of the finest verdure, wooded & watered as if only to give ideas of finished Landscapes; while the whole, from time to time, rises into still superior grandeur, by openings between the heights that terminate the view with the splendour of the British Channel. There was no going on in the carriage through such enchanting scenes; We got out upon the Hills, & walked till we could walk no longer" (*The Journals and Letters of Fanny Burney,* ed. Joyce Hemlow, 12 vols. [Oxford: Clarendon Press, 1972–1984], I, 25).

11 Charmouth, enthused John Feltham, is a "delightful village" about a mile and a half to the east of Lyme. "It occupies an elevated situation, and consequently commands many vast and beautiful prospects both of the sea and land. It has likewise the advantage of being a considerable thoroughfare, and laying so near Lyme, it is much resorted to by bathers" (Feltham, 358).

12 Up Lyme, now Uplyme, is—as the name suggests—at the top of the steep hill that rises out of Lyme.

13 Pinny, now Pinhay, lies just over a mile to the west of Lyme.

14 In her description of the "immediate environs of Lyme," Austen comes "nearer to the Romantic poets than in anything else that she wrote," declares Alethea Hayter. In particular, Hayter suggests that Austen may have been influenced in this passage by Samuel Taylor Coleridge's "Kubla Khan," a poem that was first published by Austen's own publisher, John Murray, in 1816,

Sea Bathing at Scarborough, engraved by Robert Havell (1769–1832) and Daniel Havell (d. circa 1826), after George Walker (1781–1856), 1814. Lyme was also famous for its sea bathing, and Austen herself indulged. "The Bathing was so delightful this morning," she reported to Cassandra in September 1804. But "I believe I staid in rather too long, as since the middle of the day I have felt unreasonably tired. I shall be more careful another time, & shall not bathe tomorrow, as I had before intended" (Austen, *Letters,* 95).

in the immediate environs of Lyme, to make him wish to know it better.[10] The scenes in its neighbourhood, Charmouth,[11] with its high grounds and extensive sweeps of country, and still more its sweet retired bay, backed by dark cliffs, where fragments of low rock among the sands make it the happiest spot for watching the flow of the tide, for sitting in unwearied contemplation;—the woody varieties of the cheerful village of Up Lyme,[12] and, above all, Pinny,[13] with its green chasms between romantic rocks, where the scattered forest trees and orchards of luxuriant growth declare that many a generation must have passed away since the first partial falling of the cliff[14] prepared the ground for such a state, where a scene so wonderful and so lovely is exhibited, as may more than equal any of the resembling

Samuel Taylor Coleridge, by Peter Vandyke (1729–1799), 1795. Coleridge composed "Kubla Khan" in early November 1797, but he did not publish it until 1816, and only then after Lord Byron heard him recite it and urged his publisher John Murray to put it into print.

scenes of the far-famed Isle of Wight:[15] these places must be visited, and visited again, to make the worth of Lyme understood.

The party from Uppercross passing down by the now deserted and melancholy looking rooms, and still descending, soon found themselves on the sea shore, and lingering only, as all must linger and gaze on a first return to the sea, who ever deserve[16] to look on it at all, proceeded towards the Cobb, equally their object in itself and on Captain Wentworth's account; for in a small house, near the foot of an old pier of unknown date, were the Harvilles settled. Captain

and that Austen may have read as she worked on *Persuasion.* In the poem, Coleridge writes of a

> deep romantic chasm which slanted
> Down the green hill athwart a cedarn cover!
> A savage place! as holy and inchanted
> As e'er beneath a waning moon was haunted
> By woman wailing for her demon-lover!

Hayter proposes that Austen's own memories of Lyme, coupled with her reading of Coleridge's hypnotic poem, might have cast a "strange glow" over the landscape, "and now it would be the dark cliffs, the rocky fragments, the green chasms, the forest trees, that she felt moved to describe in *Persuasion,* as the setting for Anne Elliot's 'sorrowing heart,' secretly yearning over the love that she believed she had lost for ever." The twentieth-century essayist and novelist Rebecca West (1892–1983) undoubtedly had passages such as this one in mind when she asked pointedly, "Is it really possible that anybody could read . . . *Persuasion*" without seeing behind it "a face graven with weeping?" (Hayter, "Xanadu at Lyme Regis," in *Ariel,* 1 [1970], 61, 64; Coleridge, *Poetical Works,* 6 vols., ed. J. C. C. Mays [Princeton: Princeton University Press, 2001], I, 513; West, *The Strange Necessity* [London: Jonathan Cape, 1928], 263).

15 The Isle of Wight is a large, diamond-shaped island that lies immediately off the Hampshire coast in the English Channel. It was widely celebrated for its natural beauty, "comprehending, as it does, within the space of a few miles, sublime coast views, terrific chasms formed by convulsions of Nature, richly cultivated plains, and romantic wooded seclusions" (Thomas Barber, "Preface," in *Barber's Picturesque Illustrations, of the Isle of Wight* [London: Simpkin and Marshall, 1834], i).

16 Austen reveals a great deal about her attitude toward the navy when she speaks of those "who ever deserve" to look on the sea. "*Deserve* to look on the sea?" Tony Tanner asks. "Is this Jane Austen—or Melville? Here is a shift indeed. Not the awed and humble approach to Pemberley or Mansfield Park; but the privilege, for those who deserve it, of gazing at—the sea. Jane Austen seems to be turning her back on more than just the local inanities of a Sir Walter Elliot" (Tanner, 230).

Between Lyme Regis and Charmouth, by John White Abbott (1764–1851). "One mile and half from Lyme, is the pleasant village, Charmouth, on the great road from London to Exeter," wrote M. Phillips in 1817, the same year that *Persuasion* was published. "The Mail and two other Coaches daily pass through this Village; which has many handsome lodgings, about a quarter of a mile from the Sea" (Phillips, 18).

17 Benwick would have been one of only three lieutenants on a frigate such as the *Laconia.* The first lieutenant was primarily responsible for the administration of the crew. In action, Benwick as first lieutenant would have stood by Wentworth, ready to advise or to take over if Wentworth was wounded (Lavery, 96–97).

Wentworth turned in to call on his friend; the others walked on, and he was to join them on the Cobb.

They were by no means tired of wondering and admiring; and not even Louisa seemed to feel that they had parted with Captain Wentworth long, when they saw him coming after them, with three companions, all well known already by description to be Captain and Mrs. Harville, and a Captain Benwick, who was staying with them.

Captain Benwick had some time ago been first lieutenant[17] of the Laconia; and the account which Captain Wentworth had given of him, on his return from Lyme before; his warm praise of him as an excellent young man and an officer, whom he had always valued highly, which must have stamped him well in the esteem of every listener, had been followed by a little history of his private life, which rendered him perfectly interesting in the eyes of all the ladies. He had been engaged to Captain Harville's sister, and was now mourning her loss. They had been a year or two waiting for fortune and promotion. Fortune came, his prize-money as lieutenant being great,— promotion, too, came at *last;* but Fanny Harville did not live to know it. She had died the preceding summer, while he was at sea. Captain Wentworth believed it impossible for man to be more attached to woman than poor Benwick had been to Fanny Harville, or to be more deeply afflicted under the dreadful change. He considered his disposition as of the sort which must suffer heavily, uniting very strong feelings with quiet, serious, and retiring manners, and a decided taste for reading, and sedentary pursuits. To finish the interest of the story, the friendship between him and the Harvilles seemed, if possible, augmented by the event which closed all their views of alliance, and Captain Benwick was now living with them entirely. Captain Harville had taken his present house for half a year, his taste, and his health, and his fortune all directing him to a residence unexpensive, and by the sea;[18] and the grandeur of the country, and the retirement of Lyme in the winter, appeared exactly adapted to Captain Benwick's state of mind. The sympathy and good-will excited towards Captain Benwick was very great.

"And yet," said Anne to herself, as they now moved forward to meet the party, "he has not, perhaps, a more sorrowing heart than I have. I cannot believe his prospects so blighted for ever. He is younger than I am; younger in feeling, if not in fact; younger as a man. He will rally again, and be happy with another."

They all met, and were introduced. Captain Harville was a tall, dark man, with a sensible, benevolent countenance; a little lame; and from strong features, and want of health, looking much older than Captain Wentworth. Captain Benwick looked and was the youngest of the three, and, compared with either of them, a little man. He had a pleasing face and a melancholy air, just as he ought to have, and drew back from conversation.

18 The disabled Harville has chosen to spend the winter in an inexpensive residence by the sea because he is on half pay and has no prospect of improving his fortunes with prize money. "Lodgings and boarding at Lyme are not merely reasonable, they are even cheap," John Feltham asserts; "the dissipations for the healthy, and the suitable accommodations for the sick, are within the reach of ordinary resources" (Feltham, 357).

19 What Austen calls a "great tendency to lowness" would today most likely be referred to as "depression."

20 A "nice arrangement" is one that is "agreeable, pleasant, satisfactory; attractive" *(OED)*. Austen uses the word "nice" frequently in *Persuasion,* and in a variety of different senses and contexts. Compare *Northanger Abbey* (1818), where Catherine describes Ann Radcliffe's gothic novel *The Mysteries of Udolpho* (1794) as "a nice book." "Very true," replies Henry, "and this is a very nice day, and we are taking a very nice walk, and you are two very nice young ladies. Oh! it is a very nice word indeed!—it does for every thing. Originally perhaps it was applied only to express neatness, propriety, delicacy, or refinement;—people were nice in their dress, in their sentiments, or their choice. But now every commendation on every subject is comprised in that one word" (I, 14).

Captain Harville, though not equalling Captain Wentworth in manners, was a perfect gentleman, unaffected, warm, and obliging. Mrs. Harville, a degree less polished than her husband, seemed however to have the same good feelings; and nothing could be more pleasant than their desire of considering the whole party as friends of their own, because the friends of Captain Wentworth, or more kindly hospitable than their entreaties for their all promising to dine with them. The dinner, already ordered at the inn, was at last, though unwillingly, accepted as an excuse; but they seemed almost hurt that Captain Wentworth should have brought any such party to Lyme, without considering it as a thing of course that they should dine with them.

There was so much attachment to Captain Wentworth in all this, and such a bewitching charm in a degree of hospitality so uncommon, so unlike the usual style of give-and-take invitations, and dinners of formality and display, that Anne felt her spirits not likely to be benefited by an increasing acquaintance among his brother-officers. "These would have been all my friends," was her thought; and she had to struggle against a great tendency to lowness.[19]

On quitting the Cobb, they all went indoors with their new friends, and found rooms so small as none but those who invite from the heart could think capable of accommodating so many. Anne had a moment's astonishment on the subject herself; but it was soon lost

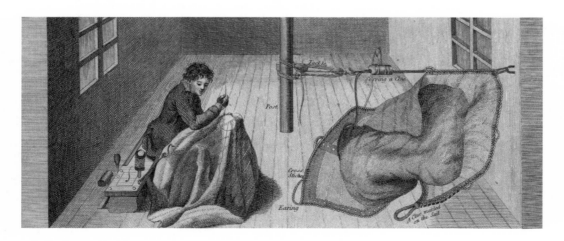

An engraving of a sailmaker at work, from David Steel's *Elements of Mastmaking, Sailmaking, and Rigging* (1794). Like Captain Harville, this sailor is not at sea, as the windows of the building reveal.

in the pleasanter feelings which sprang from the sight of all the ingenious contrivances and nice arrangements[20] of Captain Harville, to turn the actual space to the best possible account, to supply the deficiencies of lodging-house furniture, and defend the windows and doors against the winter storms to be expected. The varieties in the fitting-up of the rooms, where the common necessaries provided by the owner, in the common indifferent plight, were contrasted with some few articles of a rare species of wood, excellently worked up, and with something curious and valuable from all the distant countries Captain Harville had visited, were more than amusing to Anne: connected as it all was with his profession, the fruit of its labours, the effect of its influence on his habits, the picture of repose and domestic happiness it presented, made it to her a something more, or less, than gratification.

Captain Harville was no reader; but he had contrived excellent accommodations, and fashioned very pretty shelves, for a tolerable collection of well-bound volumes, the property of Captain Benwick. His lameness prevented him from taking much exercise; but a mind of usefulness and ingenuity seemed to furnish him with constant employment within. He drew, he varnished, he carpentered, he glued; he made toys for the children, he fashioned new netting-needles and pins with improvements; and if every thing else was done, sat down to his large fishing-net at one corner of the room.[21]

Anne thought she left great happiness behind her when they quitted the house; and Louisa, by whom she found herself walking, burst forth into raptures of admiration and delight on the character of the navy—their friendliness, their brotherliness, their openness, their uprightness; protesting that she was convinced of sailors having more worth and warmth than any other set of men in England; that they only knew how to live, and they only deserved to be respected and loved.

They went back to dress and dine; and so well had the scheme answered[22] already, that nothing was found amiss; though its being "so entirely out of the season," and the "no thorough-fare of Lyme,"[23] and the "no expectation of company," had brought many apologies from the heads of the inn.

21 Many naval men took up handicrafts to while away the time on board ship. In his discussion of how children destined for service in the navy should be educated, Richard Lovell Edgeworth (1744–1817) advises that "at seasons of the year when exercises in the open air are not convenient, the pupil may amuse himself within doors with carpenter's, smith's, and turner's tools. . . . No great apparatus of tools should at first be provided. . . . His whole stock in trade should consist . . . only of a knife, a square, a small saw, and two or three gimlets, twenty or thirty waste ends of boards of different thicknesses, and a strong stool for a workbench. With these a boy of seven or eight years old may employ himself very happily." In February 1807, Francis Austen helped with the furnishings of the Austen house in Southampton when he produced a "very nice fringe for the Drawingroom-Curtains." Later, Francis recognized that parts of Harville's character "were drawn from myself—at least some of his domestic habits, tastes and occupations bear a strong resemblance to mine." By bringing Harville so firmly within the domestic world of the cottage, Austen suggestively conflates male and female spheres: netting, for example, "was undertaken by both men and women, according to whether the product was required for female accessories and trimmings, or for sporting use as in fishing nets or rabbit snares" (Edgeworth, *Essays on Professional Education* [London: Johnson, 1809], 116; Austen, *Letters,* 123; Southam, 308; Deirdre Le Faye, *Jane Austen: The World of Her Novels* [London: Lincoln, 2002], 112).

22 Austen uses "answered" here to mean to "accomplish an end" or "suit a purpose."

23 Lyme was not on the main coaching route, so its innkeepers undoubtedly had a difficult time with the prompt delivery of fresh provisions. In November they seem to have stopped ordering for guests altogether, as the social season had passed and they had "no expectation of company."

Walter Scott, by Sir Henry Raeburn, 1822. Scott, the most famous novelist of Austen's day, was also one of her most astute contemporary critics. "That young lady had a talent for describing the involvements and feelings and characters of ordinary life which is to me the most wonderful I ever met with," he wrote in March 1826 (*The Journal of Sir Walter Scott,* ed. W. E. K. Anderson [Oxford: Clarendon Press, 1972], 114).

Lord Byron, by Richard Westall (1765–1836), 1813. Lady Caroline Lamb (1785–1828) famously described Byron as "mad—bad—and dangerous to know," but Austen herself was less intimidated: "I have read [Byron's] the Corsair, mended my petticoat, & have nothing else to do," she wrote to Cassandra in March 1814 (cited in Leslie A. Marchand, *Byron: A Biography,* 3 vols. [New York: Knopf, 1957], I, 328; Austen, *Letters,* 257).

Anne found herself by this time growing so much more hardened to being in Captain Wentworth's company than she had at first imagined could ever be, that the sitting down to the same table with him now, and the interchange of the common civilities attending on it—(they never got beyond) was become a mere nothing.

The nights were too dark for the ladies to meet again till the morrow, but Captain Harville had promised them a visit in the evening; and he came, bringing his friend also, which was more than had been expected, it having been agreed that Captain Benwick had all the appearance of being oppressed by the presence of so many strangers. He ventured among them again, however, though his spirits certainly did not seem fit for the mirth of the party in general.

While Captains Wentworth and Harville led the talk on one side of the room, and, by recurring to former days, supplied anecdotes in abundance to occupy and entertain the others, it fell to Anne's lot to be placed rather apart with Captain Benwick; and a very good impulse of her nature obliged her to begin an acquaintance with him. He was shy, and disposed to abstraction; but the engaging mildness of her countenance, and gentleness of her manners, soon had their effect; and Anne was well repaid the first trouble of exertion. He was evidently a young man of considerable taste in reading, though principally in poetry; and besides the persuasion of having given him at least an evening's indulgence in the discussion of subjects, which his usual companions had probably no concern in, she had the hope of being of real use to him in some suggestions as to the duty and benefit of struggling against affliction, which had naturally grown out of their conversation. For, though shy, he did not seem reserved; it had rather the appearance of feelings glad to burst their usual restraints; and having talked of poetry, the richness of the present age, and gone through a brief comparison of opinion as to the first-rate poets, trying to ascertain whether *Marmion* or *The Lady of the Lake*[24] were to be preferred, and how ranked the *Giaour* and *The Bride of Abydos;* and moreover, how the *Giaour* was to be pronounced,[25] he shewed himself so intimately acquainted with all the tenderest songs of the one

24 Walter Scott wrote a number of long, narrative romances set in medieval times, including *Marmion* (1808) and *The Lady of the Lake* (1810). Both poems concerned Scott's native Scotland and were hugely popular. According to her nephew James Edward Austen-Leigh, Austen derived "great pleasure" from Scott's poetry. In 1814 she was famously chagrined to discover that Scott had left off poetry and taken up as a novelist. He has "no business to write novels, especially good ones," she wrote. "—It is not fair.—He has Fame & Profit enough as a Poet, and should not be taking the bread out of other people's mouths" (Austen-Leigh, *Memoir,* 72; Austen, *Letters,* 277).

25 Lord Byron (1788–1824) published four wildly successful "Oriental tales": *The Giaour* (1813), *The Bride of Abydos* (1813), *The Corsair* (1814), and *Lara* (1814). All four poems have exotic Eastern settings and feature the Byronic hero—a handsome, disillusioned solitary haunted by guilt and sorrow. Byron signals how he intends "Giaour" to be pronounced by placing it in the poem to rhyme with "power," "bower," "hour," and "lower" ("And though to-morrow's tempest lower, /'Tis calmer than thy heart, young Giaour!"). "Giaour" is the Turkish word for "Christian" (Byron, *Poetical Works,* III, 46).

Scott and Byron dominated the literary scene during the years Austen was publishing her novels. Like Anne and Benwick, many contemporary readers engaged in lively debate over the relative merits of the two literary giants. Most famously, the brilliant radical essayist William Hazlitt (1778–1830) set them side by side as poets in his collection of essays titled *The Spirit of the Age* (1825): "Lord Byron's verse glows like a flame, consuming every thing in its way; Sir Walter Scott's glides like a river, clear, gentle, harmless. The poetry of the first scorches, that of the last scarcely warms. The light of the one proceeds from an internal source, ensanguined, sullen, fixed; the other reflects the hues of Heaven, or the face of nature, glancing vivid and various. The productions of the Northern Bard have the rust and the freshness of antiquity about them; those of the Noble Poet cease to startle from their extreme ambition of novelty, both in style and matter" (Hazlitt, *Works,* XI, 69–70).

More recently, Susan Allen Ford emphasizes the ways in which the romances of Scott and Byron are deeply congruent with the deeds and motives of Wentworth and his sailor friends: "Like the male characters valorized in *Persuasion,* the heroes of Scott and Byron are men of action—knights, pirates, sympathetic outlaws. They are not defined in terms of inheritance of land or power; instead they act in problematic relationship—covert loyalty or open revolt—to those who do hold power." Peter Knox-Shaw sees Austen's assimilation of Byron as more ambivalent, and examines the intriguing ways in which she both rejects and embraces him. "What complicates Byron's presence in *Persuasion* is that he is at once the butt of criticism and an index to the novel's quick," remarks Knox-Shaw. "He is made to preside over the meeting with Benwick in order to draw out a dark analogy between the story of the Captain whose fiancée has died and Anne's own aborted romance, and repeated allusion shows how deeply implicated he is in the novel's probing of passion and the experience of loss." *The Giaour* bears on *Persuasion* because in it "Byron devises a variety of means to evoke the sense of a life arrested and utterly transformed by an event buried in the past." Similarly, "the heroine in *The Bride of Abydos* supplies Benwick with as fit a model as the Giaour, for she loses her lover shortly after they have exchanged vows, and goes on to die of grief" (Ford, "Learning Romance from Scott and Byron: Jane Austen's Natural Sequel," in *Persuasions,* 26 [2004], 78; Knox-Shaw, "*Persuasion,* Byron, and the Turkish Tale," in *Review of English Studies,* New Series, 44 [1993], 48–49, 51).

26 Benwick's intimate acquaintance with the "tenderest songs" of Scott means that he is undoubtedly familiar with poems such as "Oh say not, my love," "The Resolve," "The Maid of Neidpath," "The Maid of Toro," and the "Song" from Canto Three of *The Lady of the Lake:*

The heath this night must be my bed,
The bracken curtain for my head,
My lullaby the warder's tread,
    Far far from love and thee, Mary;
To-morrow eve, more stilly laid,
My couch may be my bloody plaid,

My vesper song, thy wail, sweet maid!
    It will not waken me, Mary!

I may not, dare not, fancy now
The grief that clouds thy lovely brow,
I dare not think upon thy vow,
    And all it promised me, Mary.
No fond regret must Norman know;
When bursts Clan-Alpine on the foe,
His heart must be like bended bow,
    His foot like arrow free, Mary.

A time will come with feeling fraught,
For, if I fall in battle fought,
Thy hapless lover's dying thought
    Shall be a thought on thee, Mary.
And if return'd from conquer'd foes,
How blithely will the evening close,
How sweet the linnet sing repose,
    To my young bride and me, Mary!

(*Scott: Poetical Works,* ed. J. Logie Robertson [London: Oxford University Press, 1971], 236–237).

27 Byron filled his Oriental tales with "impassioned descriptions of hopeless agony." One of the most famous occurs near the opening of *The Giaour* and seems likely to have been among the passages that Benwick recites to Anne. "He who hath bent him o'er the dead," Byron writes,

Ere the first day of death is fled;
The first dark day of nothingness,
The last of danger and distress;
(Before Decay's effacing fingers
Have swept the lines where beauty lingers)
And mark'd the mild angelic air—
The rapture of repose that's there—
The fixed yet tender traits that streak
The languor of the placid cheek,
And—but for that sad shrouded eye,
    That fires not—wins not—weeps not—now—
    And but for that chill changeless brow,
Where cold Obstruction's apathy
Appals the gazing mourner's heart.

(Byron, *Poetical Works,* III, 42).

poet,[26] and all the impassioned descriptions of hopeless agony of the other;[27] he repeated, with such tremulous feeling, the various lines which imaged a broken heart, or a mind destroyed by wretchedness, and looked so entirely as if he meant to be understood, that she ventured to hope he did not always read only poetry; and to say, that she thought it was the misfortune of poetry, to be seldom safely enjoyed by those who enjoyed it completely; and that the strong feelings which alone could estimate it truly, were the very feelings which ought to taste it but sparingly.

His looks shewing him not pained, but pleased with this allusion to his situation, she was emboldened to go on; and feeling in herself the right of seniority of mind, she ventured to recommend a larger allowance of prose in his daily study; and on being requested to particularize, mentioned such works of our best moralists, such collections of the finest letters, such memoirs of characters of worth and suffering, as occurred to her at the moment as calculated to rouse and fortify the mind by the highest precepts, and the strongest examples of moral and religious endurances.[28]

Captain Benwick listened attentively, and seemed grateful for the interest implied; and though with a shake of the head, and sighs which declared his little faith in the efficacy of any books on grief like his, noted down the names of those she recommended, and promised to procure and read them.

When the evening was over, Anne could not but be amused at the idea of her coming to Lyme, to preach patience and resignation to a young man whom she had never seen before; nor could she help fearing, on more serious reflection, that, like many other great moralists and preachers, she had been eloquent on a point in which her own conduct would ill bear examination.

28 Anne does not name the moralists who can "rouse and fortify the mind by the highest precepts," but undoubtedly one of the writers she has in mind is Samuel Johnson, who in his periodical *The Rambler* dealt often with topics that spoke directly to Benwick's struggles with grief and loss. In Number 32, for example, Johnson offers "moral instruction" in "the art of bearing calamities," and "the duty of every man to furnish his mind with those principles that may enable him to act under it with decency and propriety." Sorrow, the subject of Number 47, "is to a certain point laudable, as the offspring of love, or at least pardonable as the effect of weakness; but . . . it ought not to be suffered to increase by indulgence, but must give way, after a stated time, to social duties, and the common avocations of life." Indeed, Johnson's biographer James Boswell (1740–1795) praised *The Rambler* in terms that clearly demonstrate why Anne would bring it to mind in this conversation with Benwick. "I will venture to say," Boswell declares, "that in no writings whatever can be found *more bark and steel for the mind,* if I may use the expression; more that can brace and invigorate every manly and noble sentiment" (Johnson, *Rambler,* III, 174 and 255; *Boswell's Life of Johnson,* ed. George Birkbeck Hill [Oxford: Clarendon Press, 1887], I, 215).

John Wiltshire observes that this discussion between Anne and Benwick is also notable because it reveals Austen's paradoxical attitude in *Persuasion* toward books, for Anne recommends them to strengthen Benwick at the same time that her father's obsession with the *Baronetage* has so thoroughly enervated him: "This idea of the book as fortifying the male is wonderfully parodied, and perhaps subverted, by the very first sentence of *Persuasion,* conspicuously Johnsonian in its cadence, where Sir Walter Elliot reads the Baronetage to find 'occupation for an idle hour and consolation in a distressed one'" (Wiltshire, 179).

12

1 Henrietta's conviction that "sea-air always does good" was frequently repeated in contemporary medical books and pamphlets. "Unwholesome air is a very common cause of diseases," William Buchan insisted. "Few are aware of the danger arising from it. People generally pay some attention to what they eat or drink, but seldom regard what goes into the lungs, though the latter proves often more suddenly fatal than the former." In his pamphlet on Lyme, Phillips praised the "salubrity of the air," which "occasions a still greater attraction to those who justly appreciate that greatest of blessings, *good health*" (Buchan, 51–52; Phillips, 6).

2 "Last spring twelvemonth" is "a year ago last spring."

3 By "fix at Lyme," Henrietta means that she thinks Dr. Shirley should "fix his residence permanently at Lyme."

4 Henrietta is hoping that Dr. Shirley might be persuaded to apply for a dispensation that would enable him to move away from his parish. Under the terms of such an arrangement, he would retain the income and benefits of his position while his duties would be left to Charles Hayter. Agreements of this kind were commonplace in the Church of England (Collins, 21–22).

ANNE AND HENRIETTA, FINDING THEMSELVES the earliest of the party the next morning, agreed to stroll down to the sea before breakfast.—They went to the sands, to watch the flowing of the tide, which a fine south-easterly breeze was bringing in with all the grandeur which so flat a shore admitted. They praised the morning; gloried in the sea; sympathized in the delight of the fresh-feeling breeze—and were silent; till Henrietta suddenly began again, with,

"Oh! yes,—I am quite convinced that, with very few exceptions, the sea-air always does good.[1] There can be no doubt of its having been of the greatest service to Dr. Shirley, after his illness, last spring twelvemonth.[2] He declares himself, that coming to Lyme for a month, did him more good than all the medicine he took; and, that being by the sea, always makes him feel young again. Now, I cannot help thinking it a pity that he does not live entirely by the sea. I do think he had better leave Uppercross entirely, and fix at Lyme.[3]—Do not you, Anne?—Do not you agree with me, that it is the best thing he could do, both for himself and Mrs. Shirley?—She has cousins here, you know, and many acquaintance, which would make it cheerful for her,—and I am sure she would be glad to get to a place where she could have medical attendance at hand, in case of his having another seizure. Indeed I think it quite melancholy to have such excellent people as Dr. and Mrs. Shirley, who have been doing good all their lives, wearing out their last days in a place like Uppercross, where, excepting our family, they seem shut out from all the world. I wish his friends would propose it to him. I really think they ought.

And, as to procuring a dispensation, there could be no difficulty at his time of life, and with his character.[4] My only doubt is, whether any thing could persuade him to leave his parish. He is so very strict and scrupulous in his notions; over-scrupulous, I must say. Do not you think, Anne, it is being over-scrupulous? Do not you think it is quite a mistaken point of conscience, when a clergyman sacrifices his health for the sake of duties, which may be just as well performed by another person?—And at Lyme too,—only seventeen miles off,—he would be near enough to hear, if people thought there was any thing to complain of."

Anne smiled more than once to herself during this speech,[5] and entered into the subject, as ready to do good by entering into the feelings of a young lady as of a young man,—though here it was good

The title page of M. Phillips's book *Picture of Lyme-Regis,* 1817. Phillips observes that the "amphitheatrical bay" of Lyme Regis is "one of the most enchanting spots for a Watering-place, that can be found around the British Islands.—The Scenery altogether is magnificent" (5–6).

5 Although it often goes unnoticed, Anne leavens her longing for Wentworth with an ability to see humor in the world around her, and to derive pleasure—rather than gloom—from the foibles and foolishness of others. "She is . . . more alert to find amusement in the spectacle presented by her fellow-creatures than any Austen heroine since Elizabeth Bennet," Isobel Grundy observes. "She does not wait to be loved and happy before she can feel amused; she begins to feel this way as soon as she begins to mix at large in society. Indeed, for lifting her melancholy and offering her resources, being anxiously in love seems almost as effective as being happily in love." At Lyme, Grundy adds, "Anne 'smiled more than once to herself' at Henrietta's artless self-interest on behalf of her fiancé's career; and she is variously amused by the changing attitudes of Henrietta and the other Musgroves to Lady Russell" (Grundy, "*Persuasion:* or, The Triumph of Cheerfulness," in *Persuasions,* 15 [1993], 94, 96).

A gentleman politely drew back.

Hugh Thomson, Illustrations for *Persuasion,* 1897. Mr. Elliot allows Anne and her party to pass. Captain Wentworth's affection for Anne is rekindled at this moment.

of a lower standard, for what could be offered but general acquiescence?—She said all that was reasonable and proper on the business; felt the claims of Dr. Shirley to repose, as she ought; saw how very desirable it was that he should have some active, respectable young man, as a resident curate, and was even courteous enough to hint at the advantage of such resident curate's being married.

"I wish," said Henrietta, very well pleased with her companion, "I wish Lady Russell lived at Uppercross, and were intimate with Dr. Shirley. I have always heard of Lady Russell, as a woman of the greatest influence with every body! I always look upon her as able to persuade a person to any thing! I am afraid of her, as I have told you before, quite afraid of her, because she is so very clever; but I respect her amazingly, and wish we had such a neighbour at Uppercross."

Anne was amused by Henrietta's manner of being grateful, and amused also, that the course of events and the new interests of Henrietta's views should have placed her friend at all in favour with any of the Musgrove family; she had only time, however, for a general answer, and a wish that such another woman were at Uppercross, before all subjects suddenly ceased, on seeing Louisa and Captain Wentworth coming towards them. They came also for a stroll till breakfast was likely to be ready; but Louisa recollecting, immediately afterwards, that she had something to procure at a shop, invited them all to go back with her into the town. They were all at her disposal.

When they came to the steps, leading upwards from the beach, a gentleman at the same moment preparing to come down, politely drew back, and stopped to give them way. They ascended and passed him; and as they passed, Anne's face caught his eye, and he looked at her with a degree of earnest admiration, which she could not be insensible of. She was looking remarkably well; her very regular, very pretty features, having the bloom and freshness of youth restored by the fine wind which had been blowing on her complexion, and by the animation of eye which it had also produced. It was evident that the gentleman, (completely a gentleman in manner) admired her exceedingly. Captain Wentworth looked round at her instantly in a way which shewed his noticing of it. He gave her a momentary glance,—a glance of brightness, which seemed to say, "That man is struck with you,—and even I, at this moment, see something like Anne Elliot again."

After attending Louisa through her business, and loitering about a little longer, they returned to the inn; and Anne in passing afterwards quickly from her own chamber to their dining-room, had nearly run against the very same gentleman, as he came out of an adjoining apartment. She had before conjectured him to be a stranger like themselves, and determined that a well-looking groom,[6] who was strolling about near the two inns as they came back, should be his servant. Both master and man being in mourning, assisted the idea. It was now proved that he belonged to the same inn as themselves; and this second meeting, short as it was, also proved again by the gentleman's looks, that he thought hers very lovely, and by the readiness and propriety of his apologies, that he was a man of exceedingly good manners. He seemed about thirty, and, though not handsome, had an agreeable person. Anne felt that she should like to know who he was.

They had nearly done breakfast, when the sound of a carriage, (almost the first they had heard since entering Lyme) drew half the party to the window. "It was a gentleman's carriage—a curricle—but only coming round from the stable-yard to the front door—Somebody must be going away.—It was driven by a servant in mourning."

The word curricle made Charles Musgrove jump up, that he might compare it with his own, the servant in mourning roused Anne's curiosity, and the whole six were collected to look, by the time the owner of the curricle was to be seen issuing from the door amidst the bows and civilities of the household, and taking his seat, to drive off.

"Ah!" cried Captain Wentworth, instantly, and with half a glance at Anne; "it is the very man we passed."

The Miss Musgroves agreed to it; and having all kindly watched him as far up the hill as they could, they returned to the breakfast-table. The waiter came into the room soon afterwards.

"Pray," said Captain Wentworth, immediately, "can you tell us the name of the gentleman who is just gone away?"

6 "A well-looking groom" is a "respectable looking groom."

7 Sidmouth is a small seaside resort in Devon and lies about fifteen miles to the west of Lyme.

8 Crewkherne, now Crewkerne, is an inland market town located approximately 16 miles to the northeast of Lyme. Bath is 48 miles north of Crewkerne. London is 115 miles east of Bath.

9 Austen probably borrowed the term "baronight" from Frances Burney's third novel *Camilla* (1796), where Camilla's lovable uncle Sir Hugh informs the foolish Mr. Dubster that Camilla is engaged to another. "'I know that,' replied Mr. Dubster, nodding sagaciously, 'the young gentleman having told me of the young baronight; but he said, it was all against her will, being only your over teasing, and the like.'" In *Persuasion,* the servant's reference to a "baronight" may be a malapropic combination of "baronet" and "knight" to indicate his indifference to the gradations of rank. Alternatively, as Juliet McMaster observes, "baronight" suggests that "being a baronet can be a somewhat benighted condition" (Burney, *Camilla,* ed. Edward A. Bloom and Lillian D. Bloom [Oxford: Oxford University Press, 1983], 597; McMaster, "Class," in *The Cambridge Companion to Jane Austen,* ed. Edward Copeland and Juliet McMaster [Cambridge: Cambridge University Press, 1997], 116).

10 Mr. Elliot's servant wears a coat that hangs down over the piece of cloth placed under the saddle to protect the horse's back (the "pannel"), and on which is displayed the Elliot family coat of arms.

11 Mr. Elliot is in mourning for his wife, so his servant is also dressed in black rather than in the distinctive colors of the family livery.

"Yes, Sir, a Mr. Elliot; a gentleman of large fortune,—came in last night from Sidmouth,[7]—dare say you heard the carriage, Sir, while you were at dinner; and going on now for Crewkherne,[8] in his way to Bath and London."

"Elliot!"—Many had looked on each other, and many had repeated the name, before all this had been got through, even by the smart rapidity of a waiter.

"Bless me!" cried Mary; "it must be our cousin;—it must be our Mr. Elliot, it must, indeed!—Charles, Anne, must not it? In mourning, you see, just as our Mr. Elliot must be. How very extraordinary! In the very same inn with us! Anne, must not it be our Mr. Elliot; my father's next heir? Pray Sir," (turning to the waiter), "did not you hear,—did not his servant say whether he belonged to the Kellynch family?"

"No, ma'am,—he did not mention no particular family; but he said his master was a very rich gentleman, and would be a baronight[9] some day."

"There! you see!" cried Mary, in an ecstacy, "Just as I said! Heir to Sir Walter Elliot!—I was sure that would come out, if it was so. Depend upon it, that is a circumstance which his servants take care to publish wherever he goes. But, Anne, only conceive how extraordinary! I wish I had looked at him more. I wish we had been aware in time, who it was, that he might have been introduced to us. What a pity that we should not have been introduced to each other!—Do you think he had the Elliot countenance? I hardly looked at him, I was looking at the horses; but I think he had something of the Elliot countenance. I wonder the arms did not strike me! Oh!—the greatcoat was hanging over the pannel, and hid the arms;[10] so it did, otherwise, I am sure, I should have observed them, and the livery too; if the servant had not been in mourning, one should have known him by the livery."[11]

"Putting all these very extraordinary circumstances together," said Captain Wentworth, "we must consider it to be the arrangement of Providence, that you should not be introduced to your cousin."

When she could command Mary's attention, Anne quietly tried to convince her that their father and Mr. Elliot had not, for many years, been on such terms as to make the power of attempting an introduction at all desirable.

At the same time, however, it was a secret gratification to herself to have seen her cousin, and to know that the future owner of Kellynch was undoubtedly a gentleman, and had an air of good sense. She would not, upon any account, mention her having met with him the second time; luckily Mary did not much attend to their having passed close by him in their early walk, but she would have felt quite ill-used by Anne's having actually run against him in the passage, and received his very polite excuses, while she had never been near him at all; no, that cousinly little interview must remain a perfect secret.

"Of course," said Mary, "you will mention our seeing Mr. Elliot, the next time you write to Bath. I think my father certainly ought to hear of it; do mention all about him."

Anne avoided a direct reply, but it was just the circumstance which she considered as not merely unnecessary to be communicated, but as what ought to be suppressed. The offence which had been given her father, many years back, she knew; Elizabeth's particular share in it she suspected; and that Mr. Elliot's idea always produced irritation in both, was beyond a doubt. Mary never wrote to Bath herself; all the toil of keeping up a slow and unsatisfactory correspondence with Elizabeth fell on Anne.

Breakfast had not been long over, when they were joined by Captain and Mrs. Harville, and Captain Benwick, with whom they had appointed to take their last walk about Lyme. They ought to be setting off for Uppercross by one, and in the meanwhile were to be all together, and out of doors as long as they could.

Anne found Captain Benwick getting near her, as soon as they were all fairly in the street. Their conversation, the preceding evening, did not disincline him to seek her again; and they walked together some time, talking as before of Mr. Scott and Lord Byron, and still as unable, as before, and as unable as any other two readers, to think exactly alike of the merits of either, till something occasioned

12 The "Cape" is the "Cape of Good Hope," which occupies the southern extremity of the African continent.

13 "Just made into the Grappler" means that Benwick has just been given command of the ship.

14 The "yard" or "yardarm" was a long spar that supported and spread the head of a square sail. To be "run up to the yard-arm" was to be hanged. "The victim stood on the cathead with a bag over his head. A rope was passed through a block at the fore yardarm, and the noose was put round the man's neck. A gang of sailors hauled smartly on the other end of the rope, pulling the man up to the yardarm, where he was allowed to hang for an hour." Death was often slow and painful (Lavery, 217).

15 Wentworth rushes off to help Benwick without waiting for permission from his naval superiors. In this sense Lady Russell's suspicions about his "headstrong" character seem well founded. Certainly on this and other occasions he acts in such a way as to jeopardize his own better interests. Yet at the same time, Anne is profoundly attracted to Wentworth because of his ardor and impetuosity, which inform his success as a naval officer, and which undoubtedly seem especially desirable to Anne when set against the formality and sterility of the world inhabited by her father and Elizabeth.

an almost general change amongst their party, and instead of Captain Benwick, she had Captain Harville by her side.

"Miss Elliot," said he, speaking rather low, "you have done a good deed in making that poor fellow talk so much. I wish he could have such company oftener. It is bad for him, I know, to be shut up as he is; but what can we do? we cannot part."

"No," said Anne, "that I can easily believe to be impossible; but in time, perhaps—we know what time does in every case of affliction, and you must remember, Captain Harville, that your friend may yet be called a young mourner—Only last summer, I understand."

"Ay, true enough," (with a deep sigh) "only June."

"And not known to him, perhaps, so soon."

"Not till the first week in August, when he came home from the Cape,[12]—just made into the Grappler.[13] I was at Plymouth, dreading to hear of him; he sent in letters, but the Grappler was under orders for Portsmouth. There the news must follow him, but who was to tell it? not I. I would as soon have been run up to the yard-arm.[14] Nobody could do it, but that good fellow, (pointing to Captain Wentworth.) The Laconia had come into Plymouth the week before; no danger of her being sent to sea again. He stood his chance for the rest—wrote up for leave of absence, but without waiting the return, travelled night and day till he got to Portsmouth,[15] rowed off to the Grappler that instant, and never left the poor fellow for a week; that's what he did, and nobody else could have saved poor James. You may think, Miss Elliot, whether he is dear to us!"

Anne did think on the question with perfect decision, and said as much in reply as her own feelings could accomplish, or as his seemed able to bear, for he was too much affected to renew the subject—and when he spoke again, it was of something totally different.

Mrs. Harville's giving it as her opinion that her husband would have quite walking enough by the time he reached home, determined the direction of all the party in what was to be their last walk; they would accompany them to their door, and then return and set off themselves. By all their calculations there was just time for this; but as they drew near the Cobb, there was such a general wish to walk along it once more, all were so inclined, and Louisa soon grew so determined, that the difference of a quarter of an hour, it was found, would be no difference at all, so with all the kind leave-taking, and all the kind interchange of invitations and promises which may be imagined, they parted from Captain and Mrs. Harville at their own door, and still accompanied by Captain Benwick, who seemed to cling to them to the last, proceeded to make the proper adieus to the Cobb.

Anne found Captain Benwick again drawing near her. Lord Byron's "dark blue seas"[16] could not fail of being brought forward by

16 Lord Byron uses the phrase "dark blue sea" twice in his overnight success, *Childe Harold's Pilgrimage* (1812), and two years later in *The Corsair* he begins,

> O'er the glad waters of the dark blue sea,
> Our thoughts as boundless, and our souls as free,
> Far as the breeze can bear, the billows foam,
> Survey our empire and behold our home!
>
> (Byron, *Poetical Works,* II, 35; II, 49;
> III, 150).

A. Wallis Mills, Illustrations for *Persuasion,* 1908. Captain Wentworth kneels with Louisa in his arms after her fall on the Cobb.

17 "Per force" is "by force of circumstances."

18 "Salts" here are "smelling salts," which were used to revive someone from unconsciousness.

19 Austen's description of Louisa's collapse, and of Anne's presence of mind in the moments that follow, seems to rely on at least two fictional precedents.

In Charlotte Smith's *Emmeline* (1788), the unexpected arrival of Captain William Godolphin causes his demented sister, Lady Adelina of Trelawney, to faint. Emmeline cries, "You have killed her, Sir!—She is certainly dead!" Godolphin exclaims "wildly" that he is afraid he has, and continues "after a moment's pause, during which Emmeline and the nurse were chafing the hands and temples of the dying patient—'perhaps she may recover. Send instantly for advice—run—fly—let me go myself for assistance.'

He would now have run out of the room; but Emmeline, whose admirable presence of mind this sudden scene of terror had not conquered, stopped him.

'Stay, Sir,' said she, 'I beseech you, stay. You know not wither to go. I will instantly send those who do.'"

Similarly, in Maria Edgeworth's *Belinda* (1801), Virginia falls "senseless upon the floor," and Mrs. Ormond exclaims, "She's dead!—she's dead! O, my sweet child! she's dead." Clarence announces, "her pulse is gone!"

"Lady Delacour looked at Virginia's pale lips, touched her cold hands, and with a look of horrour, cried out, 'Good Heavens! what have I done? What shall we do with her?'

'Give her air—give her air, air, air!' cried Belinda.

'You keep the air from her, Mrs. Ormond,' said Mrs. Delacour. 'Let us leave her to miss Portman; she has more presence of mind than any of us.'"

(Harris, 206, 245–246; Smith, *Works,* II, 237; Edgeworth, *Works,* II, 354–355).

Contemporary critics have commented at length on the import and effectiveness of the scene. "A common remark is that Louisa's fall is the most that Jane Austen could manage in direct drama," states Christopher Gillie, "but it illustrates a virtue of her realism and not a weakness in her imagination: in secure cir-

their present view, and she gladly gave him all her attention as long as attention was possible. It was soon drawn per force[17] another way.

There was too much wind to make the high part of the new Cobb pleasant for the ladies, and they agreed to get down the steps to the lower, and all were contented to pass quietly and carefully down the steep flight, excepting Louisa; she must be jumped down them by Captain Wentworth. In all their walks, he had had to jump her from the stiles; the sensation was delightful to her. The hardness of the pavement for her feet, made him less willing upon the present occasion; he did it, however; she was safely down, and instantly, to shew her enjoyment, ran up the steps to be jumped down again. He advised her against it, thought the jar too great; but no, he reasoned and talked in vain; she smiled and said, "I am determined I will:" he put out his hands; she was too precipitate by half a second, she fell on the pavement on the Lower Cobb, and was taken up lifeless!

There was no wound, no blood, no visible bruise; but her eyes were closed, she breathed not, her face was like death.—The horror of that moment to all who stood around!

Captain Wentworth, who had caught her up, knelt with her in his arms, looking on her with a face as pallid as her own, in an agony of silence. "She is dead! she is dead!" screamed Mary, catching hold of her husband, and contributing with his own horror to make him immoveable; and in another moment, Henrietta, sinking under the conviction, lost her senses too, and would have fallen on the steps, but for Captain Benwick and Anne, who caught and supported her between them.

"Is there no one to help me?" were the first words which burst from Captain Wentworth, in a tone of despair, and as if all his own strength were gone.

"Go to him, go to him," cried Anne, "for heaven's sake go to him. I can support her myself. Leave me, and go to him. Rub her hands, rub her temples; here are salts,[18]—take them, take them."

Captain Benwick obeyed, and Charles at the same moment, disengaging himself from his wife, they were both with him; and Louisa was raised up and supported more firmly between them, and every thing was done that Anne had prompted, but in vain; while Captain

Wentworth, staggering against the wall for his support, exclaimed in the bitterest agony,

"Oh God! her father and mother!"

"A surgeon!" said Anne.

He caught the word; it seemed to rouse him at once, and saying only "True, true, a surgeon this instant," was darting away, when Anne eagerly suggested,

"Captain Benwick, would not it be better for Captain Benwick? He knows where a surgeon is to be found."

Every one capable of thinking felt the advantage of the idea, and in a moment (it was all done in rapid moments) Captain Benwick had resigned the poor corpse-like figure entirely to the brother's care, and was off for the town with the utmost rapidity.

As to the wretched party left behind, it could scarcely be said which of the three, who were completely rational, was suffering most, Captain Wentworth, Anne, or Charles, who, really a very affectionate brother, hung over Louisa with sobs of grief, and could only turn his eyes from one sister, to see the other in a state as insensible, or to witness the hysterical agitations of his wife, calling on him for help which he could not give.

Anne, attending with all the strength and zeal, and thought, which instinct supplied, to Henrietta, still tried, at intervals, to suggest comfort to the others, tried to quiet Mary, to animate Charles, to assuage the feelings of Captain Wentworth. Both seemed to look to her for directions.

"Anne, Anne," cried Charles, "what is to be done next? What, in heaven's name, is to be done next?"

Captain Wentworth's eyes were also turned towards her.

"Had not she better be carried to the inn? Yes, I am sure, carry her gently to the inn."

"Yes, yes, to the inn," repeated Captain Wentworth, comparatively collected, and eager to be doing something. "I will carry her myself. Musgrove, take care of the others."[19]

By this time the report of the accident had spread among the workmen and boatmen about the Cobb, and many were collected near them, to be useful if wanted, at any rate, to enjoy the sight of a

cumstances of life it is precisely such an episode—a flighty young girl taking a foolish risk—that does bring tragedy. Structurally, the significance of the incident is twofold. In the first place, the risk that Louisa takes of jumping into Wentworth's arms before he is ready for her is symbolic of the risk that Anne did not take when she refused Wentworth's first offer. . . . Secondly, she is able to show the real strength of her character for the first time; it is she who keeps her head and sees what needs to be done, while the two other women respectively faint and scream hysterically, and the men are shocked into immobility" (Gillie, *Austen* [London: Longman, 1985], 158).

John Wiltshire examines Louisa's mishap at length and reads the scene from a number of different angles: "Of course, Louisa's spiritedness and Wentworth's hesitation both contribute to the accident: but that does not exhaust its significance in the novel. It is the most crucial of the many fortuitous circumstances which make up the narrative and . . . a graphic reminder that human-beings are bodies as well as minds." What is more, "there is another account of the fall's meaning that ought to be taken notice of. Perhaps it is best considered as an instance of the psychopathology of everyday life. . . . Louisa's escapade can readily be seen as a partly unconscious aspect of her courtship of Wentworth since it invites him to confirm the self-image he has helped to create, and because she is inspirited by his presence (as by the weather, the occasion, and her own bodily vitality): and his failure to reciprocate can be read erotically too. He is not feeling and responding as she is feeling: their missing each other's hands at 'the fatal moment' is a sign that he cannot 'attach himself' to her which he already unconsciously knows" (Wiltshire, 187–188).

20 As is so often the case in *Persuasion,* two groups of people have starkly differing responses to the same circumstance. After Louisa's fall, Austen brings the detached party of friends back into contact with the world around them on the Cobb, and then contrasts the intensity of their concerns with the levity of those who look on. Mary Poovey analyzes the accident scene from a political vantage point: "What is remarkable about this passage is not its proof that Austen was aware of the lower classes but the fact that it contains—at least momentarily—the workmen's point of view ('nay, two dead young ladies')." These men are "subtle reminders of the limitations" of the influence of the gentry. Mary Lascelles, however, regards the scene as essentially comedic: "the catastrophe which the spectators think they are witnessing is an illusion. Louisa is not dead—nor even injured. True, she has fallen on her head; but it had never been a very good one, and the blow seems to have cleared it" (Poovey, *The Proper Lady and the Woman Writer* [Chicago: University of Chicago Press, 1984], 234–235; Lascelles, *Jane Austen and Her Art* [Oxford: Clarendon Press, 1939], 78).

21 The "best-looking" person in this context is the "most reliable looking" person.

22 Doctors often recommended wine as a cordial. But there were stronger and more elaborate anodynes as well. "Take a thick glass or stone bottle, and put in it two quarts of the best brandy; adding the following seeds, first grossly pounded in a mortar:—Two drachms of angelica seeds, one ounce of coriander seeds, and a large pinch each of fennel seeds and aniseeds. Then squeeze in the juice of two fresh lemons, putting in also their yellow rinds; add a pound of loaf sugar; and shaking well the bottle from time to time, let the whole infuse five days. After this, to render the liquor clearer, pass it through a cotton bag, or filtering paper, and bottle it up carefully and closely corked. A small cordial glass at a time, more or less frequently, according to the circumstances, is an excellent remedy for all complaints in the stomach, indigestion, sickness, colic, obstructions, stitches of the side, spasms in the breast, diseases of the kidnies, stranguary, gravel, oppression

dead young lady, nay, two dead young ladies, for it proved twice as fine as the first report.[20] To some of the best-looking[21] of these good people Henrietta was consigned, for, though partially revived, she was quite helpless; and in this manner, Anne walking by her side, and Charles attending to his wife, they set forward, treading back with feelings unutterable, the ground which so lately, so very lately, and so light of heart, they had passed along.

They were not off the Cobb, before the Harvilles met them. Captain Benwick had been seen flying by their house, with a countenance which shewed something to be wrong; and they had set off immediately, informed and directed, as they passed, towards the spot. Shocked as Captain Harville was, he brought senses and nerves that could be instantly useful; and a look between him and his wife decided what was to be done. She must be taken to their house—all must go to their house—and wait the surgeon's arrival there. They would not listen to scruples: he was obeyed; they were all beneath his roof; and while Louisa, under Mrs. Harville's direction, was conveyed up stairs, and given possession of her own bed, assistance, cordials,[22] restoratives were supplied by her husband to all who needed them.

Louisa had once opened her eyes, but soon closed them again, without apparent consciousness. This had been a proof of life, however, of service to her sister; and Henrietta, though perfectly incapable of being in the same room with Louisa, was kept, by the agitation of hope and fear, from a return of her own insensibility. Mary, too, was growing calmer.

The surgeon[23] was with them almost before it had seemed possible. They were sick with horror while he examined; but he was not hopeless. The head had received a severe contusion, but he had seen greater injuries recovered from: he was by no means hopeless; he spoke cheerfully.

That he did not regard it as a desperate case—that he did not say a few hours must end it—was at first felt, beyond the hope of most; and the ecstasy of such a reprieve, the rejoicing, deep and silent, after a few fervent ejaculations of gratitude to Heaven had been offered, may be conceived.

The tone, the look, with which "Thank God!" was uttered by Captain Wentworth, Anne was sure could never be forgotten by her; nor the sight of him afterwards, as he sat near a table, leaning over it with folded arms, and face concealed, as if overpowered by the various feelings of his soul, and trying by prayer and reflection to calm them.[24]

Louisa's limbs had escaped. There was no injury but to the head.

It now became necessary for the party to consider what was best to be done, as to their general situation. They were now able to speak to each other, and consult. That Louisa must remain where she was, however distressing to her friends to be involving the Harvilles in such trouble, did not admit a doubt. Her removal was impossible. The Harvilles silenced all scruples; and, as much as they could, all gratitude. They had looked forward and arranged every thing, before the others began to reflect. Captain Benwick must give up his room to them, and get a bed elsewhere—and the whole was settled. They were only concerned that the house could accommodate no more; and yet perhaps by "putting the children away in the maids' room, or swinging a cot somewhere," they could hardly bear to think of not finding room for two or three besides, supposing they might wish to stay; though, with regard to any attendance on Miss Musgrove, there need not be the least uneasiness in leaving her to Mrs. Harville's care entirely. Mrs. Harville was a very experienced nurse; and her nursery-maid, who had lived with her long and gone about with her every where, was just such another. Between those two, she could want no possible attendance by day or night. And all this was said with a truth and sincerity of feeling irresistible.

Charles, Henrietta, and Captain Wentworth were the three in consultation, and for a little while it was only an interchange of perplexity and terror. "Uppercross,—the necessity of some one's going to Uppercross,—the news to be conveyed—how it could be broken to Mr. and Mrs. Musgrove—the lateness of the morning,—an hour already gone since they ought to have been off,—the impossibility of being in tolerable time." At first, they were capable of nothing more to the purpose than such exclamations; but, after a while, Captain Wentworth, exerting himself, said,

of the spleen, loathing, vertigo, rheumatism, shortness of breath, &c." (Anonymous, *The Female Instructor; or, Young Woman's Companion* [Liverpool: Nuttall, Fisher, and Dixon, 1815], 412).

23 In Austen's day, a "surgeon" was "one who practises the art of healing by manual operation; a practitioner who treats wounds, fractures, deformities, or disorders by surgical means" *(OED)*.

24 Stuart Tave underscores the significance of Wentworth's moments of "prayer and reflection." Louisa's accident is Wentworth's fault because "he has encouraged her to think that being resolute, having her own way, is a virtue. The effect of the incident upon the clear and decided Captain is to take all his strength from him and when there is assurance that her injuries are not fatal he sits over a table 'as if overpowered by the various feelings of his soul.' That overpowering is important because it is necessary for him to experience the variousness of feelings, to lose his clarity, to be plunged into confusion, before he can learn. . . . For Captain Wentworth the overpowering is the beginning of knowledge" (Tave, 277).

25 Wentworth speaks politely of "Mrs. Charles Mus-grove," and he ought to speak with the same formality of "Miss Anne Elliot." But he does not. Under duress, and with a dawning sense of her worth and his own foolishness, he calls her "Anne," a burst of emotion that reveals—despite all his attempts to convince him-self otherwise—that he still feels a close connection with her. Compare *Sense and Sensibility,* when Elinor overhears Willoughby addressing "Marianne" and con-cludes that "in the whole of the sentence, in his man-ner of pronouncing it, and in his addressing her sister by her christian name alone, she instantly saw an inti-macy so decided, a meaning so direct, as marked a per-fect agreement between them" (I, 12).

Francis Austen, by an unknown artist. Austen's fifth brother, he was educated at the Royal Navy Academy in Portsmouth and rose to the rank of admiral of the Fleet. As captain of the *Canopus,* he dined with Lord Nelson on the afternoon before the Battle of Trafalgar.

"We must be decided, and without the loss of another minute. Ev-ery minute is valuable. Some must resolve on being off for Upper-cross instantly. Musgrove, either you or I must go."

Charles agreed; but declared his resolution of not going away. He would be as little incumbrance as possible to Captain and Mrs. Har-ville; but as to leaving his sister in such a state, he neither ought, nor would. So far it was decided; and Henrietta at first declared the same. She, however, was soon persuaded to think differently. The useful-ness of her staying!—She, who had not been able to remain in Loui-sa's room, or to look at her, without sufferings which made her worse than helpless! She was forced to acknowledge that she could do no good; yet was still unwilling to be away, till touched by the thought of her father and mother, she gave it up; she consented, she was anxious to be at home.

The plan had reached this point, when Anne, coming quietly down from Louisa's room, could not but hear what followed, for the par-lour door was open.

"Then it is settled, Musgrove," cried Captain Wentworth, "that you stay, and that I take care of your sister home. But as to the rest;—as to the others;—If one stays to assist Mrs. Harville, I think it need be only one.—Mrs. Charles Musgrove will, of course, wish to get back to her children; but, if Anne will stay, no one so proper, so ca-pable as Anne!"

She paused a moment to recover from the emotion of hearing her-self so spoken of.[25] The other two warmly agreed to what he said, and she then appeared.

"You will stay, I am sure; you will stay and nurse her;" cried he, turning to her and speaking with a glow, and yet a gentleness, which seemed almost restoring the past.—She coloured deeply; and he recollected himself, and moved away.—She expressed herself most willing, ready, happy to remain. "It was what she had been think-ing of, and wishing to be allowed to do.—A bed on the floor in Loui-sa's room would be sufficient for her, if Mrs. Harville would but think so."

One thing more, and all seemed arranged. Though it was rather desirable that Mr. and Mrs. Musgrove should be previously alarmed by some share of delay; yet the time required by the Uppercross horses to take them back, would be a dreadful extension of suspense; and Captain Wentworth proposed, and Charles Musgrove agreed, that it would be much better for him to take a chaise from the inn,[26] and leave Mr. Musgrove's carriage and horses to be sent home the next morning early, when there would be the farther advantage of sending an account of Louisa's night.

Captain Wentworth now hurried off to get every thing ready on his part, and to be soon followed by the two ladies. When the plan was made known to Mary, however, there was an end of all peace in it. She was so wretched, and so vehement, complained so much of injustice in being expected to go away, instead of Anne;—Anne, who was nothing to Louisa, while she was her sister, and had the best right to stay in Henrietta's stead! Why was not she to be as useful as Anne? And to go home without Charles, too—without her husband! No, it was too unkind! And, in short, she said more than her husband could long withstand; and as none of the others could oppose when he gave way, there was no help for it: the change of Mary for Anne was inevitable.

Anne had never submitted more reluctantly to the jealous and ill-judging claims of Mary; but so it must be, and they set off for the town, Charles taking care of his sister, and Captain Benwick attending to her. She gave a moment's recollection, as they hurried along, to the little circumstances which the same spots had witnessed earlier in the morning. There she had listened to Henrietta's schemes for Dr. Shirley's leaving Uppercross; farther on, she had first seen Mr. Elliot; a moment seemed all that could now be given to any one but Louisa, or those who were wrapt up in her welfare.

Captain Benwick was most considerately attentive to her; and, united as they all seemed by the distress of the day, she felt an increasing degree of good-will towards him, and a pleasure even in thinking that it might, perhaps, be the occasion of continuing their acquaintance.

Captain Wentworth was on the watch for them, and a chaise and four in waiting, stationed for their convenience in the lowest part of the street; but his evident surprise and vexation, at the substitution

26 A four-wheeled "chaise" or "post-chaise" carried three people and could be hired from an inn. It was "intended . . . for expeditious travelling," as "lightness and simplicity are the principles on which this carriage ought to be built" (Felton, II, 66).

27 Austen's reference is to "Henry and Emma" (1709), by Matthew Prior (1664–1721). The poem recounts how Henry tests Emma's love for him by announcing that he has fallen in love with a younger and prettier woman. Emma's response is to beg to be allowed to serve her rival in order to remain near Henry. "This potent Beauty, this Triumphant Fair," cries Emma,

> This happy Object of our diff'rent Care,
> Her let me follow; Her let me attend,
> A Servant: (She may scorn the Name of Friend.)
> What She demands, incessant I'll prepare:
> I'll weave Her Garlands; and I'll pleat Her Hair:
> My busie Diligence shall deck Her Board;
> (For there, at least, I may approach my Lord).

Convinced now of Emma's love, Henry announces that no such rival exists, and then swears eternal devotion to Emma. Emily Auerbach suspects that "Emma's doormat approach . . . offended Austen's sensibility. Austen makes sure to tell us that the loyal, loving Anne Elliot could tend to Louisa's injuries faithfully but '*without* emulating the feelings of an Emma towards her Henry'" (*The Literary Works of Matthew Prior,* ed. H. Bunker Wright and Monroe K. Spears, 2 vols. [Oxford: Clarendon Press, 1959], I, 295; Auerbach, 255).

28 Anne's visit to Lyme has been brief but highly eventful, for it has afforded her the freedom to converse and to act in ways that are thwarted by the routines of Kellynch and Uppercross. "It is a setting suited to the unpretentious amiability of Wentworth's fellow officers, a place where Anne can escape from the hierarchies that constrain her inland, whether she's at home or away," Peter W. Graham notes. ". . . . If Anne can see Wentworth at his best among his peers, the friends who would have been hers had she married him, he can see her at her best in the emergency that calls forth her nerve, zeal, and thought—qualities damped down or repressed in her daily round of country life as visiting spinster sister or trapped-at-home younger daughter" (Graham, "Why Lyme Regis?" in *Persuasion,* 26 [2004], 39).

29 A "stage" was "the distance traveled between two places of rest on a road" (*OED*). The seventeen miles

of one sister for the other—the change of his countenance—the astonishment—the expressions begun and suppressed, with which Charles was listened to, made but a mortifying reception of Anne; or must at least convince her that she was valued only as she could be useful to Louisa.

She endeavoured to be composed, and to be just. Without emulating the feelings of an Emma towards her Henry,[27] she would have attended on Louisa with a zeal above the common claims of regard, for his sake; and she hoped he would not long be so unjust as to suppose she would shrink unnecessarily from the office of a friend.

In the meanwhile she was in the carriage. He had handed them both in, and placed himself between them; and in this manner, under these circumstances full of astonishment and emotion to Anne, she quitted Lyme.[28] How the long stage[29] would pass; how it was to affect their manners; what was to be their sort of intercourse, she could not foresee. It was all quite natural, however. He was devoted to Henrietta; always turning towards her; and when he spoke at all, always with the view of supporting her hopes and raising her spirits. In general, his voice and manner were studiously calm. To spare Henrietta from agitation seemed the governing principle. Once only, when she had been grieving over the last ill-judged, ill-fated walk to the Cobb, bitterly lamenting that it ever had been thought of, he burst forth, as if wholly overcome—

"Don't talk of it, don't talk of it," he cried. "Oh God! that I had not given way to her at the fatal moment! Had I done as I ought! But so eager and so resolute! Dear, sweet Louisa!"

Anne wondered whether it ever occurred to him now, to question the justness of his own previous opinion as to the universal felicity and advantage of firmness of character; and whether it might not strike him, that, like all other qualities of the mind, it should have its proportions and limits. She thought it could scarcely escape him to feel, that a persuadable temper might sometimes be as much in favour of happiness, as a very resolute character.

They got on fast. Anne was astonished to recognise the same hills and the same objects so soon. Their actual speed, heightened by some dread of the conclusion, made the road appear but half as long as on the day before. It was growing quite dusk, however, before they were in the neighbourhood of Uppercross, and there had been total silence among them for some time, Henrietta leaning back in the corner, with a shawl over her face, giving the hope of her having cried herself to sleep; when, as they were going up their last hill, Anne found herself all at once addressed by Captain Wentworth. In a low, cautious voice, he said,

"I have been considering what we had best do. She must not appear at first. She could not stand it. I have been thinking whether you had not better remain in the carriage with her, while I go in and break it to Mr. and Mrs. Musgrove. Do you think this a good plan?"

She did: he was satisfied, and said no more. But the remembrance of the appeal remained a pleasure to her—as a proof of friendship, and of deference for her judgment, a great pleasure; and when it became a sort of parting proof, its value did not lessen.

When the distressing communication at Uppercross was over, and he had seen the father and mother quite as composed as could be hoped, and the daughter all the better for being with them, he announced his intention of returning in the same carriage to Lyme; and when the horses were baited,[30] he was off.

back to Uppercross is one "long stage," so Anne, Henrietta, and Wentworth will travel without stopping.

30 "Baited" is "refreshed" and "fed."

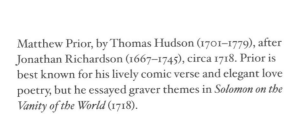

Matthew Prior, by Thomas Hudson (1701–1779), after Jonathan Richardson (1667–1745), circa 1718. Prior is best known for his lively comic verse and elegant love poetry, but he essayed graver themes in *Solomon on the Vanity of the World* (1718).

Volume II

I

THE REMAINDER OF ANNE'S TIME at Uppercross, comprehending only two days, was spent entirely at the mansion-house, and she had the satisfaction of knowing herself extremely useful there, both as an immediate companion, and as assisting in all those arrangements for the future, which, in Mr. and Mrs. Musgrove's distressed state of spirits, would have been difficulties.

They had an early account from Lyme the next morning. Louisa was much the same. No symptoms worse than before had appeared. Charles came a few hours afterwards, to bring a later and more particular account. He was tolerably cheerful. A speedy cure must not be hoped, but every thing was going on as well as the nature of the case admitted. In speaking of the Harvilles, he seemed unable to satisfy his own sense of their kindness, especially of Mrs. Harville's exertions as a nurse. "She really left nothing for Mary to do. He and Mary had been persuaded to go early to their inn last night. Mary had been hysterical again this morning. When he came away, she was going to walk out with Captain Benwick, which, he hoped, would do her good. He almost wished she had been prevailed on to come home the day before; but the truth was, that Mrs. Harville left nothing for any body to do."

Charles was to return to Lyme the same afternoon, and his father had at first half a mind to go with him, but the ladies could not consent. It would be going only to multiply trouble to the others, and increase his own distress; and a much better scheme followed and was acted upon. A chaise was sent for from Crewkherne, and Charles

1 Gentry families usually sent their sons away to school at the age of six or seven.

2 A "blain," or more commonly a "chilblain," was "an inflammatory swelling produced by exposure to cold, affecting the hands and feet, accompanied with heat and itching, and in severe cases leading to ulceration" *(OED)*. Compare Austen's immediate contemporary Percy Bysshe Shelley, whose *Revolt of Islam* appeared in the same year as *Persuasion,* and who in the poem refers to "nameless scars and lurid blains" (X, 21).

conveyed back a far more useful person in the old nursery-maid of the family, one who having brought up all the children, and seen the very last, the lingering and long-petted master Harry, sent to school after his brothers,[1] was now living in her deserted nursery to mend stockings, and dress all the blains[2] and bruises she could get near her, and who, consequently, was only too happy in being allowed to go and help nurse dear Miss Louisa. Vague wishes of getting Sarah thither, had occurred before to Mrs. Musgrove and Henrietta; but without Anne, it would hardly have been resolved on, and found practicable so soon.

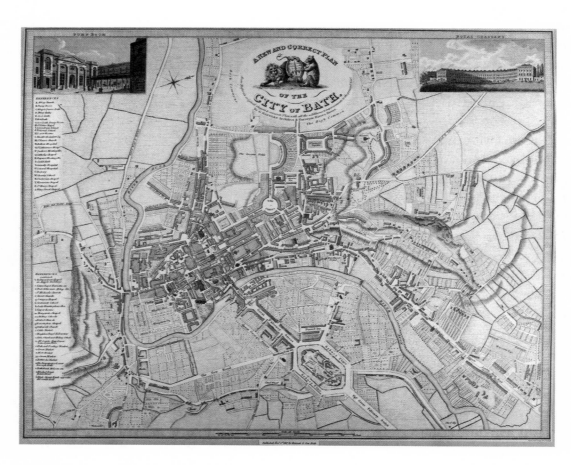

A New and Correct Plan of the City of Bath, by G. Manners. The map is from 1817, the same year that *Persuasion* was published.

They were indebted, the next day, to Charles Hayter for all the minute knowledge of Louisa, which it was so essential to obtain every twenty-four hours. He made it his business to go to Lyme, and his account was still encouraging. The intervals of sense and consciousness were believed to be stronger. Every report agreed in Captain Wentworth's appearing fixed in Lyme.

Anne was to leave them on the morrow, an event which they all dreaded. "What should they do without her? They were wretched comforters for one another!" And so much was said in this way, that Anne thought she could not do better than impart among them the general inclination to which she was privy, and persuade them all to go to Lyme at once. She had little difficulty; it was soon determined that they would go, go to-morrow, fix themselves at the inn, or get into lodgings, as it suited, and there remain till dear Louisa could be moved. They must be taking off some trouble from the good people she was with; they might at least relieve Mrs. Harville from the care of her own children; and in short they were so happy in the decision, that Anne was delighted with what she had done, and felt that she could not spend her last morning at Uppercross better than in assisting their preparations, and sending them off at an early hour, though her being left to the solitary range of the house was the consequence.

She was the last, excepting the little boys at the cottage, she was the very last, the only remaining one of all that had filled and animated both houses, of all that had given Uppercross its cheerful character. A few days had made a change indeed!

If Louisa recovered, it would all be well again. More than former happiness would be restored. There could not be a doubt, to her mind there was none, of what would follow her recovery. A few months hence, and the room now[3] so deserted, occupied but by her silent, pensive self, might be filled again with all that was happy and gay, all that was glowing and bright in prosperous love, all that was most unlike Anne Elliot!

An hour's complete leisure for such reflections as these, on a dark November day, a small[4] thick rain almost blotting out the very few objects ever to be discerned from the windows, was enough to make

3 The text has been amended here from "now room" to "room now."

4 A "small" rain is a "gentle" rain. In the opening chapter of *Quentin Durward* (1823), Walter Scott observes that "Heaven . . . works by the tempest as well as by the soft small rain" (Scott, *Quentin Durward,* ed. J. H. Alexander and G. A. M. Wood [Edinburgh: Edinburgh University Press, 2001], 26).

Camden Place, as engraved by Henry Adlard (active 1824–1869), after William Henry Bartlett (1809–1854). Given Sir Walter's obsession with appearances, it seems very likely that his home is the one below the central pediment.

5 Compare Anne's hope of being "blessed with a second spring of youth and beauty" to the fate of Maria in the closing chapter of *Mansfield Park:* "*She* must withdraw with infinitely stronger feelings to a retirement and reproach, which could allow no second spring of hope or character" (III, 17). See, too, Charlotte Smith in her *Elegiac Sonnets:* "Another May new buds and flowers shall bring;/Ah! why has happiness—no second Spring?" (Smith, *Works,* XIV, 18).

6 Camden-place, now Camden Crescent, is on the southeastern slope of Beacon Hill in the northern part of Bath. Austen does not reveal Sir Walter's precise address, but it is almost certainly number 16, which is directly under the central pediment bearing Lord Camden's coat-of-arms. Pierce Egan (1772–1849), author and sporting writer, was an enthusiastic admirer of the location: "Upper Camden-Place commands for miles a most interesting, extensive, and picturesque prospect. This fine high terrace, which is a delightful place of residence, possesses a broad pavement, a carriage-road in front of it, and [is] enclosed with iron-rails to render it perfectly safe" (Egan, 159).

the sound of Lady Russell's carriage exceedingly welcome; and yet, though desirous to be gone, she could not quit the mansion-house, or look an adieu to the cottage, with its black, dripping, and comfortless veranda, or even notice through the misty glasses the last humble tenements of the village, without a saddened heart.—Scenes had passed in Uppercross, which made it precious. It stood the record of many sensations of pain, once severe, but now softened; and of some instances of relenting feeling, some breathings of friendship and reconciliation, which could never be looked for again, and which could never cease to be dear. She left it all behind her; all but the recollection that such things had been.

Anne had never entered Kellynch since her quitting Lady Russell's house, in September. It had not been necessary, and the few occasions of its being possible for her to go to the hall she had contrived to evade and escape from. Her first return, was to resume her place in the modern and elegant apartments of the lodge, and to gladden the eyes of its mistress.

There was some anxiety mixed with Lady Russell's joy in meeting her. She knew who had been frequenting Uppercross. But happily, either Anne was improved in plumpness and looks, or Lady Russell fancied her so; and Anne, in receiving her compliments on the occasion, had the amusement of connecting them with the silent admiration of her cousin, and of hoping that she was to be blessed with a second spring of youth and beauty.[5]

When they came to converse, she was soon sensible of some mental change. The subjects of which her heart had been full on leaving Kellynch, and which she had felt slighted, and been compelled to smother among the Musgroves, were now become but of secondary interest. She had lately lost sight even of her father and sister and Bath. Their concerns had been sunk under those of Uppercross, and when Lady Russell reverted to their former hopes and fears, and spoke her satisfaction in the house in Camden-place,[6] which had been taken, and her regret that Mrs. Clay should still be with them, Anne would have been ashamed to have it known, how much more she was thinking of Lyme, and Louisa Musgrove, and all her acquaintance there; how much more interesting to her was the home and the friendship of the Harvilles and Captain Benwick, than her own father's house in Camden-place, or her own sister's intimacy with Mrs. Clay. She was actually forced to exert herself, to meet Lady Russell with any thing like the appearance of equal solicitude, on topics which had by nature the first claim on her.

There was a little awkwardness at first in their discourse on another subject. They must speak of the accident at Lyme. Lady Russell had not been arrived five minutes the day before, when a full account of the whole had burst on her; but still it must be talked of, she must make enquiries, she must regret the imprudence, lament the result, and Captain Wentworth's name must be mentioned by both. Anne was conscious of not doing it so well as Lady Russell. She could not speak the name, and look straight forward to Lady Russell's eye, till she had adopted the expedient of telling her briefly what she thought of the attachment between him and Louisa. When this was told, his name distressed her no longer.

Lady Russell had only to listen composedly, and wish them happy; but internally her heart revelled in angry pleasure, in pleased contempt, that the man who at twenty-three had seemed to understand

Looks, however, can be deceiving. Camden Place was badly planned and never finished. The promoters, explains Walter Ison, "intended to build a great crescent with wings, forming Upper Camden Place, having before it a large garden sloping towards a terrace of houses, and Lower Camden Place, forming a tangent to the crescent." The grounds were cleared in 1787, and "rapid progress" was made on the upper crescent, "when a series of alarming landslips brought the work to a standstill. That part of the building which was sited on solid rock was completed, but no further progress was made with the remaining houses." Harris concludes that "the 'lofty, dignified situation' of Camden Place does not, as Sir Walter believes, reflect his superiority. Instead, the instability of the site, the pretentiousness of the buildings, and their flawed, incomplete architecture locate him as an isolated and crumbling relic of the aristocracy. His house built upon sand confirms his folly as well as his decline as a feudal patriarch, for he exemplifies . . . a major demographic crisis of the eighteenth century, when many estates of landed families without sons were passed to more distant relatives or to new landowners. The baronetcy bought by Sir Walter's ancestors is heading for extinction, not just from the lack of a direct heir, but also because of his failure to respond to economic, agricultural, and social change. Although Austen is rarely considered to be symbolic, Sir Walter's Bath home looks startlingly emblematic" (Patricia Brückmann, "Sir Walter Elliot's Bath Address," in *Modern Philology,* 80 [1982], 58, 60; Walter Ison, *The Georgian Buildings of Bath* [London: Faber, 1948], 162–163; Harris, 164–165).

7 Anne's observation that "Kellynch-hall had passed into better hands than its owners" is perhaps the most radical statement in all of Austen, and gives the lie to the notion—famously proclaimed by Austen herself—that in her novels she worked on a "little bit (two Inches wide) of Ivory . . . with so fine a Brush, as produces little effect after much labour." On the contrary, argues Julia Prewitt Brown, "*Persuasion* registers a fundamental . . . crisis of belief in the legitimacy of social structures. . . . Established power is sustained only through a subjective belief in its legitimacy, through people believing it is legitimate and allowing themselves to be so dominated. Revolutions begin with a crisis of legitimacy. In *Persuasion* we see the beginning of a failure to support traditions, a failure that led to nineteenth-century reforms" (Austen, *Letters*, 323; Brown, 145).

somewhat of the value of an Anne Elliot, should, eight years afterwards, be charmed by a Louisa Musgrove.

The first three or four days passed most quietly, with no circumstance to mark them excepting the receipt of a note or two from Lyme, which found their way to Anne, she could not tell how, and brought a rather improving account of Louisa. At the end of that period, Lady Russell's politeness could repose no longer, and the fainter self-threatenings of the past, became in a decided tone, "I must call on Mrs. Croft; I really must call upon her soon. Anne, have you courage to go with me, and pay a visit in that house? It will be some trial to us both."

Anne did not shrink from it; on the contrary, she truly felt as she said, in observing,

"I think you are very likely to suffer the most of the two; your feelings are less reconciled to the change than mine. By remaining in the neighbourhood, I am become inured to it."

She could have said more on the subject; for she had in fact so high an opinion of the Crofts, and considered her father so very fortunate in his tenants, felt the parish to be so sure of a good example, and the poor of the best attention and relief, that however sorry and ashamed for the necessity of the removal, she could not but in conscience feel that they were gone who deserved not to stay, and that Kellynch-hall had passed into better hands than its owners.[7] These convictions must unquestionably have their own pain, and severe was its kind; but they precluded that pain which Lady Russell would suffer in entering the house again, and returning through the well-known apartments.

In such moments Anne had no power of saying to herself, "These rooms ought to belong only to us. Oh, how fallen in their destination! How unworthily occupied! An ancient family to be so driven away! Strangers filling their place!" No, except when she thought of her mother, and remembered where she had been used to sit and preside, she had no sigh of that description to heave.

Mrs. Croft always met her with a kindness which gave her the pleasure of fancying herself a favourite; and on the present occasion, receiving her in that house, there was particular attention.

The sad accident at Lyme was soon the prevailing topic; and on comparing their latest accounts of the invalid, it appeared that each lady dated her intelligence from the same hour of yester morn,[8] that Captain Wentworth had been in Kellynch yesterday—(the first time since the accident) had brought Anne the last note, which she had not been able to trace the exact steps of, had staid a few hours and then returned again to Lyme—and without any present intention of quitting it any more.—He had enquired after her, she found, particularly;—had expressed his hope of Miss Elliot's not being the worse for her exertions, and had spoken of those exertions as great.—This was handsome,—and gave her more pleasure than almost any thing else could have done.

As to the sad catastrophe[9] itself, it could be canvassed[10] only in one style by a couple of steady, sensible women, whose judgments had to work on ascertained events; and it was perfectly decided that it had been the consequence of much thoughtlessness and much imprudence; that its effects were most alarming, and that it was frightful to think, how long Miss Musgrove's recovery might yet be doubtful, and how liable she would still remain to suffer from the concussion hereafter!—The Admiral wound it all up summarily by exclaiming,

"Ay, a very bad business indeed.—A new sort of way this, for a young fellow to be making love,[11] by breaking his mistress's head!—is not it, Miss Elliot?—This is breaking a head and giving a plaister[12] truly!"

Admiral Croft's manners were not quite of the tone to suit Lady Russell, but they delighted Anne. His goodness of heart and simplicity of character were irresistible.

"Now, this must be very bad for you," said he, suddenly rousing from a little reverie, "to be coming and finding us here.—I had not recollected it before, I declare,—but it must be very bad.—But now, do not stand upon ceremony.—Get up and go over all the rooms in the house if you like it."

"Another time, Sir, I thank you, not now."

"Well, whenever it suits you.—You can slip in from the shrubbery at any time. And there you will find we keep our umbrellas, hanging

8 Writing from Lyme to Cassandra on September 14, 1804, Austen explains that she called on an acquaintance "yesterday morning," and then wonders, "ought it not in strict propriety be termed Yester-Morning?" (Austen, *Letters,* 94).

9 Austen's reference to a "sad catastrophe" echoes Charlotte Smith's use of the same phrase in *The Old Manor House,* where the looks of a distraught Orlando seem "to speak only of some sad catastrophe" (Smith, *Works,* VI, 187).

10 To "canvass" is "to discuss, criticize, scrutinize fully" *(OED)*.

11 In Austen's age, "making love" did not imply sexual intercourse.

12 "Breaking a head and giving a plaister" is a proverbial expression of fifteenth-century origin which means that the same person is both the cause and the cure of an ailment. "Plaister" is an obsolete spelling of "plaster." In Walter Scott's *Rob Roy* (1818), Baillie Jarvie burns a hole in the plaid of the Gallant Galbraith during a fight, and then promises him, "Gin I hae broken the head . . . I'se find the plaister: a new plaid sall ye hae" (Scott, *Rob Roy,* ed. David Hewitt [Edinburgh: Edinburgh University Press, 2008], 234).

13 The different locations of the umbrellas clearly indicate the different temperaments of Admiral Croft and Sir Walter. The former is practical: the umbrellas are hanging up by the door. The latter likes to be waited upon: a servant must go to the butler's room and fetch them.

14 Douglas Bush remarks that Admiral Croft's "main function in the novel is his exposure, both unconscious and conscious, of such a simulacrum of a man as Sir Walter Elliot—whose many mirrors in Kellynch Hall he puts out of sight." Compare Samuel Richardson (1689–1761) in *Sir Charles Grandison* (1753–1754), where the vain Sir Hargrave Pollexfen "forgets not to pay his respects to himself at every glass" (Bush, 184; Richardson, *Grandison,* I, 45).

up by that door. A good place, is not it? But" (checking himself) "you will not think it a good place, for yours were always kept in the butler's room.[13] Ay, so it always is, I believe. One man's ways may be as good as another's, but we all like our own best. And so you must judge for yourself, whether it would be better for you to go about the house or not."

Anne, finding she might decline it, did so, very gratefully.

"We have made very few changes either!" continued the Admiral, after thinking a moment. "Very few.—We told you about the laundry-door, at Uppercross. That has been a very great improvement. The wonder was, how any family upon earth could bear with the inconvenience of its opening as it did, so long!—You will tell Sir Walter what we have done, and that Mr. Shepherd thinks it the greatest improvement the house ever had. Indeed, I must do ourselves the justice to say, that the few alterations we have made have been all very much for the better. My wife should have the credit of them, however. I have done very little besides sending away some of the large looking-glasses from my dressing-room, which was your father's. A very good man, and very much the gentleman I am sure—but I should think, Miss Elliot" (looking with serious reflection) "I should think he must be rather a dressy man for his time of life.—Such a number of looking-glasses! oh Lord! there was no getting away from oneself. So I got Sophy to lend me a hand, and we soon shifted their quarters; and now I am quite snug, with my little shaving glass in one corner, and another great thing that I never go near."[14]

Anne, amused in spite of herself, was rather distressed for an answer, and the Admiral, fearing he might not have been civil enough, took up the subject again, to say,

"The next time you write to your good father, Miss Elliot, pray give my compliments and Mrs. Croft's, and say that we are settled here quite to our liking, and have no fault at all to find with the place. The breakfast-room chimney smokes a little, I grant you, but it is only when the wind is due north and blows hard, which may not happen three times a winter. And take it altogether, now that we have been into most of the houses hereabouts and can judge, there is not one that we like better than this. Pray say so, with my compliments. He will be glad to hear it."

Lady Russell and Mrs. Croft were very well pleased with each other; but the acquaintance which this visit began, was fated not to proceed far at present; for when it was returned, the Crofts announced themselves to be going away for a few weeks, to visit their connexions in the north of the county, and probably might not be at home again before Lady Russell would be removing to Bath.

So ended all danger to Anne of meeting Captain Wentworth at Kellynch-hall, or of seeing him in company with her friend. Every thing was safe enough and she smiled over the many anxious feelings she had wasted on the subject.

Samuel Richardson, by Joseph Highmore (1692–1780), circa 1747. Richardson's major novels are *Pamela* (1740) and *Clarissa* (1747–1748), but Austen particularly admired him for *Sir Charles Grandison*. According to her nephew James Edward Austen-Leigh, "every circumstance narrated" in the novel was "familiar to her" (Austen-Leigh, *Memoir,* 71).

2

THOUGH CHARLES AND MARY HAD REMAINED at Lyme much longer after Mr. and Mrs. Musgrove's going, than Anne conceived they could have been at all wanted, they were yet the first of the family to be at home again, and as soon as possible after their return to Uppercross, they drove over to the lodge. —They had left Louisa beginning to sit up; but her head, though clear, was exceedingly weak, and her nerves susceptible to the highest extreme of tenderness; and though she might be pronounced to be altogether doing very well, it was still impossible to say when she might be able to bear the removal home; and her father and mother, who must return in time to receive their younger children for the Christmas holidays,[1] had hardly a hope of being allowed to bring her with them.

They had been all in lodgings together. Mrs. Musgrove had got Mrs. Harville's children away as much as she could, every possible supply from Uppercross had been furnished, to lighten the inconvenience to the Harvilles, while the Harvilles had been wanting them to come to dinner every day; and in short, it seemed to have been only a struggle on each side as to which should be most disinterested[2] and hospitable.

Mary had had her evils; but upon the whole, as was evident by her staying so long, she had found more to enjoy than to suffer. —Charles Hayter had been at Lyme oftener than suited her, and when they dined with the Harvilles there had been only a maid-servant to wait, and at first, Mrs. Harville had always given Mrs. Musgrove precedence; but then, she had received so very handsome an apology from

1 The Christmas holidays stretched from Christmas Eve until Twelfth Night. "Christmas goes out in fine style, —with Twelfth Night," wrote the poet and essayist Leigh Hunt (1784–1859) in 1835. "It is a finish worthy of the time. Christmas Day was the morning of the season; New Year's Day the middle of it, or noon; Twelfth Night is the night" (*The Selected Writings of Leigh Hunt: Periodical Essays, 1822–38,* ed. Robert Morrison [London: Pickering and Chatto, 2003], 289).

2 By "disinterested," Austen means that both the Harvilles and the Musgroves are "free from selfish interest" or "unconcerned with their own advantage."

her on finding out whose daughter she was, and there had been so much going on every day, there had been so many walks between their lodgings and the Harvilles, and she had got books from the library[3] and changed them so often, that the balance had certainly been much in favour of Lyme. She had been taken to Charmouth too, and she had bathed, and she had gone to church,[4] and there were a great many more people to look at in the church at Lyme than at Uppercross,—and all this, joined to the sense of being so very useful, had made really an agreeable fortnight.

Anne enquired after Captain Benwick. Mary's face was clouded directly. Charles laughed.

"Oh! Captain Benwick is very well, I believe, but he is a very odd young man. I do not know what he would be at. We asked him to come home with us for a day or two; Charles undertook to give him some shooting, and he seemed quite delighted, and for my part, I thought it was all settled; when behold! on Tuesday night, he made a very awkward sort of excuse; 'he never shot' and he had 'been quite

3 Mary visits one of the "two well conducted Circulating Libraries" in Lyme. One was operated "by Mr. Hutchings, in Broad-street; the other by Mr. Swan, near the Rooms." Circulating libraries rented books to patrons, typically for a quarterly or annual fee, and came into existence because of the great expense of purchasing books, even for the relatively well-to-do. The commercial borrowing of books was well established by the seventeenth century and immensely fashionable by the beginning of the nineteenth. In 1821, there were about 1,500 circulating libraries located all across Britain (Phillips, 12; William St. Clair, *The Reading Nation in the Romantic Period* [Cambridge: Cambridge University Press, 2004], 237–239).

4 In Austen's day there were "three places of Worship" in Lyme, "one of the established Church, and two dissenting Chapels." Mary would unquestionably have attended the established church, which stood "on an eminence near the Cliffs; its entrance is well calculated to inspire the reflecting mind with religious awe" (Phillips, 9).

Church at Lyme Regis, by Charles Dibdin, circa 1760–1814. The picture shows the church from the northeast, with a man and woman in the churchyard by a gravestone, and the houses of the village scattered among trees on the hill.

misunderstood,'—and he had promised this and he had promised that, and the end of it was, I found, that he did not mean to come. I suppose he was afraid of finding it dull; but upon my word I should have thought we were lively enough at the Cottage for such a heart-broken man as Captain Benwick."

Charles laughed again and said, "Now Mary, you know very well how it really was.—It was all your doing," (turning to Anne.) "He fancied that if he went with us, he should find you close by; he fancied every body to be living in Uppercross; and when he discovered that Lady Russell lived three miles off, his heart failed him, and he had not courage to come. That is the fact, upon my honour. Mary knows it is."

But Mary did not give into it very graciously; whether from not considering Captain Benwick entitled by birth and situation to be in love with an Elliot, or from not wanting to believe Anne a greater attraction to Uppercross than herself, must be left to be guessed. Anne's good-will, however, was not to be lessened by what she heard. She boldly acknowledged herself flattered, and continued her enquiries.

"Oh! he talks of you," cried Charles, "in such terms,"—Mary interrupted him. "I declare, Charles, I never heard him mention Anne twice all the time I was there. I declare, Anne, he never talks of you at all."

"No," admitted Charles, "I do not know that he ever does, in a general way—but however, it is a very clear thing that he admires you exceedingly.—His head is full of some books that he is reading upon your recommendation, and he wants to talk to you about them; he has found out something or other in one of them which he thinks—Oh! I cannot pretend to remember it, but it was something very fine—I overheard him telling Henrietta all about it—and then 'Miss Elliot' was spoken of in the highest terms!—Now Mary, I declare it was so, I heard it myself, and you were in the other room.—'Elegance, sweetness, beauty,' Oh! there was no end of Miss Elliot's charms."

"And I am sure," cried Mary warmly, "it was very little to his credit, if he did. Miss Harville only died last June. Such a heart is very little worth having; is it, Lady Russell? I am sure you will agree with me."

A. Wallis Mills, Illustrations for *Persuasion,* 1908. Mary Elliot and Captain Benwick walk along the beach at Lyme.

"I must see Captain Benwick before I decide," said Lady Russell, smiling.

"And that you are very likely to do very soon, I can tell you, ma'am," said Charles. "Though he had not nerves for coming away with us and setting off again afterwards to pay a formal visit here, he will make his way over to Kellynch one day by himself, you may depend on it. I told him the distance and the road, and I told him of the church's being so very well worth seeing, for as he has a taste for those sort of things, I thought that would be a good excuse, and he listened with all his understanding and soul; and I am sure from his manner that you will have him calling here soon. So, I give you notice, Lady Russell."

"Any acquaintance of Anne's will always be welcome to me," was Lady Russell's kind answer.

"Oh! as to being Anne's acquaintance," said Mary, "I think he is rather my acquaintance, for I have been seeing him every day this last fortnight."

"Well, as your joint acquaintance, then, I shall be very happy to see Captain Benwick."

"You will not find any thing very agreeable in him, I assure you, ma'am. He is one of the dullest young men that ever lived. He has walked with me, sometimes, from one end of the sands to the other, without saying a word. He is not at all a well-bred young man. I am sure you will not like him."

"There we differ, Mary," said Anne. "I think Lady Russell would like him. I think she would be so much pleased with his mind, that she would very soon see no deficiency in his manner."

"So do I, Anne," said Charles. "I am sure Lady Russell would like him. He is just Lady Russell's sort. Give him a book, and he will read all day long."

"Yes, that he will!" exclaimed Mary, tauntingly. "He will sit poring over his book, and not know when a person speaks to him, or when one drops one's scissors, or any thing that happens. Do you think Lady Russell would like that?"

Lady Russell could not help laughing. "Upon my word," said she, "I should not have supposed that my opinion of any one could have admitted of such difference of conjecture, steady and matter of fact as I may call myself. I have really a curiosity to see the person who can give occasion to such directly opposite notions. I wish he may be induced to call here. And when he does, Mary, you may depend upon hearing my opinion; but I am determined not to judge him before-hand."

"You will not like him, I will answer for it."

Lady Russell began talking of something else. Mary spoke with animation of their meeting with, or rather missing, Mr. Elliot so ex-traordinarily.

"He is a man," said Lady Russell, "whom I have no wish to see. His declining to be on cordial terms with the head of his family, has left a very strong impression in his disfavour with me."

This decision checked Mary's eagerness, and stopped her short in the midst of the Elliot countenance.

With regard to Captain Wentworth, though Anne hazarded no enquiries, there was voluntary communication sufficient. His spirits had been greatly recovering lately, as might be expected. As Louisa improved, he had improved; and he was now quite a different crea-ture from what he had been the first week. He had not seen Louisa; and was so extremely fearful of any ill consequence to her from an interview, that he did not press for it at all; and, on the contrary, seemed to have a plan of going away for a week or ten days, till her head were stronger. He had talked of going down to Plymouth for a week, and wanted to persuade Captain Benwick to go with him; but, as Charles maintained to the last, Captain Benwick seemed much more disposed to ride over to Kellynch.

There can be no doubt that Lady Russell and Anne were both oc-casionally thinking of Captain Benwick, from this time. Lady Russell could not hear the door-bell without feeling that it might be his her-ald; nor could Anne return from any stroll of solitary indulgence in her father's grounds, or any visit of charity in the village, without wondering whether she might see him or hear of him. Captain Ben-wick came not, however. He was either less disposed for it than Charles had imagined, or he was too shy; and after giving him a week's indulgence, Lady Russell determined him to be unworthy of

5 Genteel young ladies often listed "cutting up silk and gold paper" among their accomplishments. In *Mansfield Park,* Fanny's lower-class education means that she has never even "learnt French," whereas the Miss Bertrams enjoy everything from playing duets to "making artificial flowers or wasting gold paper" (I, 2). Compare Oliver Goldsmith (1730–1774) in *The Vicar of Wakefield* (1766), where Dr. Primrose's wife, Deborah, describes the accomplishments of their daughters: "I will be bold to say my two girls have had a pretty good education, and capacity, at least the country can't shew better. They can read, write, and cast accompts; they understand their needle, breadstitch, cross and change, and all manner of plain-work; they can pink, point, and frill; and know something of music; they can do up small cloaths, work upon catgut; my eldest can cut paper, and my youngest has a very pretty manner of telling fortunes upon the cards" (*Collected Works of Oliver Goldsmith,* ed. Arthur Friedman [Oxford: Clarendon Press, 1966], IV, 63–64).

6 "Tressels," or more commonly "trestles," are braced frames that support trays and turn them into tables.

7 "Brawn" is boar or pig meat.

the interest which he had been beginning to excite.

The Musgroves came back to receive their happy boys and girls from school, bringing with them Mrs. Harville's little children, to improve the noise of Uppercross, and lessen that of Lyme. Henrietta remained with Louisa; but all the rest of the family were again in their usual quarters.

Lady Russell and Anne paid their compliments to them once, when Anne could not but feel that Uppercross was already quite alive again. Though neither Henrietta, nor Louisa, nor Charles Hayter, nor Captain Wentworth were there, the room presented as strong a contrast as could be wished, to the last state she had seen it in.

Immediately surrounding Mrs. Musgrove were the little Harvilles, whom she was sedulously guarding from the tyranny of the two children from the Cottage, expressly arrived to amuse them. On one side was a table, occupied by some chattering girls, cutting up silk and gold paper;[5] and on the other were tressels[6] and trays, bending under the weight of brawn[7] and cold pies, where riotous boys were

Tobias Smollett, by an unknown artist, circa 1770. His *Humphry Clinker* is an epistolary novel in which five characters write letters offering sometimes strikingly different views of the people and places they encounter on their travels through England and Smollett's native Scotland.

holding high revel; the whole completed by a roaring Christmas fire, which seemed determined to be heard, in spite of all the noise of the others. Charles and Mary also came in, of course, during their visit; and Mr. Musgrove made a point of paying his respects to Lady Russell, and sat down close to her for ten minutes, talking with a very raised voice, but, from the clamour of the children on his knees, generally in vain. It was a fine family-piece.

Anne, judging from her own temperament, would have deemed such a domestic hurricane a bad restorative of the nerves, which Louisa's illness must have so greatly shaken; but Mrs. Musgrove, who got Anne near her on purpose to thank her most cordially, again and again, for all her attentions to them, concluded a short recapitulation of what she had suffered herself, by observing, with a happy glance round the room, that after all she had gone through, nothing was so likely to do her good as a little quiet cheerfulness at home.

Louisa was now recovering apace. Her mother could even think of her being able to join their party at home, before her brothers and sisters went to school again. The Harvilles had promised to come with her and stay at Uppercross, whenever she returned. Captain Wentworth was gone, for the present, to see his brother in Shropshire.

"I hope I shall remember, in future," said Lady Russell, as soon as they were reseated in the carriage, "not to call at Uppercross in the Christmas holidays."

Every body has their taste in noises as well as in other matters; and sounds are quite innoxious,[8] or most distressing, by their sort rather than their quantity. When Lady Russell, not long afterwards, was entering Bath on a wet afternoon, and driving through the long course of streets from the Old Bridge to Camden-place,[9] amidst the dash[10] of other carriages, the heavy rumble of carts and drays,[11] the bawling of newsmen, muffin-men[12] and milk-men, and the ceaseless clink of pattens,[13] she made no complaint. No, these were noises which belonged to the winter pleasures;[14] her spirits rose under their influence; and, like Mrs. Musgrove, she was feeling, though not saying, that, after being long in the country, nothing could be so good for her as a little quiet cheerfulness.

8 "Innoxious" is "innocuous" or "harmless."

9 Kellynch is south of Bath, so Lady Russell and Anne enter the city by crossing the River Avon on the "Old Bridge," after which they pass through the bustling city center and then up the steep hill to Camden Place.

10 "Dash" is "splatter" or "splash."

11 A "dray" is a cart or wagon without sides and is used for hauling heavy loads.

12 An English muffin is "a small, flat, cake made from yeast batter and cooked on a hotplate, usually eaten split, toasted, and spread with butter" *(OED)*. In his epistolary verse narrative *The New Bath Guide* (1766), Christopher Anstey (1724–1805) declared that he preferred the muffins of Bath to "all the genteel Conversation I heard" (Anstey, *The New Bath Guide,* ed. Gavin Turner [Bristol: Broadcast Books, 1994], 95).

13 "Pattens" are "a kind of overshoe worn to raise an ordinary shoe above wet or muddy ground" *(OED)*. In "A Day by the Fire" (1812), Leigh Hunt recalled "a thick and rainy morning, with a sobbing wind, and the clatter of pattens along the streets" (*The Selected Writings of Leigh Hunt: Periodical Essays, 1805–14,* ed. Greg Kucich and Jeffrey N. Cox [London: Pickering and Chatto, 2003], 223).

14 Lady Russell's delight in the noises of Bath parallels Lydia Melford's in Tobias Smollett's *Humphry Clinker.* "Bath is to me a new world," exclaims Lydia. "—All is gayety, good-humour, and diversion. The eye is continually entertained with the splendour of dress and equipage; and the ear with the sound of coaches, chaises, chairs, and other carriages" (Smollett, *Humphry Clinker,* 38).

Bathwick Ferry below Camden Crescent, from an aquatint by I. Hill, after John Claude Nattes (circa 1765–1839). This picture was first published in 1805, when Austen herself was a resident of Bath.

View of Bath, engraved by T. Dixon, 1822. Although this image dates from seven years after the conclusion of events in *Persuasion,* it represents Bath very much as the characters in the novel must have known it.

Anne did not share these feelings. She persisted in a very determined, though very silent, disinclination for Bath; caught the first dim view of the extensive buildings, smoking in rain, without any wish of seeing them better; felt their progress through the streets to be, however disagreeable, yet too rapid; for who would be glad to see her when she arrived? And looked back, with fond regret, to the bustles of Uppercross and the seclusion of Kellynch.

Elizabeth's last letter had communicated a piece of news of some interest. Mr. Elliot was in Bath. He had called in Camden-place; had called a second time, a third; had been pointedly attentive: if Elizabeth and her father did not deceive themselves, had been taking as much pains to seek the acquaintance, and proclaim the value of the connection, as he had formerly taken pains to shew neglect. This was very wonderful, if it were true; and Lady Russell was in a state of very agreeable curiosity and perplexity about Mr. Elliot, already recanting the sentiment she had so lately expressed to Mary, of his being "a man whom she had no wish to see." She had a great wish to see him. If he really sought to reconcile himself like a dutiful branch, he must be forgiven for having dismembered himself from the paternal tree.

Anne was not animated to an equal pitch by the circumstance; but she felt that she would rather see Mr. Elliot again than not, which was more than she could say for many other persons in Bath.

She was put down in Camden-place; and Lady Russell then drove to her own lodgings, in Rivers-street.[15]

15 Rivers-street is located a short distance down the hill from Camden Place, close to the New Assembly Rooms.

3

1 "Laying out" is "scheming to effect some purpose." Compare Samuel Johnson, who remarked that "women are always most observed, when they seem themselves least to observe, or to lay out for observation" (Johnson, *Rambler,* IV, 155).

2 "Regretted" is "missed."

Sir Walter had taken a very good house in Camden-place, a lofty, dignified situation, such as becomes a man of consequence; and both he and Elizabeth were settled there, much to their satisfaction.

Anne entered it with a sinking heart, anticipating an imprisonment of many months, and anxiously saying to herself, "Oh! when shall I leave you again?" A degree of unexpected cordiality, however, in the welcome she received, did her good. Her father and sister were glad to see her, for the sake of shewing her the house and furniture, and met her with kindness. Her making a fourth, when they sat down to dinner, was noticed as an advantage.

Mrs. Clay was very pleasant, and very smiling; but her courtesies and smiles were more a matter of course. Anne had always felt that she would pretend what was proper on her arrival; but the complaisance of the others was unlooked for. They were evidently in excellent spirits, and she was soon to listen to the causes. They had no inclination to listen to her. After laying out[1] for some compliments of being deeply regretted[2] in their old neighbourhood, which Anne could not pay, they had only a few faint enquiries to make, before the talk must be all their own. Uppercross excited no interest, Kellynch very little, it was all Bath.

They had the pleasure of assuring her that Bath more than answered their expectations in every respect. Their house was undoubtedly the best in Camden-place; their drawing-rooms had many decided advantages over all the others which they had either seen or heard of; and the superiority was not less in the style of the fitting-up,[3] or the taste of the furniture. Their acquaintance was exceedingly sought after. Every body was wanting to visit them. They had drawn back from many introductions, and still were perpetually having cards left by people of whom they knew nothing.[4]

Here were funds of enjoyment! Could Anne wonder that her father and sister were happy? She might not wonder, but she must sigh that her father should feel no degradation in his change; should see nothing to regret in the duties and dignity of the resident landholder; should find so much to be vain of[5] in the littlenesses of a town; and she must sigh, and smile, and wonder too, as Elizabeth threw open the folding-doors, and walked with exultation from one drawing-room to the other, boasting of their space, at the possibility of that woman, who had been mistress of Kellynch Hall, finding extent to be proud of between two walls, perhaps thirty feet asunder.

But this was not all which they had to make them happy. They had Mr. Elliot, too. Anne had a great deal to hear of Mr. Elliot. He was not only pardoned, they were delighted with him. He had been in Bath about a fortnight; (he had passed through Bath in November, in his way to London, when the intelligence of Sir Walter's being settled there had of course reached him, though only twenty-four hours in the place, but he had not been able to avail himself of it): but he had now been a fortnight in Bath, and his first object, on arriving, had been to leave his card in Camden-place, following it up by such assiduous endeavours to meet, and, when they did meet, by such great openness of conduct, such readiness to apologize for the past, such solicitude to be received as a relation again, that their former good understanding was completely re-established.

They had not a fault to find in him. He had explained away all the appearance of neglect on his own side. It had originated in misapprehension entirely. He had never had an idea of throwing himself off; he had feared that he was thrown off, but knew not why; and delicacy had kept him silent. Upon the hint of having spoken disrespectfully or carelessly of the family, and the family honours, he was quite indignant. He, who had ever boasted of being an Elliot, and whose feelings, as to connection, were only too strict to suit the unfeudal[6] tone of the present day! He was astonished, indeed! But his character and

3 The "fitting-up" is the "interior decoration."

4 By 1800, the French practice of leaving a card at someone's home as a way of initiating an acquaintance had become common in Britain. Cards were left in lieu of a personal visit and were usually displayed in the hall to let other callers see who had preceded them: "Ideally a lady seated in her carriage handed her card to her servant who took it to the door and handed it to the servant of the house who took it to his mistress who could then decide whether or not she was 'At Home' to the caller." The practice developed as a way of monitoring the bounds of "good society": the Elliots did not have to return the compliment if they did not want to, and they undoubtedly did not in cases where the cards were "left by people of whom they knew nothing." In some instances, the practice of leaving a card went on for years without the two parties actually meeting, "for as leaving your name on a card at the door, is considered as a visit, this may go on reciprocally for a length of time, and if such visitors never meet at home, they do not personally know each other, when they chance to meet at any common friend's house, or elsewhere; and of course such meeting would be very awkward" (Leonore Davidoff, *The Best Circles: Society Etiquette and the Season* [London: Cresset, 1986], 42; Trusler, 30–31).

5 "To be vain of" is "to disregard, to treat with contempt" *(OED).*

6 "Unfeudal" is a rare usage and suggests the ways in which democratic and reformist elements in England are undermining the prestige of the traditional landed elites. The years following the French Revolution brought men such as Croft and Wentworth to prominence and introduced the prospect of vast changes to the social structure. "But," remarks Claudia Johnson, "the causes and the processes of such transformation are not themselves the subject of *Persuasion.* Instead they are the pervasive backdrop Austen establishes throughout *Persuasion* in order to consider the psychological impact that social arrangements have on women and the apparent possibilities which the 'unfeudal tone of the present day' may hold out for them" (Johnson, 148).

Marlborough Buildings, from a steel engraving by J. Hollway, circa 1845. In *Persuasion,* Colonel and Mrs. Wallis live here "in very good style."

general conduct must refute it. He could refer Sir Walter to all who knew him; and, certainly, the pains he had been taking on this, the first opportunity of reconciliation, to be restored to the footing of a relation and heir-presumptive, was a strong proof of his opinions on the subject.

The circumstances of his marriage too were found to admit of much extenuation. This was an article[7] not to be entered on by himself; but a very intimate friend of his, a Colonel Wallis, a highly respectable man, perfectly the gentleman, (and not an ill-looking man, Sir Walter added) who was living in very good style in Marlborough Buildings,[8] and had, at his own particular request, been admitted to their acquaintance through Mr. Elliot, had mentioned one or two things relative to the marriage, which made a material difference in the discredit of it.

Colonel Wallis had known Mr. Elliot long, had been well acquainted also with his wife, had perfectly understood the whole story. She was certainly not a woman of family, but well educated, accomplished, rich, and excessively in love with his friend. There had been the charm. She had sought him. Without that attraction, not all her money would have tempted Elliot, and Sir Walter was, moreover, assured of her having been a very fine[9] woman. Here was a great deal to soften the business. A very fine woman, with a large fortune, in love with him! Sir Walter seemed to admit it as complete apology, and though Elizabeth could not see the circumstance in quite so favourable a light, she allowed it be a great extenuation.

Mr. Elliot had called repeatedly, had dined with them once, evidently delighted by the distinction of being asked, for they gave no dinners in general;[10] delighted, in short, by every proof of cousinly notice, and placing his whole happiness in being on intimate terms in Camden-place.

Anne listened, but without quite understanding it. Allowances, large allowances, she knew, must be made for the ideas of those who spoke. She heard it all under embellishment. All that sounded extravagant or irrational in the progress of the reconciliation might have no origin but in the language of the relators. Still, however, she had the sensation of there being something more than immediately appeared, in Mr. Elliot's wishing, after an interval of so many years, to be well received by them. In a worldly view, he had nothing to gain by being on terms with Sir Walter, nothing to risk by a state of variance. In all probability he was already the richer of the two, and the Kellynch estate would as surely be his hereafter as the title. A sensible man! and he had looked like a *very* sensible man, why should it be an object to him? She could only offer one solution; it was, perhaps, for Elizabeth's sake. There might really have been a liking formerly, though convenience and accident had drawn him a different way, and now that he could afford to please himself, he might mean to pay his addresses to her. Elizabeth was certainly very handsome, with well-bred, elegant manners, and her character might never have been penetrated by Mr. Elliot, knowing her but in public, and when very young himself. How her temper and understanding might bear the investigation of his present keener time of life was another concern, and rather a fearful one. Most earnestly did she wish that he might not be too nice,[11] or too observant, if Elizabeth were his object; and that Elizabeth was disposed to believe herself so, and that her friend

9 "Fine" in this context means "attractive" or "good-looking."

10 The Elliots probably "gave no dinners in general" because they were living on a budget, which would have been apparent had they invited company to dine with them.

11 "Too nice" is a common expression in Austen, meaning "particular, strict, or careful with regard to a specific point or thing" *(OED)*. In *Mansfield Park,* for example, Edmund complains to Fanny, "You and Miss Crawford have made me too nice" (III, 4).

12 "Under-hung" means that the lower jaw projects beyond the upper.

13 A woman's "confinement" was the prescribed period of rest immediately before and following child-
birth.

14 Bond Street is immediately below Milsom Street in
the heart of Bath and is famous for its shopping.

Mrs. Clay was encouraging the idea, seemed apparent by a glance or
two between them, while Mr. Elliot's frequent visits were talked of.

Anne mentioned the glimpses she had had of him at Lyme, but
without being much attended to. "Oh! yes, perhaps, it had been Mr.
Elliot. They did not know. It might be him, perhaps." They could not
listen to her description of him. They were describing him themselves; Sir Walter especially. He did justice to his very gentlemanlike
appearance, his air of elegance and fashion, his good shaped face, his
sensible eye, but, at the same time, "must lament his being very much
under-hung,[12] a defect which time seemed to have increased; nor
could he pretend to say that ten years had not altered almost every
feature for the worse. Mr. Elliot appeared to think that he (Sir Walter) was looking exactly as he had done when they last parted;" but
Sir Walter had "not been able to return the compliment entirely,
which had embarrassed him. He did not mean to complain, however.
Mr. Elliot was better to look at than most men, and he had no objection to being seen with him any where."

Mr. Elliot, and his friends in Marlborough Buildings, were talked
of the whole evening. "Colonel Wallis had been so impatient to be
introduced to them! and Mr. Elliot so anxious that he should!" And
there was a Mrs. Wallis, at present only known to them by description, as she was in daily expectation of her confinement;[13] but Mr.
Elliot spoke of her as "a most charming woman, quite worthy of being known in Camden-place," and as soon as she recovered, they
were to be acquainted. Sir Walter thought much of Mrs. Wallis; she
was said to be an excessively pretty woman, beautiful. "He longed to
see her. He hoped she might make some amends for the many very
plain faces he was continually passing in the streets. The worst of
Bath was, the number of its plain women. He did not mean to say
that there were no pretty women, but the number of the plain was
out of all proportion. He had frequently observed, as he walked, that
one handsome face would be followed by thirty, or five and thirty
frights; and once, as he had stood in a shop in Bond-street,[14] he had
counted eighty-seven women go by, one after another, without there
being a tolerable face among them. It had been a frosty morning, to
be sure, a sharp frost, which hardly one woman in a thousand could

stand the test of. But still, there certainly were a dreadful multitude of ugly women in Bath; and as for the men! they were infinitely worse. Such scarecrows as the streets were full of! It was evident how little the women were used to the sight of any thing tolerable, by the effect which a man of decent appearance produced. He had never walked any where arm in arm with Colonel Wallis, (who was a fine military figure, though sandy-haired)[15] without observing that every woman's eye was upon him; every woman's eye was sure to be upon Colonel Wallis." Modest Sir Walter! He was not allowed to escape, however. His daughter and Mrs. Clay united in hinting that Colonel Wallis's companion might have as good a figure as Colonel Wallis, and certainly was not sandy-haired.

"How is Mary looking?" said Sir Walter, in the height of his good humour. "The last time I saw her, she had a red nose, but I hope that may not happen every day."

"Oh! no, that must have been quite accidental. In general she has been in very good health, and very good looks since Michaelmas."

"If I thought it would not tempt her to go out in sharp winds, and grow coarse, I would send her a new hat and pelisse."

15 As with Mrs. Clay's freckles, Sir Walter regards Colonel Wallis's sandy hair as a physical blemish.

Lansdown Crescent, by David Cox (1783–1859), 1820.
Mr. Elliot dines here but does not stay late, for by
10 o'clock he is with the Elliots in Camden Place.

16 Lansdown Crescent is a fashionable area located one-third of a mile northwest of Camden Crescent, with spectacular views of the surrounding countryside. "The *Crescent*," enthused Pierce Egan, "is a noble pile of building; and its extraordinary elevation is the admiration of every spectator" (Egan, 160).

17 Sir Walter is clearly economizing, for Mr. Elliot is greeted, not by a raft of servants, but by a butler and—instead of a liveried and more expensive footman—a menial footboy.

Anne was considering whether she should venture to suggest that a gown, or a cap, would not be liable to any such misuse, when a knock at the door suspended every thing. "A knock at the door! and so late! It was ten o'clock. Could it be Mr. Elliot? They knew he was to dine in Lansdown Crescent.[16] It was possible that he might stop in his way home, to ask them how they did. They could think of no one else. Mrs. Clay decidedly thought it Mr. Elliot's knock." Mrs. Clay was right. With all the state which a butler and foot-boy[17] could give, Mr. Elliot was ushered into the room.

It was the same, the very same man, with no difference but of dress. Anne drew a little back, while the others received his compliments, and her sister his apologies for calling at so unusual an hour, but "he could not be so near without wishing to know that neither she nor her friend had taken cold the day before, &c. &c." which was all as politely done, and as politely taken as possible, but her part must follow then. Sir Walter talked of his youngest daughter; "Mr. Elliot must give him leave to present him to his youngest daughter"—(there was no occasion for remembering Mary) and Anne, smiling and blushing, very becomingly shewed to Mr. Elliot the pretty features which he had by no means forgotten, and instantly saw, with amusement at his little start of surprise, that he had not been at all aware of who she was. He looked completely astonished, but not more astonished than pleased; his eyes brightened, and with the most perfect alacrity he welcomed the relationship, alluded to the past, and entreated to be received as an acquaintance already. He was quite as good-looking as he had appeared at Lyme, his countenance improved by speaking, and his manners were so exactly what they ought to be, so polished, so easy, so particularly agreeable, that she could compare them in excellence to only one person's manners. They were not the same, but they were, perhaps, equally good.

He sat down with them, and improved their conversation very much. There could be no doubt of his being a sensible man. Ten minutes were enough to certify that. His tone, his expressions, his choice of subject, his knowing where to stop,—it was all the operation of a sensible, discerning mind. As soon as he could, began to talk to her of Lyme, wanting to compare opinions respecting the place, but especially wanting to speak of the circumstance of their happening to be guests in the same inn at the same time, to give his own route, understand something of hers, and regret that he should have lost such an opportunity of paying his respects to her. She gave him a short account of her party, and business at Lyme. His regret increased as he listened. He had spent his whole solitary evening in the room adjoining theirs; had heard voices—mirth continually; thought they must be a most delightful set of people—longed to be with them; but certainly without the smallest suspicion of his possessing the shadow of a right to introduce himself. If he had but asked who the party were! The name of Musgrove would have told him enough. "Well, it would serve to cure him of an absurd practice of never asking a question at an inn, which he had adopted, when quite a young man, on the principle of its being very ungenteel to be curious.

"The notions of a young man of one or two and twenty," said he, "as to what is necessary in manners to make him quite the thing, are more absurd, I believe, than those of any other set of beings in the world. The folly of the means they often employ is only to be equalled by the folly of what they have in view."

But he must not be addressing his reflections to Anne alone; he knew it; he was soon diffused again among the others, and it was only at intervals that he could return to Lyme.

His enquiries, however, produced at length an account of the scene she had been engaged in there, soon after his leaving the place. Having alluded to "an accident," he must hear the whole. When he questioned, Sir Walter and Elizabeth began to question also; but the difference in their manner of doing it could not be unfelt. She could only compare Mr. Elliot to Lady Russell, in the wish of really comprehending what had passed, and in the degree of concern for what she must have suffered in witnessing it.

He staid an hour with them. The elegant little clock on the mantel-piece had struck "eleven with its silver sounds,"[18] and the watchman[19] was beginning to be heard at a distance telling the same tale, before Mr. Elliot or any of them seemed to feel that he had been there long.

Anne could not have supposed it possible that her first evening in Camden-place could have passed so well!

18 No exact source for this quotation has been identified. Several commentators have suggested that Austen has in mind Alexander Pope's *Rape of the Lock* (1714), I, 15–18:

> Now lapdogs give themselves the rowzing Shake,
> And sleepless Lovers, just at Twelve, awake:
> Thrice rung the Bell, the Slipper knock'd the
>   Ground,
> And the press'd Watch return'd a silver Sound.
>
> (Pope, II, 146)

19 The "watchman" was "one of a body of men formerly appointed to keep watch and ward in all towns from sunset to sunrise; later, a constable of the watch who, before the Police Act of 1839, patrolled the streets by night to safeguard life and property" *(OED)*.

4

THERE WAS ONE POINT WHICH ANNE, on returning to her family, would have been more thankful to ascertain, even than Mr. Elliot's being in love with Elizabeth, which was, her father's not being in love with Mrs. Clay; and she was very far from easy about it, when she had been at home a few hours. On going down to breakfast the next morning, she found there had just been a decent pretence on the lady's side of meaning to leave them. She could imagine Mrs. Clay to have said, that "now Miss Anne was come, she could not suppose herself at all wanted;" for Elizabeth was replying, in a sort of whisper, "That must not be any reason, indeed. I assure you I feel it none. She is nothing to me, compared with you;" and she was in full time to hear her father say, "My dear Madam, this must not be. As yet, you have seen nothing of Bath. You have been here only to be useful. You must not run away from us now. You must stay to be acquainted with Mrs. Wallis, the beautiful Mrs. Wallis. To your fine mind, I well know the sight of beauty is a real gratification."

He spoke and looked so much in earnest, that Anne was not surprised to see Mrs. Clay stealing a glance at Elizabeth and herself. Her countenance, perhaps, might express some watchfulness; but the praise of the fine mind did not appear to excite a thought in her sister. The lady could not but yield to such joint entreaties, and promise to stay.

In the course of the same morning, Anne and her father chancing to be alone together, he began to compliment her on her improved looks; he thought her "less thin in her person, in her cheeks; her skin, her complexion, greatly improved—clearer, fresher. Had she been using any thing in particular?" "No, nothing." "Merely Gowland," he supposed. "No, nothing at all." "Ha! he was surprised at that;"[1] and added, "certainly you cannot do better than continue as you are; you cannot be better than well; or I should recommend Gowland, the constant use of Gowland, during the spring months. Mrs. Clay has been using it at my recommendation, and you see what it has done for her. You see how it has carried away her freckles."[2]

He began to compliment her on her improved looks.

Hugh Thomson, Illustrations for *Persuasion,* 1897. Sir Walter finds that Anne's beauty is returning.

1 This exchange between Anne and her father is an example of Austen's famous practice of free indirect speech, where she blends the descriptions of the narrator with the speech or thought-processes of her characters, sometimes with and sometimes without quotation marks.

2 John Gowland (d. 1776) invented Gowland's Lotion in about 1740 as a cure for a celebrated beauty named Elizabeth Chudleigh (circa 1720–1788), who had developed blotches on her face. The lotion produced miraculous results, and Gowland soon became a very wealthy man. Nearly fifty years later his lotion was said to be "without a single rival to dispute its claim, as the specific for all cutaneous diseases and impurities, from a freckle or tetter to a mask of carbuncles" (Thomas Vincent and Robert Dickinson, *On the Power and Effects of Gowland's Lotion* [London: printed for the proprietors, 1794], 13).

What Gowland was actually selling, however, was hardly curative. His lotion was composed mainly of bitter almonds and sugar, but it also contained a small quantity of mercuric chloride, which is a derivative of sulphuric acid, and which is strong enough to remove the top layer of the skin. Women, in effect, were trying to improve their complexion by chemically peeling their skin away. By 1810, John Corry (fl. 1792–1836) knew the truth: "There's the lotion of Gowland that flays ladies' faces, / Distorting the features of our modern graces." T. A. B. Corley concludes that Austen had two reasons for introducing Gowland's Lotion into *Persuasion* at this point. The first was that "she wished to show how the boost in Anne's self-esteem, through being courted by two rivals, Captain Wentworth and Mr. Elliot, significantly helped to improve her looks." The second was that if Austen knew of the dangers of Gowland's, "then Sir Walter's remarks were further evidence of his vacuous character" (Corley, "The Shocking History of Gowland's Lotion," in *Jane Austen Society Report* [1999], 37–41).

In 1983, Nora Crook pointed out that Gowland's Lotion contained "corrosive sublimate" of mercury, which "had a particular connection with the old-fashioned treatment of syphilis." "Readers of *Persuasion* will readily remember Sir Walter Elliot's recommendation of Gowland's to Anne, on the strength of its supposed benefits to Mrs. Clay's freckles," Crook declares. ". . . . I do not suppose that Jane Austen is telling us that Mrs. Clay had once contracted syphilis, but her name, suggesting both 'the weaker vessel' and 'corruption,' implies that she is morally flawed, and her freckles are likewise symbolic. That she would 'taint' the Elliot family were she to marry into it is certainly to be understood." Yet while Mrs. Clay's character and motives are unquestionably suspect, Sir Walter's recommendation of Gowland's to his own daughter thoroughly undermines the notion that it was widely understood as a remedy for venereal disease (Crook, "Gowland's Lotion," in *Times Literary Supplement* [October 7, 1983], 1089).

3 Drinking the hot spring waters of Bath was believed to ameliorate a long list of ailments. "It is unnecessary to give minute directions for drinking the waters," asserted John Mansford in *The Invalid's Companion to Bath* (1820); "as this must in every case be determined by the medical attendant. In general, however, it may be observed, that a quarter of a pint is at first to be entered upon before breakfast, and repeated about noon; and by the effects of this quantity, its increase is to be regulated." In June 1799, Austen was in Bath with her ailing brother Edward, and she wrote to tell Cassandra of the steps he was taking to improve his health: "He drinks at the Hetling Pump, is to bathe tomorrow, & try Electricity on Tuesday" (Mansford, 25; Austen, *Letters,* 42).

4 "Candid" is used here in an obsolete sense, meaning "free from malice" or "kindly disposed."

5 Alistair Duckworth finds this description of Mr. Elliot particularly troubling. "Social decorum had always, of course, been available to the hypocrite as a mask for selfish ends, but the mask was usually visible in the earlier novels," he notes. "In *Persuasion* the mask is often indistinguishable from the face." Mr. Elliot seems "to bring together in one catalogue most of the characteristics of social and moral excellence," yet he is "as insidious a character as is to be seen" anywhere in Austen's work (Duckworth, *The Improvement of the Estate* [Baltimore: Johns Hopkins University Press, 1971], 181–182).

If Elizabeth could but have heard this! Such personal praise might have struck her, especially as it did not appear to Anne that the freckles were at all lessened. But every thing must take its chance. The evil of the marriage would be much diminished, if Elizabeth were also to marry. As for herself, she might always command a home with Lady Russell.

Lady Russell's composed mind and polite manners were put to some trial on this point, in her intercourse in Camden-place. The sight of Mrs. Clay in such favour, and of Anne so overlooked, was a perpetual provocation to her there; and vexed her as much when she was away, as a person in Bath who drinks the water,[3] gets all the new publications, and has a very large acquaintance, has time to be vexed.

As Mr. Elliot became known to her, she grew more charitable, or more indifferent, towards the others. His manners were an immediate recommendation; and on conversing with him she found the solid so fully supporting the superficial, that she was at first, as she told Anne, almost ready to exclaim, "Can this be Mr. Elliot?" and could not seriously picture to herself a more agreeable or estimable man. Every thing united in him; good understanding, correct opinions, knowledge of the world, and a warm heart. He had strong feelings of family-attachment and family-honour, without pride or weakness; he lived with the liberality of a man of fortune, without display; he judged for himself in every thing essential, without defying public opinion in any point of worldly decorum. He was steady, observant, moderate, candid;[4] never run away with by spirits or by selfishness, which fancied itself strong feeling; and yet, with a sensibility to what was amiable and lovely, and a value for all the felicities of domestic life, which characters of fancied enthusiasm and violent agitation seldom really possess.[5] She was sure that he had not been happy in marriage. Colonel Wallis said it, and Lady Russell saw it; but it had been no unhappiness to sour his mind, nor (she began pretty soon to suspect) to prevent his thinking of a second choice. Her satisfaction in Mr. Elliot outweighed all the plague of Mrs. Clay.

It was now some years since Anne had begun to learn that she and her excellent friend could sometimes think differently; and it did not surprise her, therefore, that Lady Russell should see nothing suspicious or inconsistent, nothing to require more motives than appeared, in Mr. Elliot's great desire of a reconciliation. In Lady Russell's view, it was perfectly natural that Mr. Elliot, at a mature time of life, should feel it a most desirable object, and what would very generally recommend him, among all sensible people, to be on good terms with the head of his family; the simplest process in the world of time upon a head naturally clear, and only erring in the heyday of youth. Anne presumed, however, still to smile about it; and at last to mention "Elizabeth." Lady Russell listened, and looked, and made only this cautious reply: "Elizabeth! Very well. Time will explain."

It was a reference to the future, which Anne, after a little observation, felt she must submit to. She could determine nothing at present. In that house Elizabeth must be first; and she was in the habit of such general observance as "Miss Elliot," that any particularity of attention seemed almost impossible. Mr. Elliot, too, it must be remembered, had not been a widower seven months. A little delay on his side might be very excusable. In fact, Anne could never see the crape round his hat,[6] without fearing that she was the inexcusable one, in attributing to him such imaginations; for though his marriage had not been very happy, still it had existed so many years that she could not comprehend a very rapid recovery from the awful impression of its being dissolved.

However it might end, he was without any question their pleasantest acquaintance in Bath; she saw nobody equal to him; and it was a great indulgence now and then to talk to him about Lyme, which he seemed to have as lively a wish to see again, and to see more of, as herself. They went through the particulars of their first meeting a great many times. He gave her to understand that he had looked at her with some earnestness. She knew it well; and she remembered another person's look also.

They did not always think alike. His value for rank and connexion she perceived to be greater than hers. It was not merely complaisance, it must be a liking to the cause, which made him enter warmly into her father and sister's solicitudes on a subject which she thought unworthy to excite them. The Bath paper one morning announced

6 Crape was a kind of black silk gauze. Mr. Elliot wears it round his hat as a sign of mourning. Compare Mary Elizabeth Braddon (1837–1915) in her novel *Lady Audley's Secret* (1861), where George Talboys is informed of his wife's death and wears a "deep band of crape about his hat" for a full year, the customary time period for a widower to mourn. Mr. Elliot's wife has been dead only seven months, and already he seems in pursuit of other women; certainly he was ogling Anne when they passed each other in Lyme. His display of the crape seems a mockery of—rather than a genuine expression of grief over—the loss of his wife, and contrasts tellingly with the enduring sorrow Anne privately feels over the loss of Wentworth (Braddon, *Lady Audley's Secret,* ed. David Skilton [Oxford: Oxford University Press, 2008], 49).

7 Newcomers to Bath had their names announced in the *Bath Chronicle and Weekly Gazette.* In May 1799, Austen herself was in Bath, from where she informed Cassandra that "there was a very long list of Arrivals here, in the Newspaper yesterday, so that we need not immediately dread absolute Solitude" (Austen, *Letters,* 41). The word "Dowager" indicates that Lady Dalrymple is a widow. Like Sir Walter, Lady Russell, Mr. Elliot, and Mrs. Smith, she has lost her spouse.

8 Lady Dalrymple is the widow of a viscount, so both she and her daughter are members of the nobility, and a good deal higher up the social scale than Sir Walter, who ranks as a commoner, and whose baronetcy is the lowest of all hereditary titles. For this reason, introducing himself to Lady Dalrymple is a matter of some delicacy, as Sir Walter needs to find an intermediary who might speak to her on his behalf, or devise some other means of determining whether she wished to be addressed by him.

Yet while Lady Dalrymple is the highest-ranking member of society in the novel, Austen complicates her stature by making her an Irish viscountess, and thus a member of what John Wiltshire refers to as the "fringe" aristocracy. Austen herself appears to have shared in the general disdain that many Britons felt for the Irish nobility. Writing from Lyme in September 1804, she reported to Cassandra that if she had chosen to stay longer at a ball she might have danced "with a new, odd looking Man who had been eyeing me for some time, & at last without any introduction asked me if I meant to dance again.—I think he must be Irish by his ease, & because I imagine him to belong to the Honble Barnwalls, who are the son & son's wife of an Irish Viscount—bold, queerlooking people, just fit to be Quality at Lyme" (Wiltshire, 160; Austen, *Letters,* 94).

In Austen's era, the word "cousins" meant the close family connection we associate with it today, but it was also used more broadly to refer to "a kinsman or kinswoman, a relative" *(OED).*

9 "Letters of ceremony" were formal letters sent on family occasions such as births, marriages, and deaths.

the arrival of the Dowager Viscountess Dalrymple, and her daughter, the Honourable Miss Carteret;[7] and all the comfort of No. —, Camden-place, was swept away for many days; for the Dalrymples (in Anne's opinion, most unfortunately) were cousins of the Elliots; and the agony was, how to introduce themselves properly.[8]

Anne had never seen her father and sister before in contact with nobility, and she must acknowledge herself disappointed. She had hoped better things from their high ideas of their own situation in life, and was reduced to form a wish which she had never foreseen—a wish that they had more pride; for "our cousins Lady Dalrymple and Miss Carteret;" "our cousins, the Dalrymples," sounded in her ears all day long.

Sir Walter had once been in company with the late Viscount, but had never seen any of the rest of the family, and the difficulties of the case arose from there having been a suspension of all intercourse by letters of ceremony,[9] ever since the death of that said late Viscount, when, in consequence of a dangerous illness of Sir Walter's at the same time, there had been an unlucky omission at Kellynch. No letter of condolence had been sent to Ireland. The neglect had been visited on the head of the sinner, for when poor Lady Elliot died herself, no letter of condolence was received at Kellynch, and, consequently, there was but too much reason to apprehend that the Dalrymples considered the relationship as closed. How to have this anxious business set to rights, and be admitted as cousins again, was the question; and it was a question which, in a more rational manner, neither Lady Russell nor Mr. Elliot thought unimportant. "Family connexions were always worth preserving, good company always worth seeking; Lady Dalrymple had taken a house, for three months, in Laura-place,[10] and would be living in style. She had been at Bath the year before, and Lady Russell had heard her spoken of as a charming woman. It was very desirable that the connexion should be renewed, if it could be done, without any compromise of propriety on the side of the Elliots."

Sir Walter, however, would choose his own means, and at last wrote a very fine letter of ample explanation, regret and entreaty, to his right honourable cousin. Neither Lady Russell nor Mr. Elliot could admire the letter; but it did all that was wanted, in bringing three lines of scrawl from the Dowager Viscountess. "She was very much honoured, and should be happy in their acquaintance." The toils of the business were over, the sweets began. They visited in Laura-place, they had the cards of Dowager Viscountess Dalrymple, and the Hon. Miss Carteret, to be arranged wherever they might be most visible; and "Our cousins in Laura-place," — "Our cousins, Lady Dalrymple and Miss Carteret," were talked of to every body.

Anne was ashamed. Had Lady Dalrymple and her daughter even been very agreeable, she would still have been ashamed of the agitation they created, but they were nothing. There was no superiority of manner, accomplishment, or understanding. Lady Dalrymple had acquired the name of "a charming woman," because she had a smile and a civil answer for every body. Miss Carteret, with still less to say, was so plain and so awkward, that she would never have been tolerated in Camden-place but for her birth.

Lady Russell confessed that she had expected something better; but yet "it was an acquaintance worth having," and when Anne ventured to speak her opinion of them to Mr. Elliot, he agreed to their being nothing in themselves, but still maintained that as a family connexion, as good company, as those who would collect good company around them, they had their value. Anne smiled and said,

"My idea of good company, Mr. Elliot, is the company of clever, well-informed people, who have a great deal of conversation; that is what I call good company."

"You are mistaken," said he gently, "that is not good company, that is the best. Good company requires only birth, education and manners, and with regard to education is not very nice. Birth and good manners are essential; but a little learning is by no means a dangerous thing[11] in good company, on the contrary, it will do very well. My cousin, Anne, shakes her head. She is not satisfied. She is fastidious. My dear cousin, (sitting down by her) you have a better right to be fastidious than almost any other woman I know; but will it answer? Will it make you happy? Will it not be wiser to accept the society of these good ladies in Laura-place, and enjoy all the advantages of the connexion as far as possible? You may depend upon it, that they will

10 Laura Place in Bath is the most prestigious of all the carefully graded addresses in the novel. It is a small square linked to Pulteney Bridge and built on an angle, with a street running diagonally out of each of its four corners. In January 1801, as her parents searched for a permanent residence in Bath, Austen informed Cassandra that she thought "some of the short streets leading from Laura Place or Pulteney Street" would be "above our price." Eventually the Austens moved to Sidney Place, which is located off the northern end of Pulteney Street (Austen, *Letters,* 67).

11 Mr. Elliot inverts Alexander Pope's well-known axiom from *An Essay on Criticism* (1711), 215–218:

> A *little Learning* is a dang'rous Thing;
> Drink deep, or taste not the *Pierian* Spring:
> There *shallow Draughts* intoxicate the Brain,
> And drinking *largely* sobers us again.
>
> (Pope, I, 264–265)

12 Anne is punning on "place" as both a physical location and a social position.

Alexander Pope, oil on canvas, from the studio of Michael Dahl (1659–1743), circa 1727. In *An Essay on Man* (1733–1734), Pope observes that "One truth is clear, / Whatever is, is right." Austen puns on the line in an October 1813 letter to Cassandra. "'Whatever is, is best,'" she assures her sister. "There has been one infallible Pope in the World" (Austen, *Letters*, 245).

move in the first set in Bath this winter, and as rank is rank, your being known to be related to them will have its use in fixing your family (our family let me say) in that degree of consideration which we must all wish for."

"Yes," sighed Anne, "we shall, indeed, be known to be related to them!"—then recollecting herself, and not wishing to be answered, she added, "I certainly do think there has been by far too much trouble taken to procure the acquaintance. I suppose (smiling) I have more pride than any of you; but I confess it does vex me, that we should be so solicitous to have the relationship acknowledged, which we may be very sure is a matter of perfect indifference to them."

"Pardon me, my dear cousin, you are unjust to your own claims. In London, perhaps, in your present quiet style of living, it might be as you say; but in Bath, Sir Walter Elliot and his family will always be worth knowing, always acceptable as acquaintance."

"Well," said Anne, "I certainly am proud, too proud to enjoy a welcome which depends so entirely upon place."12

"I love your indignation," said he; "it is very natural. But here you are in Bath, and the object is to be established here with all the credit and dignity which ought to belong to Sir Walter Elliot. You talk of being proud, I am called proud I know, and I shall not wish to believe myself otherwise, for our pride, if investigated, would have the same object, I have no doubt, though the kind may seem a little different. In one point, I am sure, my dear cousin, (he continued, speaking lower, though there was no one else in the room) in one point, I am sure, we must feel alike. We must feel that every addition to your father's society, among his equals or superiors, may be of use in diverting his thoughts from those who are beneath him."

He looked, as he spoke, to the seat which Mrs. Clay had been lately occupying, a sufficient explanation of what he particularly meant; and though Anne could not believe in their having the same sort of pride, she was pleased with him for not liking Mrs. Clay; and her conscience admitted that his wishing to promote her father's getting great acquaintance, was more than excusable in the view of defeating her.

5

WHILE SIR WALTER AND ELIZABETH WERE assiduously pushing their good fortune in Laura-place, Anne was renewing an acquaintance of a very different description.

She had called on her former governess, and had heard from her of there being an old school-fellow in Bath, who had the two strong claims on her attention, of past kindness and present suffering. Miss Hamilton, now Mrs. Smith, had shewn her kindness in one of those periods of her life when it had been most valuable. Anne had gone unhappy to school, grieving for the loss of a mother whom she had dearly loved, feeling her separation from home, and suffering as a girl of fourteen, of strong sensibility and not high spirits, must suffer at such a time; and Miss Hamilton, three years older than herself, but still from the want of near relations and a settled home, remaining another year at school, had been useful and good to her in a way which had considerably lessened her misery, and could never be remembered with indifference.

Miss Hamilton had left school, had married not long afterwards, was said to have married a man of fortune, and this was all that Anne had known of her, till now that their governess's account brought her situation forward in a more decided but very different form.

She was a widow, and poor. Her husband had been extravagant; and at his death, about two years before, had left his affairs dreadfully involved. She had had difficulties of every sort to contend with, and in addition to these distresses, had been afflicted with a severe rheumatic fever, which finally settling in her legs, had made her for

1 The "Hot Bath" and the "Cross Bath" were located in the lower southwestern section of the town, a short distance from Mrs. Smith's lodgings. The Romans bathed in these hot mineral springs and praised them for their medicinal qualities. John Mansford asserts that the "warm bath judiciously used, will be found a powerful adjunct in the treatment of many disorders. It softens the skin, determines to the surface, and thus relieves internal congestion; tranquillizes an excited system; reduces the velocity, and equalizes the distribution of the circulating fluids; relieves female obstructions; promotes the action of the absorbents; and furthers the design of many medicines" (Mansford, 113).

2 Westgate Buildings lie immediately to the west of the Hot and Cross Baths. Sir Walter disapproves of the location—it is far down the hill from Camden Place and much lower down the social scale, as it was several blocks away from the fashionable center of the town and in close proximity to some of Bath's shadier areas. Yet there was still a good deal to recommend the location. Pierce Egan called Westgate Buildings "a plain neat row of houses," and in early 1801 Austen herself praised them: "Westgate Buildings, tho' quite in the lower part of the Town are not badly situated themselves; the street is broad, & has rather a good appearance." Jocelyn Harris observes that there are good reasons behind Mrs. Smith's decision to live there: "Because the baths offered little accommodation for dressing and undressing, invalids had to live nearby. From her lodgings in Westgate Buildings, Mrs. Smith is 'conveyed into the warm bath' in 'specially made sedan chairs, which are quite small and low, bowed out below so as to give room, and with very short poles, for the purpose of carrying the people straight out of their beds, in their bathing costume, right into their baths'—the short poles allowed chairmen to traverse close and winding stairs" (Egan, 91; Austen, *Letters*, 67; Harris, 174).

Lady Russell's willingness to escort Anne to Mrs. Smith's lodgings reveals the central paradox of her character: her deference to rank makes her impercep-

The Cross Bath, from an aquatint after John Claude Nattes. In October 1813 Austen reported to Cassandra that the Dowager Lady Bridges was "going to try the Hot pump, the Cross Bath being about to be painted" (Austen, *Letters*, 238).

the present a cripple. She had come to Bath on that account, and was now in lodgings near the hot-baths,[1] living in a very humble way, unable even to afford herself the comfort of a servant, and of course almost excluded from society.

Their mutual friend answered for the satisfaction which a visit from Miss Elliot would give Mrs. Smith, and Anne therefore lost no time in going. She mentioned nothing of what she had heard, or what she intended, at home. It would excite no proper interest there. She only consulted Lady Russell, who entered thoroughly into her sentiments, and was most happy to convey her as near to Mrs. Smith's lodgings in Westgate-buildings,[2] as Anne chose to be taken.

The visit was paid, their acquaintance re-established, their interest in each other more than re-kindled. The first ten minutes had its awkwardness and its emotion. Twelve years were gone since they had parted, and each presented a somewhat different person from what the other had imagined. Twelve years had changed Anne from the blooming, silent, unformed girl of fifteen, to the elegant little woman of seven and twenty, with every beauty excepting bloom, and with manners as consciously right as they were invariably gentle; and twelve years had transformed the fine-looking, well-grown Miss Hamilton, in all the glow of health and confidence of superiority, into a poor, infirm, helpless widow, receiving the visit of her former protegée as a favour; but all that was uncomfortable in the meeting had soon passed away, and left only the interesting charm of remembering former partialities and talking over old times.

Anne found in Mrs. Smith the good sense and agreeable manners which she had almost ventured to depend on, and a disposition to converse and be cheerful beyond her expectation. Neither the dissipations of the past—and she had lived very much in the world, nor the restrictions of the present; neither sickness nor sorrow seemed to have closed her heart or ruined her spirits.

In the course of a second visit she talked with great openness, and Anne's astonishment increased. She could scarcely imagine a more cheerless situation in itself than Mrs. Smith's. She had been very fond of her husband,—she had buried him. She had been used to affluence,—it was gone. She had no child to connect her with life and happiness again, no relations to assist in the arrangement of perplexed affairs, no health to make all the rest supportable. Her accommodations were limited to a noisy parlour, and a dark bed-room behind, with no possibility of moving from one to the other without assistance, which there was only one servant in the house to afford, and she never quitted the house but to be conveyed into the warm bath.—Yet, in spite of all this, Anne had reason to believe that she had moments only of languor and depression, to hours of occupation and enjoyment. How could it be?—She watched—observed—reflected—and finally determined that this was not a case of fortitude or of resignation only.—A submissive spirit might be patient, a strong understanding would supply resolution, but here was something more; here was that elasticity of mind,[3] that disposition to be comforted, that power of turning readily from evil to good, and of finding employment which carried her out of herself, which was from

tive and unhelpful on several occasions, yet she enters "thoroughly" into Anne's "sentiments" concerning the poverty and isolation of Mrs. Smith, and she is "most happy to convey her as near to Mrs. Smith's lodgings in Westgate-buildings, as Anne chose to be taken."

3 Austen's use of the phrase "elasticity of mind" echoes Walter Scott's use of the same phrase to describe Captain Brown in *Guy Mannering* (1815): "Brown . . . had been from infancy a ball for fortune to spurn at; but nature had given him that elasticity of mind, which rises higher from the rebound" (Scott, *Guy Mannering*, ed. Peter Garside [Edinburgh: Edinburgh University Press, 1999], 110).

4 "Card-racks" were racks for holding visiting cards. These items were part of the stock-in-trade of the nineteenth-century women who attempted to raise money through handicraft and cottage industry. Compare Charlotte Brontë (1816–1855) in *Shirley* (1849), where "a monster collection of pincushions, needle-books, card-racks, work-bags, [and] articles of infant-wear" are made by "the willing or reluctant hands of the Christian ladies of a parish, and sold perforce to the heathenish gentlemen thereof, at prices unblushingly exorbitant" (Brontë, *Shirley,* ed. Herbert Rosengarten and Margaret Smith [Oxford: Clarendon Press, 1979], 125).

5 Though impoverished herself, Mrs. Smith maintains her status as a gentlewoman by dispensing charity to "one or two very poor families" in her neighborhood. Austen here also seems to glimpse a world in which women are free to exercise their entrepreneurial skills and instincts.

Nature alone. It was the choicest gift of Heaven; and Anne viewed her friend as one of those instances in which, by a merciful appointment, it seems designed to counterbalance almost every other want.

There had been a time, Mrs. Smith told her, when her spirits had nearly failed. She could not call herself an invalid now, compared with her state on first reaching Bath. Then, she had indeed been a pitiable object—for she had caught cold on the journey, and had hardly taken possession of her lodgings, before she was again confined to her bed, and suffering under severe and constant pain; and all this among strangers—with the absolute necessity of having a regular nurse, and finances at that moment particularly unfit to meet any extraordinary expense. She had weathered it however, and could truly say that it had done her good. It had increased her comforts by making her feel herself to be in good hands. She had seen too much of the world, to expect sudden or disinterested attachment any where, but her illness had proved to her that her landlady had a character to preserve, and would not use her ill; and she had been particularly fortunate in her nurse, as a sister of her landlady, a nurse by profession, and who had always a home in that house when unemployed, chanced to be at liberty just in time to attend her.—"And she," said Mrs. Smith, "besides nursing me most admirably, has really proved an invaluable acquaintance.—As soon as I could use my hands, she taught me to knit, which has been a great amusement; and she put me in the way of making these little thread-cases, pincushions and card-racks,[4] which you always find me so busy about, and which supply me with the means of doing a little good to one or two very poor families in this neighbourhood.[5] She has a large acquaintance, of course professionally, among those who can afford to buy, and she disposes of my merchandize. She always takes the right time for applying. Every body's heart is open, you know, when they have recently escaped from severe pain, or are recovering the blessing of health, and nurse Rooke thoroughly understands when to speak. She is a shrewd, intelligent, sensible woman. Hers is a line for seeing human nature; and she has a fund of good sense and observation which, as a companion, make her infinitely superior to thousands of those who having only received 'the best education in the world,' know nothing worth attending to. Call it gossip if you will; but when nurse Rooke has half an hour's leisure to bestow on me, she is sure to have something to relate that is entertaining and profitable, something that makes one know one's species better. One likes to hear what is going on, to be *au fait*[6] as to the newest modes of being trifling and silly. To me, who live so much alone, her conversation I assure you, is a treat."

Anne, far from wishing to cavil at the pleasure, replied, "I can easily believe it. Women of that class have great opportunities, and if they are intelligent may be well worth listening to. Such varieties of human nature as they are in the habit of witnessing! And it is not merely in its follies, that they are well read; for they see it occasionally under every circumstance that can be most interesting or affecting. What instances must pass before them of ardent, disinterested, self-denying attachment, of heroism, fortitude, patience, resignation—of all the conflicts and all the sacrifices that ennoble us most. A sick chamber may often furnish the worth of volumes."

"Yes," said Mrs. Smith more doubtingly, "sometimes it may, though I fear its lessons are not often in the elevated style you describe. Here and there, human nature may be great in times of trial, but generally speaking it is its weakness and not its strength that appears in a sick chamber; it is selfishness and impatience rather than generosity and fortitude, that one hears of.[7] There is so little real friendship in the world!—and unfortunately" (speaking low and tremulously) "there are so many who forget to think seriously till it is almost too late."

Anne saw the misery of such feelings. The husband had not been what he ought, and the wife had been led among that part of mankind which made her think worse of the world, than she hoped it deserved. It was but a passing emotion however with Mrs. Smith, she shook it off, and soon added in a different tone,

"I do not suppose the situation my friend Mrs. Rooke is in at present, will furnish much either to interest or edify me.—She is only nursing Mrs. Wallis of Marlborough-buildings—a mere pretty, silly, expensive, fashionable woman, I believe—and of course will have

6 "Au fait" is a French phrase meaning "fully informed." Mrs. Smith's use of a foreign language reveals her fashionable education.

7 Anne's tendency to romanticize is clearly exposed in this passage when her exalted notions of the "heroism" to be found among the wounded and the ill are subverted by Mrs. Smith's practical knowledge of the harsher realities of life, and her insistence that, "generally speaking," it is the weakness of human nature and "not its strength that appears in a sick chamber."

nothing to report but of lace and finery.—I mean to make my profit of Mrs. Wallis, however. She has plenty of money, and I intend she shall buy all the high-priced things I have in hand now."

Anne had called several times on her friend, before the existence of such a person was known in Camden-place. At last, it became necessary to speak of her.—Sir Walter, Elizabeth and Mrs. Clay returned one morning from Laura-place, with a sudden invitation from Lady Dalrymple for the same evening, and Anne was already engaged, to spend that evening in Westgate-buildings. She was not sorry for the excuse. They were only asked, she was sure, because Lady Dalrymple being kept at home by a bad cold, was glad to make use of the relationship which had been so pressed on her,—and she declined on her own account with great alacrity—"She was engaged to spend the evening with an old schoolfellow." They were not much interested in any thing relative to Anne, but still there were questions enough asked, to make it understood what this old schoolfellow was; and Elizabeth was disdainful, and Sir Walter severe.

"Westgate-buildings!" said he; "and who is Miss Anne Elliot to be visiting in Westgate-buildings?—A Mrs. Smith. A widow Mrs. Smith,—and who was her husband? One of the five thousand Mr. Smiths whose names are to be met with every where. And what is her attraction? That she is old and sickly.—Upon my word, Miss Anne Elliot, you have the most extraordinary taste! Every thing that revolts other people, low company, paltry rooms, foul air, disgusting associations are inviting to you. But surely, you may put off this old lady till to-morrow. She is not so near her end, I presume, but that she may hope to see another day. What is her age? Forty?"

"No, Sir, she is not one and thirty; but I do not think I can put off my engagement, because it is the only evening for some time which will at once suit her and myself.—She goes into the warm bath to-morrow, and for the rest of the week you know we are engaged."

"But what does Lady Russell think of this acquaintance?" asked Elizabeth.

"She sees nothing to blame in it," replied Anne; "on the contrary, she approves it; and has generally taken me, when I have called on Mrs. Smith."

"Westgate-buildings must have been rather surprised by the appearance of a carriage drawn up near its pavement!" observed Sir Walter.—"Sir Henry Russell's widow, indeed, has no honours to distinguish her arms;[8] but still, it is a handsome equipage, and no doubt is well known to convey a Miss Elliot.—A widow Mrs. Smith, lodging in Westgate-buildings!—A poor widow, barely able to live, between thirty and forty—a mere Mrs. Smith, an every day Mrs. Smith, of all people and all names in the world, to be the chosen friend of Miss Anne Elliot, and to be preferred by her, to her own family connections among the nobility of England and Ireland! Mrs. Smith, such a name!"[9]

Mrs. Clay, who had been present while all this passed, now thought it advisable to leave the room, and Anne could have said much and did long to say a little, in defence of *her* friend's not very dissimilar claims to theirs, but her sense of personal respect to her father prevented her.[10] She made no reply. She left it to himself to recollect, that Mrs. Smith was not the only widow in Bath between thirty and forty, with little to live on, and no sirname[11] of dignity.

Anne kept her appointment; the others kept theirs, and of course she heard the next morning that they had had a delightful evening.—She had been the only one of the set absent; for Sir Walter and Elizabeth had not only been quite at her ladyship's service themselves, but had actually been happy to be employed by her in collecting others, and had been at the trouble of inviting both Lady Russell and Mr. Elliot; and Mr. Elliot had made a point of leaving Colonel Wallis early, and Lady Russell had fresh arranged all her evening engagements in order to wait on her. Anne had the whole history of all that such an evening could supply, from Lady Russell. To her, its greatest interest must be, in having been very much talked of between her friend and Mr. Elliot, in having been wished for, regretted, and at the same time honoured for staying away in such a cause.—Her kind, compassionate visits to this old schoolfellow, sick and reduced, seemed to have quite delighted Mr. Elliot. He thought her a most extraordinary young woman; in her temper, manners, mind, a model of female excellence. He could meet even Lady Russell in a discussion of her merits; and Anne could not be given to understand so

8 A coat-of-arms is painted on Lady Russell's carriage to denote that she was married to a knight. But as Sir Walter is quick to point out, there are no additional embellishments "to distinguish" the arms, which means that there were no special achievements after the original knighthood was awarded.

9 As a man of property and wealth, Sir Walter is supposed to take a paternalistic interest in disadvantaged and impoverished people such as Mrs. Smith. His scornful response to her plight illuminates how out of touch he is with his social duties, and why Anne's generosity and concern make her both a more fitting representative of the landed gentry and a woman who identifies strongly with the self-reliance, courage, and sense of duty that she sees exemplified in the men and women of the navy.

10 Andor Gomme wonders at the regard Anne can still feel for her father. "What can be said in favour of such a man?" he asks. "Yet it is surely of some importance that he should not be merely an object to scoff at. For we find that, after his very nasty outburst about Mrs. Smith . . . Anne is kept from speaking her mind by 'her sense of personal respect for her father.' That Anne should stop short of telling her father what she thinks of him is understandable; that by this time she should feel a *respect* which is *personal* for the man he has been shown to be is not" (Gomme, 177).

11 "Sirname" is an obsolete spelling of "surname."

much by her friend, could not know herself to be so highly rated by a sensible man, without many of those agreeable sensations which her friend meant to create.

Lady Russell was now perfectly decided in her opinion of Mr. Elliot. She was as much convinced of his meaning to gain Anne in time, as of his deserving her; and was beginning to calculate the number of weeks which would free him from all the remaining restraints of widowhood, and leave him at liberty to exert his most open powers of pleasing. She would not speak to Anne with half the certainty she felt on the subject, she would venture on little more than hints of what might be hereafter, of a possible attachment on his side, of the desirableness of the alliance, supposing such attachment to be real, and returned. Anne heard her, and made no violent exclamations. She only smiled, blushed, and gently shook her head.

"I am no match-maker, as you well know," said Lady Russell, "being much too well aware of the uncertainty of all human events and calculations. I only mean that if Mr. Elliot should some time hence pay his addresses to you, and if you should be disposed to accept him, I think there would be every possibility of your being happy together. A most suitable connection every body must consider it—but I think it might be a very happy one."

"Mr. Elliot is an exceedingly agreeable man, and in many respects I think highly of him," said Anne; "but we should not suit."

Lady Russell let this pass, and only said in rejoinder, "I own that to be able to regard you as the future mistress of Kellynch, the future Lady Elliot—to look forward and see you occupying your dear mother's place, succeeding to all her rights, and all her popularity, as well as to all her virtues, would be the highest possible gratification to me.—You are your mother's self in countenance and disposition; and if I might be allowed to fancy you such as she was, in situation, and name, and home, presiding and blessing in the same spot, and only superior to her in being more highly valued! My dearest Anne, it would give me more delight than is often felt at my time of life!"

Anne was obliged to turn away, to rise, to walk to a distant table, and, leaning there in pretended employment, try to subdue the feelings this picture excited. For a few moments her imagination and her heart were bewitched. The idea of becoming what her mother had been; of having the precious name of "Lady Elliot" first revived in herself; of being restored to Kellynch, calling it her home again, her home for ever, was a charm which she could not immediately resist. Lady Russell said not another word, willing to leave the matter to its own operation; and believing that, could Mr. Elliot at that moment with propriety have spoken for himself!—She believed, in short, what Anne did not believe. The same image of Mr. Elliot speaking for himself, brought Anne to composure again. The charm of Kellynch and of "Lady Elliot" all faded away. She never could accept him. And it was not only that her feelings were still adverse to any man save one; her judgment, on a serious consideration of the possibilities of such a case, was against Mr. Elliot.

Though they had now been acquainted a month, she could not be satisfied that she really knew his character. That he was a sensible man, an agreeable man,—that he talked well, professed good opinions, seemed to judge properly and as a man of principle,—this was all clear enough. He certainly knew what was right, nor could she fix on any one article of moral duty evidently transgressed; but yet she would have been afraid to answer for his conduct. She distrusted the past, if not the present. The names which occasionally dropt of former associates, the allusions to former practices and pursuits, suggested suspicions not favourable of what he had been. She saw that there had been bad habits; that Sunday-travelling[12] had been a common thing; that there had been a period of his life (and probably not a short one) when he had been, at least, careless on all serious matters; and, though he might now think very differently, who could answer for the true sentiments of a clever, cautious man, grown old enough to appreciate a fair character?[13] How could it ever be ascertained that his mind was truly cleansed?

Mr. Elliot was rational, discreet, polished,—but he was not open. There was never any burst of feeling, any warmth of indignation or delight, at the evil or good of others. This, to Anne, was a decided imperfection. Her early impressions were incurable. She prized the frank, the open-hearted, the eager character beyond all others. Warmth and enthusiasm did captivate her still. She felt that she

12 Sunday traveling had been a contentious issue for centuries. In *A Serious Call to a Devout and Holy Life* (1728), the devotional writer William Law (1686–1761) made clear that on the Lord's day Christians should abstain "from many innocent and lawful things, as *travelling, visiting, common conversation,* and discoursing upon *worldly matters,* as *trade, news,* and the like." Instead, they "should devote the day, besides public worship, to greater retirement, reading, devotion, instruction, and works of Charity." By the nineteenth century, however, the practice of Sunday traveling was common, though still frequently censured. For example, in *The Newcomes* (1853–1855), William Makepeace Thackeray (1811–1863) has Miss Honeyman snap, "Innocent or not, this house is not intended for assignations, Clive! As long as Sir Brian Newcome lodges here, you will be pleased to keep away from it, sir; and though I don't approve of Sunday travelling, I think the very best thing you can do is to put yourself in the train and go back to London." Nearly four decades later, in a pamphlet in the British Library stamped December 10, 1892, the Anti-Sunday-Travelling Union announced that it had "for its object the suppression of Sunday travelling. It is the combined influence of the many individual Sunday travellers of Great Britain, which keeps at work over two hundred thousand railway, tram, omnibus, cab, and steam-boat men, during the day which God has appointed for their rest" (Law, *A Serious Call to a Devout and Holy Life* [London: Innys, 1729], 105; Thackeray, *The Newcomes,* ed. David Pascoe [London: Penguin Book, 1996], 447; Anonymous, *The Anti-Sunday-Travelling Union* [London: Private Printing, n.d.], 1).

Austen's prudish-sounding strictures on Sunday traveling have been taken by many commentators as evidence of her increasing attachment to evangelical Christianity in the closing years of her life. "I am by no means convinced that we ought not all to be Evangelicals," she declared in November 1814, less than a year before she began to write *Persuasion.* Observes Marilyn Butler: "The Evangelical colouring of [Austen's] Christianity in the later novels blends imperceptibly with her earlier conservatism, since the goal of Evangelicalism was generally to fortify middle-class life by arming it from within" (Austen, *Letters,* 280; Butler, 285).

13 "Character" in this context is "reputation."

Charles Austen, by an unknown artist. Austen's sixth and youngest brother, he was educated at the Royal Navy Academy in Portsmouth and rose to the rank of rear-admiral. During the same months covered by the plotline of *Persuasion,* his first wife, Fanny, died, and he served in the Mediterranean aboard the *Phoenix.*

could so much more depend upon the sincerity of those who sometimes looked or said a careless or a hasty thing, than of those whose presence of mind never varied, whose tongue never slipped.

Mr. Elliot was too generally agreeable. Various as were the tempers in her father's house, he pleased them all. He endured too well,—stood too well with everybody. He had spoken to her with some degree of openness of Mrs. Clay; had appeared completely to see what Mrs. Clay was about, and to hold her in contempt; and yet Mrs. Clay found him as agreeable as anybody.

Lady Russell saw either less or more than her young friend, for she saw nothing to excite distrust. She could not imagine a man more exactly what he ought to be than Mr. Elliot; nor did she ever enjoy a sweeter feeling than the hope of seeing him receive the hand of her beloved Anne in Kellynch church, in the course of the following autumn.

6

It was the beginning of February; and Anne, having been a month in Bath, was growing very eager for news from Uppercross and Lyme. She wanted to hear much more than Mary communicated. It was three weeks since she had heard at all. She only knew that Henrietta was at home again; and that Louisa, though considered to be recovering fast, was still at Lyme; and she was thinking of them all very intently one evening, when a thicker letter than usual from Mary was delivered to her, and, to quicken the pleasure and surprise, with Admiral and Mrs. Croft's compliments.[1]

The Crofts must be in Bath! A circumstance to interest her. They were people whom her heart turned to very naturally.

"What is this?" cried Sir Walter. "The Crofts arrived in Bath? The Crofts who rent Kellynch? What have they brought you?"

"A letter from Uppercross Cottage, Sir."

"Oh! those letters are convenient passports. They secure an introduction. I should have visited Admiral Croft, however, at any rate. I know what is due to my tenant."

Anne could listen no longer; she could not even have told how the poor Admiral's complexion escaped; her letter engrossed her. It had been begun several days back.

"February 1st,——.

"My Dear Anne,
"I make no apology for my silence, because I know how little people think of letters in such a place as Bath. You must

[1] In Austen's day, there were no manufactured envelopes or adhesive postage stamps, and the recipient of a letter—rather than the sender—paid the postage. Most letters were written on a single sheet of "legal-sized paper, folded to make four pages about eight-by-eleven inches. . . . The center third of page 4, when the letter was folded from top and bottom, became the front of the 'envelope' for the address and hand-stamped postmarks, while the folded-over sides were sealed with a wax wafer." The cost of the letter depended on the number of sheets and how far it traveled. In 1812, a single letter cost fourpence for fifteen miles or less. More sheets cost more money. As the Crofts are traveling to Bath, Mary has saved Anne the expense of the letter by asking the Crofts to carry it to her. Anne receives the letter with a brief note from the Crofts (their "compliments"), for social protocol required them to announce their arrival in Bath to friends and acquaintances (Jo Modert, "Post/Mail," in Grey, 345–346).

2 Mary's point is that in the country around Upper-cross the rain often makes the roads and footpaths im-passable, whereas the "nice pavements" of Bath allow movement about town even when there has been in-clement weather. Mary, however, is again feeling sorry for herself. Her complaints about the rain are not shared by Elizabeth Bennet, who in *Pride and Prejudice* walks three miles through muddy fields to visit her ail-ing sister Jane, though her actions shock the squeamish Mrs. Hurst: "I hope you saw her petticoat, six inches deep in mud, I am absolutely certain" (I, 8). Further, the pavements in Bath are not all that Mary believes them to be. For centuries, British roads had been built at great expense using large paving stones that were soon dislodged or broken by the pressure of the car-riages that passed over them. In *Northanger Abbey*, for example, Catherine and Isabella are prevented from crossing the street in Bath "by the approach of a gig, driven along on bad pavement by a most knowing-looking coachman" (I, 7). Yet the situation was about to improve dramatically, for as Austen wrote *Persuasion*, John Loudon McAdam (1756–1836) began to revolu-tionize the construction of British roads by using smaller stones on the road surface, a method that pro-duced a much stronger and smoother road, and that used the weight of the carriages to consolidate—rather than destroy—the road surface, as McAdam docu-mented in works such as *Remarks on the Present System of Road-Making* (1816) and *Practical Essay on the Scientific Repair and Preservation of Roads* (1819).

3 As always, Mary's conversation bristles with contra-dictions and a painful lack of self-awareness. She has just condemned Mrs. Harville as "an odd mother" for leaving her children at Uppercross over the Christmas holidays, yet she herself is happy to imagine parting with her own children "for a month or six weeks" while she enjoys a trip to Bath.

be a great deal too happy to care for Uppercross, which, as you well know, affords little to write about. We have had a very dull Christmas; Mr. and Mrs. Musgrove have not had one dinner-party all the holidays. I do not reckon the Hay-ters as any body. The holidays, however, are over at last: I be-lieve no children ever had such long ones. I am sure I had not. The house was cleared yesterday, except of the little Harvilles; but you will be surprised to hear that they have never gone home. Mrs. Harville must be an odd mother to part with them so long. I do not understand it. They are not at all nice children, in my opinion; but Mrs. Musgrove seems to like them quite as well, if not better, than her grand-children. What dreadful weather we have had! It may not be felt in Bath, with your nice pavements; but in the country it is of some consequence.[2] I have not had a creature call on me since the second week in January, except Charles Hayter, who has been calling much oftener than was welcome. Be-tween ourselves, I think it a great pity Henrietta did not re-main at Lyme as long as Louisa; it would have kept her a little out of his way. The carriage is gone to-day, to bring Louisa and the Harvilles to-morrow. We are not asked to dine with them, however, till the day after, Mrs. Musgrove is so afraid of her being fatigued by the journey, which is not very likely, considering the care that will be taken of her; and it would be much more convenient to me to dine there to-morrow. I am glad you find Mr. Elliot so agreeable, and wish I could be ac-quainted with him too; but I have my usual luck, I am always out of the way when any thing desirable is going on; always the last of my family to be noticed. What an immense time Mrs. Clay has been staying with Elizabeth! Does she never mean to go away? But perhaps if she were to leave the room vacant we might not be invited. Let me know what you think of this. I do not expect my children to be asked, you know. I can leave them at the Great House very well, for a month or six weeks.[3] I have this moment heard that the Crofts are going to Bath almost immediately; they think the admiral gouty.[4] Charles heard it quite by chance: they have not had the civility to give me any notice, or offer to take any thing. I do not think they improve at all as neighbours. We see nothing of them, and this is really an instance of gross inattention. Charles joins me in love, and every thing proper. Yours, affectionately,

"Mary M———."

"I am sorry to say that I am very far from well; and Jemima has just told me that the butcher says there is a bad sore-throat very much about. I dare say I shall catch it; and my sore-throats, you know, are always worse than anybody's."

So ended the first part, which had been afterwards put into an envelop, containing nearly as much more.

"I kept my letter open, that I might send you word how Louisa bore her journey, and now I am extremely glad I did, having a great deal to add. In the first place, I had a note from Mrs. Croft yesterday, offering to convey any thing to you; a very kind, friendly note indeed, addressed to me, just as it ought; I shall therefore be able to make my letter as long as I like. The admiral does not seem very ill, and I sincerely hope Bath will do him all the good he wants. I shall be truly glad to have them back again. Our neighbourhood cannot spare such a pleasant family. But now for Louisa. I have something to communicate that will astonish you not a little. She and the Harvilles came on Tuesday very safely, and in the evening we went to ask her how she did, when we were rather surprised not to find Captain Benwick of the party, for he had been invited as well as the Harvilles; and what do you think was the reason? Neither more nor less than his being in love with Louisa, and not choosing to venture to Uppercross till he had had an answer from Mr. Musgrove; for it was all settled between him and her before she came away, and he had written to her father by Captain Harville. True, upon my

4 In modern medicine, "gout" is a form of arthritis characterized by deposits of urates in and around the joints, and especially in the feet. "Excess and idleness" were long thought to be "the true sources from whence it originally sprung, and all who would avoid it must be *active* and *temperate*." William Buchan provides a vivid outline of the symptoms and onset of the disease: "a fit of the gout is generally preceded by indigestion, drowsiness, belching of wind, a slight head-ach, sickness, and sometimes vomiting. . . . The regular gout generally makes its attack in the spring, or beginning of winter, and in the following manner: About two or three in the morning the patient is seized with a pain in his great toe, sometimes in the heel, and at other times in the ancle, or calf of the leg. This pain is accompanied with a sensation as if cold water were poured upon the part, which is succeeded by a shivering, with some degree of fever. Afterwards the pain increases, and fixing among the small bones of the foot, the patient feels all the different kinds of torture, as if the part were stretched, burnt, squeezed, gnawed, or torn in pieces." Unfortunately, Buchan adds, "there are no medicines yet known that will cure the gout," but he does have one strong recommendation: "Such as can afford to go to Bath, will find great benefit from bathing and drinking the water. It both promotes digestion, and invigorates the habit." In Tobias Smollett's *Humphry Clinker,* the cantankerous Matthew Bramble arrives in Bath and immediately declares himself "invested with the gout in his right foot" (Buchan, 264–265, 268; Smollett, *Humphry Clinker,* 29).

honour. Are not you astonished? I shall be surprised at least if you ever received a hint of it, for I never did. Mrs. Musgrove protests solemnly that she knew nothing of the matter. We are all very well pleased, however; for though it is not equal to her marrying Captain Wentworth, it is infinitely better than Charles Hayter; and Mr. Musgrove has written his consent, and Captain Benwick is expected to-day. Mrs. Harville says her husband feels a good deal on his poor sister's account; but, however, Louisa is a great favourite with both. Indeed Mrs. Harville and I quite agree that we love her the better for having nursed her. Charles wonders what Captain Wentworth will say; but if you remember, I never thought him attached to Louisa; I never could see any thing of it. And this is the end, you see, of Captain Benwick's being supposed to be an admirer of yours. How Charles could take such a thing into his head was always incomprehensible to me. I hope he will be more agreeable now. Certainly not a great match for Louisa Musgrove; but a million times better than marrying among the Hayters."

Mary need not have feared her sister's being in any degree prepared for the news. She had never in her life been more astonished. Captain Benwick and Louisa Musgrove! It was almost too wonderful for belief; and it was with the greatest effort that she could remain in the room, preserve an air of calmness, and answer the common questions of the moment. Happily for her, they were not many. Sir Walter wanted to know whether the Crofts travelled with four horses, and whether they were likely to be situated in such a part of Bath as it might suit Miss Elliot and himself to visit in; but had little curiosity beyond.

"How is Mary?" said Elizabeth; and without waiting for an answer, "And pray what brings the Crofts to Bath?"

"They come on the Admiral's account. He is thought to be gouty."

"Gout and decrepitude!" said Sir Walter. "Poor old gentleman."

"Have they any acquaintance here?" asked Elizabeth.

"I do not know; but I can hardly suppose that, at Admiral Croft's time of life, and in his profession, he should not have many acquaintance in such a place as this."

"I suspect," said Sir Walter coolly, "that Admiral Croft will be best known in Bath as the renter of Kellynch-hall. Elizabeth, may we venture to present him and his wife in Laura-place?"

"Oh! no, I think not. Situated as we are with Lady Dalrymple, cousins, we ought to be very careful not to embarrass her with acquaintance she might not approve. If we were not related, it would not signify; but as cousins, she would feel scrupulous as to any proposal of ours. We had better leave the Crofts to find their own level. There are several odd-looking men walking about here, who, I am told, are sailors. The Crofts will associate with them!"

This was Sir Walter and Elizabeth's share of interest in the letter; when Mrs. Clay had paid her tribute of more decent attention, in an enquiry after Mrs. Charles Musgrove, and her fine little boys, Anne was at liberty.

In her own room she tried to comprehend it. Well might Charles wonder how Captain Wentworth would feel! Perhaps he had quitted the field, had given Louisa up, had ceased to love, had found he did not love her. She could not endure the idea of treachery or levity, or

The Junction of Milsom Street and Bond Street with Portraits of Bath Swells, as drawn and engraved by Robert Cruikshank (1789–1856), 1825. A "swell" was a person dressed in the height of fashion.

any thing akin to ill-usage between him and his friend. She could not endure that such a friendship as theirs should be severed unfairly.

Captain Benwick and Louisa Musgrove! The high-spirited, joyous talking Louisa Musgrove, and the dejected, thinking, feeling, reading Captain Benwick, seemed each of them every thing that would not suit the other. Their minds most dissimilar! Where could have been the attraction? The answer soon presented itself. It had been in situation. They had been thrown together several weeks; they had been living in the same small family party; since Henrietta's coming away, they must have been depending almost entirely on each other, and Louisa, just recovering from illness, had been in an interesting state, and Captain Benwick was not inconsolable. That was a point which Anne had not been able to avoid suspecting before; and instead of drawing the same conclusion as Mary, from the present course of events, they served only to confirm the idea of his having felt some dawning of tenderness toward herself. She did not mean, however, to derive much more from it to gratify her vanity, than Mary might have allowed. She was persuaded that any tolerably pleasing young woman who had listened and seemed to feel for him, would have received the same compliment. He had an affectionate heart. He must love somebody.

She saw no reason against their being happy. Louisa had fine naval fervour to begin with, and they would soon grow more alike. He would gain cheerfulness, and she would learn to be an enthusiast for Scott and Lord Byron; nay, that was probably learnt already; of course they had fallen in love over poetry. The idea of Louisa Musgrove turned into a person of literary taste, and sentimental reflection, was amusing, but she had no doubt of its being so. The day at Lyme, the fall from the Cobb, might influence her health, her nerves, her courage, her character to the end of her life, as thoroughly as it appeared to have influenced her fate.

The conclusion of the whole was, that if the woman who had been sensible of[5] Captain Wentworth's merits could be allowed to prefer another man, there was nothing in the engagement to excite lasting wonder; and if Captain Wentworth lost no friend by it, certainly nothing to be regretted. No, it was not regret which made Anne's

In earnest contemplation of some print.

Charles Edmund Brock, Illustrations for *Persuasion,* 1898. Anne approaches Admiral Croft as he stares through the printshop window.

6 Gay Street runs parallel to Milsom Street and links Queen Square with the Circus. It was a fashionable enough location to impress Sir Walter, but not so far up the town as to challenge his own address in Camden Place. When house-hunting in Bath in 1801, Austen described Gay Street as "too high, except only the lower house on the left hand side as you ascend," an observation in which she seems to refer both to the high rents along the street and to its elevation, which would have put significant physical strain on her aging parents. Tobias Smollett describes Gay Street as "so difficult, steep, and slippery, that, in wet weather, it must be exceedingly dangerous, both for those that ride in carriages, and those that walk a-foot" (Austen, *Letters,* 67; Smollett, *Humphry Clinker,* 35).

After the death of her father in 1805, Austen, her mother, and Cassandra lived briefly at number 25 Gay Street.

7 Milsom Street runs from George Street down to where it connects with both New and Old Bond Street. Pierce Egan described it as "the very magnet of Bath, and if there is any company or *movement* in the City, *Milsom-Street* is the *pulse* of it." In the height of the season, it is "the promenade of the gentlemen, and the *shopping* of the ladies." Until the "hour of dinner-time . . . the familiar *nod,* and the *'how do you do?'* are repeated fifty times." The street itself, "from its ascent, is elegant and imposing," and "all is bustle and gaiety: numerous dashing equipages passing and repassing, others gracing the doors of the tradesmen; sprinkled here and there with the invalids in the comfortable sedans and easy two-wheeled carriages, all anxious to participate in this active part of Bath" (Egan, 140, 68–69).

Anne's walk from "the lower part of the town" through Milsom Street and then up to Camden Place is a steep one, and it indicates that, after several years in which she appeared "faded and thin," her vitality is now returning.

8 A "cockleshell" is a light, flimsy boat. Compare Maria Edgeworth in *Patronage,* where Captain Hungerford writes home immediately after a battle at sea with the French: "Dear mother—English victorious—of course. . . . In the cockleshell I have—could do noth-

heart beat in spite of herself, and brought the colour into her cheeks when she thought of Captain Wentworth unshackled and free. She had some feelings which she was ashamed to investigate. They were too much like joy, senseless joy!

She longed to see the Crofts, but when the meeting took place, it was evident that no rumour of the news had yet reached them. The visit of ceremony was paid and returned, and Louisa Musgrove was mentioned, and Captain Benwick too, without even half a smile.

The Crofts had placed themselves in lodgings in Gay-street,[6] perfectly to Sir Walter's satisfaction. He was not at all ashamed of the acquaintance, and did, in fact, think and talk a great deal more about the Admiral, than the Admiral ever thought or talked about him.

The Crofts knew quite as many people in Bath as they wished for, and considered their intercourse with the Elliots as a mere matter of form, and not in the least likely to afford them any pleasure. They brought with them their country habit of being almost always together. He was ordered to walk, to keep off the gout, and Mrs. Croft seemed to go shares with him in every thing, and to walk for her life, to do him good. Anne saw them wherever she went. Lady Russell took her out in her carriage almost every morning, and she never failed to think of them, and never failed to see them. Knowing their feelings as she did, it was a most attractive picture of happiness to her. She always watched them as long as she could; delighted to fancy she understood what they might be talking of, as they walked along in happy independence, or equally delighted to see the Admiral's hearty shake of the hand when he encountered an old friend, and observe their eagerness of conversation when occasionally forming into a little knot of the navy, Mrs. Croft looking as intelligent and keen as any of the officers around her.

Anne was too much engaged with Lady Russell to be often walking herself, but it so happened that one morning, about a week or ten days after the Crofts' arrival, it suited her best to leave her friend, or her friend's carriage, in the lower part of the town, and return alone to Camden-place; and in walking up Milsom-street,[7] she had the good fortune to meet with the Admiral. He was standing by himself, at a printshop window, with his hands behind him, in earnest contemplation of some print, and she not only might have passed him unseen, but was obliged to touch as well as address him before she could catch his notice. When he did perceive and acknowledge her, however, it was done with all his usual frankness and good humour. "Ha! is it you? Thank you, thank you. This is treating me like a friend. Here I am, you see, staring at a picture. I can never get by this shop without stopping. But what a thing here is, by way of a boat. Do look at it. Did you ever see the like? What queer fellows your fine painters must be, to think that any body would venture their lives in such a shapeless old cockleshell[8] as that. And yet, here are two gentlemen stuck up in it mightily at their ease, and looking about them at the rocks and mountains, as if they were not to be upset the next moment, which they certainly must be. I wonder where that boat was built!" (laughing heartily) "I would not venture over a horsepond[9] in it. Well," (turning away) "now, where are you bound? Can I go any where for you, or with you? Can I be of any use?"

"None, I thank you, unless you will give me the pleasure of your company the little way our road lies together. I am going home."

"That I will, with all my heart, and farther too. Yes, yes, we will have a snug walk together; and I have something to tell you as we go along. There, take my arm; that's right; I do not feel comfortable if I have not a woman there. Lord! what a boat it is!" taking a last look at the picture, as they began to be in motion.

"Did you say that you had something to tell me, sir?"

"Yes, I have. Presently. But here comes a friend, Captain Brigden; I shall only say, 'How d'ye do,' as we pass, however. I shall not stop. 'How d'ye do.' Brigden stares to see anybody with me but my wife. She, poor soul, is tied by the leg. She has a blister on one of her heels, as large as a three shilling piece.[10] If you look across the street, you will see Admiral Brand coming down and his brother. Shabby fellows, both of them! I am glad they are not on this side of the way. Sophy cannot bear them. They played me a pitiful trick once—got away some of my best men.[11] I will tell you the whole story another time. There comes old Sir Archibald Drew and his grandson. Look, he sees us; he kisses his hand to you; he takes you for my wife. Ah! the peace has come too soon for that younker.[12] Poor old Sir Archibald!

ing worth mentioning—but am promised a ship soon" (Edgeworth, *Works,* VI, 173).

9 The picture that Admiral Croft is examining has not been conclusively identified, but it may be that he is "interpreting in his own fashion a painting such as Turner's famous sea-piece *Shipwreck* of 1805 . . . from which prints made by the engraver Charles Turner were issued in 1807," as Peter Sabor conjectures (Sabor, "'Staring in Astonishment': Portraits and Prints in *Persuasion,"* in *Jane Austen's Business,* ed. Juliet McMaster and Bruce Stovel [London: Macmillan, 1996], 24–25). A "horsepond" was "a pond for watering and washing horses," but it was also "proverbial as a ducking-place for obnoxious persons" *(OED).*

10 Technically speaking, the "three shilling piece" was a silver token, not a coin. It was only produced between 1811 and 1816 as the government responded to wartime shortages of small change and worked out the creation of a new silver coinage (eventually introduced early in 1817). The three-shilling piece was just under an inch and a half in diameter, so poor Mrs. Croft has a dreadfully large blister, even if her husband is exaggerating a little in his description of it. Though it is plain that the admiral and Mrs. Croft are deeply in love, Austen makes them both remarkably *un*romantic figures, as they hobble about Bath, he with the gout and she with a painful blister.

11 The "pitiful trick" played by Admiral Brand on Admiral Croft may well have involved what was known as a "press-gang," a detachment of men under the command of an officer who were empowered to round up men and force them into military service. Civilians were usually the target of these raids, but in this instance Admiral Brand seems to have "pressed" men from a fellow officer. The practice was widespread and brutal. In 1803, the teenaged Thomas De Quincey (1785–1859) stood in a crowd that watched a press-gang make its way toward the docks after a successful sweep through the streets of Liverpool. Among "their booty" was a man "who hid his face to conceal his emotions: his two sisters stood on the pier among the crowd—weeping and telling his story to the spectators. . . .

On this general tribute of sympathy and affection, the poor fellow, who had hitherto hid his face to stifle or conceal his grief, could bear it no longer; but, sobbing aloud, lifted up his eyes and fixed them with such mingling expressions of agony—gratitude—mournful remembrance on his friends—relations—and his dear countrymen (whom very likely he was now gazing at for the last time) as roused indignation against the pressers and pity for the pressed in every bosom." In Maria Edgeworth's *Patronage,* Alfred explains to Caroline that the wife of his friend O'Brien has just been to see him: "She was in the greatest distress about her husband; he had, she said, in going to see her, been seized by a press gang, and put on board a tender now on the Thames. Moved by the poor Irish woman's agony of grief, and helpless state, I went to Greenwich where the tender was lying, to speak to the Captain, and to offer what money might be necessary to obtain O'Brien's release" (*The Works of Thomas De Quincey: Writings, 1799–1820,* ed. Barry Symonds [London: Pickering and Chatto, 2000], 25–26; Edgeworth, *Works,* VI, 237).

12 The "peace has come too soon" for Sir Archibald's grandson because much of the navy has been stood down, and there are now no further opportunities for prize money. A "younker" is "a boy or junior seaman on board ship" (*OED*).

How do you like Bath, Miss Elliot? It suits us very well. We are always meeting with some old friend or other; the streets full of them every morning; sure to have plenty of chat; and then we get away from them all, and shut ourselves into our lodgings, and draw in our chairs, and are as snug as if we were at Kellynch, ay, or as we used to be even at North Yarmouth and Deal. We do not like our lodgings here the worse, I can tell you, for putting us in mind of those we first had at North Yarmouth. The wind blows through one of the cupboards just in the same way."

When they were got a little farther, Anne ventured to press again for what he had to communicate. She had hoped, when clear of Milsom-street, to have her curiosity gratified; but she was still obliged to wait, for the Admiral had made up his mind not to begin,

Jack in the Bilboes, engraved by William Ward (1766–1826), after George Morland (1763–1804), circa 1790. In this picture, a press gang abducts a waterman, while his two upper-class passengers watch in horror. Perhaps Admiral Brand "got away" some of Admiral Croft's best men using similarly brutal tactics. A bilbo is "a long iron bar, furnished with sliding shackles to confine the ankles of prisoners, and a lock by which to fix one end of the bar to the floor or ground" (*OED*).

till they had gained the greater space and quiet of Belmont,[13] and as she was not really Mrs. Croft, she must let him have his own way. As soon as they were fairly ascending Belmont, he began,

"Well, now you shall hear something that will surprise you. But first of all, you must tell me the name of the young lady I am going to talk about. That young lady, you know, that we have all been so concerned for. The Miss Musgrove, that all this has been happening to. Her christian name—I always forget her christian name."

Anne had been ashamed to appear to comprehend so soon as she really did; but now she could safely suggest the name of "Louisa."

"Ay, ay, Miss Louisa Musgrove, that is the name. I wish young ladies had not such a number of fine christian names. I should never be out, if they were all Sophys, or something of that sort. Well, this Miss Louisa, we all thought, you know, was to marry Frederick. He was courting her week after week. The only wonder was, what they could be waiting for, till the business at Lyme came; then, indeed, it was clear enough that they must wait till her brain was set to right. But even then, there was something odd in their way of going on. Instead of staying at Lyme, he went off to Plymouth, and then he went off to see Edward. When we came back from Minehead,[14] he was gone down to Edward's, and there he has been ever since. We have seen nothing of him since November. Even Sophy could not understand it. But now, the matter has taken the strangest turn of all; for this young lady, this same Miss Musgrove, instead of being to marry Frederick, is to marry James Benwick. You know James Benwick."

"A little. I am a little acquainted with Captain Benwick."

"Well, she is to marry him. Nay, most likely they are married already, for I do not know what they should wait for."

"I thought Captain Benwick a very pleasing young man," said Anne, "and I understand that he bears an excellent character."

"Oh! yes, yes, there is not a word to be said against James Benwick. He is only a commander, it is true, made[15] last summer, and these are bad times for getting on, but he has not another fault that I know of. An excellent, good-hearted fellow, I assure you, a very active, zealous officer too, which is more than you would think for, perhaps, for that soft sort of manner does not do him justice."

13 Belmont is the steep stretch of road leading up Lansdown Hill to Camden Place.

14 Minehead is a port in West Somerset on the southern shore of the Bristol Channel.

15 "Made" is "promoted."

"Indeed you are mistaken there, sir. I should never augur want of spirit from Captain Benwick's manners. I thought them particularly pleasing, and I will answer for it they would generally please."

"Well, well, ladies are the best judges; but James Benwick is rather too piano[16] for me, and though very likely it is all our partiality, Sophy and I cannot help thinking Frederick's manners better than his. There is something about Frederick more to our taste."

Anne was caught. She had only meant to oppose the too-common idea of spirit and gentleness being incompatible with each other, not at all to represent Captain Benwick's manners as the very best that could possibly be, and, after a little hesitation, she was beginning to say, "I was not entering into any comparison of the two friends," but the Admiral interrupted her with,

"And the thing is certainly true. It is not a mere bit of gossip. We have it from Frederick himself. His sister had a letter from him yesterday, in which he tells us of it, and he had just had it in a letter from Harville, written upon the spot, from Uppercross. I fancy they are all at Uppercross."

This was an opportunity which Anne could not resist; she said, therefore, "I hope, Admiral, I hope there is nothing in the style of Captain Wentworth's letter to make you and Mrs. Croft particularly uneasy. It did certainly seem, last autumn, as if there were an attachment between him and Louisa Musgrove; but I hope it may be understood to have worn out on each side equally, and without violence. I hope his letter does not breathe the spirit of an ill-used man."

"Not at all, not at all; there is not an oath or a murmur from beginning to end."

Anne looked down to hide her smile.

"No, no; Frederick is not a man to whine and complain; he has too much spirit for that. If the girl likes another man better, it is very fit she should have him."

"Certainly. But what I mean is, that I hope there is nothing in Captain Wentworth's manner of writing to make you suppose he thinks himself ill-used by his friend, which might appear, you know, without its being absolutely said. I should be very sorry that such a friendship as has subsisted between him and Captain Benwick should be destroyed, or even wounded, by a circumstance of this sort."

"Yes, yes, I understand you. But there is nothing at all of that nature in the letter. He does not give the least fling at Benwick; does not so much as say, 'I wonder at it, I have a reason of my own for wondering at it.' No, you would not guess, from his way of writing, that he had ever thought of this Miss (what's her name?) for himself. He very handsomely hopes they will be happy together, and there is nothing very unforgiving in that, I think."

Anne did not receive the perfect conviction which the Admiral meant to convey, but it would have been useless to press the enquiry farther. She, therefore, satisfied herself with common-place remarks, or quiet attention, and the Admiral had it all his own way.

"Poor Frederick!" said he at last. "Now he must begin all over again with somebody else. I think we must get him to Bath. Sophy must write, and beg him to come to Bath. Here are pretty girls enough, I am sure. It would be of no use to go to Uppercross again, for that other Miss Musgrove, I find, is bespoke by[17] her cousin, the young parson. Do not you think, Miss Elliot, we had better try to get him to Bath?"

17 "Bespoke by" means "engaged to."

7

1 Molland's was a fashionable sweetshop at 2 Milsom Street.

2 A "barouche" was a luxury vehicle that featured a four-wheeled carriage with a driver's seat high in front, two double seats inside facing each other, and a folding top over the back seat. The grandeur of the vehicle suits Lady Dalrymple, but when Austen herself rode in one, she seemed decidedly uncomfortable. "I could not but feel that I had naturally small right to be parading about London in a Barouche," she told Cassandra in May 1813 (Austen, *Letters,* 214).

WHILE ADMIRAL CROFT WAS TAKING this walk with Anne, and expressing his wish of getting Captain Wentworth to Bath, Captain Wentworth was already on his way thither. Before Mrs. Croft had written, he was arrived; and the very next time Anne walked out, she saw him.

Mr. Elliot was attending his two cousins and Mrs. Clay. They were in Milsom-street. It began to rain, not much, but enough to make shelter desirable for women, and quite enough to make it very desirable for Miss Elliot to have the advantage of being conveyed home in Lady Dalrymple's carriage, which was seen waiting at a little distance; she, Anne, and Mrs. Clay, therefore, turned into Molland's,[1] while Mr. Elliot stepped to Lady Dalrymple, to request her assistance. He soon joined them again, successful, of course; Lady Dalrymple would be most happy to take them home, and would call for them in a few minutes.

Her ladyship's carriage was a barouche,[2] and did not hold more than four with any comfort. Miss Carteret was with her mother; consequently it was not reasonable to expect accommodation for all the three Camden-place ladies. There could be no doubt as to Miss Elliot. Whoever suffered inconvenience, she must suffer none, but it occupied a little time to settle the point of civility between the other two. The rain was a mere trifle, and Anne was most sincere in preferring a walk with Mr. Elliot. But the rain was also a mere trifle to Mrs. Clay; she would hardly allow it even to drop at all, and her boots were so thick! much thicker than Miss Anne's; and, in short, her civility rendered her quite as anxious to be left to walk with Mr. Elliot, as Anne could be, and it was discussed between them with a generosity so polite and so determined, that the others were obliged to settle it for them; Miss Elliot maintaining that Mrs. Clay had a little cold already, and Mr. Elliot deciding on appeal, that his cousin Anne's boots were rather the thickest.

It was fixed accordingly that Mrs. Clay should be of the party in the carriage; and they had just reached this point when Anne, as she sat near the window, descried, most decidedly and distinctly, Captain Wentworth walking down the street.[3]

Her start was perceptible only to herself; but she instantly felt that she was the greatest simpleton in the world, the most unaccountable and absurd! For a few minutes she saw nothing before her. It was all confusion. She was lost; and when she had scolded back her senses, she found the others still waiting for the carriage, and Mr. Elliot (always obliging) just setting off for Union-street[4] on a commission of Mrs. Clay's.

3 Wentworth is free to move where he chooses, while Anne must sit passively in a shop window. The rituals of courtship play out in much the same way throughout Austen. Men command. Women wait. Men inherit. Women wait. Men enjoy. Women wait. In this scene, "as at Lyme, Anne has to allow arrangements to be made for her, this time by William Elliot," Roger Sales remarks. "The severe restrictions on her movement are in marked contrast to Wentworth's ability to please himself. . . . There is no overt comment about the gendered nature of transport and movement. The scene is graphic enough nevertheless: Anne has to wait in the shop like a commodity while . . . Wentworth is unexpectedly walking in the street outside" (Sales, 192–193).

4 Union Street lies below Milsom Street and is reached by passing through New Bond Street and Burton Street.

A barouche from 1825. The vehicle was a status symbol. In *Sense and Sensibility,* Edward Ferrars's sister longs "to see him distinguished . . . but in the mean while . . . it would have quieted her ambition to see him driving a barouche" (I, 3).

5 "Know" is used here in the sense of "recognize" or "acknowledge."

She now felt a great inclination to go to the outer door; she wanted to see if it rained. Why was she to suspect herself of another motive? Captain Wentworth must be out of sight. She left her seat, she would go, one half of her should not be always so much wiser than the other half, or always suspecting the other of being worse than it was. She would see if it rained. She was sent back, however, in a moment by the entrance of Captain Wentworth himself, among a party of gentlemen and ladies, evidently his acquaintance, and whom he must have joined a little below Milsom-street. He was more obviously struck and confused by the sight of her, than she had ever observed before; he looked quite red. For the first time, since their renewed acquaintance, she felt that she was betraying the least sensibility of the two. She had the advantage of him, in the preparation of the last few moments. All the overpowering, blinding, bewildering, first effects of strong surprise were over with her. Still, however, she had enough to feel! It was agitation, pain, pleasure, a something between delight and misery.

He spoke to her, and then turned away. The character of his manner was embarrassment. She could not have called it either cold or friendly, or any thing so certainly as embarrassed.

After a short interval, however, he came towards her and spoke again. Mutual enquiries on common subjects passed; neither of them, probably, much the wiser for what they heard, and Anne continuing fully sensible of his being less at ease than formerly. They had, by dint of being so very much together, got to speak to each other with a considerable portion of apparent indifference and calmness; but he could not do it now. Time had changed him, or Louisa had changed him. There was consciousness of some sort or other. He looked very well, not as if he had been suffering in health or spirits, and he talked of Uppercross, of the Musgroves, nay, even of Louisa, and had even a momentary look of his own arch significance as he named her; but yet it was Captain Wentworth not comfortable, not easy, not able to feign that he was.

It did not surprise, but it grieved Anne to observe that Elizabeth would not know[5] him. She saw that he saw Elizabeth, that Elizabeth saw him, that there was complete internal recognition on each side; she was convinced that he was ready to be acknowledged as an acquaintance, expecting it, and she had the pain of seeing her sister turn away with unalterable coldness.

Lady Dalrymple's carriage, for which Miss Elliot was growing very impatient, now drew up; the servant came in to announce it. It was beginning to rain again, and altogether there was a delay, and a bustle, and a talking, which must make all the little crowd in the shop understand that Lady Dalrymple was calling to convey Miss Elliot. At last Miss Elliot and her friend, unattended but by the servant, (for there was no cousin returned)[6] were walking off; and Captain Wentworth, watching them, turned again to Anne, and by manner, rather than words, was offering his services to her.

"I am much obliged to you," was her answer, "but I am not going with them. The carriage would not accommodate so many. I walk. I prefer walking."

"But it rains."

"Oh! very little. Nothing that I regard."

After a moment's pause he said, "Though I came only yesterday, I have equipped myself properly for Bath already, you see," (pointing to a new umbrella)[7] "I wish you would make use of it, if you are determined to walk; though, I think, it would be more prudent to let me get you a chair."[8]

She was very much obliged to him, but declined it all, repeating her conviction, that the rain would come to nothing at present, and adding, "I am only waiting for Mr. Elliot. He will be here in a moment, I am sure."

She had hardly spoken the words, when Mr. Elliot walked in. Captain Wentworth recollected him perfectly. There was no difference between him and the man who had stood on the steps at Lyme, admiring Anne as she passed, except in the air and look and manner of the privileged relation and friend. He came in with eagerness, appeared to see and think only of her, apologised for his stay, was grieved to have kept her waiting, and anxious to get her away without further loss of time, and before the rain increased; and in another

6 Several commentators have wondered: why does Mrs. Clay send Mr. Elliot to Union Street, what does he do for her there, and what does this tell us about their relationship? Austen does not explain it.

7 In Tobias Smollett's *Humphry Clinker,* Matthew Bramble bemoans the fact that there is "almost perpetual" rain in Bath. A number of umbrella-makers set up shop in the city in Austen's day, including Mr. Payne at "10, Trim Street," Mr. Scovell in "Wade's-passage," and Mr. Turnbull at "1, New Bond-street-buildings" (Smollett, *Humphry Clinker,* 35; *Gye's Bath Directory, Corrected to January 1819* [Bath: Gye, 1819], 84, 90, 98).

8 Hired "sedan chairs" were covered, portable chairs mounted on four poles, with side windows, and a hinged doorway. They seated one person and were carried by two servants.

View along Pulteney Street, by John Claude Nattes.
Austen and her parents went house hunting in Bath
in January 1801. There were three areas of the city in
which they were particularly interested: "Westgate
Buildings, Charles Street, & some of the short streets
leading from Laura Place or Pulteney St." (Austen,
Letters, 66–67).

moment they walked off together, her arm under his, a gentle and
embarrassed glance, and a "good morning to you," being all that she
had time for, as she passed away.

As soon as they were out of sight, the ladies of Captain Wentworth's party began talking of them.

"Mr. Elliot does not dislike his cousin, I fancy?"

"Oh! no, that is clear enough. One can guess what will happen
there. He is always with them; half lives in the family, I believe. What
a very good-looking man!"

"Yes, and Miss Atkinson, who dined with him once at the Wallises,
says he is the most agreeable man she ever was in company with."

"She is pretty, I think; Anne Elliot; very pretty, when one comes to
look at her. It is not the fashion to say so, but I confess I admire her
more than her sister."

"Oh! so do I."

"And so do I. No comparison. But the men are all wild after Miss
Elliot. Anne is too delicate for them."

Anne would have been particularly obliged to her cousin, if he
would have walked by her side all the way to Camden-place, without
saying a word. She had never found it so difficult to listen to him,
though nothing could exceed his solicitude and care, and though his
subjects were principally such as were wont to be always interesting—praise, warm, just, and discriminating, of Lady Russell, and in-
sinuations highly rational against Mrs. Clay. But just now she could
think only of Captain Wentworth. She could not understand his
present feelings, whether he were really suffering much from disappointment or not; and till that point were settled, she could not be
quite herself.

She hoped to be wise and reasonable in time; but alas! alas! she
must confess to herself that she was not wise yet.

Another circumstance very essential for her to know, was how
long he meant to be in Bath; he had not mentioned it, or she could
not recollect it. He might be only passing through. But it was more
probable that he should be come to stay. In that case, so liable as
every body was to meet every body in Bath, Lady Russell would in

all likelihood see him somewhere.—Would she recollect him? How would it all be?

She had already been obliged to tell Lady Russell that Louisa Musgrove was to marry Captain Benwick. It had cost her something to encounter Lady Russell's surprise; and now, if she were by any chance to be thrown into company with Captain Wentworth, her imperfect knowledge of the matter might add another shade of prejudice against him.

The following morning Anne was out with her friend, and for the first hour, in an incessant and fearful sort of watch for him in vain; but at last, in returning down Pulteney-street,[9] she distinguished him on the right hand pavement at such a distance as to have him in view the greater part of the street. There were many other men about him, many groups walking the same way, but there was no mistaking him. She looked instinctively at Lady Russell; but not from any mad idea of her recognising him so soon as she did herself. No, it was not to be supposed that Lady Russell would perceive him till they were nearly opposite. She looked at her however, from time to time, anxiously; and when the moment approached which must point him out, though not daring to look again (for her own countenance she knew was unfit to be seen), she was yet perfectly conscious of Lady Russell's eyes being turned exactly in the direction for him, of her being in short intently observing him. She could thoroughly comprehend the sort of fascination he must possess over Lady Russell's mind, the difficulty it must be for her to withdraw her eyes, the astonishment she must be feeling that eight or nine years should have passed over him, and in foreign climes and in active service too, without robbing him of one personal grace!

At last, Lady Russell drew back her head.—"Now, how would she speak of him?"

"You will wonder," said she, "what has been fixing my eye so long; but I was looking after some window-curtains, which Lady Alicia and Mrs. Frankland were telling me of last night. They described the drawing-room window-curtains of one of the houses on this side of the way, and this part of the street, as being the handsomest and best

9 Completed in 1793, "Pulteney Street," or "Great Pulteney Street," is a wide and impressive thoroughfare on the eastern side of Bath. It connects Laura Place with Sydney Place. Enthused John Feltham: "On the farther side of the [River] Avon is a new creation of architectural beauties, which may vie with any thing in the world. Laura-Place and its accompaniments; and Great Pulteney-Street, terminated by Sydney-gardens, present an assemblage of fine buildings, which do honour to the present age" (Feltham, 59). In *Northanger Abbey*, Catherine Morland and the Allens settle "in comfortable lodgings in Pulteney-street" (I, 2).

10 In this exchange between Anne and Lady Russell, "one wonders whom to laugh at most," Andor Gomme remarks, "—Anne for assuming that everyone must see through her own eyes, or Lady Russell for simply not seeing at all." Joseph Duffy concludes that "the smile of 'pity and disdain' which Anne gives immediately afterwards is either for 'her friend or herself.' The reader, caught up in the complex irony which deflates the two figures, feels something of each for both women" (Gomme, 180; Duffy, 286).

11 The "theatre" was the splendid new "Theatre Royal," which opened in October 1805 in Beaufort Square. "The exterior is handsome," Pierce Egan reported; "but its interior is finished in such a high state of excellence, as to vie with any building of a similar description. . . . The decorations are very splendid; and the colouring and gift mouldings executed with much taste and effect" (Egan, 143). The "rooms" were not the "Lower Assembly Rooms," located in Terrace Walk in the southeastern section of the town, but the "New" or "Upper Assembly Rooms," which were completed in 1771, and which lie just to the east of the Circus. Here people gathered for regular evenings of gambling, music, and dancing.

12 The Elliots undoubtedly rejected the Assembly Rooms as "not fashionable enough" because people from much further down the social scale were openly welcomed. In Tobias Smollett's *Humphry Clinker,* Matthew Bramble, so unlike Sir Walter in so many ways, shares with him an adamantine belief in maintaining the distinctions of rank, and he is correspondingly distressed by the broad social interaction he witnesses in the Assembly Rooms. Bramble's nephew Jery Melford explains that in Bath there is a "general mixture of all degrees assembled in our public rooms. . . . This is what my uncle reprobates, as a monstrous jumble of heterogeneous principles; a vile mob of noise and impertinence, without decency or subordination" (Smollett, *Humphry Clinker,* 47).

hung of any in Bath, but could not recollect the exact number, and I have been trying to find out which it could be; but I confess I can see no curtains hereabouts that answer their description."

Anne sighed and blushed and smiled, in pity and disdain, either at her friend or herself.[10]—The part which provoked her most, was that in all this waste of foresight and caution, she should have lost the right moment for seeing whether he saw them.

A day or two passed without producing any thing.—The theatre or the rooms,[11] where he was most likely to be, were not fashionable enough for the Elliots,[12] whose evening amusements were solely in the elegant stupidity of private parties, in which they were getting more and more engaged;[13] and Anne, wearied of such a state of stagnation, sick of knowing nothing, and fancying herself stronger because her strength was not tried, was quite impatient for the concert evening. It was a concert for the benefit of a person patronised by Lady Dalrymple. Of course they must attend. It was really expected to be a good one, and Captain Wentworth was very fond of music. If she could only have a few minutes conversation with him again, she fancied she should be satisfied; and as to the power of addressing

New Theatre Royal, from a copper engraving by an unknown artist, 1807. The theater, located in Beaufort Square, opened in October 1805 with a performance of Shakespeare's *Richard III*.

him she felt all over courage if the opportunity occurred. Elizabeth had turned from him, Lady Russell overlooked him; her nerves were strengthened by these circumstances; she felt that she owed him attention.

She had once partly promised Mrs. Smith to spend the evening with her; but in a short hurried call she excused herself and put it off, with the more decided promise of a longer visit on the morrow. Mrs. Smith gave a most good-humoured acquiescence.

"By all means," said she; "only tell me all about it, when you do come. Who is your party?"

Anne named them all. Mrs. Smith made no reply; but when she was leaving her, said, and with an expression half serious, half arch, "Well, I heartily wish your concert may answer; and do not fail me to-morrow if you can come; for I begin to have a foreboding that I may not have many more visits from you."

Anne was startled and confused, but after standing in a moment's suspense, was obliged, and not sorry to be obliged, to hurry away.

13 Austen herself thought little of private parties in Bath. In May 1801, she complained to Cassandra of "another stupid party last night; perhaps if larger they might be less intolerable, but here there were only just enough to make one card table, with six people to look over, & talk nonsense to each other" (Austen, *Letters,* 85).

The Shipwreck, mezzotint on paper, by Charles Turner (1774–1857), after J. M. W. Turner, 1807. It is not known whether this painting was inspired by an actual shipwreck.

8

1 The octagon room was in the center of the Upper Assembly Rooms. People gathered there before balls, concerts, and parties, for it opened directly onto the building's three main rooms: the ballroom, the card room, and the tea room (which also served as the concert room).

SIR WALTER, HIS TWO DAUGHTERS, and Mrs. Clay, were the earliest of all their party, at the rooms in the evening; and as Lady Dalrymple must be waited for, they took their station by one of the fires in the octagon room.[1] But hardly were they so settled, when the door opened again, and Captain Wentworth walked in alone. Anne was the nearest to him, and making yet a little advance, she instantly spoke. He was preparing only to bow and pass on, but her gentle "How do you do?" brought him out of the straight line to stand near her, and make enquiries in return, in spite of the formidable father and sister in the back ground. Their being in the back ground was a support to Anne; she knew nothing of their looks, and felt equal to every thing which she believed right to be done.

While they were speaking, a whispering between her father and Elizabeth caught her ear. She could not distinguish, but she must guess the subject; and on Captain Wentworth's making a distant bow, she comprehended that her father had judged so well as to give him that simple acknowledgment of acquaintance, and she was just in time by a side glance to see a slight curtsey from Elizabeth herself. This, though late and reluctant and ungracious, was yet better than nothing, and her spirits improved.

After talking however of the weather and Bath and the concert, their conversation began to flag, and so little was said at last, that she was expecting him to go every moment; but he did not; he seemed in no hurry to leave her; and presently with renewed spirit, with a little smile, a little glow, he said,

"I have hardly seen you since our day at Lyme. I am afraid you must have suffered from the shock, and the more from its not overpowering you at the time."

She assured him that she had not.

"It was a frightful hour," said he, "a frightful day!" and he passed his hand across his eyes, as if the remembrance were still too painful; but in a moment half smiling again, added, "The day has produced some effects however—has had some consequences which must be considered as the very reverse of frightful.—When you had the presence of mind to suggest that Benwick would be the properest person to fetch a surgeon, you could have little idea of his being eventually one of those most concerned in her recovery."

"Certainly I could have none. But it appears—I should hope it would be a very happy match. There are on both sides good principles and good temper."

"Yes," said he, looking not exactly forward[2]—"but there I think ends the resemblance. With all my soul I wish them happy, and rejoice over every circumstance in favour of it. They have no difficulties to contend with at home, no opposition, no caprice, no delays.—The Musgroves are behaving like themselves, most honour-

2 "Looking not exactly forward" is "not looking directly at her."

The Concert Room or Tea Room at the New Assembly Rooms, by John Claude Nattes. The New or Upper Assembly Rooms were completed in 1771 and offered regular evening entertainments, including balls and concerts. In *Northanger Abbey*, Catherine Morland arrives in Bath and must soon face "the important evening . . . which was to usher her into the Upper Rooms" (I, 2).

3 "Gratitude" was a loaded word in the heated early nineteenth-century debates about love and gender. In his immensely influential conduct book, *A Father's Legacy to His Daughters* (1774), the physician and writer John Gregory (1724–1773) insisted that what women "commonly called love . . . is rather gratitude," and then detailed the key role it played in the development of a romantic attachment. "As . . . Nature has not given you that unlimited range in your choice which we enjoy," explained Gregory, "she has wisely and benevolently assigned to you a greater flexibility of taste on this subject. Some agreeable qualities recommend a gentleman to your common good liking and friendship. In the course of his acquaintance, he contracts an attachment to you. When you perceive it, it excites your gratitude; this gratitude rises into a preference, and this preference perhaps at last advances to some degree of attachment, especially if it meets with crosses and difficulties; for these, and a state of suspense, are very great incitements to attachment, and are the food of love in both sexes" (Gregory, *A Father's Legacy to His Daughters* [London: Strahan and Cadell, 1774], 80–83).

In expressing gratitude to the hero for his kindness and assistance, and then confessing that these emotions have led to deeper feelings of love for him, heroines in the novels of Austen and many of her female contemporaries follow the path marked out for them by Gregory. At the close of *Pride and Prejudice,* for example, Elizabeth tells Darcy that "her sentiments had undergone so material a change . . . as to make her receive with gratitude and pleasure, his present assurances" (III, 16). Wentworth clearly thinks that the relationship between Benwick and Louisa would be stronger if it had originated in gratitude. But ironically, as Laurence Lerner points out, gratitude is not an emotion at the heart of Wentworth's relationship with Anne. "In Lydia Bennet briefly, in Mary Crawford more thoroughly, and in Marianne with full and passionate intensity," he argues, "we can see the anti-Jane who lived unquelled in the moralist, and tore her books apart: until, in the end, she won her mistress over. For in Jane Austen's last novel, *Persuasion* . . . intensity of feeling moves nearer to the centre of the book's professed values. It is Jane Austen's one romantic novel:

ably and kindly, only anxious with true parental hearts to promote their daughter's comfort. All this is much, very much in favour of their happiness; more than perhaps—"

He stopped. A sudden recollection seemed to occur, and to give him some taste of that emotion which was reddening Anne's cheeks and fixing her eyes on the ground.—After clearing his throat, however, he proceeded thus,

"I confess that I do think there is a disparity, too great a disparity, and in a point no less essential than mind.—I regard Louisa Musgrove as a very amiable, sweet-tempered girl, and not deficient in understanding; but Benwick is something more. He is a clever man, a reading man—and I confess that I do consider his attaching himself to her, with some surprise. Had it been the effect of gratitude,[3] had he learnt to love her, because he believed her to be preferring him, it would have been another thing. But I have no reason to suppose it so. It seems, on the contrary, to have been a perfectly spontaneous, untaught feeling on his side, and this surprises me. A man like him, in his situation![4] With a heart pierced, wounded, almost broken! Fanny Harville was a very superior creature; and his attachment to her was indeed attachment. A man does not recover from such a devotion of the heart to such a woman!—He ought not—he does not."

Either from the consciousness, however, that his friend had recovered, or from some other consciousness, he went no farther; and Anne, who, in spite of the agitated voice in which the latter part had been uttered, and in spite of all the various noises of the room, the almost ceaseless slam of the door, and ceaseless buzz of persons walking through, had distinguished every word, was struck, gratified, confused, and beginning to breathe very quick, and feel an hundred things in a moment. It was impossible for her to enter on such a subject; and yet, after a pause, feeling the necessity of speaking, and having not the smallest wish for a total change, she only deviated so far as to say,

"You were a good while at Lyme, I think?"

"About a fortnight. I could not leave it till Louisa's doing well was quite ascertained. I had been too deeply concerned in the mischief to be soon at peace. It had been my doing—solely mine. She would not have been obstinate if I had not been weak. The country round Lyme is very fine. I walked and rode a great deal; and the more I saw, the more I found to admire."

"I should very much like to see Lyme again," said Anne.

"Indeed! I should not have supposed that you could have found any thing in Lyme to inspire such a feeling. The horror and distress you were involved in—the stretch of mind, the wear of spirits!—I should have thought your last impressions of Lyme must have been strong disgust."

"The last few hours were certainly very painful," replied Anne: "but when pain is over, the remembrance of it often becomes a pleasure. One does not love a place the less for having suffered in it, unless it has been all suffering, nothing but suffering—which was by no

the one book in which love is not the product of gratitude and esteem" (Lerner, *The Truthtellers* [London: Chatto & Windus, 1967], 166).

4 Wentworth refers to the fact that Benwick's fiancée, Fanny Harville, has been dead less than a year.

With all the eagerness compatible with anxious elegance.

Hugh Thomson, Illustrations for *Persuasion*, 1897. Sir Walter and Elizabeth greet Lady Dalrymple and Miss Carteret.

means the case at Lyme. We were only in anxiety and distress during the last two hours; and, previously, there had been a great deal of enjoyment. So much novelty and beauty! I have travelled so little, that every fresh place would be interesting to me—but there is real beauty at Lyme: and in short" (with a faint blush at some recollections) "altogether my impressions of the place are very agreeable."

As she ceased, the entrance door opened again, and the very party appeared for whom they were waiting. "Lady Dalrymple, Lady Dalrymple," was the rejoicing sound; and with all the eagerness compatible with anxious elegance, Sir Walter and his two ladies stepped forward to meet her. Lady Dalrymple and Miss Carteret, escorted by Mr. Elliot and Colonel Wallis, who had happened to arrive nearly at the same instant, advanced into the room. The others joined them, and it was a group in which Anne found herself also necessarily included. She was divided from Captain Wentworth. Their interesting, almost too interesting conversation must be broken up for a time; but slight was the penance compared with the happiness which brought it on! She had learnt, in the last ten minutes, more of his feelings towards Louisa, more of all his feelings, than she dared to think of! and she gave herself up to the demands of the party, to the needful civilities of the moment, with exquisite, though agitated sensations. She was in good humour with all. She had received ideas which disposed her to be courteous and kind to all, and to pity every one, as being less happy than herself.

The delightful emotions were a little subdued, when, on stepping back from the group, to be joined again by Captain Wentworth, she saw that he was gone. She was just in time to see him turn into the concert room. He was gone—he had disappeared: she felt a moment's regret. But "they should meet again. He would look for her—he would find her out long before the evening were over—and at present, perhaps, it was as well to be asunder. She was in need of a little interval for recollection."

Upon Lady Russell's appearance soon afterwards, the whole party was collected, and all that remained, was to marshal themselves, and proceed into the concert room; and be of all the consequence in their

Comforts of Bath, by Thomas Rowlandson, 1798. Rowlandson, a painter and caricaturist, illustrated life in late eighteenth-century Bath in a series of vivid comic images, including this scene of an evening concert.

power, draw as many eyes, excite as many whispers, and disturb as many people as they could.

Very, very happy were both Elizabeth and Anne Elliot as they walked in. Elizabeth, arm in arm with Miss Carteret, and looking on the broad back of the dowager Viscountess Dalrymple before her, had nothing to wish for which did not seem within her reach; and Anne——but it would be an insult to the nature of Anne's felicity, to draw any comparison between it and her sister's; the origin of one all selfish vanity, of the other all generous attachment.

Anne saw nothing, thought nothing of the brilliancy of the room. Her happiness was from within. Her eyes were bright, and her cheeks glowed,—but she knew nothing about it. She was thinking only of the last half hour, and as they passed to their seats, her mind took a hasty range over it. His choice of subjects, his expressions, and still more his manner and look, had been such as she could see in only one light. His opinion of Louisa Musgrove's inferiority, an opinion

5 Anne's cautious but thrilling realization that Wentworth "must love her" connects her with a past that had once—and not too long ago—seemed dead and gone. "*Persuasion* is a book about a longed-for and impossible return," Gillian Beer observes. "It is, in that sense, a ghost story, and Frederick Wentworth a revenant. Like *The Winter's Tale* it is about love restored against all likelihood. It is as if the beloved dead come back. The gap of loss can be closed up, youth and beauty retrieved, dead affection revived. The work is both domestic and uncanny, offering to Anne and the reader at last paradisal relief" (Beer, "Introduction," in Jane Austen, *Persuasion,* ed. Gillian Beer [London: Penguin, 2003], xxix).

6 The "interval" is the "intermission."

7 A knowledge of Italian was an "accomplishment" of many genteel women. Compare *Pride and Prejudice,* where Caroline Bingley insists that "a woman must have a thorough knowledge of music, singing, drawing, dancing, and the modern languages" to deserve to be known as "accomplished." Shortly thereafter, Caroline sits at the piano-forte and plays "some Italian songs" as evidence of her own refinement (I, 8, 10).

8 The "concert bill" was the "program."

which he had seemed solicitous to give, his wonder at Captain Benwick, his feelings as to a first, strong attachment,—sentences begun which he could not finish—his half averted eyes, and more than half expressive glance,—all, all declared that he had a heart returning to her at least; that anger, resentment, avoidance, were no more; and that they were succeeded, not merely by friendship and regard, but by the tenderness of the past; yes, some share of the tenderness of the past. She could not contemplate the change as implying less.— He must love her.[5]

These were thoughts, with their attendant visions, which occupied and flurried her too much to leave her any power of observation; and she passed along the room without having a glimpse of him, without even trying to discern him. When their places were determined on, and they were all properly arranged, she looked round to see if he should happen to be in the same part of the room, but he was not, her eye could not reach him; and the concert being just opening, she must consent for a time to be happy in an humbler way.

The party was divided, and disposed of on two contiguous benches: Anne was among those on the foremost, and Mr. Elliot had manœuvred so well, with the assistance of his friend Colonel Wallis, as to have a seat by her. Miss Elliot, surrounded by her cousins, and the principal object of Colonel Wallis's gallantry, was quite contented.

Anne's mind was in a most favourable state for the entertainment of the evening: it was just occupation enough: she had feelings for the tender, spirits for the gay, attention for the scientific, and patience for the wearisome; and had never liked a concert better, at least during the first act. Towards the close of it, in the interval[6] succeeding an Italian song,[7] she explained the words of the song to Mr. Elliot.—They had a concert bill[8] between them.

"This," said she, "is nearly the sense, or rather the meaning of the words, for certainly the sense of an Italian love-song must not be talked of,—but it is as nearly the meaning as I can give; for I do not pretend to understand the language. I am a very poor Italian scholar."

"Yes, yes, I see you are. I see you know nothing of the matter. You have only knowledge enough of the language, to translate at sight these inverted, transposed, curtailed Italian lines, into clear, comprehensible, elegant English. You need not say anything more of your ignorance.—Here is complete proof."

"I will not oppose such kind politeness; but I should be sorry to be examined by a real proficient."

"I have not had the pleasure of visiting in Camden-place so long," replied he, "without knowing something of Miss Anne Elliot; and I do regard her as one who is too modest, for the world in general to be aware of half her accomplishments, and too highly accomplished for modesty to be natural in any other woman."

"For shame! for shame!—this is too much of flattery. I forget what we are to have next," turning to the bill.

"Perhaps," said Mr. Elliot, speaking low, "I have had a longer acquaintance with your character than you are aware of."

"Indeed!—How so? You can have been acquainted with it only since I came to Bath, excepting as you might hear me previously spoken of in my own family."

"I knew you by report long before you came to Bath. I had heard you described by those who knew you intimately. I have been acquainted with you by character many years. Your person, your disposition, accomplishments, manner—they were all described, they were all present to me."

Mr. Elliot was not disappointed in the interest he hoped to raise. No one can withstand the charm of such a mystery. To have been described long ago to a recent acquaintance, by nameless people, is irresistible; and Anne was all curiosity. She wondered, and questioned him eagerly—but in vain. He delighted in being asked, but he would not tell.

"No, no—some time or other perhaps, but not now. He would mention no names now; but such, he could assure her, had been the fact. He had many years ago received such a description of Miss Anne Elliot, as had inspired him with the highest idea of her merit, and excited the warmest curiosity to know her."

9 Mr. Elliot is diverting Anne with teasing and rumor, but at the same time he has a serious purpose in mind. In breathing his wishes that her "name might never change," he is in effect proposing to her, for if she agreed to become his wife, her last name would remain Elliot. But if Mr. Elliot had hoped to use this subtle profession as a means of gauging Anne's feelings for him, he is disappointed. Anne is not even sure that she has heard his words correctly, and before she has any time to consider them her attention is preoccupied by the conversation between her father and Lady Dalrymple. Had she had the time or inclination to challenge Mr. Elliot, however, the situation would not necessarily be any clearer, for he has cunningly couched his proposal in such a way as to risk little personal injury or insult to his pride, since he might respond by plausibly insisting that—far from a proposal—he had merely intended to indicate the long-standing "charm" the name "Anne Elliot" had held for him. In this passage, the two are working from very different vantage points. Mr. Elliot may feel genuine affection for Anne, but he is also a trifler and an opportunist who knows exactly what he is doing in floating a proposal of marriage that he can easily claim was nothing of the sort. For her part, Anne is remarkably self-aware at many points in the novel, but here she does not know her own mind, and her actions bring about the very reverse of what she intends. Her flirtatious conversation with Mr. Elliot in front of Wentworth emboldens the man she does not want to marry and upsets the man she does.

10 Lady Dalrymple views Wentworth through the lens of her own vanity. He is a "very fine young man indeed," so she concludes that he must be Irish like herself.

Anne could think of no one so likely to have spoken with partiality of her many years ago, as the Mr. Wentworth, of Monkford, Captain Wentworth's brother. He might have been in Mr. Elliot's company, but she had not courage to ask the question.

"The name of Anne Elliot," said he, "has long had an interesting sound to me. Very long has it possessed a charm over my fancy; and, if I dared, I would breathe my wishes that the name might never change."[9]

Such she believed were his words; but scarcely had she received their sound, than her attention was caught by other sounds immediately behind her, which rendered every thing else trivial. Her father and Lady Dalrymple were speaking.

"A well-looking man," said Sir Walter, "a very well-looking man."

"A very fine young man indeed!" said Lady Dalrymple. "More air than one often sees in Bath.—Irish, I dare say."[10]

"No, I just know his name. A bowing acquaintance. Wentworth—Captain Wentworth of the navy. His sister married my tenant in Somersetshire,—the Croft, who rents Kellynch."

Before Sir Walter had reached this point, Anne's eyes had caught the right direction, and distinguished Captain Wentworth, standing among a cluster of men at a little distance. As her eyes fell on him, his seemed to be withdrawn from her. It had that appearance. It seemed as if she had been one moment too late; and as long as she dared observe, he did not look again: but the performance was recommencing, and she was forced to seem to restore her attention to the orchestra, and look straight forward.

When she could give another glance, he had moved away. He could not have come nearer to her if he would; she was so surrounded and shut in: but she would rather have caught his eye.

Mr. Elliot's speech too distressed her. She had no longer any inclination to talk to him. She wished him not so near her.

The first act was over. Now she hoped for some beneficial change; and, after a period of nothing-saying amongst the party, some of them did decide on going in quest of tea. Anne was one of the few who did not choose to move. She remained in her seat, and so did Lady Russell; but she had the pleasure of getting rid of Mr. Elliot;

and she did not mean, whatever she might feel on Lady Russell's account, to shrink from conversation with Captain Wentworth, if he gave her the opportunity. She was persuaded by Lady Russell's countenance that she had seen him.

He did not come however. Anne sometimes fancied she discerned him at a distance, but he never came. The anxious interval wore away unproductively. The others returned, the room filled again, benches were reclaimed and re-possessed, and another hour of pleasure or of penance was to be set out, another hour of music was to give delight or the gapes,[11] as real or affected taste for it prevailed. To Anne, it chiefly wore the prospect of an hour of agitation. She could not quit that room in peace without seeing Captain Wentworth once more, without the interchange of one friendly look.

In re-settling themselves, there were now many changes, the result of which was favourable for her. Colonel Wallis declined sitting down again, and Mr. Elliot was invited by Elizabeth and Miss Carteret, in a manner not to be refused, to sit between them; and by some other removals, and a little scheming of her own, Anne was enabled to place herself much nearer the end of the bench than she had been before, much more within reach of a passer-by. She could not do so, without comparing herself with Miss Larolles,[12] the inimitable Miss Larolles,—but still she did it, and not with much happier effect; though by what seemed prosperity in the shape of an early abdication in her next neighbours, she found herself at the very end of the bench before the concert closed.

Such was her situation, with a vacant space at hand, when Captain Wentworth was again in sight. She saw him not far off. He saw her too; yet he looked grave, and seemed irresolute, and only by very slow degrees came at last near enough to speak to her. She felt that something must be the matter. The change was indubitable. The difference between his present air and what it had been in the octagon room was strikingly great.—Why was it? She thought of her father—of Lady Russell. Could there have been any unpleasant glances? He began by speaking of the concert, gravely; more like the Captain Wentworth of Uppercross; owned himself disappointed, had expected better singing; and, in short, must confess that he should not

11 "Gapes" is slang for "a fit of yawning."

12 Miss Larolles is a minor character in Frances Burney's *Cecilia* (1782). During a concert in London she informs Cecilia that she has not been able to draw Mr. Meadows into a conversation, though "I sat at the outside on purpose to speak to a person or two, that I knew would be strolling about; for if one sits on the inside, there's no speaking to a creature, you know, so I never do it. . . . It's the shockingest thing you can conceive to be made sit in the middle of those forms; one might as well be at home, for nobody can speak to one" (Burney, *Cecilia,* ed. Peter Sabor and Margaret Anne Doody [Oxford: Oxford University Press, 1988], 286).

In *Northanger Abbey,* Austen famously describes *Cecilia*—along with Burney's *Camilla* and Edgeworth's *Belinda*—as novels "in which the greatest powers of the mind are displayed, in which the most thorough knowledge of human nature, the happiest delineation of its varieties, the liveliest effusions of wit and humour are conveyed to the world in the best chosen language" (I, 5).

be sorry when it was over. Anne replied, and spoke in defence of the performance so well, and yet in allowance for his feelings, so pleasantly, that his countenance improved, and he replied again with almost a smile. They talked for a few minutes more; the improvement held; he even looked down towards the bench, as if he saw a place on it well worth occupying; when, at that moment, a touch on her shoulder obliged Anne to turn round. — It came from Mr. Elliot. He begged her pardon, but she must be applied to, to explain Italian again. Miss Carteret was very anxious to have a general idea of what was next to be sung. Anne could not refuse; but never had she sacrificed to politeness with a more suffering spirit.

A few minutes, though as few as possible, were inevitably consumed; and when her own mistress again, when able to turn and look as she had done before, she found herself accosted by Captain Wentworth, in a reserved yet hurried sort of farewell. "He must wish her good night. He was going — he should get home as fast as he could."

"Is not this song worth staying for?" said Anne, suddenly struck by an idea which made her yet more anxious to be encouraging.

"No!" he replied impressively, "there is nothing worth my staying for;" and he was gone directly.

Jealousy of Mr. Elliot! It was the only intelligible motive. Captain Wentworth jealous of her affection! Could she have believed it a week ago — three hours ago! For a moment the gratification was exquisite. But alas! there were very different thoughts to succeed. How was such jealousy to be quieted? How was the truth to reach him? How, in all the peculiar disadvantages of their respective situations, would he ever learn her real sentiments? It was misery to think of Mr. Elliot's attentions. — Their evil was incalculable.

9

Anne recollected with pleasure the next morning her promise of going to Mrs. Smith; meaning that it should engage her from home at the time when Mr. Elliot would be most likely to call; for to avoid Mr. Elliot was almost a first object.

She felt a great deal of good will towards him. In spite of the mischief of his attentions, she owed him gratitude and regard, perhaps compassion. She could not help thinking much of the extraordinary circumstances attending their acquaintance; of the right which he seemed to have to interest her, by every thing in situation, by his own sentiments, by his early prepossession. It was altogether very extraordinary.—Flattering, but painful. There was much to regret. How she might have felt, had there been no Captain Wentworth in the case, was not worth enquiry; for there was a Captain Wentworth: and be the conclusion of the present suspense good or bad, her affection would be his for ever. Their union, she believed, could not divide her more from other men, than their final separation.

Prettier musings of high-wrought love and eternal constancy, could never have passed along the streets of Bath, than Anne was sporting with from Camden-place to Westgate-buildings. It was almost enough to spread purification and perfume all the way.[1]

She was sure of a pleasant reception; and her friend seemed this morning particularly obliged to her for coming, seemed hardly to have expected her, though it had been an appointment.

An account of the concert was immediately claimed; and Anne's recollections of the concert were quite happy enough to animate her

[1] Anne's pretty "musings of high-wrought love and eternal constancy" have elicited sharply differing interpretations, and as is so often the case in Austen criticism, at stake is the issue of irony. Julia Prewitt Brown observes that "Marvin Mudrick, in general so stringent an interpreter of Austen's irony, sees this passage as a sincere 'burst of affection' from Jane Austen herself. 'We share the author's overt sympathy,' he writes, in an instance of 'unalloyed joy.' I confess to bafflement at such an interpretation. The passage seems to me directly and passionately hostile in its irony; nothing could be more antithetical to Austen's conception of love than the image of purification and perfume. The statement is another example of the sudden, uncontrolled outburst of the authorial mind. As in the Dick Musgrove passage, the hostility is pathological but understandable. Anne is on her way to visit Mrs. Smith, who has no suitors to choose from, no money, and few friends. It seems a grotesque luxury for Anne to insist that, given her choice of suitors, she would only choose Wentworth and love him eternally. The passage is an angry defence of those who have to make do with what they have" (Brown, 135).

The little Durands were there.

Hugh Thomson, Illustrations for *Persuasion,* 1897. The Durands enjoy the concert, open-mouthed and on the edges of their seats.

features, and make her rejoice to talk of it. All that she could tell, she told most gladly; but the all was little for one who had been there, and unsatisfactory for such an enquirer as Mrs. Smith, who had already heard, through the short cut of a laundress and a waiter, rather more of the general success and produce of the evening than Anne could relate; and who now asked in vain for several particulars of the company. Every body of any consequence or notoriety in Bath was well known by name to Mrs. Smith.

"The little Durands were there, I conclude," said she, "with their mouths open to catch the music; like unfledged sparrows ready to be fed. They never miss a concert."

"Yes. I did not see them myself, but I heard Mr. Elliot say they were in the room."

"The Ibbotsons—were they there? and the two new beauties, with the tall Irish officer, who is talked of for one of them."

"I do not know.—I do not think they were."

"Old Lady Mary Maclean? I need not ask after her. She never misses, I know; and you must have seen her. She must have been in your own circle, for as you went with Lady Dalrymple, you were in the seats of grandeur; round the orchestra, of course."

"No, that was what I dreaded. It would have been very unpleasant to me in every respect. But happily Lady Dalrymple always chooses to be farther off; and we were exceedingly well placed—that is for hearing; I must not say for seeing, because I appear to have seen very little."

"Oh! you saw enough for your own amusement.—I can understand. There is a sort of domestic enjoyment to be known even in a crowd, and this you had. You were a large party in yourselves, and you wanted nothing beyond."

"But I ought to have looked about me more," said Anne, conscious while she spoke, that there had in fact been no want of looking about; that the object only had been deficient.

"No, no—you were better employed. You need not tell me that you had a pleasant evening. I see it in your eye. I perfectly see how the hours passed—that you had always something agreeable to listen to. In the intervals of the concert, it was conversation."

Anne half smiled and said, "Do you see that in my eye?"

"Yes, I do. Your countenance perfectly informs me that you were in company last night with the person, whom you think the most agreeable in the world, the person who interests you at this present time, more than all the rest of the world put together."

A blush overspread Anne's cheeks. She could say nothing.

"And such being the case," continued Mrs. Smith, after a short pause, "I hope you believe that I do know how to value your kindness in coming to me this morning. It is really very good of you to come and sit with me, when you must have so many pleasanter demands upon your time."

Anne heard nothing of this. She was still in the astonishment and confusion excited by her friend's penetration, unable to imagine how any report of Captain Wentworth could have reached her. After another short silence—

"Pray," said Mrs. Smith, "is Mr. Elliot aware of your acquaintance with me? Does he know that I am in Bath?"

"Mr. Elliot!" repeated Anne, looking up surprised. A moment's reflection shewed her the mistake she had been under. She caught it instantaneously; and, recovering courage with the feeling of safety, soon added, more composedly, "are you acquainted with Mr. Elliot?"

"I have been a good deal acquainted with him," replied Mrs. Smith, gravely, "but it seems worn out now. It is a great while since we met."

"I was not at all aware of this. You never mentioned it before. Had I known it, I would have had the pleasure of talking to him about you."

"To confess the truth," said Mrs. Smith, assuming her usual air of cheerfulness, "that is exactly the pleasure I want you to have. I want you to talk about me to Mr. Elliot. I want your interest with him. He can be of essential service to me; and if you would have the goodness, my dear Miss Elliot, to make it an object to yourself, of course it is done."

"I should be extremely happy—I hope you cannot doubt my willingness to be of even the slightest use to you," replied Anne; "but I suspect that you are considering me as having a higher claim on Mr.

Elliot—a greater right to influence him, than is really the case. I am sure you have, somehow or other, imbibed such a notion. You must consider me only as Mr. Elliot's relation. If in that light, if there is any thing which you suppose his cousin might fairly ask of him, I beg you would not hesitate to employ me."

Mrs. Smith gave her a penetrating glance, and then, smiling, said,

"I have been a little premature, I perceive. I beg your pardon. I ought to have waited for official information. But now, my dear Miss Elliot, as an old friend, do give me a hint as to when I may speak. Next week? To be sure by next week I may be allowed to think it all settled, and build my own selfish schemes on Mr. Elliot's good fortune."

"No," replied Anne, "nor next week, nor next, nor next. I assure you that nothing of the sort you are thinking of will be settled any week. I am not going to marry Mr. Elliot. I should like to know why you imagine I am."

Mrs. Smith looked at her again, looked earnestly, smiled, shook her head, and exclaimed,

"Now, how I do wish I understood you! How I do wish I knew what you were at! I have a great idea that you do not design to be cruel, when the right moment comes. Till it does come, you know, we women never mean to have any body. It is a thing of course among us, that every man is refused—till he offers. But why should you be cruel? Let me plead for my—present friend I cannot call him—but for my former friend. Where can you look for a more suitable match? Where could you expect a more gentlemanlike, agreeable man? Let me recommend Mr. Elliot. I am sure you hear nothing but good of him from Colonel Wallis; and who can know him better than Colonel Wallis?"

"My dear Mrs. Smith, Mr. Elliot's wife has not been dead much above half a year. He ought not to be supposed to be paying his addresses to any one."

"Oh! if these are your only objections," cried Mrs. Smith, archly, "Mr. Elliot is safe, and I shall give myself no more trouble about him. Do not forget me when you are married, that's all. Let him know me to be a friend of yours, and then he will think little of the trouble required, which it is very natural for him now, with so many affairs and engagements of his own, to avoid and get rid of as he can—very natural, perhaps. Ninety-nine out of a hundred would do the same. Of course, he cannot be aware of the importance to me. Well, my dear Miss Elliot, I hope and trust you will be very happy. Mr. Elliot has sense to understand the value of such a woman. Your peace will not be shipwrecked as mine has been. You are safe in all worldly matters, and safe in his character. He will not be led astray, he will not be misled by others to his ruin."

"No," said Anne, "I can readily believe all that of my cousin. He seems to have a calm, decided temper, not at all open to dangerous impressions. I consider him with great respect. I have no reason, from any thing that has fallen within my observation, to do otherwise. But I have not known him long; and he is not a man, I think, to be known intimately soon. Will not this manner of speaking of him, Mrs. Smith, convince you that he is nothing to me? Surely, this must be calm enough. And, upon my word, he is nothing to me. Should he ever propose to me (which I have very little reason to imagine he has any thought of doing), I shall not accept him. I assure you I shall not. I assure you Mr. Elliot had not the share which you have been supposing, in whatever pleasure the concert of last night might afford:— not Mr. Elliot; it is not Mr. Elliot that—"

She stopped, regretting with a deep blush that she had implied so much; but less would hardly have been sufficient. Mrs. Smith would hardly have believed so soon in Mr. Elliot's failure, but from the perception of there being a somebody else. As it was, she instantly submitted, and with all the semblance of seeing nothing beyond; and Anne, eager to escape farther notice, was impatient to know why Mrs. Smith should have fancied she was to marry Mr. Elliot, where she could have received the idea, or from whom she could have heard it.

"Do tell me how it first came into your head."

"It first came into my head," replied Mrs. Smith, "upon finding how much you were together, and feeling it to be the most probable thing in the world to be wished for by everybody belonging to either of you; and you may depend upon it that all your acquaintance have

2 In the early nineteenth century, "intimately" meant "closely acquainted," and the sexual charge the word now carries was much weaker. Compare Samuel Richardson in *Sir Charles Grandison:* "like minds will be intimate at first sight" (Richardson, *Grandison,* I, 147).

disposed of you in the same way. But I never heard it spoken of till two days ago."

"And has it indeed been spoken of?"

"Did you observe the woman who opened the door to you, when you called yesterday?"

"No. Was not it Mrs. Speed, as usual, or the maid? I observed no one in particular."

"It was my friend, Mrs. Rooke—Nurse Rooke, who, by the by, had a great curiosity to see you, and was delighted to be in the way to let you in. She came away from Marlborough-buildings only on Sunday; and she it was who told me you were to marry Mr. Elliot. She had had it from Mrs. Wallis herself, which did not seem bad authority. She sat an hour with me on Monday evening, and gave me the whole history."

"The whole history!" repeated Anne, laughing. "She could not make a very long history, I think, of one such little article of unfounded news."

Mrs. Smith said nothing.

"But," continued Anne, presently, "though there is no truth in my having this claim on Mr. Elliot, I should be extremely happy to be of use to you, in any way that I could. Shall I mention to him your being in Bath? Shall I take any message?"

"No, I thank you: no, certainly not. In the warmth of the moment, and under a mistaken impression, I might, perhaps, have endeavoured to interest you in some circumstances. But not now: no, I thank you, I have nothing to trouble you with."

"I think you spoke of having known Mr. Elliot many years?"

"I did."

"Not before he married, I suppose?"

"Yes; he was not married when I knew him first."

"And—were you much acquainted?"

"Intimately."[2]

"Indeed! Then do tell me what he was at that time of life. I have a great curiosity to know what Mr. Elliot was as a very young man. Was he at all such as he appears now?"

"I have not seen Mr. Elliot these three years," was Mrs. Smith's answer, given so gravely that it was impossible to pursue the subject farther; and Anne felt that she had gained nothing but an increase of curiosity. They were both silent—Mrs. Smith very thoughtful. At last,

"I beg your pardon, my dear Miss Elliot," she cried, in her natural tone of cordiality, "I beg your pardon for the short answers I have been giving you, but I have been uncertain what I ought to do. I have been doubting and considering as to what I ought to tell you. There were many things to be taken into the account. One hates to be officious, to be giving bad impressions, making mischief. Even the smooth surface of family-union seems worth preserving, though there may be nothing durable beneath. However, I have determined; I think I am right; I think you ought to be made acquainted with Mr. Elliot's real character. Though I fully believe that, at present, you have not the smallest intention of accepting him, there is no saying what may happen. You might, some time or other, be differently affected towards him. Hear the truth, therefore, now, while you are unprejudiced. Mr. Elliot is a man without heart or conscience; a designing, wary, cold-blooded being, who thinks only of himself; who, for his own interest or ease, would be guilty of any cruelty, or any treachery, that could be perpetrated without risk of his general character. He has no feeling for others. Those whom he has been the chief cause of leading into ruin, he can neglect and desert without the smallest compunction. He is totally beyond the reach of any sentiment of justice or compassion. Oh! he is black at heart, hollow and black!"

Anne's astonished air, and exclamation of wonder, made her pause, and in a calmer manner she added,

"My expressions startle you. You must allow for an injured, angry woman. But I will try to command myself. I will not abuse him. I will only tell you what I have found him. Facts shall speak. He was the intimate friend of my dear husband, who trusted and loved him, and thought him as good as himself. The intimacy had been formed before our marriage. I found them most intimate friends; and I, too,

3 "Excessively" here means "exceedingly."

4 Mr. Elliot resided in an area of London known as the Temple, which housed two of the four Inns of Court and contained lodgings reserved for students of the law and members of the legal profession. In Austen's time, many leisured young men lived in the Temple, which had become a cross between an educational establishment and a fashionable club.

5 A "farthing" was a British coin equal to one-quarter of a penny.

became excessively[3] pleased with Mr. Elliot, and entertained the highest opinion of him. At nineteen, you know, one does not think very seriously, but Mr. Elliot appeared to me quite as good as others, and much more agreeable than most others, and we were almost always together. We were principally in town, living in very good style. He was then the inferior in circumstances, he was then the poor one; he had chambers in the Temple,[4] and it was as much as he could do to support the appearance of a gentleman. He had always a home with us whenever he chose it; he was always welcome; he was like a brother. My poor Charles, who had the finest, most generous spirit in the world, would have divided his last farthing[5] with him; and I know that his purse was open to him; I know that he often assisted him."

"This must have been about that very period of Mr. Elliot's life," said Anne, "which has always excited my particular curiosity. It must have been about the same time that he became known to my father and sister. I never knew him myself, I only heard of him, but there was a something in his conduct then with regard to my father and sister, and afterwards in the circumstances of his marriage, which I never could quite reconcile with present times. It seemed to announce a different sort of man."

"I know it all, I know it all," cried Mrs. Smith. "He had been introduced to Sir Walter and your sister before I was acquainted with him, but I heard him speak of them for ever. I know he was invited and encouraged, and I know he did not choose to go. I can satisfy you, perhaps, on points which you would little expect; and as to his marriage, I knew all about it at the time. I was privy to all the fors and againsts, I was the friend to whom he confided his hopes and plans, and though I did not know his wife previously, (her inferior situation in society, indeed, rendered that impossible) yet I knew her all her life afterwards, or, at least, till within the last two years of her life, and can answer any question you wish to put."

"Nay," said Anne, "I have no particular enquiry to make about her. I have always understood they were not a happy couple. But I should like to know why, at that time of his life, he should slight my father's acquaintance as he did. My father was certainly disposed to take very kind and proper notice of him. Why did Mr. Elliot draw back?"

"Mr. Elliot," replied Mrs. Smith, "at that period of his life, had one object in view—to make his fortune, and by a rather quicker process than the law. He was determined to make it by marriage. He was determined, at least, not to mar it by an imprudent marriage; and I know it was his belief, (whether justly or not, of course I cannot decide) that your father and sister, in their civilities and invitations, were designing a match between the heir and the young lady; and it was impossible that such a match should have answered his ideas of wealth and independance. That was his motive for drawing back, I can assure you. He told me the whole story. He had no concealments with me. It was curious, that having just left you behind me in Bath, my first and principal acquaintance on marrying, should be your cousin; and that, through him, I should be continually hearing of your father and sister. He described one Miss Elliot, and I thought very affectionately of the other."

"Perhaps," cried Anne, struck by a sudden idea, "you sometimes spoke of me to Mr. Elliot?"

"To be sure I did, very often. I used to boast of my own Anne Elliot, and vouch for your being a very different creature from—"

She checked herself just in time.

"This accounts for something which Mr. Elliot said last night," cried Anne. "This explains it. I found he had been used to hear of me. I could not comprehend how. What wild imaginations one forms, where dear self is concerned! How sure to be mistaken! But I beg your pardon; I have interrupted you. Mr. Elliot married, then, completely for money? The circumstance, probably, which first opened your eyes to his character."

Mrs. Smith hesitated a little here. "Oh! those things are too common. When one lives in the world, a man or woman's marrying for money is too common to strike one as it ought. I was very young, and associated only with the young and we were a thoughtless, gay set, without any strict rules of conduct. We lived for enjoyment. I think differently now; time and sickness, and sorrow, have given me other

Charles Edmund Brock, Illustrations for *Persuasion,* 1898. Anne is shocked by
William Elliot's letter to Charles Smith.

notions; but, at that period, I must own I saw nothing reprehensible in what Mr. Elliot was doing. 'To do the best for himself,' passed as a duty."

"But was not she a very low woman?"[6]

"Yes; which I objected to, but he would not regard. Money, money, was all that he wanted. Her father was a grazier,[7] her grandfather had been a butcher, but that was all nothing. She was a fine woman, had had a decent education, was brought forward by some cousins, thrown by chance into Mr. Elliot's company, and fell in love with him; and not a difficulty or a scruple was there on his side, with respect to her birth. All his caution was spent in being secured of the real amount of her fortune,[8] before he committed himself. Depend upon it, whatever esteem Mr. Elliot may have for his own situation in life now, as a young man he had not the smallest value for it. His chance of the Kellynch estate was something, but all the honour of the family he held as cheap as dirt. I have often heard him declare, that if baronetcies were saleable, any body should have his for fifty pounds, arms and motto, name and livery included; but I will not pretend to repeat half that I used to hear him say on that subject. It would not be fair. And yet you ought to have proof; for what is all this but assertion? and you shall have proof."

"Indeed, my dear Mrs. Smith, I want none," cried Anne;[9] "You have asserted nothing contradictory to what Mr. Elliot appeared to be some years ago. This is all in confirmation, rather, of what we used to hear and believe. I am more curious to know why he should be so different now?"

"But for my satisfaction; if you will have the goodness to ring for Mary—stay, I am sure you will have the still greater goodness of going yourself into my bedroom, and bringing me the small inlaid box which you will find on the upper shelf of the closet."

Anne, seeing her friend to be earnestly bent on it, did as she was desired. The box was brought and placed before her, and Mrs. Smith, sighing over it as she unlocked it, said,

"This is full of papers belonging to him, to my husband, a small portion only of what I had to look over when I lost him. The letter I am looking for, was one written by Mr. Elliot to him before our

6 A "very low woman" was a woman from the lower ranks of society.

7 A "grazier" was a person who grazed sheep and cattle.

8 Mr. Elliot wants to be certain ("secured") that he knows how much his wife is worth, and that after their marriage he will have access to her entire fortune. He probably achieved these ends, as he has studied the law, and his father-in-law is at the lower end of the social scale and almost certainly uneducated. The law stipulated that, once married, the woman's property became the man's: "By marriage those chattels which belonged to the woman before marriage, are by act of law vested in the husband . . . and this is founded on the notion of an unity of person subsisting between husband and wife; it being held in law that they are one person, so that the very being and essence of the woman is suspended during the coverture, or entirely merged and incorporated in that of the husband" (Anonymous, *The Laws Respecting Women* [London: Johnson, 1777], 149).

9 Susan Morgan examines the limitations of Mrs. Smith's narrative mode. "In a novel intensely and almost solely focused on the ways we can see into other hearts, Mrs. Smith offers the wrong way," states Morgan. "For her the ways of knowing are those in which the 'Facts shall speak.' She believes that Anne 'ought to have proof' and 'shall have proof,' in spite of Anne's claim that she has no need of it. At the same time Mrs. Smith's narrative style is distinctly gothic. Her method is as exaggeratedly scientific as it is sentimental" (Morgan, *In the Meantime: Character and Perception in Jane Austen's Fiction* [Chicago: University of Chicago Press, 1980], 177–178).

10 Tunbridge Wells is a small spa town in Kent, about thirty miles southeast of London. Throughout the eighteenth century it was—after Bath—the chief resort of fashionable London society. In *Northanger Abbey,* for example, Isabella Thorpe compares "the balls of Bath with those of Tunbridge" (I, 4).

11 "Give me joy" is "congratulate me."

12 Mr. Elliot means that the first time he visits Kellynch will be after Sir Walter's death, when the property will belong to him, and he will be free to sell it by auction ("bring it with best advantage to the hammer").

13 The "reversion" is the right to succeed to Sir Walter's title and estate. Mr. Elliot would lose this right if Sir Walter were to remarry and produce a son. But— Mr. Elliot reasons—at least that would mean he was no longer plagued by Sir Walter's designs to marry him to Elizabeth.

14 "Walter" is the ancestral Christian name of the owner of Kellynch.

marriage, and happened to be saved; why, one can hardly imagine. But he was careless and immethodical, like other men, about those things; and when I came to examine his papers, I found it with others still more trivial from different people scattered here and there, while many letters and memorandums of real importance had been destroyed. Here it is. I would not burn it, because being even then very little satisfied with Mr. Elliot, I was determined to preserve every document of former intimacy. I have now another motive for being glad that I can produce it."

This was the letter, directed to "Charles Smith, Esq. Tunbridge Wells,"[10] and dated from London, as far back as July, 1803.

> "Dear Smith,
> "I have received yours. Your kindness almost overpowers me. I wish nature had made such hearts as yours more common, but I have lived three and twenty years in the world, and have seen none like it. At present, believe me, I have no need of your services, being in cash again. Give me joy:[11] I have got rid of Sir Walter and Miss. They are gone back to Kellynch, and almost made me swear to visit them this summer, but my first visit to Kellynch will be with a surveyor, to tell me how to bring it with best advantage to the hammer.[12] The baronet, nevertheless, is not unlikely to marry again; he is quite fool enough. If he does, however, they will leave me in peace, which may be a decent equivalent for the reversion.[13] He is worse than last year.
> "I wish I had any name but Elliot. I am sick of it. The name of Walter[14] I can drop, thank God! and I desire you will never insult me with my second W. again, meaning, for the rest of my life, to be only yours truly,
> Wm. Elliot."

Such a letter could not be read without putting Anne in a glow; and Mrs. Smith, observing the high colour in her face, said,

"The language, I know, is highly disrespectful. Though I have forgot the exact terms, I have a perfect impression of the general mean-

ing. But it shews you the man. Mark his professions to my poor husband. Can any thing be stronger?"

Anne could not immediately get over the shock and mortification
of finding such words applied to her father. She was obliged to recollect that her seeing the letter was a violation of the laws of honour,
that no one ought to be judged or to be known by such testimonies,
that no private correspondence could bear the eye of others, before
she could recover calmness enough to return the letter which she
had been meditating over, and say,

"Thank you. This is full proof undoubtedly, proof of every thing
you were saying. But why be acquainted with us now?"

"I can explain this too," cried Mrs. Smith, smiling.

"Can you really?"

"Yes. I have shewn you Mr. Elliot, as he was a dozen years ago, and
I will shew him as he is now. I cannot produce written proof again,
but I can give as authentic oral testimony as you can desire, of what
he is now wanting, and what he is now doing. He is no hypocrite now.
He truly wants to marry you. His present attentions to your family
are very sincere, quite from the heart. I will give you my authority;
his friend Colonel Wallis."

"Colonel Wallis! are you acquainted with him?"

"No. It does not come to me in quite so direct a line as that; it
takes a bend or two, but nothing of consequence. The stream is as
good as at first; the little rubbish it collects in the turnings, is easily
moved away. Mr. Elliot talks unreservedly to Colonel Wallis of his
views on you—which said Colonel Wallis I imagine to be in himself a
sensible, careful, discerning sort of character; but Colonel Wallis has
a very pretty silly wife, to whom he tells things which he had better
not, and he repeats it all to her. She, in the overflowing spirits of her
recovery, repeats it all to her nurse; and the nurse, knowing my acquaintance with you, very naturally brings it all to me. On Monday
evening my good friend Mrs. Rooke let me thus much into the se-
crets of Marlborough-buildings. When I talked of a whole history
therefore, you see, I was not romancing so much as you supposed."

"My dear Mrs. Smith, your authority is deficient. This will not do.
Mr. Elliot's having any views on me will not in the least account for

the efforts he made towards a reconciliation with my father. That was all prior to my coming to Bath; I found them on the most friendly terms when I arrived."

"I know you did; I know it all perfectly, but" –

"Indeed, Mrs. Smith, we must not expect to get real information in such a line. Facts or opinions which are to pass through the hands of so many, to be misconceived by folly in one, and ignorance in another, can hardly have much truth left."

"Only give me a hearing. You will soon be able to judge of the general credit due, by listening to some particulars which you can yourself immediately contradict or confirm. Nobody supposes that you were his first inducement. He had seen you indeed, before he came to Bath and admired you, but without knowing it to be you. So says my historian at least. Is this true? Did he see you last summer or autumn, 'somewhere down in the west,' to use her own words, without knowing it to be you?"

"He certainly did. So far it is very true. At Lyme; I happened to be at Lyme."

"Well," continued Mrs. Smith triumphantly, "grant my friend the credit due to the establishment of the first point asserted. He saw you then at Lyme, and liked you so well as to be exceedingly pleased to meet with you again in Camden-place, as Miss Anne Elliot, and from that moment, I have no doubt, had a double motive in his visits there. But there was another, and an earlier; which I will now explain. If there is any thing in my story which you know to be either false or improbable, stop me. My account states, that your sister's friend, the lady now staying with you, whom I have heard you mention, came to Bath with Miss Elliot and Sir Walter as long ago as September, (in short when they first came themselves) and has been staying there ever since; that she is a clever, insinuating, handsome woman, poor and plausible, and altogether such in situation and manner, as to give a general idea among Sir Walter's acquaintance, of her meaning to be Lady Elliot, and as general a surprise that Miss Elliot should be apparently blind to the danger."

Here Mrs. Smith paused a moment; but Anne had not a word to say, and she continued,

"This was the light in which it appeared to those who knew the family, long before your return to it; and Colonel Wallis had his eye upon your father enough to be sensible of it, though he did not then visit in Camden-place; but his regard for Mr. Elliot gave him an interest in watching all that was going on there, and when Mr. Elliot came to Bath for a day or two, as he happened to do a little before Christmas, Colonel Wallis made him acquainted with the appearance of things, and the reports beginning to prevail.—Now you are to understand that time had worked a very material change in Mr. Elliot's opinions as to the value of a baronetcy. Upon all points of blood and connexion,[15] he is a completely altered man. Having long had as much money as he could spend, nothing to wish for on the side of avarice or indulgence, he has been gradually learning to pin his happiness upon the consequence he is heir to. I thought it coming on, before our acquaintance ceased, but it is now a confirmed feeling. He cannot bear the idea of not being Sir William. You may guess therefore that the news he heard from his friend, could not be very agreeable,[16] and you may guess what it produced; the resolution of coming back to Bath as soon as possible, and of fixing himself here for a time, with the view of renewing his former acquaintance and recovering such a footing in the family, as might give him the means of ascertaining the degree of his danger, and of circumventing the lady if he found it material. This was agreed upon between the two friends, as the only thing to be done; and Colonel Wallis was to assist in every way that he could. He was to be introduced, and Mrs. Wallis was to be introduced, and every body was to be introduced. Mr. Elliot came back accordingly; and on application was forgiven, as you know, and re-admitted into the family; and there it was his constant object, and his only object (till your arrival added another motive) to watch Sir Walter and Mrs. Clay. He omitted no opportunity of being with them, threw himself in their way, called at all hours—but I need not be particular on this subject. You can imagine what an artful man would do; and with this guide, perhaps, may recollect what you have seen him do."

"Yes," said Anne, "you tell me nothing which does not accord with what I have known, or could imagine. There is always something of-

15 "Blood and connexion" refer to an "honorable lineage" and a "distinguished kinship," as well as more broadly to all the social advantages that accrue to members of prominent old families.

16 Mr. Elliot finds Colonel Wallis's news of the goings-on at Camden Place not very agreeable because, if Sir Walter marries Mrs. Clay and produces a son, Mr. Elliot will not get the baronetcy he now has his heart set on.

Fanny Knight, from a watercolor by Cassandra Austen. Fanny was the eldest daughter of Edward Austen Knight (1767–1852), Austen's third brother. Austen was immensely fond of her. "You are inimitable, irresistable," she wrote to Fanny in February 1817. "You are the delight of my Life" (Austen, *Letters,* 328).

17 The "marriage articles" were a private legal document, written up before the marriage, that detailed such arrangements as property rights between the husband and wife, the regular allowance (or "pin money") that the husband was to pay to the wife, and the future rights of succession. Compare *Pride and Prejudice,* where "five thousand pounds was settled by marriage articles on Mrs. Bennet and the children" (III, 8).

fensive in the details of cunning. The manœuvres of selfishness and duplicity must ever be revolting, but I have heard nothing which really surprises me. I know those who would be shocked by such a representation of Mr. Elliot, who would have difficulty in believing it; but I have never been satisfied. I have always wanted some other motive for his conduct than appeared.—I should like to know his present opinion, as to the probability of the event he has been in dread of; whether he considers the danger to be lessening or not."

"Lessening, I understand," replied Mrs. Smith. "He thinks Mrs. Clay afraid of him, aware that he sees through her, and not daring to proceed as she might do in his absence. But since he must be absent some time or other, I do not perceive how he can ever be secure, while she holds her present influence. Mrs. Wallis has an amusing idea, as nurse tells me, that it is to be put into the marriage articles[17] when you and Mr. Elliot marry, that your father is not to marry Mrs. Clay. A scheme, worthy of Mrs. Wallis's understanding, by all accounts; but my sensible nurse Rooke sees the absurdity of it.— 'Why, to be sure, ma'am,' said she, 'it would not prevent his marrying any body else.' And indeed, to own the truth, I do not think nurse in her heart is a very strenuous opposer of Sir Walter's making a second match. She must be allowed to be a favourer of matrimony you know, and (since self will intrude) who can say that she may not have some flying visions of attending the next Lady Elliot, through Mrs. Wallis's recommendation?"

"I am very glad to know all this," said Anne, after a little thoughtfulness. "It will be more painful to me in some respects to be in company with him, but I shall know better what to do. My line of conduct will be more direct. Mr. Elliot is evidently a disingenuous, artificial, worldly man, who has never had any better principle to guide him than selfishness."

But Mr. Elliot was not yet done with. Mrs. Smith had been carried away from her first direction, and Anne had forgotten, in the interest of her own family concerns, how much had been originally implied against him; but her attention was now called to the explanation of those first hints, and she listened to a recital which, if it did not perfectly justify the unqualified bitterness of Mrs. Smith, proved him to have been very unfeeling in his conduct towards her, very deficient both in justice and compassion.

She learned that (the intimacy between them continuing unimpaired by Mr. Elliot's marriage) they had been as before always together, and Mr. Elliot had led his friend into expenses much beyond his fortune. Mrs. Smith did not want to take blame to herself, and was most tender of throwing any on her husband; but Anne could collect that their income had never been equal to their style of living, and that from the first, there had been a great deal of general and joint extravagance. From his wife's account of him, she could discern Mr. Smith to have been a man of warm feelings, easy temper, careless habits, and not strong understanding, much more amiable than his friend, and very unlike him—led by him, and probably despised by him. Mr. Elliot, raised by his marriage to great affluence, and disposed to every gratification of pleasure and vanity which could be commanded without involving[18] himself, (for with all his self-indulgence he had become a prudent man) and beginning to be rich, just as his friend ought to have found himself to be poor, seemed to have had no concern at all for that friend's probable finances, but, on the contrary, had been prompting and encouraging expenses, which could end only in ruin. And the Smiths accordingly had been ruined.

The husband had died just in time to be spared the full knowledge of it. They had previously known embarrassments[19] enough to try the friendship of their friends, and to prove that Mr. Elliot's had better not be tried; but it was not till his death that the wretched state of his affairs was fully known. With a confidence in Mr. Elliot's regard, more creditable to his feelings than his judgment, Mr. Smith had appointed him the executor of his will; but Mr. Elliot would not act, and the difficulties and distresses which this refusal had heaped on her, in addition to the inevitable sufferings of her situation, had been such as could not be related without anguish of spirit, or listened to without corresponding indignation.[20]

Anne was shewn some letters of his on the occasion, answers to urgent applications from Mrs. Smith, which all breathed the same stern resolution of not engaging in a fruitless trouble, and, under a cold civility, the same hard-hearted indifference to any of the evils it

18 In this context, "involving" means to become entangled in troubles or perplexities, "to engage in circumstances from which it is difficult to withdraw" (OED).

19 "Embarrassments" are "financial difficulties."

20 As a husband and wife were considered to be one person in the eyes of the law, a woman who lost her husband had no legal status as a person, which meant that she was forced to rely on male relatives or friends to initiate legal proceedings on her behalf. The situation became even more complicated and precarious for the woman when—as is the case for Mrs. Smith—the executor of the husband's will neglects or ignores his responsibilities.

21 Property in the West Indies meant involvement with the slave trade, which was legal throughout the region, and which produced the large profits that underwrote the fortunes of many British families. Britain abolished the slave trade in 1807, a decision that would have deepened the financial insecurity of Mrs. Smith during the years of her widowhood, though the overall effect of the Napoleonic Wars was to increase the number of Britain's colonial possessions. Slavery itself remained legal in the British Empire until 1833. In *Persuasion,* Tim Fulford notes, the British gentry "has been renewed by the careers that its less wealthy sons have taken up. It has been revitalized by opportunities that empire gives for character-building employment. That it has also been renewed by the income stemming from the ownership of slave colonies is a point that Mrs. Smith's case raises but that Austen chooses not to pursue." Austen is more forthright about the issue of slavery in *Mansfield Park,* where the Bertrams unexpectedly find themselves in financial difficulties after "some recent losses" on Sir Thomas's "West India Estate" (I, 3). Many commentators have suggested that the underlying cause of these "losses" is the political and economic disruption brought about by the passage of the 1807 Abolition Bill (Fulford, "Romanticizing the Empire: The Naval Heroes of Southey, Coleridge, Austen and Marryat," in *Modern Language Quarterly,* 60 [1999], 190).

Slavery was an issue that touched the Austen family as well. Austen's father was trustee of a plantation in Antigua. Her brother Francis, a confirmed Evangelical, served on British ships in the West Indies, where he saw firsthand "the harshness and despotism which has been so justly attributed to the conduct of land-holders or their managers," and recorded his regret that "any trace of it should be found to exist in countries dependent on England, or colonised by her subjects." Austen herself identified closely with the abolitionists and greatly approved of one of their most important leaders, Thomas Clarkson (1760–1846), whose works include *An Essay on the Slavery and Commerce of the Human Species* (1786) and *History of the Rise, Progress, and Accom-*

might bring on her. It was a dreadful picture of ingratitude and inhumanity; and Anne felt at some moments, that no flagrant open crime could have been worse. She had a great deal to listen to; all the particulars of past sad scenes, all the minutiæ of distress upon distress, which in former conversations had been merely hinted at, were dwelt on now with a natural indulgence. Anne could perfectly comprehend the exquisite relief, and was only the more inclined to wonder at the composure of her friend's usual state of mind.

There was one circumstance in the history of her grievances of particular irritation. She had good reason to believe that some property of her husband in the West Indies,[21] which had been for many years under a sort of sequestration for the payment of its own incumbrances,[22] might be recoverable by proper measures; and this property, though not large, would be enough to make her comparatively rich. But there was nobody to stir in it.[23] Mr. Elliot would do nothing, and she could do nothing herself, equally disabled from personal exertion by her state of bodily weakness, and from employing others by her want of money. She had no natural connexions to assist her even with their counsel, and she could not afford to purchase the assistance of the law. This was a cruel aggravation of actually streightened[24] means. To feel that she ought to be in better circumstances, that a little trouble in the right place might do it, and to fear that delay might be even weakening her claims, was hard to bear!

It was on this point that she had hoped to engage Anne's good offices with Mr. Elliot. She had previously, in the anticipation of their marriage, been very apprehensive of losing her friend by it; but on being assured that he could have made no attempt of that nature, since he did not even know her to be in Bath, it immediately occurred, that something might be done in her favour by the influence of the woman he loved, and she had been hastily preparing to interest Anne's feelings, as far as the observances due to Mr. Elliot's character would allow, when Anne's refutation of the supposed engagement changed the face of every thing, and while it took from her the new-formed hope of succeeding in the object of her first anxiety, left her at least the comfort of telling the whole story her own way.

After listening to this full description of Mr. Elliot, Anne could not but express some surprise at Mrs. Smith's having spoken of him so favourably in the beginning of their conversation. "She had seemed to recommend and praise him!"

"My dear," was Mrs. Smith's reply, "there was nothing else to be done. I considered your marrying him as certain, though he might not yet have made the offer, and I could no more speak the truth of him, than if he had been your husband. My heart bled for you, as I talked of happiness. And yet, he is sensible, he is agreeable, and with such a woman as you, it was not absolutely hopeless. He was very unkind to his first wife. They were wretched together. But she was too ignorant and giddy for respect, and he had never loved her. I was willing to hope that you must fare better."

Anne could just acknowledge within herself such a possibility of having been induced to marry him, as made her shudder at the idea of the misery which must have followed. It was just possible that she might have been persuaded by Lady Russell! And under such a supposition, which would have been most miserable, when time had disclosed all, too late?

It was very desirable that Lady Russell should be no longer deceived; and one of the concluding arrangements of this important conference, which carried them through the greater part of the morning, was, that Anne had full liberty to communicate to her friend every thing relative to Mrs. Smith, in which his conduct was involved.

plishment of the Abolition of the African Slave Trade by the British Parliament (1808) (Southam, 189–190).

22 The "payment of its own incumbrances" means that the property in the West Indies produces an income, but that it has been appropriated by Mr. Smith's creditors to pay off his remaining debts.

23 "To stir in it" is "to pursue it."

24 "Streightened" is "straitened" or "reduced."

IO

ANNE WENT HOME TO THINK OVER all that she had heard. In one point, her feelings were relieved by this knowledge of Mr. Elliot. There was no longer any thing of tenderness due to him. He stood, as opposed to Captain Wentworth, in all his own unwelcome obtrusiveness; and the evil of his attentions last night, the irremediable mischief he might have done, was considered with sensations unqualified, unperplexed.—Pity for him was all over. But this was the only point of relief. In every other respect, in looking around her, or penetrating forward, she saw more to distrust and to apprehend. She was concerned for the disappointment and pain Lady Russell would be feeling, for the mortifications which must be hanging over her father and sister, and had all the distress of foreseeing many evils, without knowing how to avert any one of them.—She was most thankful for her own knowledge of him. She had never considered herself as entitled to reward for not slighting an old friend like Mrs. Smith, but here was a reward indeed springing from it!—Mrs. Smith had been able to tell her what no one else could have done. Could the knowledge have been extended through her family!—But this was a vain idea. She must talk to Lady Russell, tell her, consult with her, and having done her best, wait the event[1] with as much composure as possible; and after all, her greatest want of composure would be in that quarter of the mind which could not be opened to Lady Russell, in that flow of anxieties and fears which must be all to herself.

She found, on reaching home, that she had, as she intended, escaped seeing Mr. Elliot; that he had called and paid them a long morning visit; but hardly had she congratulated herself, and felt safe till to-morrow, when she heard that he was coming again in the evening.

"I had not the smallest intention of asking him," said Elizabeth, with affected carelessness, "but he gave so many hints; so Mrs. Clay says, at least."

"Indeed I do say it. I never saw any body in my life spell[2] harder for an invitation. Poor man! I was really in pain for him; for your hard-hearted sister, Miss Anne, seems bent on cruelty."

"Oh!" cried Elizabeth, "I have been rather too much used to the game to be soon overcome by a gentleman's hints. However, when I found how excessively he was regretting that he should miss my father this morning, I gave way immediately, for I would never really omit an opportunity of bringing him and Sir Walter together. They appear to so much advantage in company with each other! Each behaving so pleasantly! Mr. Elliot looking up with so much respect!"

"Quite delightful!" cried Mrs. Clay, not daring, however, to turn her eyes towards Anne. "Exactly like father and son! Dear Miss Elliot, may I not say father and son?"

"Oh! I lay no embargo on any body's words. If you will have such ideas! But, upon my word, I am scarcely sensible of his attentions being beyond those of other men."

"My dear Miss Elliot!" exclaimed Mrs. Clay, lifting up her hands and eyes, and sinking all the rest of her astonishment in a convenient silence.

"Well, my dear Penelope, you need not be so alarmed about him. I did invite him, you know. I sent him away with smiles. When I found he was really going to his friends at Thornberry-park[3] for the whole day to-morrow, I had compassion on him."

Anne admired the good acting of the friend, in being able to shew such pleasure as she did, in the expectation, and in the actual arrival of the very person whose presence must really be interfering with her prime object. It was impossible but that Mrs. Clay must hate the sight of Mr. Elliot; and yet she could assume a most obliging, placid look, and appear quite satisfied with the curtailed license of devot-

2 To "spell" is "to intimate or suggest a desire *for* something; to ask *for,* either by hints or direct request" *(OED).*

3 Austen may be thinking here of Thornbury (not "Thornberry") Park. But if she is, she has misremembered how far away it is from Bath, for we soon learn that Mr. Elliot's engagement is "seven miles off," whereas Thornbury Park is located fifteen miles north of Bristol, which is twelve miles northwest of Bath.

4 "Eclat" derives from the French "faire éclat," which means to "create a stir or scandal."

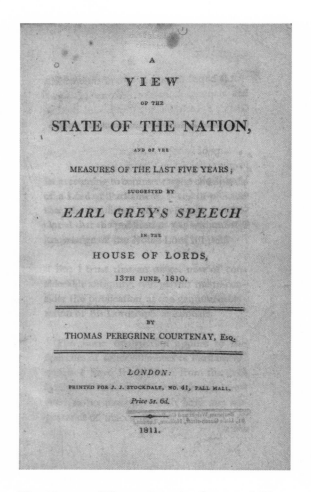

The title page of Thomas Peregrine Courtenay's *View of the State of the Nation*. Courtenay was a staunch conservative who served both William Pitt (1759–1806) and the duke of Wellington (1769–1852) during his long political career. His *Commentaries on the Historic Plays of Shakespeare* appeared in 1840.

ing herself only half as much to Sir Walter as she would have done otherwise.

To Anne herself it was most distressing to see Mr. Elliot enter the room; and quite painful to have him approach and speak to her. She had been used before to feel that he could not be always quite sincere, but now she saw insincerity in every thing. His attentive deference to her father, contrasted with his former language, was odious; and when she thought of his cruel conduct towards Mrs. Smith, she could hardly bear the sight of his present smiles and mildness, or the sound of his artificial good sentiments. She meant to avoid any such alteration of manners as might provoke a remonstrance on his side. It was a great object with her to escape all enquiry or eclat;[4] but it was her intention to be as decidedly cool to him as might be compatible with their relationship, and to retrace, as quietly as she could, the few steps of unnecessary intimacy she had been gradually led along. She was accordingly more guarded, and more cool, than she had been the night before.

He wanted to animate her curiosity again as to how and where he could have heard her formerly praised; wanted very much to be gratified by more solicitation; but the charm was broken: he found that the heat and animation of a public room were necessary to kindle his modest cousin's vanity; he found, at least, that it was not to be done now, by any of those attempts which he could hazard among the too-commanding claims of the others. He little surmised that it was a subject acting now exactly against his interest, bringing immediately into her thoughts all those parts of his conduct which were least excusable.

She had some satisfaction in finding that he was really going out of Bath the next morning, going early, and that he would be gone the greater part of two days. He was invited again to Camden-place the very evening of his return; but from Thursday to Saturday evening his absence was certain. It was bad enough that a Mrs. Clay should be always before her; but that a deeper hypocrite should be added to their party, seemed the destruction of every thing like peace and comfort. It was so humiliating to reflect on the constant deception practised on her father and Elizabeth; to consider the various sources

The White Hart, by William Lewis, after John Charles Maggs (1819–1896). Austen's friend and relation Fanny Cage may have served as a model for Louisa Musgrove, for both women suffered from nerves after a bad accident, and both were particularly susceptible to noise during their subsequent stay at the White Hart. "Poor F. Cage," Austen wrote to Cassandra in 1813, ". . . the noise of the White Hart was terrible to her" (Austen, *Letters,* 221, 420).

5 "So complicate" is, literally, "so folded together."

6 "Compounded" is "settled amicably."

7 "New poems" included *The Excursion,* by William Wordsworth; *Roderick, the Last of the Goths,* by Robert Southey (1774–1843); *Jacqueline,* by Samuel Rogers (1763–1855); and *The Corsair* and *Lara,* both by Lord Byron. All five of these poems were published in 1814. There were also many recent pamphlets and books on the state of the nation, such as *A View of the State of the Nation, and of the measures of the last five years* (1811), by Thomas Peregrine Courtenay (1782–1841); *A Series of Letters on the Political and Financial State of the Nation* (1814), by Francis Perceval Eliot (1755–1818); and the anonymous *View of the State of the Nation, at the present crisis* (1814).

of mortification preparing for them! Mrs. Clay's selfishness was not so complicate[5] nor so revolting as his; and Anne would have compounded[6] for the marriage at once, with all its evils, to be clear of Mr. Elliot's subtleties, in endeavouring to prevent it.

On Friday morning she meant to go very early to Lady Russell, and accomplish the necessary communication; and she would have gone directly after breakfast but that Mrs. Clay was also going out on some obliging purpose of saving her sister trouble, which determined her to wait till she might be safe from such a companion. She saw Mrs. Clay fairly off, therefore, before she began to talk of spending the morning in Rivers-street.

"Very well," said Elizabeth, "I have nothing to send but my love. Oh! you may as well take back that tiresome book she would lend me, and pretend I have read it through. I really cannot be plaguing myself for ever with all the new poems and states of the nation[7] that come out. Lady Russell quite bores one with her new publications.

8 *Arrangé* is "artificial."

9 "The White Hart" was located on the western side of the Abbey Churchyard and was Bath's principal coaching inn. It was demolished in 1869. Compare Charles Dickens in *The Pickwick Papers* (1836–1837), where "Mr. Pickwick and his friends . . . respectively retired to their private sitting-rooms at the White Hart Hotel, opposite the great pump room, Bath, where the waiters, from their costume, might be mistaken for Westminster boys, only they destroy the illusion by behaving themselves so much better" (Dickens, *The Pickwick Papers,* ed. James Kinsley [Oxford: Oxford University Press, 1988, 445]).

10 "Regular" is "sensible."

You need not tell her so, but I thought her dress hideous the other night. I used to think she had some taste in dress, but I was ashamed of her at the concert. Something so formal and *arrangé*[8] in her air! and she sits so upright! My best love, of course."

"And mine," added Sir Walter. "Kindest regards. And you may say, that I mean to call upon her soon. Make a civil message. But I shall only leave my card. Morning visits are never fair by women at her time of life, who make themselves up so little. If she would only wear rouge, she would not be afraid of being seen; but last time I called, I observed the blinds were let down immediately."

While her father spoke, there was a knock at the door. Who could it be? Anne, remembering the preconcerted visits, at all hours, of Mr. Elliot, would have expected him, but for his known engagement seven miles off. After the usual period of suspense, the usual sounds of approach were heard, and "Mr. and Mrs. Charles Musgrove" were ushered into the room.

Surprise was the strongest emotion raised by their appearance; but Anne was really glad to see them; and the others were not so sorry but that they could put on a decent air of welcome; and as soon as it became clear that these, their nearest relations, were not arrived with any views of accommodation in that house, Sir Walter and Elizabeth were able to rise in cordiality, and do the honours of it very well. They were come to Bath for a few days with Mrs. Musgrove, and were at the White Hart.[9] So much was pretty soon understood; but till Sir Walter and Elizabeth were walking Mary into the other drawing-room, and regaling themselves with her admiration, Anne could not draw upon Charles's brain for a regular[10] history of their coming, or an explanation of some smiling hints of particular business, which had been ostentatiously dropped by Mary, as well as of some apparent confusion as to whom their party consisted of.

She then found that it consisted of Mrs. Musgrove, Henrietta, and Captain Harville, beside their two selves. He gave her a very plain, intelligible account of the whole; a narration in which she saw a great deal of most characteristic proceeding. The scheme had received its first impulse by Captain Harville's wanting to come to Bath on business. He had begun to talk of it a week ago; and by way of doing something, as shooting was over, Charles had proposed coming with him, and Mrs. Harville had seemed to like the idea of it very much, as an advantage to her husband; but Mary could not bear to be left, and had made herself so unhappy about it that, for a day or two, every thing seemed to be in suspense, or at an end. But then, it had been taken up by his father and mother. His mother had some old friends in Bath, whom she wanted to see; it was thought a good opportunity for Henrietta to come and buy wedding-clothes for herself and her sister; and, in short, it ended in being his mother's party, that every thing might be comfortable and easy to Captain Harville; and he and Mary were included in it, by way of general convenience. They had arrived late the night before. Mrs. Harville, her children, and Captain Benwick, remained with Mr. Musgrove and Louisa at Uppercross.

Anne's only surprise was, that affairs should be in forwardness enough for Henrietta's wedding-clothes to be talked of: she had imagined such difficulties of fortune to exist there as must prevent the marriage from being near at hand; but she learned from Charles that, very recently, (since Mary's last letter to herself) Charles Hayter had been applied to by a friend to hold a living for a youth who could not possibly claim it under many years;[11] and that, on the strength of this present income, with almost a certainty of something more permanent long before the term in question, the two families had consented to the young people's wishes, and that their marriage was likely to take place in a few months, quite as soon as Louisa's. "And a very good living it was," Charles added, "only five-and-twenty miles from Uppercross, and in a very fine country—fine part of Dorsetshire. In the centre of some of the best preserves[12] in the kingdom, surrounded by three great proprietors, each more careful and jealous[13] than the other; and to two of the three, at least, Charles Hayter might get a special recommendation. Not that he will value it as he ought," he observed, "Charles is too cool about sporting. That's the worst of him."

"I am extremely glad, indeed," cried Anne, "particularly glad that this should happen: and that of two sisters, who both deserve equally well, and who have always been such good friends, the pleasant pros-

11 Charles Hayter has agreed to serve as an interim pastor in a parish that has been promised to a person who is not yet twenty-three years old, the minimum age for ordination in the Church of England (Collins, 20).

12 "Preserves" were sections of large estates set aside for the purpose of sustaining populations of game animals. Hunting was a major activity in Austen's day, and many country gentlemen thought of themselves as existing solely "to hunt and shoot and raise the price of corn" (R. J. White, *Life in Regency England* [London: Batsford, 1963], 53). In *Mansfield Park,* Tom and Edmund go pheasant hunting and bring home "six brace" between them (II, 1), while in *Pride and Prejudice* Mrs. Bennet anxiously assures Mr. Bingley that he may come and shoot birds on Mr. Bennet's estate after he has "killed" all the birds on his own (III, 11). Fox hunting was a national pastime. In *Northanger Abbey,* Catherine must suffer in silence while John Thorpe boasts to her of "some famous day's sport, with the foxhounds, in which his foresight and skill in directing the dogs had repaired the mistakes of the most experienced huntsman, and in which the boldness of his riding, though it had never endangered his own life for a moment, had been constantly leading others into difficulties" (I, 9). Charles Musgrove is of course especially interested in the game preserves because he does "nothing with much zeal, but sport."

13 "Jealous" is "vigilant."

14 Mr. Musgrove is under financial strain because he has to find the money for two dowries at the same time.

15 Typically, the daughter brought to the marriage any money she might have inherited, together with whatever portion of her parents' estate she was entitled to.

16 "As times go" in the nineteenth century, more and more couples married for love and compatibility rather than as a way of consolidating family property and wealth. In *The History of Sexuality,* Michel Foucault examines this fundamental shift in values and posits two competing systems of marriage: the "deployment of alliance" and a newer arrangement created "particularly from the eighteenth century onward," the "deployment of sexuality." In *Pride and Prejudice,* when Darcy first proposes to Elizabeth, he is in effect torn between these two systems, between what he owes his rank (the "deployment of alliance") and what he owes his own passions (the "deployment of sexuality"). In *Persuasion,* Sir Walter, Elizabeth, and Mary are all committed to the "deployment of alliance," whereas Charles Hayter and Henrietta—like Anne herself—choose a partner on the basis of desire and individual preference (Foucault, *The History of Sexuality,* vol. 1, trans. Robert Hurley [New York: Random House, 1978], 106).

'*Sits at her elbow, reading verses.*'

Hugh Thomson, Illustrations for *Persuasion,* 1897. Captain Benwick reads to his fiancée Louisa Musgrove.

pects of one should not be dimming those of the other—that they should be so equal in their prosperity and comfort. I hope your father and mother are quite happy with regard to both."

"Oh! yes. My father would be as well pleased if the gentlemen were richer, but he has no other fault to find. Money, you know, coming down with money—two daughters at once—it cannot be a very agreeable operation, and it streightens him as to many things.[14] However, I do not mean to say they have not a right to it. It is very fit they should have daughters' shares;[15] and I am sure he has always been a very kind, liberal father to me. Mary does not above half like Henrietta's match. She never did, you know. But she does not do him justice, nor think enough about Winthrop. I cannot make her attend to the value of the property. It is a very fair match, as times go;[16] and I have liked Charles Hayter all my life, and I shall not leave off now."

"Such excellent parents as Mr. and Mrs. Musgrove," exclaimed Anne, "should be happy in their children's marriages. They do every thing to confer happiness, I am sure. What a blessing to young people to be in such hands! Your father and mother seem so totally free from all those ambitious feelings which have led to so much misconduct and misery, both in young and old! I hope you think Louisa perfectly recovered now?"

He answered rather hesitatingly, "Yes, I believe I do—very much recovered; but she is altered: there is no running or jumping about, no laughing or dancing; it is quite different. If one happens only to shut the door a little hard, she starts and wriggles like a young dab chick[17] in the water; and Benwick sits at her elbow, reading verses, or whispering to her, all day long."

Anne could not help laughing. "That cannot be much to your taste, I know," said she; "but I do believe him to be an excellent young man."

"To be sure he is. Nobody doubts it; and I hope you do not think I am so illiberal as to want every man to have the same objects and pleasures as myself. I have a great value for Benwick; and when one can but get him to talk, he has plenty to say. His reading has done him no harm, for he has fought as well as read. He is a brave fellow. I got more acquainted with him last Monday than ever I did before. We had a famous set-to at rat-hunting all the morning, in my father's great barns;[18] and he played his part so well, that I have liked him the better ever since."

Here they were interrupted by the absolute necessity of Charles's following the others to admire mirrors and china; but Anne had heard enough to understand the present state of Uppercross, and rejoice in its happiness; and though she sighed as she rejoiced, her sigh had none of the ill-will of envy in it. She would certainly have risen to their blessings if she could, but she did not want to lessen theirs.

The visit passed off altogether in high good humour. Mary was in excellent spirits, enjoying the gaiety and the change; and so well satisfied with the journey in her mother-in-law's carriage with four

17 A "dab-chick" is a small grebe noted for its diving. Austen seems to recall Alexander Pope in *The Dunciad* (1728), II, 59–60: "As when a dab-chick waddles thro' the copse, / On feet and wings, and flies, and wades, and hops" (Pope, V, 105).

18 William Makepeace Thackeray gives a vivid account of rat hunting in his masterpiece *Vanity Fair,* a novel published in 1847–1848, but set like *Persuasion* during the Regency. One "most blissful morning," Thackeray writes, "Mr. James, the Colonel, and Horn . . . taking little Rawdon with them . . . partook of the amusement of rat-hunting in a barn, than which sport Rawdon as yet had never seen anything so noble. They stopped up the ends of certain drains in the barn, into the other openings of which ferrets were inserted; and then stood silently aloof with uplifted stakes in their hands, and an anxious little terrier (Mr. James's celebrated 'dawg' Forceps, indeed,) scarcely breathing from excitement, listening motionless on three legs, to the faint squeaking of the rats below. Desperately bold at last, the persecuted animals bolted above-ground: the terrier accounted for one, the keeper for another, Rawdon, from flurry and excitement missed his rat, but on the other hand he half-murdered a ferret" (Thackeray, *Vanity Fair,* ed. Peter Shillingsburg [New York: Garland, 1989], 405).

Charles Edmund Brock, Illustrations for *Persuasion,* 1898. Charles Musgrove and Captain Benwick enjoy a morning together hunting rats.

horses, and with her own complete independence of Camden-place, that she was exactly in a temper to admire every thing as she ought, and enter most readily into all the superiorities of the house, as they were detailed to her. She had no demands on her father or sister, and her consequence was just enough increased by their handsome drawing-rooms.

Elizabeth was, for a short time, suffering a good deal. She felt that Mrs. Musgrove and all her party ought to be asked to dine with them, but she could not bear to have the difference of style, the reduction of servants, which a dinner must betray, witnessed by those who had been always so inferior to the Elliots of Kellynch.[19] It was a struggle between propriety and vanity; but vanity got the better, and then Elizabeth was happy again. These were her internal persuasions.— "Old fashioned notions—country hospitality—we do not profess to give dinners—few people in Bath do—Lady Alicia never does; did not even ask her own sister's family, though they were here a month: and I dare say it would be very inconvenient to Mrs. Musgrove—put her quite out of her way. I am sure she would rather not come—she cannot feel easy with us. I will ask them all for an evening; that will be much better—that will be a novelty and a treat. They have not seen two such drawing rooms before. They will be delighted to come to-morrow evening. It shall be a regular party—small, but most elegant." And this satisfied Elizabeth: and when the invitation was given to the two present, and promised for the absent, Mary was as completely satisfied. She was particularly asked to meet Mr. Elliot, and be introduced to Lady Dalrymple and Miss Carteret, who were fortunately already engaged to come; and she could not have received a more gratifying attention. Miss Elliot was to have the honour of calling on Mrs. Musgrove in the course of the morning, and Anne walked off with Charles and Mary, to go and see her and Henrietta directly.

Her plan of sitting with Lady Russell must give way for the present. They all three called in Rivers-street for a couple of minutes; but Anne convinced herself that a day's delay of the intended communication could be of no consequence, and hastened forward to the White Hart, to see again the friends and companions of the last au-

19 Elizabeth's reluctance to invite members of her family to dine in Camden Place contrasts strikingly with the hospitality of the Harvilles, who a few months earlier had eagerly invited their friends to dine in their small cottage at Lyme. Elizabeth cannot bear the reduced circumstances "which a dinner must betray." The Harvilles "invite from the heart."

tumn, with an eagerness of good will which many associations contributed to form.

They found Mrs. Musgrove and her daughter within, and by themselves, and Anne had the kindest welcome from each. Henrietta was exactly in that state of recently-improved views, of fresh-formed happiness, which made her full of regard and interest for every body she had ever liked before at all; and Mrs. Musgrove's real affection had been won by her usefulness when they were in distress. It was a heartiness, and a warmth, and a sincerity which Anne delighted in the more, from the sad want of such blessings at home. She was intreated to give them as much of her time as possible, invited for every day and all day long, or rather claimed as a part of the family; and in return, she naturally fell into all her wonted ways of attention and assistance, and on Charles's leaving them together, was listening to Mrs. Musgrove's history of Louisa, and to Henrietta's of herself, giving opinions on business, and recommendations to shops; with intervals of every help which Mary required, from altering her ribbon to settling her accounts, from finding her keys, and assorting her

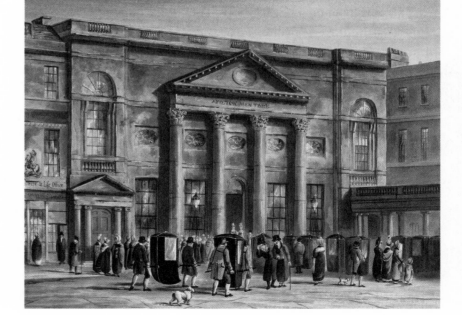

The Pump Room, by David Cox, 1820. The name derived from the pump that drew up the mineral water that so many flocked to Bath to drink in the hope of finding a cure for their particular ailment. "Taking the waters" was also an essential part of social life in Bath.

trinkets, to trying to convince her that she was not ill used by any body; which Mary, well amused as she generally was in her station at a window overlooking the entrance to the pump-room,[20] could not but have her moments of imagining.

A morning of thorough confusion was to be expected. A large party in an hotel ensured a quick-changing, unsettled scene. One five minutes brought a note, the next a parcel, and Anne had not been there half an hour, when their dining-room, spacious as it was, seemed more than half filled: a party of steady old friends were seated round Mrs. Musgrove, and Charles came back with Captains Harville and Wentworth. The appearance of the latter could not be more than the surprise of the moment. It was impossible for her to have forgotten to feel, that this arrival of their common friends must be soon bringing them together again. Their last meeting had been most important in opening his feelings; she had derived from it a delightful conviction; but she feared from his looks, that the same unfortunate persuasion,[21] which had hastened him away from the concert room, still governed. He did not seem to want to be near enough for conversation.

She tried to be calm, and leave things to take their course; and tried to dwell much on this argument of rational dependance— "Surely, if there be constant attachment on each side, our hearts must understand each other ere[22] long. We are not boy and girl, to be captiously[23] irritable, misled by every moment's inadvertence, and wantonly playing with our own happiness." And yet, a few minutes afterwards, she felt as if their being in company with each other, under their present circumstances, could only be exposing them to inadvertencies[24] and misconstructions of the most mischievous[25] kind.

"Anne," cried Mary, still at her window, "there is Mrs. Clay, I am sure, standing under the colonnade, and a gentleman with her. I saw them turn the corner from Bath-street[26] just now. They seem deep in talk. Who is it?—Come, and tell me. Good heavens! I recollect.—It is Mr. Elliot himself."

"No," cried Anne quickly, "it cannot be Mr. Elliot, I assure you. He was to leave Bath at nine this morning, and does not come back till to-morrow."

20 The "Pump Room" was situated between Bath Abbey to the east and the White Hart Inn to the west and was the center of social activity in Bath. "Here an excellent company of musicians perform every morning, during the full season," John Feltham reports; "and a numerous assemblage of ladies and gentlemen, walking up and down in social converse, during the performance, presents a picture of animation which nothing can exceed. All persons who are decently dressed, without any regard to fashion, may freely perambulate the Pump-room. Those who drink the waters, however, are expected to pay about a guinea a month, besides a gratuity to the pumper" (Feltham, 47). In *Northanger Abbey,* Catherine soon discovers that every morning in Bath "brought its regular duties;—shops were to be visited; some new part of the town to be looked at; and the Pump-room to be attended, where they paraded up and down for an hour, looking at every body and speaking to no one" (I, 3).

21 In this context, "persuasion" means "a belief, conviction, or opinion" *(OED).*

22 "Ere" is "before."

23 "Captiously" is used here in the sense of "apt to catch at faults or take exception to actions" *(OED).*

24 "Inadvertencies" are "acts of inattention or heedlessness."

25 "Mischievous" in this sense is "harmful" or "destructive."

26 Bath Street lies immediately to the south of the White Hart Inn, and opens into the Abbey Churchyard.

27 In the early nineteenth century, a handshake between a man and a woman was a highly suggestive ges-
ture that indicated a close degree of familiarity. "At no
time" ought a woman "to volunteer shaking hands with
a male acquaintance, who holds not any particular
bond of esteem with regard to herself or family," *The
Mirror of Graces* sternly instructed. "A touch, a pressure
of the hands, are the only external signs a woman can
give of entertaining a particular regard for certain individuals. And to lavish this valuable power of expression
upon all comers, upon the impudent and contemptible, is an indelicate extravagance which, I hope, needs
only to be exposed, to be put for ever out of countenance." The handshake between Mr. Elliot and Mrs.
Clay is yet another clear sign that an intimate relationship is developing between them. What is more,
though it is happening right under the noses of the Elliots, they are all oblivious to it. They see Mr. Elliot
only as he relates to their particular situation and
serves to help or hinder their own particular interests.
Here—because she is so absorbed in proving to Wentworth that she has no interest in Mr. Elliot's activities—Anne fails to recognize the significance of Mr.
Elliot being in Bath when he said he would be away, of
his meeting with Mrs. Clay when she is on her own,
and of his shaking hands with her when they part. As is
so often the case, perception is at the heart of persuasion (A Lady of Distinction, *The Mirror of the Graces*
[London: Crosby, 1811], 170).

28 Pierce Egan enthusiastically described the boxes
at the new Theatre Royal: "There are three tier of
boxes. The private ones, which are twenty-six in number, are enclosed with gilt lattices. . . . The private
boxes have also an elegant suite of retiring rooms"
(Egan, 143–144).

As she spoke, she felt that Captain Wentworth was looking at her;
the consciousness of which vexed and embarrassed her, and made
her regret that she had said so much, simple as it was.

Mary, resenting that she should be supposed not to know her own
cousin, began talking very warmly about the family features, and
protesting still more positively that it was Mr. Elliot, calling again
upon Anne to come and look herself; but Anne did not mean to stir,
and tried to be cool and unconcerned. Her distress returned, however, on perceiving smiles and intelligent glances pass between two
or three of the lady visitors, as if they believed themselves quite in
the secret. It was evident that the report concerning her had spread;
and a short pause succeeded, which seemed to ensure that it would
now spread farther.

"Do come, Anne," cried Mary, "come and look yourself. You will
be too late, if you do not make haste. They are parting, they are shaking hands.[27] He is turning away. Not know Mr. Elliot, indeed!—You
seem to have forgot all about Lyme."

To pacify Mary, and perhaps screen her own embarrassment, Anne
did move quietly to the window. She was just in time to ascertain
that it really was Mr. Elliot (which she had never believed), before
he disappeared on one side, as Mrs. Clay walked quickly off on the
other; and checking the surprise which she could not but feel at such
an appearance of friendly conference between two persons of totally
opposite interests, she calmly said, "Yes, it is Mr. Elliot certainly. He
has changed his hour of going, I suppose, that is all—or I may be mistaken; I might not attend;" and walked back to her chair, recomposed,
and with the comfortable hope of having acquitted herself well.

The visitors took their leave; and Charles, having civilly seen them
off, and then made a face at them, and abused them for coming, began with—

"Well, mother, I have done something for you that you will like. I
have been to the theatre, and secured a box[28] for tomorrow night.
A'n't I a good boy? I know you love a play; and there is room for us all.
It holds nine. I have engaged Captain Wentworth. Anne will not be
sorry to join us, I am sure. We all like a play. Have not I done well,
mother?"

Mrs. Musgrove was good humouredly beginning to express her perfect readiness for the play, if Henrietta and all the others liked it, when Mary eagerly interrupted her by exclaiming,

"Good heavens, Charles! how can you think of such a thing? Take a box for to-morrow night! Have you forgot that we are engaged to Camden-place to-morrow night? and that we were most particularly asked on purpose to meet Lady Dalrymple and her daughter, and Mr. Elliot—all the principal family connexions—on purpose to be introduced to them? How can you be so forgetful?"

"Phoo! phoo!" replied Charles, "what's an evening party? Never worth remembering. Your father might have asked us to dinner, I think, if he had wanted to see us. You may do as you like, but I shall go to the play."

"Oh! Charles, I declare it will be too abominable if you do! when you promised to go."

"No, I did not promise. I only smirked and bowed, and said the word 'happy.' There was no promise."

"But you must go, Charles. It would be unpardonable to fail. We were asked on purpose to be introduced. There was always such a great connexion between the Dalrymples and ourselves. Nothing ever happened on either side that was not announced immediately. We are quite near relations, you know: and Mr. Elliot too, whom you ought so particularly to be acquainted with! Every attention is due to Mr. Elliot. Consider, my father's heir—the future representative of the family."

"Don't talk to me about heirs and representatives," cried Charles. "I am not one of those who neglect the reigning power to bow to the rising sun. If I would not go for the sake of your father, I should think it scandalous to go for the sake of his heir. What is Mr. Elliot to me?"[29]

The careless expression was life to Anne, who saw that Captain Wentworth was all attention, looking and listening with his whole soul; and that the last words brought his enquiring eyes from Charles to herself.

Charles and Mary still talked on in the same style; he, half serious and half jesting, maintaining the scheme for the play; and she, invari-

29 It is a critical commonplace to divide *Persuasion* into two social groups: the old and largely sterile world of the landed gentry and the new world of the rising professional classes represented by the women and men of the navy. However, Charles Musgrove's defiant question—"What is Mr. Elliot to me?"—plainly shows that there are important connections between the navy class of Wentworth and the Crofts, and those elements of the country gentry that still prized confidence, generosity, and independence.

ably serious, most warmly opposing it, and not omitting to make it known, that however determined to go to Camden-place herself, she should not think herself very well used, if they went to the play without her. Mrs. Musgrove interposed.

"We had better put it off. Charles, you had much better go back, and change the box for Tuesday. It would be a pity to be divided, and we should be losing Miss Anne too, if there is a party at her father's; and I am sure neither Henrietta nor I should care at all for the play, if Miss Anne could not be with us."

Anne felt truly obliged to her for such kindness; and quite as much so, moreover, for the opportunity it gave her of decidedly saying—

"If it depended only on my inclination, ma'am, the party at home (excepting on Mary's account) would not be the smallest impediment. I have no pleasure in the sort of meeting, and should be too happy to change it for a play, and with you. But, it had better not be attempted, perhaps."

She had spoken it; but she trembled when it was done, conscious that her words were listened to, and daring not even to try to observe their effect.

It was soon generally agreed that Tuesday should be the day, Charles only reserving the advantage of still teasing his wife, by persisting that he would go to the play to-morrow, if nobody else would.

Captain Wentworth left his seat, and walked to the fireplace; probably for the sake of walking away from it soon afterwards, and taking a station, with less barefaced design, by Anne.

"You have not been long enough in Bath," said he, "to enjoy the evening parties of the place."

"Oh! no. The usual character of them has nothing for me. I am no card-player."

"You were not formerly, I know. You did not use to like cards; but time makes many changes."

"I am not yet so much changed," cried Anne, and stopped, fearing she hardly knew what misconstruction. After waiting a few moments he said—and as if it were the result of immediate feeling—"It is a period, indeed! Eight years and a half is a period!"

Whether he would have proceeded farther was left to Anne's imagination to ponder over in a calmer hour; for while still hearing the sounds he had uttered, she was startled to other subjects by Henrietta, eager to make use of the present leisure for getting out, and calling on her companions to lose no time, lest somebody else should come in.

They were obliged to move. Anne talked of being perfectly ready, and tried to look it; but she felt that could Henrietta have known the regret and reluctance of her heart in quitting that chair, in preparing to quit the room, she would have found, in all her own sensations for her cousin, in the very security of his affection, wherewith[30] to pity her.

Their preparations, however, were stopped short. Alarming sounds[31] were heard; other visitors approached, and the door was thrown open for Sir Walter and Miss Elliot, whose entrance seemed to give a general chill. Anne felt an instant oppression, and, wherever she looked, saw symptoms of the same. The comfort, the freedom, the gaiety of the room was over, hushed into cold composure, determined silence, or insipid talk, to meet the heartless elegance of her father and sister. How mortifying to feel that it was so!

Her jealous eye was satisfied in one particular. Captain Wentworth was acknowledged again by each, by Elizabeth more graciously than before. She even addressed him once, and looked at him more than once. Elizabeth was, in fact, revolving a great measure. The sequel explained it. After the waste of a few minutes in saying the proper nothings, she began to give the invitation which was to comprise all the remaining dues of the Musgroves. "To-morrow evening, to meet a few friends, no formal party." It was all said very gracefully, and the cards with which she had provided herself, the "Miss Elliot at home,"[32] were laid on the table, with a courteous, comprehensive smile to all; and one smile and one card more decidedly for Captain Wentworth. The truth was, that Elizabeth had been long enough in Bath, to understand the importance of a man of such an air and appearance as his. The past was nothing. The present was that Captain Wentworth would move about well in her drawing-room. The card

30 "Wherewith" is "the means" or "the resources."

31 "Alarming sounds" in this context are sounds that "arouse or attract attention" *(OED)*.

32 A card announcing that a person was "at home" was "used as a formula" to invite company "to an informal reception" *(OED)*.

33 Anne and Wentworth have been in each other's company for weeks, but there has been so little direct dialogue between them that he seems an almost ghostly presence in her life. Yet between them there has also been strong, nonverbal communication, and slowly it is working to bring them back together again. In an 1821 assessment in the *Quarterly Review,* Richard Whately emphasizes Anne's keen observations of Wentworth, and then comments on the difference between the distance that divided them for so many years, and "her involuntary sympathy with all his feelings, and instant comprehension of all his thoughts, of the meaning of every glance of his eye, and curl of his lip." More recently, Juliet McMaster notes that *Persuasion* has a great deal to offer "the observer of body language, since Anne Elliot is an astute reader, observing the frankly expressive facial motions of Wentworth, and herself vividly legible, though no one but the reader is observing the signs. . . . And since the two principals in this love story are estranged and cannot relate through speech—except through overhearing speech addressed to others—the body motions and signals are their best route to understanding and reconcilement" (*Critical Heritage,* 103; McMaster, *Reading the Body in the Eighteenth-Century Novel* [London: Palgrave, 2004], 172).

34 "She felt unequal to move" has been amended by several editors to read "she felt unequal to more," a change that seems plausible.

was pointedly given, and Sir Walter and Elizabeth arose and disappeared.

The interruption had been short, though severe; and ease and animation returned to most of those they left, as the door shut them out, but not to Anne. She could think only of the invitation she had with such astonishment witnessed; and of the manner in which it had been received, a manner of doubtful meaning, of surprise rather than gratification, of polite acknowledgement rather than acceptance. She knew him; she saw disdain in his eye, and could not venture to believe that he had determined to accept such an offering, as atonement for all the insolence of the past. Her spirits sank. He held the card in his hand after they were gone, as if deeply considering it.

"Only think of Elizabeth's including every body!" whispered Mary very audibly. "I do not wonder Captain Wentworth is delighted! You see he cannot put the card out of his hand."

Anne caught his eye, saw his cheeks glow, and his mouth form itself into a momentary expression of contempt, and turned away, that she might neither see nor hear more to vex her.[33]

The party separated. The gentlemen had their own pursuits, the ladies proceeded on their own business, and they met no more while Anne belonged to them. She was earnestly begged to return and dine, and give them all the rest of the day; but her spirits had been so long exerted, that at present she felt unequal to move,[34] and fit only for home, where she might be sure of being as silent as she chose.

Promising to be with them the whole of the following morning, therefore, she closed the fatigues of the present, by a toilsome walk to Camden-place, there to spend the evening chiefly in listening to the busy arrangements of Elizabeth and Mrs. Clay for the morrow's party, the frequent enumeration of the persons invited, and the continually improving detail of all the embellishments which were to make it the most completely elegant of its kind in Bath, while harassing herself in secret with the never-ending question, of whether Captain Wentworth would come or not? They were reckoning him as certain, but, with her, it was a gnawing solicitude never appeased for five minutes together. She generally thought he would come, because she generally thought he ought; but it was a case which she could not so shape into any positive act of duty or discretion, as inevitably to defy the suggestions of very opposite feelings.

She only roused herself from the broodings of this restless agitation, to let Mrs. Clay know that she had been seen with Mr. Elliot three hours after his being supposed to be out of Bath; for having watched in vain for some intimation of the interview from the lady herself, she determined to mention it; and it seemed to her that there was guilt in Mrs. Clay's face as she listened. It was transient, cleared away in an instant, but Anne could imagine she read there the consciousness of having, by some complication of mutual trick, or some overbearing authority of his, been obliged to attend (perhaps for half an hour) to his lectures and restrictions on her designs on Sir Walter. She exclaimed, however, with a very tolerable imitation of nature,

"Oh dear! very true. Only think, Miss Elliot, to my great surprise I met with Mr. Elliot in Bath-street! I was never more astonished. He turned back and walked with me to the Pump-yard. He had been prevented setting off for Thornberry, but I really forget by what— for I was in a hurry, and could not much attend, and I can only answer for his being determined not to be delayed in his return. He wanted to know how early he might be admitted to-morrow. He was full of 'to-morrow;' and it is very evident that I have been full of it too ever since I entered the house, and learnt the extension of your plan, and all that had happened, or my seeing him could never have gone so entirely out my head."

II

1 "Plighted" is "pledged."

2 The Sultaness Scheherazade is a character in *The Arabian Nights' Entertainment.* To avenge himself for the infidelity of his first wife, a sultan vows to marry a new woman every evening and execute her the following day. When he meets Scheherazade, however, she tells him such interesting stories that he keeps delaying her execution from day to day until finally he falls in love with her and revokes his vow. Compare Maria Edgeworth in *Belinda,* where Lady Delacour turns to the eponymous heroine and asks "with a forced smile . . . 'Now shall the princess Scheherazade go on with her story?'" (Edgeworth, *Works,* II, 42).

3 The text has been amended here from "friend's account" to "friends' account."

ONE DAY ONLY HAD PASSED since Anne's conversation with Mrs. Smith; but a keener interest had succeeded, and she was now so little touched by Mr. Elliot's conduct, except by its effects in one quarter, that it became a matter of course the next morning, still to defer her explanatory visit in Rivers-street. She had promised to be with the Musgroves from breakfast to dinner. Her faith was plighted,[1] and Mr. Elliot's character, like the Sultaness Scheherazade's head,[2] must live another day.

She could not keep her appointment punctually, however; the weather was unfavourable, and she had grieved over the rain on her friends' account,[3] and felt it very much on her own, before she was able to attempt the walk. When she reached the White Hart, and made her way to the proper apartment, she found herself neither arriving quite in time, nor the first to arrive. The party before her were Mrs. Musgrove, talking to Mrs. Croft, and Captain Harville to Captain Wentworth, and she immediately heard that Mary and Henrietta, too impatient to wait, had gone out the moment it had cleared, but would be back again soon, and that the strictest injunctions had been left with Mrs. Musgrove, to keep her there till they returned. She had only to submit, sit down, be outwardly composed, and feel herself plunged at once in all the agitations which she had merely laid her account of tasting a little before the morning closed. There was no delay, no waste of time. She was deep in the happiness of such misery, or the misery of such happiness, instantly. Two minutes after her entering the room, Captain Wentworth said,

"We will write the letter we were talking of, Harville, now, if you will give me materials."

Materials were all at hand, on a separate table; he went to it, and nearly turning his back on them all, was engrossed by writing.

Mrs. Musgrove was giving Mrs. Croft the history of her eldest daughter's engagement, and just in that inconvenient tone of voice which was perfectly audible while it pretended to be a whisper. Anne felt that she did not belong to the conversation, and yet, as Captain Harville seemed thoughtful and not disposed to talk, she could not avoid hearing many undesirable particulars, such as "how Mr. Musgrove and my brother Hayter had met again and again to talk it over; what my brother Hayter had said one day, and what Mr. Musgrove had proposed the next, and what had occurred to my sister Hayter, and what the young people had wished, and what I said at first I never could consent to, but was afterwards persuaded to think might do very well," and a great deal in the same style of open-hearted communication—Minutiæ which, even with every advantage of taste and delicacy which good Mrs. Musgrove could not give, could be properly interesting only to the principals. Mrs. Croft was attending with great good humour, and whenever she spoke at all, it was very sensibly. Anne hoped the gentlemen might each be too much self-occupied to hear.

"And so, ma'am, all these thing considered," said Mrs. Musgrove in her powerful whisper, "though we could have wished it different, yet altogether we did not think it fair to stand out any longer; for Charles Hayter was quite wild about it, and Henrietta was pretty near as bad; and so we thought they had better marry at once, and make the best of it, as many others have done before them. At any rate, said I, it will be better than a long engagement."

"That is precisely what I was going to observe," cried Mrs. Croft. "I would rather have young people settle on a small income at once, and have to struggle with a few difficulties together, than be involved in a long engagement. I always think that no mutual—"

"Oh! dear Mrs. Croft," cried Mrs. Musgrove, unable to let her finish her speech, "there is nothing I so abominate for young people as a long engagement. It is what I always protested against for my chil-

Anna Letitia Barbauld, by Sir Emery Walker (1851–1933), after Henry Meyer. Barbauld produced voluminously as an editor and reviewer. Her literary anthology for young women, *The Female Speaker,* appeared in 1811, the same year as Austen's *Sense and Sensibility.* Barbauld's most ambitious poem, *Eighteen Hundred and Eleven,* was published in 1812 and vigorously condemned Britain's participation in the wars against Napoleon.

dren. It is all very well, I used to say, for young people to be engaged, if there is a certainty of their being able to marry in six months, or even in twelve, but a long engagement!"

"Yes, dear ma'am," said Mrs. Croft, "or an uncertain engagement; an engagement which may be long. To begin without knowing that at such a time there will be the means of marrying, I hold to be very unsafe and unwise, and what, I think, all parents should prevent as far as they can."

Anne found an unexpected interest here. She felt its application to herself, felt it in a nervous thrill all over her, and at the same moment that her eyes instinctively glanced towards the distant table, Captain Wentworth's pen ceased to move, his head was raised, pausing, listening, and he turned round the next instant to give a look—one quick, conscious look at her.

The two ladies continued to talk, to re-urge the same admitted truths, and enforce them with such examples of the ill effect of a contrary practice, as had fallen within their observation, but Anne

A youth of the Busby family, by Jacob Fruman. The miniature of himself that Captain Benwick had painted for Fanny Harville would have been similar to this one. Fruman may also have painted the miniature of Austen's sailor brother Francis circa 1806, for Fruman was working in South Africa at the time Francis was engaged in long-distance convoying to the Cape of Good Hope.

heard nothing distinctly; it was only a buzz of words in her ear, her mind was in confusion.

Captain Harville, who had in truth been hearing none of it, now left his seat, and moved to a window; and Anne seeming to watch him, though it was from thorough absence of mind, became gradually sensible[4] that he was inviting her to join him where he stood. He looked at her with a smile, and a little motion of the head, which expressed, "Come to me, I have something to say;" and the unaffected, easy kindness of manner which denoted the feelings of an older acquaintance than he really was, strongly enforced the invitation. She roused herself and went to him. The window at which he stood, was at the other end of the room from where the two ladies were sitting, and though nearer to Captain Wentworth's table, not very near. As she joined him, Captain Harville's countenance reassumed the serious, thoughtful expression which seemed its natural character.

"Look here," said he, unfolding a parcel in his hand, and displaying a small miniature painting, "do you know who that is?"

"Certainly, Captain Benwick."

"Yes, and you may guess who it is for. But (in a deep tone) it was not done for her. Miss Elliot, do you remember our walking together at Lyme, and grieving for him? I little thought then—but no matter. This was drawn at the Cape. He met with a clever young German artist at the Cape,[5] and in compliance with a promise to my poor sister, sat to him, and was bringing it home for her. And I have now the charge of getting it properly set for another! It was a commission to me! But who else was there to employ? I hope I can allow for him. I am not sorry, indeed, to make it over to another. He undertakes it—(looking towards Captain Wentworth) he is writing about it now." And with a quivering lip he wound up the whole by adding, "Poor Fanny! she would not have forgotten him so soon!"

"No," replied Anne, in a low feeling voice. "That, I can easily believe."

"It was not in her nature. She doated on him."

"It would not be the nature of any woman who truly loved."

Captain Harville smiled, as much as to say, "Do you claim that for your sex?" and she answered the question, smiling also, "Yes. We

4 "Sensible" is "aware."

5 The "clever young German artist at the Cape" has been tentatively identified as Jacob Frieman or Fruman (Harris, 84, 216–217).

6 Critics have found sources for Anne's claims about the differing fates of female and male lovers in writings from Geoffrey Chaucer (circa 1342–1400) and William Shakespeare to Richard Steele (1672–1729) and Mary Wollstonecraft. In *The Rambler*, Number 85, Samuel Johnson writes that he has "always admired the wisdom" of teaching "every woman of whatever condition . . . some arts of manufacture, by which the vacuities of recluse and domestick leisure may be filled up. These arts are more necessary as the weakness of their sex and the general system of life debar ladies from many employments which by diversifying the circumstances of men, preserve them from being cankered by the rust of their own thoughts" and victimized by "chimeras, fears, sorrows and desires." The author and editor Anna Letitia Barbauld (1743–1825) makes a similar point in her 1810 essay titled "The Origin and Progress of Novel-Writing": "Why is it that women when they write are apt to give a melancholy tinge to their compositions? Is it that they suffer more, and have fewer resources against melancholy? Is it that men, mixing at large in society, have a brisker flow of ideas, and, seeing a greater variety of characters, introduce more of the business and pleasures of life into their productions? Is it that humour is a scarcer product of the mind than sentiment, and more congenial to the stronger powers of man? Is it that women nurse those feelings in secrecy and silence and diversify the expression of them with endless shades of sentiment, which are more transiently felt, and with fewer modifications of delicacy, by the other sex?" (Johnson, *Rambler*, IV, 85–86; *Anna Letitia Barbauld: Selected Poetry and Prose*, ed. William McCarthy and Elizabeth Kraft [Peterborough, ON: Broadview, 2002], 405–406).

Further, in her personal copy of *Persuasion*, Maria Edgeworth wrote in the margin beside this passage that "our mind is continually fixt on one object." Similarly, Lord Byron, in the conclusion to Canto One of *Don Juan* (1819), echoes Austen when he has Donna Julia pour out her grief over her separation from Don Juan:

"Man's love is of his life a thing apart,
   'Tis woman's whole existence; man may range

certainly do not forget you, so soon as you forget us. It is, perhaps, our fate rather than our merit. We cannot help ourselves. We live at home, quiet, confined, and our feelings prey upon us. You are forced on exertion. You have always a profession, pursuits, business of some sort or other, to take you back into the world immediately, and continual occupation and change soon weaken impressions."[6]

"Granting your assertion that the world does all this so soon for men, (which, however, I do not think I shall grant) it does not apply to Benwick. He has not been forced upon any exertion. The peace turned him on shore at the very moment, and he has been living with us, in our little family-circle, ever since."

"True," said Anne, "very true; I did not recollect; but what shall we say now, Captain Harville? If the change be not from outward circumstances, it must be from within; it must be nature, man's nature, which has done the business for Captain Benwick."[7]

"No, no, it is not man's nature. I will not allow it to be more man's nature than woman's to be inconstant and forget those they do love, or have loved. I believe the reverse. I believe in a true analogy between our bodily frames and our mental; and that as our bodies are the strongest, so are our feelings; capable of bearing most rough usage, and riding out the heaviest weather."

"Your feelings may be the strongest," replied Anne, "but the same spirit of analogy will authorise me to assert that ours are the most tender. Man is more robust than woman, but he is not longer-lived; which exactly explains my view of the nature of their attachments. Nay, it would be too hard upon you, if it were otherwise. You have difficulties, and privations, and dangers enough to struggle with. You are always labouring and toiling, exposed to every risk and hardship. Your home, country, friends, all quitted. Neither time, nor health, nor life, to be called your own. It would be too hard indeed" (with a faltering voice) "if woman's feelings were to be added to all this."

"We shall never agree upon this question"— Captain Harville was beginning to say, when a slight noise called their attention to Captain Wentworth's hitherto perfectly quiet division of the room. It was nothing more than that his pen had fallen down, but Anne was startled at finding him nearer than she had supposed, and half inclined

to suspect that the pen had only fallen, because he had been occupied by them, striving to catch sounds, which yet she did not think
he could have caught.

"Have you finished your letter?" said Captain Harville.

"Not quite, a few lines more. I shall have done in five minutes."

"There is no hurry on my side. I am only ready whenever you
are.—I am in very good anchorage here," (smiling at Anne) "well supplied, and want for nothing.—No hurry for a signal at all.—Well,
Miss Elliot," (lowering his voice) "as I was saying, we shall never agree
I suppose upon this point. No man and woman would, probably. But
let me observe that all histories are against you, all stories, prose and
verse. If I had such a memory as Benwick, I could bring you fifty
quotations in a moment on my side the argument, and I do not think
I ever opened a book in my life which had not something to say upon
woman's inconstancy. Songs and proverbs, all talk of woman's fickle-
ness. But perhaps you will say, these were all written by men."

"Perhaps I shall.—Yes, yes, if you please, no reference to examples
in books. Men have had every advantage of us in telling their own
story. Education has been theirs in so much higher a degree; the pen
has been in their hands. I will not allow books to prove any thing."[8]

"But how shall we prove any thing?"

"We never shall. We never can expect to prove any thing upon
such a point. It is a difference of opinion which does not admit of
proof. We each begin probably with a little bias towards our own sex,
and upon that bias build every circumstance in favour of it which has
occurred within our own circle; many of which circumstances (perhaps those very cases which strike us the most) may be precisely such
as cannot be brought forward[9] without betraying a confidence, or in
some respect saying what should not be said."

"Ah!" cried Captain Harville, in a tone of strong feeling, "if I could
but make you comprehend what a man suffers when he takes a last
look at his wife and children, and watches the boat that he has sent
them off in, as long as it is in sight, and then turns away and says,
'God knows whether we ever meet again!' And then, if I could convey to you the glow of his soul when he does see them again; when,
coming back after a twelvemonth's absence perhaps, and obliged to

The court, camp, church, the vessel, and the mart,
  Sword, gown, gain, glory, offer in exchange
Pride, fame, ambition, to fill up his heart,
  And few there are whom these can not estrange;
Man has all these resources, we but one,
  To love again, and be again undone."

(Johnson, 160; Byron, *Poetical
Works*, V, 71).

7 Anne's belief that "man's nature" is at the heart
of Benwick's inconstancy invokes the Duke's famous
words to Viola in Shakespeare's *Twelfth Night* (circa
1601), II, iv, 32–35:

For, boy, however we do praise ourselves,
Our fancies are more giddy and unfirm,
More longing, wavering, sooner lost and worn,
Than women's are.

Austen's affinities with Shakespeare have been frequently discussed. One of her finest nineteenth-
century critics, Richard Simpson (1820–1876), observed in 1870 that "Anne Elliot is Shakespeare's Viola
translated into an English girl of the nineteenth century. Like Viola, she never tells her love, or rather never
talks of it after its extinguishing, but sits like patience
on a monument smiling at grief; the green and yellow
melancholy feeds on her, and wastes her beauty. Like
Viola, too, she meekly ministers to the woman who is
unknowingly her rival" (*Critical Heritage*, 256).

8 Anne maintains a paradoxical attitude toward the
efficacy of reading. Earlier, when walking in Lyme, she
had recommended a series of books to Benwick because she thought he would benefit from "examples of
moral and religious endurance," whereas now in Bath
she "will not allow books to prove any thing." Austen,
at least at this point in her career, seems to question
the value of reading and whether the written word can
exert any influence beyond the realm of art.

9 "Brought forward" is "used as examples."

10 Brian Southam points out that Harville's reference to "that 'last look,' of sad parting and fond farewell, is a recurrent theme in the poetry of the sea," and that "in ships at sea, 'these treasures of his existence' were the traditional toast for Saturday night." Southam also highlights the ways in which in this scene Austen draws on the experiences of her two sailor brothers, Francis and Charles Austen (1779–1852). Parting "marked" their lives, he asserts. "Francis recalled 'leaving his wife in an advanced state of pregnancy at home' on joining the *St. Albans* at Sheerness only weeks before the birth of his first daughter, Mary Jane, on 27 April 1807. For Charles, it was more painful still, leaving his three children for the *Phoenix* in October 1814, their mother, Fanny Palmer, having died only weeks before, following the death of a fourth child, an infant three weeks old. Francis's Memoir is tight-lipped and reveals little of his feelings. But Charles's diaries tell us of his loneliness at sea and the dreams of Fanny and their children crowding night after night to haunt him" (Southam, 296).

11 Anne and Harville both speak from the depths of their own experience in this emotional exchange about constancy and hope. Yet as Christopher Ricks has finely observed, there is a large and revealing gap between what Harville says and what Anne replies: "Captain Harville's impassioned speech has at its heart the words 'wife and children', which then becomes the insistent 'them' as he asks Anne to imagine his imaginings. . . . And what is so sad in Anne Elliot's entirely honourable reply is its entire inability to engage with that part of what is being said, with 'wife *and children*'. She speaks with great feeling, and she grants that a good man is capable of everything great and good in his married life; but, in the urgency of her love for Wentworth, she can think only in terms of *one* object: 'I believe you equal to every important exertion, and to every domestic forbearance, so long as—if I may be allowed the expression, so long as you have an object. I mean while the woman you love lives, and lives for you.' It is so different from anything that Captain Harville was speaking of as to make it unignorable that even the most generous and just of people may *need* not fully to

put into another port, he calculates how soon it be possible to get them there, pretending to deceive himself, and saying, 'They cannot be here till such a day,' but all the while hoping for them twelve hours sooner, and seeing them arrive at last, as if Heaven had given them wings, by many hours sooner still! If I could explain to you all this, and all that a man can bear and do, and glories to do for the sake of these treasures of his existence![10] I speak, you know, only of such men as have hearts!" pressing his own with emotion.

"Oh!" cried Anne eagerly, "I hope I do justice to all that is felt by you, and by those who resemble you. God forbid that I should undervalue the warm and faithful feelings of any of my fellow-creatures. I should deserve utter contempt if I dared to suppose that true attachment and constancy were known only by woman. No, I believe you capable of every thing great and good in your married lives. I believe you equal to every important exertion, and to every domestic forbearance, so long as—if I may be allowed the expression, so long as you have an object. I mean, while the woman you love lives, and lives for you. All the privilege I claim for my own sex (it is not a very enviable one, you need not covet it) is that of loving longest, when existence or when hope is gone."[11]

She could not immediately have uttered another sentence; her heart was too full, her breath too much oppressed.

"You are a good soul," cried Captain Harville, putting his hand on her arm quite affectionately. "There is no quarrelling with you.—And when I think of Benwick, my tongue is tied."

Their attention was called towards the others.—Mrs. Croft was taking leave.

"Here, Frederick, you and I part company, I believe," said she. "I am going home, and you have an engagement with your friend.—To-night we may have the pleasure of all meeting again, at your party," (turning to Anne.) "We had your sister's card yesterday, and I understood Frederick had a card too, though I did not see it—and you are disengaged, Frederick, are you not, as well as ourselves?"

Captain Wentworth was folding up a letter in great haste, and either could not or would not answer fully.

Placed it before Anne.

Hugh Thomson, Illustrations for *Persuasion*, 1897. Captain
Wentworth draws his letter from among the scattered papers
on the writing desk and leaves it for Anne.

attend." Anne has an enormous capacity for sharing in
the sorrows of others, but in this instance her desperate desire to articulate her grief over Wentworth con-
sumes her, and she overlooks Harville's anguish in
order to voice her own (Ricks, "Jane Austen and the
Business of Mothering," in *Essays in Appreciation* [Ox-
ford: Clarendon Press, 1996], 105).

"Yes," said he, "very true; here we separate, but Harville and I shall
soon be after you, that is, Harville, if you are ready, I am in half a minute. I know you will not be sorry to be off. I shall be at your service in
half a minute."

Mrs. Croft left them, and Captain Wentworth, having sealed his
letter with great rapidity, was indeed ready, and had even a hurried,
agitated air, which shewed impatience to be gone. Anne knew not
how to understand it. She had the kindest "Good morning, God
bless you," from Captain Harville, but from him not a word, nor a
look. He had passed out of the room without a look!

She had only time, however, to move closer to the table where he had been writing, when footsteps were heard returning; the door opened; it was himself. He begged their pardon, but he had forgotten his gloves, and instantly crossing the room to the writing table, and standing with his back towards Mrs. Musgrove, he drew out a letter from under the scattered paper, placed it before Anne with eyes of glowing entreaty fixed on her for a moment, and hastily collecting his gloves, was again out of the room, almost before Mrs. Musgrove was aware of his being in it—the work of an instant!

The revolution which one instant had made in Anne, was almost beyond expression. The letter, with a direction hardly legible, to "Miss A. E——." was evidently the one which he had been folding so hastily. While supposed to be writing only to Captain Benwick, he had been also addressing her! On the contents of that letter depended all which this world could do for her! Any thing was possible, any thing might be defied rather than suspense. Mrs. Musgrove had little arrangements of her own at her own table; to their protection she must trust, and sinking into the chair which he had occupied, succeeding to the very spot where he had leaned and written, her eyes devoured the following words:

"I can listen no longer in silence. I must speak to you by such means as are within my reach. You pierce my soul. I am half agony, half hope. Tell me not that I am too late, that such precious feelings are gone for ever. I offer myself to you again with a heart even more your own, than when you almost broke it eight years and a half ago. Dare not say that man forgets sooner than woman, that his love has an earlier death. I have loved none but you. Unjust I may have been, weak and resentful I have been, but never inconstant. You alone have brought me to Bath. For you alone I think and plan.—Have you not seen this? Can you fail to have understood my wishes?—I had not waited even these ten days, could I have read your feelings, as I think you must have penetrated mine. I can hardly write. I am every instant hearing something which overpowers me. You sink your voice, but I can distinguish the tones of that voice, when they would be lost on others.—Too good, too excellent creature! You do us justice indeed. You do believe that there is true attachment and constancy among men. Believe it to be most fervent, most undeviating in

　　F. W."

　　"I must go, uncertain of my fate; but I shall return hither, or follow your party, as soon as possible. A word, a look will be enough to decide whether I enter your father's house this evening, or never."[12]

Such a letter was not to be soon recovered from. Half an hour's solitude and reflection might have tranquillized her; but the ten minutes only, which now passed before she was interrupted, with all the restraints of her situation, could do nothing towards tranquillity. Every moment rather brought fresh agitation. It was an overpowering happiness. And before she was beyond the first stage of full sensation, Charles, Mary, and Henrietta all came in.

　　The absolute necessity of seeming like herself produced then an immediate struggle; but after a while she could do no more. She began not to understand a word they said, and was obliged to plead indisposition and excuse herself. They could then see that she looked very ill—were shocked and concerned—and would not stir without her for the world. This was dreadful! Would they only have gone away, and left her in the quiet possession of that room, it would have been her cure; but to have them all standing or waiting around her was distracting, and, in desperation, she said she would go home.

　　"By all means, my dear," cried Mrs. Musgrove, "go home directly and take care of yourself, that you may be fit for the evening. I wish Sarah was here to doctor you, but I am no doctor myself. Charles, ring and order a chair. She must not walk."

　　But the chair would never do. Worse than all! To lose the possibility of speaking two words to Captain Wentworth in the course of her quiet, solitary progress up the town (and she felt almost certain of meeting him) could not be borne. The chair was earnestly protested

12 Wentworth's letter, as well as the dialogue that leads up to it, is a drastic revision of the original manuscript ending (see Appendix A) and is the most poignant scene in all of Austen. Critics have discussed the letter at great length and from a variety of perspectives. Some have described its emotional impact with memorable concision. Stuart Tave notes that one way of summarizing the action of *Persuasion* is "to say that it begins when Anne's word has no weight and it ends when her word pierces a man's soul." Roger Gard states that *Persuasion* opens with "what seems a reversion" to the "earlier, simpler, lighter art" of Austen's first novels, "but the reader of the final pages is in tears" (Tave, 256; Gard, *Jane Austen's Novels: The Art of Clarity* [New Haven: Yale University Press, 1992], 182).

　　Other critics have written more expansively on specific aspects of the scene. Deidre Lynch highlights the phrase "the revolution which one instant had made in Anne," and notes that Austen's "choice of the word 'revolution' works as so much else in *Persuasion* does— to place Anne in the midst of the historical life of an era that had just begun and did not know where it was going" (Lynch, "Introduction," in *Persuasion,* ed. Deidre Lynch [Oxford: Oxford University Press, 2004], xxxiii).

　　Mary Favret explores the interplay between what Anne is saying and what Wentworth is writing: "Wentworth's letter literally hangs on Anne's every word. His message is governed by her expressions: the full meaning of his 'half'-way language requires the recipient's remembering her concurrent discussion with Captain Harville. This interdependence replaces the less vulnerable compositions of Austen's other male writers. The careful narrative provided by a Darcy, for example, might have provoked Anne's rejection of men's 'history'. . . . Significantly, the letter functions as the vehicle for this social-sexual revolution. Like Anne's consciousness, Wentworth's letter defies limits and devours the words in the air about it. As the stories of Benwick, Harville's sister, and the Musgrove daughters fade away, the letter affirms and intensifies the language, the unique understanding, shared by Anne and Wentworth" (Favret, *Romantic Correspondence: Women,*

Politics, and the Fiction of Letters [Cambridge: Cambridge University Press, 1993], 171–172).

John Wiltshire examines the ways in which the scene reverses the roles of Anne and Wentworth. Earlier, when Wentworth spoke to Louisa in the hedgerow above Winthrop, Anne had sat listening intently to his every word, many of which he clearly spoke with her in mind. Now, she speaks to Harville with Wentworth at the forefront of her thoughts, and he strains to hear her. "The length and eloquence of Captain Harville's and Anne Elliot's speeches form a consummate duet, almost operatic in its final affirmative intensity, on the theme of constancy," writes Wiltshire. "That their dialogue fulfils the desire, repressed or suppressed throughout the novel, for Anne to speak, to be eloquent, that Anne and Wentworth change their typical narrative positions—she speaking, he hanging on her words, she narrating (if indirectly) her deepest experience of life, actively speaking her passive experience, he the dependent listener, at that moment performing a service for a colleague . . . affirms the experience of women" (Wiltshire, 191–192).

For Tony Tanner, the most important moment in the scene is when Wentworth drops his pen. As Anne is "arguing with Harville—and of course her words have a double target and dual purpose, as she hopes that the nearby Wentworth, seated and writing, will hear them and detect the personal message contained in the general statements—a 'slight noise' draws their attention to Wentworth. 'It was nothing more than that his pen had fallen down.' Nothing more—in many ways it is the most quietly dramatic and loaded incident in the book. The pen may, generally speaking, be in 'their hands'; but at this crucial moment the pen—a specific one—had dropped from *his*—specific—hand. However unintentionally, however momentarily, he is disproving the generalisation which Anne is enunciating. . . . Wentworth at this critical moment has . . . dropped . . . that instrument which is at once a tool and a symbol of men's dominance over women; the means by which they rule women's destinies, literally *write* . . . their lives. It is as if he is open to a more equal (unscripted) relationship in which the old patterns of

against; and Mrs. Musgrove, who thought only of one sort of illness, having assured herself, with some anxiety, that there had been no fall in the case; that Anne had not, at any time lately, slipped down, and got a blow on her head; that she was perfectly convinced of having had no fall, could part with her cheerfully, and depend on finding her better at night.

Anxious to omit no possible precaution, Anne struggled, and said,

"I am afraid, ma'am, that it is not perfectly understood. Pray be so good as to mention to the other gentlemen that we hope to see your whole party this evening. I am afraid there has been some mistake; and I wish you particularly to assure Captain Harville, and Captain Wentworth, that we hope to see them both."

"Oh! my dear, it is quite understood, I give you my word. Captain Harville has no thought but of going."

"Do you think so? But I am afraid; and I should be so very sorry! Will you promise me to mention it, when you see them again? You will see them both again this morning, I dare say. Do promise me."

"To be sure I will, if you wish it. Charles, if you see Captain Harville any where, remember to give Miss Anne's message. But indeed, my dear, you need not be uneasy. Captain Harville holds himself quite engaged, I'll answer for it; and Captain Wentworth the same, I dare say."

Anne could do no more; but her heart prophesied some mischance, to damp the perfection of her felicity. It could not be very lasting, however. Even if he did not come to Camden-place himself, it would be in her power to send an intelligible sentence by Captain Harville.

Another momentary vexation occurred. Charles, in his real concern and good-nature, would go home with her; there was no preventing him. This was almost cruel! But she could not be long ungrateful; he was sacrificing an engagement at a gunsmith's to be of use to her; and she set off with him, with no feeling but gratitude apparent.

They were in Union-street, when a quicker step behind, a something of familiar sound, gave her two moments preparation for the sight of Captain Wentworth. He joined them; but, as if irresolute whether to join or to pass on, said nothing—only looked. Anne could command herself enough to receive that look, and not repulsively. The cheeks which had been pale now glowed, and the movements which had hesitated were decided. He walked by her side. Presently, struck by a sudden thought, Charles said,

"Captain Wentworth, which way are you going? only to Gay-street, or farther up the town?"

"I hardly know," replied Captain Wentworth, surprised.

"Are you going as high as Belmont? Are you going near Camden-place? Because if you are, I shall have no scruple in asking you to take my place, and give Anne your arm to her father's door. She is rather done for this morning, and must not go so far without help. And I ought to be at that fellow's in the market-place. He promised me the sight of a capital gun he is just going to send off; said he would keep it unpacked to the last possible moment, that I might see it; and if I do not turn back now, I have no chance. By his description, a good deal like the second-sized double-barrel of mine, which you shot with one day, round Winthrop."

There could not be an objection. There could be only a most proper alacrity, a most obliging compliance for public view; and smiles reined in and spirits dancing in private rapture. In half a minute, Charles was at the bottom of Union-street again, and the other two proceeding together; and soon words enough had passed between them to decide their direction towards the comparatively quiet and retired gravel-walk,[13] where the power of conversation would make the present hour a blessing indeed; and prepare it for all the immortality which the happiest recollections of their own future lives could bestow. There they exchanged again those feelings and those promises which had once before seemed to secure every thing, but which had been followed by so many, many years of division and estrangement. There they returned again into the past, more exquisitely happy, perhaps, in their re-union, than when it had been first projected; more tender, more tried, more fixed in a knowledge of each other's character, truth, and attachment; more equal to act, more justified in acting. And there, as they slowly paced the

dominance and deference are abandoned, deleted—dropped" (Tanner, 241).

13 The "gravel-walk" connects Queen Square with the Royal Crescent. At its southern end it runs parallel to Gay Street before bending west behind Brock Street.

gradual ascent, heedless of every group around them, seeing neither sauntering politicians, bustling house-keepers, flirting girls, nor nursery-maids and children, they could indulge in those retrospections and acknowledgments, and especially in those explanations of what had directly preceded the present moment, which were so poignant and so ceaseless in interest. All the little variations of the last week were gone through; and of yesterday and to-day there could scarcely be an end.

She had not mistaken him. Jealousy of Mr. Elliot had been the retarding weight, the doubt, the torment. That had begun to operate in the very hour of first meeting her in Bath; that had returned, after a short suspension, to ruin the concert; and that had influenced him in every thing he had said and done, or omitted to say and do, in the last four-and-twenty hours. It had been gradually yielding to the better hopes which her looks, or words, or actions occasionally encouraged; it had been vanquished at last by those sentiments and those tones which had reached him while she talked with Captain Harville; and under the irresistible governance of which he had seized a sheet of paper, and poured out his feelings.

Of what he had then written, nothing was to be retracted or qualified. He persisted in having loved none but her. She had never been supplanted. He never even believed himself to see her equal. Thus much indeed he was obliged to acknowledge — that he had been constant unconsciously, nay unintentionally; that he had meant to forget her, and believed it to be done. He had imagined himself indifferent, when he had only been angry; and he had been unjust to her merits, because he had been a sufferer from them. Her character was now fixed on his mind as perfection itself, maintaining the loveliest medium of fortitude and gentleness; but he was obliged to acknowledge that only at Uppercross had he learnt to do her justice, and only at Lyme had he begun to understand himself.

At Lyme, he had received lessons of more than one sort. The passing admiration of Mr. Elliot had at least roused him, and the scenes on the Cobb, and at Captain Harville's, had fixed her superiority.

In his preceding attempts to attach himself to Louisa Musgrove (the attempts of angry pride), he protested that he had for ever felt it to be impossible; that he had not cared, could not care for Louisa; though, till that day, till the leisure for reflection which followed it, he had not understood the perfect excellence of the mind with which Louisa's could so ill bear a comparison; or the perfect, unrivalled hold it possessed over his own. There, he had learnt to distinguish between the steadiness of principle and the obstinacy of self-will, between the darings of heedlessness and the resolution of a collected mind. There, he had seen every thing to exalt in his estimation the woman he had lost, and there begun to deplore the pride, the folly, the madness of resentment, which had kept him from trying to regain her when thrown in his way.

From that period his penance had become severe. He had no sooner been free from the horror and remorse attending the first few days of Louisa's accident, no sooner begun to feel himself alive again, than he had begun to feel himself, though alive, not at liberty.

"I found," said he, "that I was considered by Harville an engaged man! That neither Harville nor his wife entertained a doubt of our mutual attachment. I was startled and shocked. To a degree, I could contradict this instantly; but, when I began to reflect that others might have felt the same—her own family, nay, perhaps herself, I was no longer at my own disposal. I was hers in honour if she wished it. I had been unguarded. I had not thought seriously on this subject before. I had not considered that my excessive intimacy must have its danger of ill consequence in many ways; and that I had no right to be trying whether I could attach myself to either of the girls, at the risk of raising even an unpleasant report, were there no other ill effects. I had been grossly wrong, and must abide the consequences."

He found too late, in short, that he had entangled himself; and that precisely as he became fully satisfied of his not caring for Louisa at all, he must regard himself as bound to her, if her sentiments for him were what the Harvilles supposed. It determined him to leave Lyme, and await her complete recovery elsewhere. He would gladly weaken, by any fair means, whatever feelings or speculations concerning him might exist; and he went, therefore, to his brother's,

Unfinished sketch of Jane Austen, by Cassandra Austen, circa 1811. This is the only authentic likeness of Austen's face. Charlotte-Maria Beckford remembered Austen at about this time "as a tall thin *spare* person, with very high cheek bones, great colour—sparkling Eyes not large but joyous & intelligent" (cited in Park Honan, *Jane Austen* [New York: St. Martin's, 1987], 270).

meaning after a while to return to Kellynch, and act as circumstances might require.

"I was six weeks with Edward," said he, "and saw him happy. I could have no other pleasure. I deserved none. He enquired after you very particularly; asked even if you were personally altered, little suspecting that to my eye you could never alter."

Anne smiled, and let it pass. It was too pleasing a blunder for a reproach. It is something for a woman to be assured, in her eight-and-twentieth year, that she has not lost one charm of earlier youth: but the value of such homage was inexpressibly increased to Anne, by comparing it with former words, and feeling it to be the result, not the cause of a revival of his warm attachment.

He had remained in Shropshire, lamenting the blindness of his own pride, and the blunders of his own calculations, till at once released from Louisa by the astonishing and felicitous intelligence of her engagement with Benwick.

"Here," said he, "ended the worst of my state; for now I could at least put myself in the way of happiness, I could exert myself, I could do something. But to be waiting so long in inaction, and waiting only for evil, had been dreadful. Within the first five minutes I said, 'I will be at Bath on Wednesday,' and I was. Was it unpardonable to think it worth my while to come? and to arrive, with some degree of hope? You were single. It was possible that you might retain the feelings of the past, as I did; and one encouragement happened to be mine. I could never doubt that you would be loved and sought by others, but I knew to a certainty that you had refused one man at least, of better pretensions than myself: and I could not help often saying, Was this for me?"

Their first meeting in Milsom-street afforded much to be said, but the concert still more. That evening seemed to be made up of exquisite moments. The moment of her stepping forward in the octagon-room to speak to him, the moment of Mr. Elliot's appearing and tearing her away, and one or two subsequent moments, marked by returning hope or increasing despondence, were dwelt on with energy.

"To see you," cried he, "in the midst of those who could not be my well-wishers, to see your cousin close by you, conversing and smiling, and feel all the horrible eligibilities and proprieties of the match! To consider it as the certain wish of every being who could hope to influence you! Even, if your own feelings were reluctant or indifferent, to consider what powerful supports would be his! Was it not enough to make the fool of me which I appeared? How could I look on without agony? Was not the very sight of the friend who sat behind you, was not the recollection of what had been, the knowledge of her influence, the indelible, immoveable impression of what persuasion had once done—was it not all against me?"

"You should have distinguished," replied Anne. "You should not have suspected me now; the case so different, and my age so different. If I was wrong in yielding to persuasion once, remember that it was to persuasion exerted on the side of safety, not of risk. When I yielded, I thought it was to duty; but no duty could be called in aid here. In marrying a man indifferent to me,[14] all risk would have been incurred, and all duty violated."

"Perhaps I ought to have reasoned thus," he replied, "but I could not. I could not derive benefit from the late knowledge I had acquired of your character. I could not bring it into play: it was overwhelmed, buried, lost in those earlier feelings which I had been smarting under year after year. I could think of you only as one who had yielded, who had given me up, who had been influenced by any one rather than by me. I saw you with the very person who had guided you in that year of misery. I had no reason to believe her of less authority now.—The force of habit was to be added."

"I should have thought," said Anne, "that my manner to yourself might have spared you much or all of this."

"No, no! your manner might be only the ease which your engagement to another man would give. I left you in this belief; and yet—I was determined to see you again. My spirits rallied with the morning, and I felt that I had still a motive for remaining here."

At last Anne was at home again, and happier than any one in that house could have conceived. All the surprise and suspense, and every

14 Anne means that she was indifferent to Mr. Elliot (not that he was indifferent to her).

15 Anne's celebration of Wentworth's "being there" always marks a moment of enormous relief, for the two can now address each other with an intimacy and openness that was lost eight years ago, and that has stood in sharp contrast to the misgivings and side-glances of their more recent exchanges. Linda Bree remarks that "the sexuality inherent in the concept of conversation, and latent throughout the various conversations between Anne and Wentworth even at their least communicative, bubbles to the surface here, as the happy lovers achieve at last a state of unmediated communication and, in prospect, consummation—the ultimate belonging" (Bree, "Belonging to the Conversation in *Persuasion*," in *The Talk in Jane Austen,* ed. Bruce Stovel and Lynn Weinlos Gregg [Edmonton: University of Alberta Press, 2002], 164).

16 Anne rationalizes that taking Lady Russell's counsel on Wentworth's initial marriage proposal was "one of those cases in which advice is good or bad only as the event decides." "This is an extraordinary statement!" cries Robert Hopkins. "How can a subsequent event be the determinant of whether a moral decision is right or wrong? Suppose, for example, that Captain Wentworth had married Anne, returned to sea, been severely wounded in battle and then returned to Anne, like Rochester in *Jane Eyre,* blinded, and, in addition, destitute? Would this scenario have proved Lady Russell morally right? Or suppose Anne had married and had a daughter, and Wentworth had died at sea but had not yet earned his fortune? . . . Is Anne Elliot merely assuming a providential universe in which whatever happens is right? . . . And is Jane Austen projecting into her last novel a reconsideration of the moral implications of her earlier prudential plots that, in spite of her hard-boiled, no-nonsense vision, reward her heroines with marriage and with fortune?" (Hopkins, 144–145).

other painful part of the morning dissipated by this conversation, she re-entered the house so happy as to be obliged to find an alloy in some momentary apprehensions of its being impossible to last. An interval of meditation, serious and grateful, was the best corrective of every thing dangerous in such high-wrought felicity; and she went to her room, and grew steadfast and fearless in the thankfulness of her enjoyment.

The evening came, the drawing-rooms were lighted up, the company assembled. It was but a card-party, it was but a mixture of those who had never met before, and those who met too often—a commonplace business, too numerous for intimacy, too small for variety; but Anne had never found an evening shorter. Glowing and lovely in sensibility and happiness, and more generally admired than she thought about or cared for, she had cheerful or forbearing feelings for every creature around her. Mr. Elliot was there; she avoided, but she could pity him. The Wallises; she had amusement in understanding them. Lady Dalrymple and Miss Carteret; they would soon be innoxious cousins to her. She cared not for Mrs. Clay, and had nothing to blush for in the public manners of her father and sister. With the Musgroves, there was the happy chat of perfect ease; with Captain Harville, the kind-hearted intercourse of brother and sister; with Lady Russell, attempts at conversation, which a delicious consciousness cut short; with Admiral and Mrs. Croft, every thing of peculiar cordiality and fervent interest, which the same consciousness sought to conceal;—and with Captain Wentworth, some moments of communication continually occurring, and always the hope of more, and always the knowledge of his being there![15]

It was in one of these short meetings, each apparently occupied in admiring a fine display of green-house plants, that she said—

"I have been thinking over the past, and trying impartially to judge of the right and wrong, I mean with regard to myself; and I must believe that I was right, much as I suffered from it, that I was perfectly right in being guided by the friend whom you will love better than you do now. To me, she was in the place of a parent. Do not mistake me, however. I am not saying that she did not err in her advice.

It was, perhaps, one of those cases in which advice is good or bad only as the event decides;[16] and for myself, I certainly never should, in any circumstance of tolerable similarity, give such advice. But I mean, that I was right in submitting to her, and that if I had done otherwise, I should have suffered more in continuing the engagement than I did even in giving it up, because I should have suffered in my conscience. I have now, as far as such a sentiment is allowable in human nature, nothing to reproach myself with; and if I mistake not, a strong sense of duty is no bad part of a woman's portion."

He looked at her, looked at Lady Russell, and looking again at her, replied, as if in cool deliberation,

"Not yet. But there are hopes of her being forgiven in time. I trust to being in charity with her soon. But I too have been thinking over the past, and a question has suggested itself, whether there may not have been one person more my enemy even than that lady? My own self. Tell me if, when I returned to England in the year eight, with a few thousand pounds, and was posted into the Laconia, if I had then written to you, would you have answered my letter? would you, in short, have renewed the engagement then?"

"Would I!" was all her answer; but the accent was decisive enough.[17]

"Good God!" he cried, "you would! It is not that I did not think of it, or desire it, as what could alone crown all my other success. But I was proud, too proud to ask again. I did not understand you. I shut my eyes, and would not understand you, or do you justice. This is a recollection which ought to make me forgive every one sooner than myself. Six years of separation and suffering might have been spared. It is a sort of pain, too, which is new to me. I have been used to the gratification of believing myself to earn every blessing that I enjoyed. I have valued myself on honourable toils and just rewards. Like other great men under reverses," he added with a smile, "I must endeavour to subdue my mind to my fortune. I must learn to brook being happier than I deserve."

17 Anne is made in this closing dialogue to draw the moral of *Persuasion,* yet her own position remains contradictory. She declares—as she has already done in Chapter 4—that she was right in taking the advice of Lady Russell, even though the advice was wrong, and in a similar situation she herself would never have given it. Douglas Bush accepts that this "earnest assertion" comes from "a person of the finest moral sensitivity and integrity," but he points out that "it seems to be directly opposed to what had also been an earlier conviction, that, while defending Lady Russell and herself, 'she should yet have been a happier woman in maintaining the engagement, than she had been in the sacrifice of it.' Indeed she had been ready to reject her elder's advice two years after she had taken it: in this last dialogue, when Wentworth . . . says that he had perhaps been a worse enemy to himself than Lady Russell, and asks whether, when he returned to England in 1808 with a few thousand pounds, she would have renewed the engagement then, 'Would I!' was all her answer." Anne thus declares that she was "perfectly right" to be guided by Lady Russell's opinion in refusing Wentworth, and yet she also asserts that had Wentworth asked for her hand two years later she would have rejected Lady Russell's counsel and married him (Bush, 179–180).

1 In the opinion of the *British Critic,* Austen's concerns about her "bad morality" were justified. *Persuasion* contained "parts of very great merit," it declared in 1818, but among them it "certainly should not number its *moral,* which seems to be, that young people should always marry according to their own inclinations and upon their own judgment; for that if in consequence of listening to grave counsels, they defer their marriage, till they have wherewith to live upon, they will be laying the foundation for years of misery, such as only the heroes and heroines of novels can reasonably hope ever to see the end of" (*Critical Heritage,* 84).

Austen's commitment to "bad morality" in her own age, however, is a large part of what makes her so appealing in ours. "Like *Northanger Abbey, Persuasion* reflects on its own refusal to ratify received notions," Claudia Johnson declares: "the narrator validates the perseverance of young people in carrying their points even though doing so is, as she says, 'bad morality to conclude with.'" Robert Hopkins agrees. "Had Anne and Wentworth married eight years sooner, they would have been poor, imprudent,—and very much in love. All the weight of the narrative—the Crofts, Captain and Mrs. Harville, Captain Benwick and his deceased fiancee—argues in favor of Anne and Wentworth marrying earlier. Given a choice between prudential morality and the truth of love, *Persuasion* argues for love" (Johnson, 155; Hopkins, 154).

2 According to Marilyn Butler, in elevating Wentworth from "nobody" to "somebody," Austen reveals ethical

WHO CAN BE IN DOUBT OF WHAT FOLLOWED? When any two young people take it into their heads to marry, they are pretty sure by perseverance to carry their point, be they ever so poor, or ever so imprudent, or ever so little likely to be necessary to each other's ultimate comfort. This may be bad morality to conclude with, but I believe it to be truth;[1] and if such parties succeed, how should a Captain Wentworth and an Anne Elliot, with the advantage of maturity of mind, consciousness of right, and one independent fortune between them, fail of bearing down every opposition? They might in fact have borne down a great deal more than they met with, for there was little to distress them beyond the want of graciousness and warmth.—Sir Walter made no objection, and Elizabeth did nothing worse than look cold and unconcerned. Captain Wentworth, with five-and-twenty thousand pounds, and as high in his profession as merit and activity could place him, was no longer nobody.[2] He was now esteemed quite worthy to address[3] the daughter of a foolish, spendthrift baronet, who had not had principle or sense enough to maintain himself in the situation in which Providence had placed him, and who could give his daughter at present but a small part of the share of ten thousand pounds which must be hers hereafter.[4]

Sir Walter indeed, though he had no affection for Anne, and no vanity flattered, to make him really happy on the occasion, was very far from thinking it a bad match for her. On the contrary, when he saw more of Captain Wentworth, saw him repeatedly by daylight and eyed him well, he was very much struck by his personal claims,

A. Wallis Mills, Illustrations for *Persuasion,* 1908. Sir Walter records the marriage of Captain Wentworth and Anne in his beloved *Baronetage.*

rather than political intentions. She is not concerned with the "radical" contention that "the gentry are no longer fit to rule." Instead, "she puts her sailors Captain Wentworth and Admiral Croft into the novel to make an entirely moral point, that the old system absolutely depended upon its belief in the gentleman as a leader. By the last year of her life, when the gentry successfully got a new Corn Law through Parliament, they were no longer representing themselves as heads of the local community, and as custodians for all its members; they were openly pursuing their own material interests, as individuals or as a class. It is the abdication of the governors that Jane Austen depicts in her final years as a writer" (Butler, *Romantics, Rebels and Reactionaries* [Oxford: Oxford University Press, 1981], 108).

3 "Address" is "court" or "propose marriage to."

4 The law of primogeniture provided for younger children with what was known as a "portion." Most daughters received their portion when they married, but because of the mortgage on Kellynch, Anne receives from her father only "a small part of the share of ten thousand pounds which must be hers hereafter." Paying his daughter in installments exposes the mismanagement and excess of the "foolish, spendthrift baronet." When Anne's "share" has been paid in full, it will yield her a handsome annual income of approximately five hundred pounds. For more information, see John Habakkuk, *Marriage, Debt, and the Estates System: English Landownership, 1650–1950* (Oxford: Clarendon Press, 1994).

and felt that his superiority of appearance might be not unfairly balanced against her superiority of rank; and all this, assisted by his well-sounding name, enabled Sir Walter at last to prepare his pen with a very good grace for the insertion of the marriage in the volume of honour.

The only one among them, whose opposition of feeling could excite any serious anxiety, was Lady Russell. Anne knew that Lady Russell must be suffering some pain in understanding and relinquishing Mr. Elliot, and be making some struggles to become truly acquainted with, and do justice to Captain Wentworth. This however was what Lady Russell had now to do. She must learn to feel that she had been mistaken with regard to both; that she had been unfairly influenced by appearances in each; that because Captain Wentworth's manners had not suited her own ideas, she had been too quick in suspecting them to indicate a character of dangerous impetuosity; and that because Mr. Elliot's manners had precisely pleased her in their propriety and correctness, their general politeness and suavity, she had been too quick in receiving them as the certain result of the most

A landaulette, by an unknown artist, 1816. At the end of *Persuasion,* Austen is no longer concerned with who owns the land or inhabits the great house. Her interest now is in the possibilities of happiness and order in a world of mutability and chance. Mary clings to calcified notions of title and property. But Anne and Wentworth are most deeply committed to each other, and they are ready to start a new life of duty, travel, and opportunity.

correct opinions and well regulated mind. There was nothing less for Lady Russell to do, than to admit that she had been pretty completely wrong, and to take up a new set of opinions and of hopes.

There is a quickness of perception in some, a nicety in the discernment of character, a natural penetration, in short, which no experience in others can equal, and Lady Russell had been less gifted in this part of understanding than her young friend. But she was a very good woman, and if her second object was to be sensible and well-judging, her first was to see Anne happy. She loved Anne better than she loved her own abilities; and when the awkwardness of the beginning was over, found little hardship in attaching herself as a mother to the man who was securing the happiness of her other child.

Of all the family, Mary was probably the one most immediately gratified by the circumstance. It was creditable to have a sister married, and she might flatter herself with having been greatly instrumental to the connexion, by keeping Anne with her in the autumn; and as her own sister must be better than her husband's sisters, it was very agreeable that Captain Wentworth should be a richer man than either Captain Benwick or Charles Hayter. — She had something to suffer perhaps when they came into contact again, in seeing Anne restored to the rights of seniority,[5] and the mistress of a very pretty landaulette;[6] but she had a future to look forward to, of powerful consolation. Anne had no Uppercross-hall before her, no landed estate, no headship of a family; and if they could but keep Captain Wentworth from being made a baronet,[7] she would not change situations with Anne.

It would be well for the eldest sister if she were equally satisfied with her situation, for a change is not very probable there. She had soon the mortification of seeing Mr. Elliot withdraw; and no one of proper condition has since presented himself to raise even the unfounded hopes which sunk with him.

The news of his cousin Anne's engagement burst on Mr. Elliot most unexpectedly. It deranged his best plan of domestic happiness, his best hope of keeping Sir Walter single by the watchfulness which a son-in-law's rights would have given. But, though discomfited and disappointed, he could still do something for his own interest and

5 Mary had taken precedence over Anne because, though younger, she was married and Anne was not. But with her marriage to Wentworth, Anne is once again restored to "the rights of seniority." Compare *Pride and Prejudice,* where after her marriage to Wickham, Lydia informs her older sister Jane, "I take your place now, and you must go lower, because I am a married woman" (III, 9).

6 A "landaulette," or a "demi-landau," was a light, four-wheeled carriage for two passengers, with a top that could be let down or thrown back. William Felton asserted that no carriage exceeded the landaulette "for country use," and estimated that with all the "extras" and fittings ("A footman cushion," "Lace covered glass frames," "Venetian blinds," "A pair of Italian lamps," and so on), the total cost of the vehicle was just over £155 (Felton, II, 73–76).

7 Mary has cause for concern. Wentworth stood a realistic chance of being made a baronet, for "the Order . . . has of late years assumed an increased brilliancy, by having been so frequently made the reward of naval and military merit" (John Debrett, *The Baronetage of England* [London: Rivington, 1815], iv).

8 Love and friendship are key terms in Austen. In weighing the obligations couples have both to themselves and to their friends, Eric C. Walker writes illuminatingly about Mrs. Smith and the ways in which her story disturbs the marriage settlement between Wentworth and Anne. "Mrs. Smith is a major preoccupation of the novel in its closing paragraphs," he observes. "But I am not inclined to sum her up in the terms of several recent readings, as, pejoratively, a self-interested cog in colonialist machinery, or, honorifically, along any one of several utopian vectors—as a story, for example, of emergent property rights for women, or of a 'third sphere' of self-sufficient women." Rather, Walker argues, "in the narrative behavior of the final paragraphs, the novel digs in its heels against pressures both to rule friends out of the conjugal frame or to blend them without hitch into the companionate marriage settlement. . . . At its close, the novel remembers [Mrs. Smith] with a vengeance." (Walker, *Marriage, Writing, and Romanticism: Wordsworth and Austen after War* [Stanford: Stanford University Press, 2009], 174, 176).

9 Anne would have had a serious scare soon after her reunion with Wentworth. On March 1, 1815—Sir Walter's fifty-fifth birthday—Napoleon escaped from his exile on the island of Elba, returned to Paris, and attempted to recapture his empire. Allied forces, under the command of the duke of Wellington, vanquished him on June 18, 1815, at the Battle of Waterloo, after which he was banished to St. Helena, where he died six years later.

10 The circumstances faced by wives of military men were often discussed in contemporary conduct books. In a time of war, the wife of a naval officer is "left to endure the anxieties of a long separation from her husband, while he is toiling on the ocean," declared the devotional writer Thomas Gisborne. ". . . The state of tremulous suspense, when the mind is ignorant of the fate of the object which it holds most dear, and knows not but that the next post may confirm the most dreadful of its apprehensions, can be calmed only by those consolations which look beyond the present world" (Gisborne, *An Enquiry into the Duties of the Female Sex* [London: Cadell and Davies, 1801], 366).

his own enjoyment. He soon quitted Bath; and on Mrs. Clay's quitting it likewise soon afterwards, and being next heard of as established under his protection in London, it was evident how double a game he had been playing, and how determined he was to save himself from being cut out by one artful woman, at least.

Mrs. Clay's affections had overpowered her interest, and she had sacrificed, for the young man's sake, the possibility of scheming longer for Sir Walter. She has abilities, however, as well as affections; and it is now a doubtful point whether his cunning, or hers, may finally carry the day; whether, after preventing her from being the wife of Sir Walter, he may not be wheedled and caressed at last into making her the wife of Sir William.

It cannot be doubted that Sir Walter and Elizabeth were shocked and mortified by the loss of their companion, and the discovery of their deception in her. They had their great cousins, to be sure, to resort to for comfort; but they must long feel that to flatter and follow others, without being flattered and followed in turn, is but a state of half enjoyment.

Anne, satisfied at a very early period of Lady Russell's meaning to love Captain Wentworth as she ought, had no other alloy to the happiness of her prospects than what arose from the consciousness of having no relations to bestow on him which a man of sense could value. There she felt her own inferiority keenly. The disproportion in their fortune was nothing; it did not give her a moment's regret; but to have no family to receive and estimate him properly; nothing of respectability, of harmony, of good-will to offer in return for all the worth and all the prompt welcome which met her in his brothers and sisters, was a source of as lively pain as her mind could well be sensible of, under circumstances of otherwise strong felicity. She had but two friends in the world to add to his list, Lady Russell and Mrs. Smith. To those, however, he was very well disposed to attach himself. Lady Russell, in spite of all her former transgressions, he could now value from his heart. While he was not obliged to say that he believed her to have been right in originally dividing them, he was ready to say almost every thing else in her favour; and as for Mrs.

Smith, she had claims of various kinds to recommend her quickly and permanently.

Her recent good offices by Anne had been enough in themselves; and their marriage, instead of depriving her of one friend, secured her two. She was their earliest visitor in their settled life; and Captain Wentworth, by putting her in the way of recovering her husband's property in the West Indies; by writing for her, acting for her, and seeing her through all the petty difficulties of the case, with the activity and exertion of a fearless man and a determined friend, fully requited the services which she had rendered, or ever meant to render, to his wife.[8]

Mrs. Smith's enjoyments were not spoiled by this improvement of income, with some improvement of health, and the acquisition of such friends to be often with, for her cheerfulness and mental alacrity did not fail her; and while these prime supplies of good remained, she might have bid defiance even to greater accessions of worldly prosperity. She might have been absolutely rich and perfectly healthy, and yet be happy. Her spring of felicity was in the glow of her spirits, as her friend Anne's was in the warmth of her heart. Anne was tenderness itself, and she had the full worth of it in Captain Wentworth's affection. His profession was all that could ever make her friends wish that tenderness less; the dread of a future war[9] all that could dim her sunshine. She gloried in being a sailor's wife, but she must pay the tax of quick alarm for belonging to that profession which is, if possible, more distinguished in its domestic virtues than in its national importance.[10]

THE END.

Contemporary critics have also commented on these final lines, and how Anne and Wentworth's public duties both burden and enrich their private lives. "*Persuasion*'s first readers could safely imagine Captain Wentworth forsaking the public for the private sphere, exchanging war for domestic joy," Harris remarks. "But in her last sentence, Austen celebrates martial achievements. . . . Her phrase about the 'national importance' of the navy reminds contemporary readers just how much Britain's imperial power and safety still depended upon the naval profession." Elvira Casal adds that "one of the great ironies in *Persuasion* is that although the function of the navy is often to distance men from their home communities and families, the navy is ultimately identified with a sense of community and security. The ships which, in Captain Wentworth's mind at the beginning of the novel, are no place for women become, by the end, the center for a new type of community characterized by its 'domestic virtues.' This transformation is only possible, however, because Captain Wentworth himself is transformed." For Ruth Perry, the close of *Persuasion* reveals an "inexorable historical movement" in which "the claustrophobia of the consanguineal family contrasts with the opening vistas promised by the new sort of marriage. Sir Walter Elliot and Elizabeth, with their disdain for any but their own consanguineal relatives—including the pallid Lady Dalrymple and plain and awkward Miss Carteret—must give way to Anne and Wentworth, the new couple who make their way alone, independent of any relations, loyal to the disembodied State rather than to any particular kin. Conjugality trumps consanguinity in this last novel." Tony Tanner sees the conclusion this way: "Anne's 'alarm' is indefinite and in the future—an integral part of her happy marriage, out of an old society and into a new one, far away from the abandoned 'paternal abode,' with nothing assured except her joy in her reciprocated love. . . . The final words of *Persuasion* effectively point to that radical redefinition and relocation of values which marks the whole novel" (Harris, 85; Casal, "More Distinguished in His Domestic Virtues: Captain Wentworth Comes Home," in *Persuasions,* 26 [2004], 154; Perry, *Novel Relations: The Transformation of Kinship in English Literature and Culture, 1748–1818* [Cambridge University Press, 2004], 406–407; Tanner, 245).

APPENDIXES

FURTHER READING

ILLUSTRATION CREDITS

ACKNOWLEDGMENTS

Appendix A

The Original Ending of *Persuasion*

Austen originally concluded *Persuasion* in July 1816 with the following two manuscript chapters, which she cancelled and replaced three weeks later with the final three chapters of the published novel. Austen's original ending "did not satisfy her," explained her nephew James Edward Austen-Leigh. "She thought it tame and flat, and was desirous of producing something better. This weighed upon her mind, the more so probably on account of the weak state of her health; so that one night she retired to rest in very low spirits. But such depression was little in accordance with her nature, and was soon shaken off. The next morning she awoke to more cheerful views and brighter inspirations: the sense of power revived; and imagination resumed its course" (Austen-Leigh, *Memoir,* 125). The two cancelled chapters are the only section from any of her published novels to have survived in manuscript, and they offer highly illuminating evidence of her methods of composition and revision.

The manuscript of these chapters is now housed in the British Library (Egerton MS. 3038). In the transcription, I have retained Austen's abbreviations, as well as her various irregularities in punctuation and spelling ("releif" instead of "relief," for example). The manuscript is sometimes very difficult to read because of words that Austen has crossed out or written over. In these instances, I have checked my transcription against—and on occasion revised it in light of—the readings found in three key sources: *The Manuscript Chapters of "Persuasion,"* ed. R. W. Chapman (Oxford: Clarendon Press, 1926); Arthur M. Axelrad, *Jane Austen Caught in the Act of Greatness* (n.p.: 1st Books, 2003), 5–131; and Harris, 36–62.

First manuscript page of the two cancelled chapters of *Persuasion*. As the many excisions and alterations in the manuscript make plain, Austen worked hard to produce the precision and vitality of her prose.

JULY 8
CHAP. 10.

With all this knowledge of M[r]. E— & this authority to impart it, Anne left Westgate Build[gs]—her mind deeply busy in revolving what she had heard, feeling, thinking, recalling & forseeing every thing, shocked at M[r]. Elliot—sighing over future Kellynch, and pained for Lady Russell, whose confidence in him had been entire.—The Embarrassment which must be felt from this hour in his presence!—How to behave to him?—how to get rid of him?—What to do by any of the Party at home?—where to be blind?—where to be active?—It was altogether a confusion of Images & Doubts—a perplexity, an agitation, which she could not see the end of—and she was in Gay S[t]—& still so much engrossed, that she started on being addressed by Adm[l]. Croft, as if he were a person unlikely to be met there. It was within a few steps of his own door.—"You are going to call upon my wife, said he, she will be very glad to see you."—Anne denied it. "No—she really had not time, she was in her way home"—but while she spoke, the Adm[l]. had stepped back & knocked at the door, calling out, "Yes, yes, do go in; she is all alone—go in & rest yourself."—Anne felt so little disposed at this time to be in company of any sort, that it vexed her to be thus constrained—but she was obliged to stop. "Since you are so very kind, said she, I will just ask M[rs]. Croft how she does, but I really cannot stay 5 minutes.—You are sure she is quite alone." The possibility of Capt. W. had occurred—and most fearfully anxious was she to be assured—either that he was within or that he was not;—*which,* might have been a question.—"Oh! yes, quite alone—Nobody but her Mantuamaker[1] with her, & they have been shut up together this half hour, so it must be over soon."—"Her Mantuamaker!—then I am sure my calling now, w[d]. be most inconvenient.—Indeed you must allow me to leave my Card & be so good as to explain it afterwards to M[rs]. C." "No, no, not at all, not at all. She will be very happy to see you. Mind—I will not swear that she has not something particular to say to you—but *that* will all come out in the right place. I give no hints.—Why, Miss Elliot, we begin to hear strange things of you—(smiling in her face)—But you have not much the look of it—as Grave as a little Judge."[2]—Anne blushed.—"Aye, aye, that will do. Now, it is right. I *thought* we were not mistaken." She was left to guess at the direction of his Suspicions;—the first wild idea had been of some disclosure from his B[r] in law—but she was ashamed the next moment—& felt how far more probable that he should be meaning M[r]. E.—The door was opened—& the Man evidently beginning to *deny* his Mistress, when the sight of his Master stopped him. The Adm[l]. enjoyed the joke exceedingly. Anne thought his triumph over Stephen rather too long. At last however, he was able to invite her upstairs, & stepping before her said—"I will just go up with you myself & shew you in—. I cannot stay, because I must go to the P. office, but if you will only sit down for 5 minutes I am sure Sophy will come—and you will find nobody to disturb you—there is nobody but Frederick here—" opening the door as he spoke.—Such a person to be passed over as a No-

body to *her!*—After being allowed to feel quite secure—indifferent—at her ease, to
have it burst on her that she was to be the next moment in the same room with
him!—No time for recollection!—for planning behaviour, or regulating manners!—
There was time only to turn pale, before she had passed through the door, & met
the astonished eyes of Capt. W—— who was sitting by the fire pretending to read &
prepared for no greater surprise than the Admiral's hasty return.—Equally unexpected was the meeting, on each side. There was nothing to be done however, but to
stifle feelings & be quietly polite;—and the Admiral was too much on the alert, to
leave any troublesome pause.—He repeated again what he had said before about his
wife & everybody insisted on Anne's sitting down & being perfectly comfortable,
was sorry he must leave her himself, but was sure M^{rs}. Croft w^d. be down very soon,
& w^d. go upstairs & give her notice directly.—Anne *was* sitting down, but now she
arose again—to entreat him not to interrupt M^{rs}. C– & re-urge the wish of going
away & calling another time.—But the Adm^l. would not hear of it;—and if she did
not return to the charge with unconquerable Perseverance, or did not with a more
passive Determination walk quietly out of the room—(as certainly she might have
done) may she not be pardoned?—If she *had* no horror of a few minutes Tète a Tète
with Capt. W——, may she not be pardoned for not wishing to give him the idea that
she had?—She reseated herself, & The Adm^l. took leave;—but on reaching the door,
said, "Frederick, a word with *you, if you please*". Capt. W—— went to him; and instantly, before they were well out of the room, the Adm^l. continued, "As I am going
to leave you together, it is but fair I should give you something to talk of—& so, if
you please—". Here the door was very firmly closed; she could guess by which of the
two; and she lost entirely what immediately followed; but it was impossible for her
not to distinguish parts of the rest, for the Adm^l. on the strength of the Door's being
shut was speaking without any management of voice, tho' she c^d. hear his companion trying to check him.—She could not doubt their being speaking of her. She
heard her own name & *Kellynch* repeatedly—she was very much distressed.—She
knew not what to do, or what to expect—and among other agonies felt the possibility of Capt. W——'s not returning into the room at all, which after *her* consenting to
stay would have been—too bad for Language.—They seemed to be talking of the
Adm^{ls}. Lease of Kellynch. She heard him say something of "the Lease being signed
or not signed"—*that* was not likely to be a very agitating subject—but then followed
"I hate to be at an uncertainty—I must know at once—Sophy thinks the same"—
Then, in a lower tone, Capt. W—— seemed remonstrating—wanting to be excused—
wanting to put something off. "Phoo, Phoo—answered the Admiral now is the Time.
If *you* will not speak, I will stop & speak myself."—"Very well Sir, very well Sir," followed with some impatience, from his companion, opening the door as he spoke.—
"You will then—you promise you will?" replied the Admiral, in all the power of his
natural voice, unbroken even by one thin door.—"Yes—Sir—Yes." And the Adm^l.
was hastily left, the door was closed, and the moment arrived in which Anne was

alone with Capt. W——. She could not attempt to see how he looked; but he walked immediately to a window, as if irresolute & embarrassed;—and for about the space of 5 seconds, she repented what she had done—censured it as unwise, blushed over it as indelicate.—She longed to be able to speak of the weather or the Concert—but could only compass the releif of taking a Newspaper in her hand.—The distressing pause was soon over however; he turned round in half a minute, & coming towards the Table where she sat, said, in a voice of effort & constraint—"You must have heard too much already Madam, to be in any doubt of my having promised Adm^l. Croft to speak to you on some particular subject—& this conviction determines me to do it—however repugnant to my—to all my sense of propriety, to be taking so great a liberty.—You will acquit *me* of Impertinence I trust, by considering me as speaking only for another, & speaking by Necessity;—and the Adm^l. is a Man who can never be thought Impertinent by one who knows him as you do—. His Intentions are always the Kindest & the Best;—and you will perceive that he is actuated by none other, in the application which I am now with—with very peculiar feelings—obliged to make."—He stopped—but merely to recover breath;—not seeming to expect any answer.—Anne listened, as if her Life depended on the issue of his Speech.—He proceeded, with a forced alacrity.—"The Adm^l., Madam, was this morning confidently informed that you were—upon my word I am quite at a loss, ashamed—(breathing & speaking quick)—the awkwardness of *giving* Information of this sort to one of the Parties—You can be at no loss to understand me—It was very confidently said that M^r. Elliot—that everything was settled in the family for an Union between M^r. Elliot—& yourself. It was added that you were to live at Kellynch—that Kellynch was to be given up. This, the Admiral knew could not be correct—But it occurred to him that it might be the *wish* of the Parties. And my commission from him Madam, is to say, that if the Family-wish is such, his Lease of Kellynch shall be cancel'd, & he & my sister will provide themselves with another home, without imagining themselves to be doing anything which under similar circumstances w^d. not be done for *them*.—This is all Madam.—A very few words in reply from you will be sufficient.—That *I* should be the person commissioned on this subject is extraordinary!—and beleive me Madam, it is no less painful.—A very few words however will put an end to the awkwardness & distress we may *both* be feeling." Anne spoke a word or two, but they were un-intelligible—And before she could command herself, he added—"If you only tell me that the Adm^l. *may* address a Line to Sir Walter, it will be enough.—Pronounce only the words, *he may.*—I shall immediately follow him with your message.—" This was spoken, as with a fortitude which seemed to meet the message.—"No Sir—said Anne—. There is no message.—You are misin—the Adm^l. is misinformed.—I do justice to the kindness of his Intentions, but he is quite mistaken. There is no Truth in any such report."—He was a moment silent.—She turned her eyes towards him for the first time since his reentering the room. His colour was varying—& he was looking at her with all the

Power & Keenness, which she beleived no other eyes than his possessed.—"*No* Truth in any such report!—he repeated.—No Truth in any *part* of it?—" "None."—He had been standing by a chair—enjoying the releif of leaning on it—or of playing with it;—he now sat down—drew it a little nearer to her—& looked, with an expression which had something more than penetration in it, something softer.—Her Countenance did not discourage.—It was a silent, but a very powerful Dialogue;—on his side, Supplication, on her's acceptance.—Still, a little nearer—and a hand taken and pressed—and "Anne, my own dear Anne!"—bursting forth in the fullness of exquisite feeling—and all Suspense & Indecision were over—. They were re-united. They were restored to all that had been lost. They were carried back to the past, with only an increase of attachment & confidence, & only such a flutter of present Delight as made them little fit for the interruption of M^{rs}. Croft, when she joined them not long afterwards.—*She* probably, in the observations of the next ten minutes, saw something to suspect—& tho' it was hardly possible for a woman of her description to wish the Mantuamaker had imprisoned her longer, she might be very likely wishing for some excuse to run about the house, some storm to break the windows above, or a summons to the Admiral's Shoemaker below.—Fortune favoured them all however in another way—in a gentle, steady rain—just happily set in as the Admiral returned & Anne rose to go.—She was earnestly invited to stay dinner;—a note was dispatched to Camden Place—and she staid;—staid till 10 at night. And during that time, the Husband & wife, either by the wife's contrivance, or by simply going on in their usual way, were frequently out of the room together—gone up stairs to hear a noise, or down stairs to settle their accounts, or upon the Landing place to trim the Lamp.—And these precious moments were turned to so good an account that all the most anxious feelings of the past were gone through.—Before they parted at night, Anne had the felicity of being assured in the first place that—(so far from being altered for the worse!)—she had *gained* inexpressibly in personal Loveliness; & that as to Character—her's was now fixed on his Mind as Perfection itself—maintaining the just Medium of Fortitude & Gentleness;—that he had never ceased to love & prefer her, though it had been only at Uppercross that he had learn't to do her Justice—& only at Lyme that he had begun to understand his own sensations;—that at Lyme he had received Lessons of more than one kind;—the passing admiration of M^{r}. Elliot had at least *roused* him, and the scenes on the Cobb & at Capt. Harville's had fixed her superiority. In his preceeding *attempts* to attach himself to Louisa Musgrove, (the attempts of Anger & Pique)—he protested that he had continually felt the impossibility of really caring for Louisa, though till *that day,* till the leisure for reflection which followed it, he had not understood the perfect excellence of the Mind, with which Louisa's could so ill bear a comparison, or the perfect, the unrivalled hold it possessed over his own.—There he had learnt to distinguish between the steadiness of Principle & the Obstinacy of Self-will, between the Darings of Heedlessness, & the Resolution of a collected Mind—there he had seen everything to exalt in his estimation the Woman he had lost, & there begun to deplore the pride, the folly, the madness of resentment which had kept him from trying to regain her, when thrown in his way. From that period to the present had his penance been the most severe.—He had no sooner been free from the horror & remorse attending the first few days of Louisa's accident, no sooner begun to feel himself alive again, than he had begun to feel himself though alive, not at liberty.—He found that he was considered by his friend Harville, as an engaged Man. The Harvilles entertained not a doubt of a mutual attachment between him & Louisa—and though this, to *a degree,* was contradicted instantly—it yet made him feel that perhaps by *her* family, by everybody, by *herself* even, the same idea might be held—and that he was not *free* in honour—though, if such were to be the conclusion, too free alas! in Heart.—He had never thought justly on this subject before—he had not sufficiently considered that his excessive Intimacy at Uppercross must have it's danger of ill consequence in many ways, and that while trying whether he c^d. attach himself to either of the Girls, he might be exciting unpleasant reports, if not, raising unrequited regard!—He found, too late, that he had entangled himself—and that precisely as he became thoroughly satisfied of his not *caring* for Louisa at all, he must regard himself as bound to her, if her feelings for him, were what the Harvilles supposed.—It determined him to leave Lyme—& await her perfect recovery elsewhere. He would gladly weaken, by any *fair* means, whatever sentiments or speculations concerning him might exist; and he went therefore into Shropshire, meaning after a while, to return to the Crofts at Kellynch, & act as he found requisite.—He had remained in Shropshire, lamenting the Blindness of his own Pride, & the Blunders of his own Calculations, till at once released from Louisa by the astonishing felicity of her engagement with Benwicke. Bath, Bath—had instantly followed, in *Thought;* & not long after, in *fact.* To Bath, to arrive with Hope, to be torn by Jealousy at the first sight of M^r. E——, to experience all the changes of each at the Concert, to be miserable by this morning's circumstantial report, to be now, more happy than Language could express, or any heart but his own be capable of.

He was very eager & very delightful in the description of what he had felt at the Concert.—The Even^g. seemed to have been made up of exquisite moments;—the moment of her stepping forward in the Octagon Room to speak to him—the moment of M^r. E's appearing & tearing her away, & one or two subsequent moments, marked by returning hope, or increasing Despondence, were all dwelt on with energy. "To see you, cried he, in the midst of those who could not be *my* well-wishers, to see your Cousin close by you—conversing & smiling—& feel all the horrible Eligibilities & Proprieties of the Match!—to consider it as the certain wish of every being who could hope to influence you—even, if your own feelings were reluctant, or indifferent—to consider what powerful supports would be his!—Was not it enough to make the fool of me, which my behaviour expressed?—How could I look on without agony?—Was not the very sight of the *Friend* who sat behind you?—was not the recollection of what *had* been—the knowledge of her Influence—the indelible, immoveable Impression of what *Persuasion* had *once* done, was not it all against me?"—"You should have distinguished—replied Anne—You should not have suspected me *now;*—The case so different, & my age so different!—If I *was* wrong, in yeilding to Persuasion once, remember that it was to Persuasion exerted on the side of Safety, not of Risk. When I yeilded, I thought it was to *Duty.*—But no *Duty* could be called in aid here.—In marrying a Man indifferent to me, all Risk would have been incurred, & all Duty violated."—"Perhaps I ought to have reasoned thus, he replied, but I could not.—I could not derive benefit from the later knowledge of your Character which I had acquired, I could not bring it into play, it was overwhelmed, buried, lost in those earlier feelings, which I had been smarting under Year after Year.—I could think of you only as one who *had* yeilded, who *had* given me up, who *had* been influenced by any one rather than by *me*—I saw you with the very Person who had guided you in that year of Misery—I had no reason to think her of less authority now;—The force of Habit was to be added."—"I should have thought, said Anne, that my Manner to yourself, might have spared you much, or all of this.—" "No—No—Your manner might be only the ease, which your engagement to another Man would give.—I left you with this beleif.—And yet—I was determined to see you again.—My spirits rallied with the morning, & I felt that I had still a motive for remaining here.—The Admiral's news indeed, was a revulsion. Since that moment, I have been decided what to do—and had it been confirmed, This would have been my *last day* in Bath."

There was time for all this to pass,—with such Interruptions only as enhanced the charm of the communication—and Bath c^d. scarcely contain any other two Beings at once so rationally & so rapturously happy as during that even^g. occupied the Sopha of M^rs. Croft's Drawing room in Gay S^t.

Capt. W.—had taken care to meet the Adm^l.—as he returned into the house, to satisfy him as to M^r. E—& Kellynch;—and the delicacy of the Admiral's good nature kept him from saying another word on the subject to Anne.—He was quite concerned lest he might have been giving her pain by touching a tender part. Who could say?—She might be liking her Cousin, better than he liked her.—And indeed, upon recollection, if they had been to marry at all why should they have waited so long? –

When the Even^g. closed it is probable that the Adm^l received some new Ideas from his wife;—whose particularly friendly manner in parting with her, gave Anne the gratifying persuasion of her seeing & approving.

It had been such a day to Anne!—the hours which had passed since her leaving Camden Place, had done so much!—She was almost bewildered, almost too happy in looking back.—It was necessary to sit up half the Night & lie awake the remainder to comprehend with composure her present state, & pay for the overplus of Bliss, by Headake & Fatigue.—

CHAPTER 11.

Who can be in doubt of what followed?—When any two Young People take it into their heads to marry, they are pretty sure by perseverance to carry their point—be they ever so poor, or ever so imprudent, or ever so little likely to be necessary to each other's ultimate comfort. This may be bad Morality to conclude with, but I beleive it to be Truth—and if such parties succeed, how should a Capt W– & an Anne E——, with the advantage of maturity of Mind, consciousness of Right, & one Independant Fortune between them, fail of bearing down every opposition? They might in fact, have born down a great deal more than they met with, for there was little to distress them beyond the want of Graciousness & Warmth. Sir W. made no objection, & Eliz[th] did nothing worse than look cold & unconcerned.—Capt. W—with £25,000—& as high in his Profession as Merit & Activity c[d] place him, was no longer nobody. He was now esteemed quite worthy to address the Daughter of a foolish spend thrift Baronet, who had not had Principle or sense enough to maintain himself in the Situation in which Providence had placed him, & who c[d]. give his Daughter but a small part of the Share of ten Thousand pounds which must be her's hereafter.—Sir Walter indeed tho' he had no affection for his Daughter & no vanity flattered to make him really happy on the occasion, was very far from thinking it a bad match for her.—On the contrary when he saw more of Capt. W.—& eyed him well, he was very much struck by his personal claims & felt that *his* superiority of appearance might be not unfairly balanced against *her* superiority of Rank;—and all this, together with his well-sounding name, enabled Sir W. at last to prepare his pen with a very good grace for the insertion of the Marriage in the volume of Honour.— The only person among them whose opposition of feelings c[d]. excite any serious anxiety, was Lady Russel.—Anne knew that Lady R—must be suffering some pain in understanding & relinquishing M[r]. E—& be making some struggles to become truly acquainted with & do justice to Capt W.—This however, was what Lady R— had now to do. She must learn to feel that she had been mistaken with regard to both—that she had been unfairly influenced by appearances in each—that, because Capt. W.'s manners had not suited her own ideas, she had been too quick in suspecting them to indicate a Character of dangerous Impetuosity, & that because M[r]. Elliot's manners had precisely pleased her in their propriety & correctness, their general politeness & suavity, she had been too quick in receiving them as the certain result of the most correct opinions & well regulated Mind.—There was nothing less for Lady R. to do than to admit that she had been pretty completely wrong, & to take up a new set of opinions & hopes.—There *is* a quickness of perception in some, a nicety in the discernment of character—a natural Penetration in short, which no Experience in others can equal—and Lady R. had been less gifted in this part of Understanding than her Young friend;—but she was a very good Woman; & if her second object was to be sensible & well-judging, her first was to see Anne happy. She loved Anne better than she loved her own abilities—and when the awkwardness of the Beginning was over, found little hardship in attaching herself as a Mother to the Man who was securing the happiness of her Child. Of all the family, Mary was probably the one most immediately gratified by the circumstance.—It was creditable to have a Sister married, and she might flatter herself that she had been greatly instrumental to the connection, by having Anne staying with her in the Autumn; & as her own Sister must be better than her Husbands Sisters, it was very agreeable that Captn. W—should be a richer Man than either Capt. B. or Charles Hayter.—She had something to suffer perhaps when they came into contact again, in seeing Anne restored to the rights of Seniority & the Mistress of a very pretty Landaulet—but *she* had a *future* to look forward to, of powerful consolation—Anne had no Uppercross Hall before her, no Landed Estate, no Headship of a family, and if they could but keep Capt. W—from being made a Baronet, she would not change situations with Anne.—It would be well for the *Eldest* Sister if she were equally satisfied with *her* situation, for a change is not very probable there.—She had soon the mortification of seeing M^r. E. withdraw, & no one of proper condition has since presented himself to raise even the unfounded hopes which sunk with *him*. The news of his Cousin Anne's engagement burst on M^r. Elliot most unexpectedly. It deranged his best plan of domestic Happiness, his best hopes of keeping Sir Walter single by the watchfulness which a son in law's rights w^d. have given.—But tho' discomfited & disappointed, he c^d. still do something for his own Interest & his own enjoyment. He soon quitted Bath and on M^rs. Clay's quitting it likewise soon afterwards & being next heard of, as established under his Protection in London, it was evident how double a Game he had been playing, & how determined he was to save himself from being cut out by *one* artful woman at least.—M^rs. Clay's affections had overpowered her Interest, & she had sacrificed for the Young Man's sake, the possibility of scheming longer for Sir Walter;—she has Abilities however as well as Affections, and it is now a doubtful point whether his cunning or hers may finally carry the day, whether, after preventing her from being the wife of Sir Walter, he may not be wheedled & caressed at last into making her the wife of Sir William.—

It cannot be doubted that Sir Walter & Eliz: were shocked & mortified by the loss of their companion & the discovery of their deception in her. They had their great cousins to be sure, to resort to for comfort—but they must long feel that to flatter & follow others, without being flattered & followed themselves is but a state of half enjoyment.

Anne, satisfied at a very early period, of Lady Russel's *meaning* to love Capt. W—as she ought, had no other alloy to the happiness of her prospects, than what arose from the consciousness of having no relations to bestow on him which a Man of sense could value.—There, she felt her own Inferiority keenly.—The disproportion in their fortunes was nothing;—it did not give her a moment's regret;—but to have no Family to receive & estimate him properly, nothing of respectability, of Harmony, of—Goodwill to offer in return for all the Worth & all the prompt welcome which met her in his Brothers & Sisters, was a source of as lively pain, as her Mind could well be sensible of, under circumstances of otherwise strong felicity.—She had but two friends in the World, to add to his List, Lady R. & M[rs]. Smith.—To those however, he was very well-disposed to attach himself. Lady R—inspite of all her former transgressions, he could now value from his heart;—while he was not obliged to say that he beleived her to have been right in originally dividing them, he was ready to say almost anything else in her favour;—& as for M[rs]. Smith, she had claims of various kinds to recommend her quickly & permanently.—Her recent good offices by Anne had been enough in themselves—and their marriage, instead of depriving her of one friend secured her two. She was one of their first visitors in their settled Life—and Capt. Wentworth, by putting her in the way of recovering her Husband's property in the W. Indies, by writing for her, acting for her, & seeing her through all the petty Difficulties of the case, with the activity & exertion of a fearless Man, & a determined friend, fully requited the services she had rendered, or had ever meant to render, to his Wife. M[rs]. Smith's enjoyments were not *spoiled* by this improvement of Income, with some improvement of health, & the acquisition of such friends to be often with, for her chearfulness & mental Activity did not fail her, & while those prime supplies of Good remained, she might have bid defiance even to greater accessions of worldly Prosperity. She might have been absolutely rich & perfectly healthy, & yet be happy.—*Her* spring of Felicity was in the glow of her Spirits—as her friend Anne's was in the warmth of her Heart.—Anne was Tenderness itself;—and she had the full worth of it in Capt[n]. Wentworth's affection. His Profession was all that could ever make her friends wish *that* Tenderness less; the dread of a future War, all that could dim her Sunshine.—She gloried in being a Sailor's wife, but she must pay the tax of quick alarm, for belonging to that Profession which is—if possible—more distinguished in it's Domestic Virtues, than in it's National Importance.—

Finis

July 18.–1816.

Notes

1 A "mantuamaker" is a "dressmaker."

2 "Grave as a judge" is proverbial. Compare Charles Lamb (1775–1834) in his 1821 essay "My First Play," where he describes sitting in a theater "as grave as a judge," watching an actress whose "hysteric affectations" moved him "like some solemn tragic passion" (Lamb, *Elia and the Last Essays of Elia,* ed. Jonathan Bate (Oxford: Oxford University Press, 1987), 113).

Appendix B

Biographical Notice of the Author

BY HENRY AUSTEN

Austen's fourth and favorite brother, Henry, attended Oxford University, served in the Oxfordshire militia, made a romantic marriage, was for a time a banker, and finished his career as a clergyman. Of all her siblings, Henry took the greatest interest in Austen's writings and dealt often with publishers on her behalf. He composed this "Biographical Notice" of his sister shortly after her death in July 1817. The "Notice" marks the first time the public was presented with information about Austen's life and learned that she was the author of four previously published novels. Henry's idealized image of his sister shaped not only the early reception of *Persuasion* but also the ways in which Austen was read and understood throughout the nineteenth century.

Henry first published the "Notice" as a preface to *Northanger Abbey: and Persuasion,* 4 vols. (London: Murray, 1818), I, iii–xix. The copytext here is taken from this edition.

⁓

THE FOLLOWING PAGES are the production of a pen which has already contributed in no small degree to the entertainment of the public. And when the public, which has not been insensible to the merits of "Sense and Sensibility," "Pride and Prejudice," "Mansfield Park," and "Emma," shall be informed that the hand which guided that pen[1] is now mouldering in the grave, perhaps a brief account of Jane Austen will be read with a kindlier sentiment than simple curiosity.

Henry Austen, by an unknown artist, circa 1820. He was the funniest and most charming of Austen's six brothers. "His hopefulness of temperament," wrote one of his nieces, "in adjusting itself to all circumstances, even the adverse, seemed to create a perpetual sunshine" (cited in Cecil, 37).

Short and easy will be the task of the mere biographer. A life of usefulness, literature, and religion, was not by any means a life of event. To those who lament their irreparable loss, it is consolatory to think that, as she never deserved disapprobation, so, in the circle of her family and friends, she never met reproof; that her wishes were not only reasonable, but gratified; and that to the little disappointments incidental to human life was never added, even for a moment, an abatement of good-will from any who knew her.

Jane Austen was born on the 16th of December, 1775, at Steventon, in the county of Hants. Her father was Rector of that parish upwards of forty years. There he resided, in the conscientious and unassisted discharge of his ministerial duties, until he was turned of seventy years. Then he retired with his wife, our authoress, and her sister, to Bath, for the remainder of his life, a period of about four years.[2] Being not only a profound scholar, but possessing a most exquisite taste in every species of literature, it is not wonderful[3] that his daughter Jane should, at a very early age, have become sensible to the charms of style, and enthusiastic in the cultivation of her own language. On the death of her father she removed, with her mother and sister, for a short time, to Southampton,[4] and finally, in 1809, to the pleasant village of Chawton,[5] in the same county. From this place she sent into the world those novels, which by many have been placed on the same shelf as the works of a D'Arblay and an Edgeworth.[6] Some of these novels had been the gradual performances of her previous life. For though in composition she was equally rapid and correct, yet an invincible distrust of her own judgement induced her to withhold her works from the public, till time and many perusals had satisfied her that the charm of recent composition was dissolved. The natural constitution, the regular habits, the quiet and happy occupations of our authoress, seemed to promise a long succession of amusement to the public, and a gradual increase of reputation to herself. But the symptoms of a decay, deep and incurable, began to shew themselves in the commencement of 1816.[7] Her decline was at first deceitfully slow; and until the spring of this present year, those who knew their happiness to be involved in her existence could not endure to despair. But in the month of May, 1817, it was found advisable that she should be removed to Winchester[8] for the benefit of constant medical aid, which none even then dared to hope would be permanently beneficial. She supported, during two months, all the varying pain, irksomeness, and tedium, attendant on decaying nature, with more than resignation, with a truly elastic cheerfulness. She retained her faculties, her memory, her fancy, her temper, and her affections, warm, clear, and unimpaired, to the last. Neither her love of God, nor of her fellow creatures flagged for a moment. She made a point of receiving the sacrament before excessive bodily weakness might have rendered her perception unequal to her wishes. She wrote whilst she could hold a pen, and with a pencil when a pen was become too laborious. The day preceding her death she composed some stanzas replete with fancy and vigour.[9] Her last voluntary speech conveyed thanks to her medical attendant; and to the final question asked of her, purporting to know her wants, she replied, "I want nothing but death."

She expired shortly after, on Friday the 18th of July, 1817, in the arms of her sister, who, as well as the relator of these events, feels too surely that they shall never look upon her like again.

Jane Austen was buried on the 24th of July, 1817, in the cathedral church of Winchester, which, in the whole catalogue of its mighty dead, does not contain the ashes of a brighter genius or a sincerer Christian.

Of personal attractions she possessed a considerable share. Her stature was that of true elegance. It could not have been increased without exceeding the middle height. Her carriage and deportment were quiet, yet graceful. Her features were separately good. Their assemblage produced an unrivalled expression of that cheerfulness, sensibility, and benevolence, which were her real characteristics. Her complexion was of the finest texture. It might with truth be said, that her eloquent blood spoke through her modest cheek.[10] Her voice was extremely sweet. She delivered herself with fluency and precision. Indeed she was formed for elegant and rational society, excelling in conversation as much as in composition. In the present age it is hazardous to mention accomplishments. Our authoress would, probably, have been inferior to few in such acquirements, had she not been so superior to most in higher things. She had not only an excellent taste for drawing, but, in her earlier days, evinced great power of hand in the management of the pencil. Her own musical attainments she held very cheap. Twenty years ago they would have been thought more of, and twenty years hence many a parent will expect their daughters to be applauded for meaner performances. She was fond of dancing, and excelled in it. It remains now to add a few observations on that which her friends deemed more important, on those endowments which sweetened every hour of their lives.

If there be an opinion current in the world, that perfect placidity of temper is not reconcileable to the most lively imagination, and the keenest relish for wit, such an opinion will be rejected for ever by those who have had the happiness of knowing the authoress of the following works. Though the frailties, foibles, and follies of others could not escape her immediate detection, yet even on their vices did she never trust herself to comment with unkindness. The affectation of candour is not uncommon; but she had no affectation. Faultless herself, as nearly as human nature can be, she always sought, in the faults of others, something to excuse, to forgive or forget. Where extenuation was impossible, she had a sure refuge in silence. She never uttered either a hasty, a silly, or a severe expression. In short, her temper was as polished as her wit. Nor were her manners inferior to her temper. They were of the happiest kind. No one could be often in her company without feeling a strong desire of obtaining her friendship, and cherishing a hope of having obtained it. She was tranquil without reserve or stiffness; and communicative without intrusion or self-sufficiency. She became an authoress entirely from taste and inclination. Neither the hope of fame nor profit mixed with her early motives.[11] Most of her works, as before observed, were composed many years previous to their publication.[12] It was with extreme difficulty that her friends, whose partiality she suspected whilst she honoured their judgement, could prevail on her to publisher her first work. Nay, so persuaded was she that its sale would not repay the expense of publication, that she actually made a reserve from her very moderate income to meet the expected loss. She could scarcely believe what she termed her great good fortune when "Sense and Sensibility" produced a clear profit of about £150. Few so gifted were so truly unpretending. She regarded the above sum as a prodigious recompense for that which had cost her nothing. Her readers, perhaps, will wonder that such a work produced so little at a time when some authors have received more guineas than they have written lines. The works of our authoress, however, may live as long as those which have burst on the world with more éclat. But the public has not been unjust; and our authoress was far from thinking it so. Most gratifying to her was the applause which from time to time reached her ears from those who were competent to discriminate. Still, in spite of such applause, so much did she shrink for notoriety, that no accumulation of fame would have induced her, had she lived, to affix her name to any productions of her pen. In the bosom of her own family she talked of them freely, thankful for praise, open to remark, and submissive to criticism. But in public she turned away from any allusion to the character of an authoress. She read aloud with very great taste and effect. Her own works, probably, were never heard to so much advantage as from her own mouth; for she partook largely in all the best gifts of the comic muse. She was a warm and judicious admirer of landscape, both in nature and on canvass. At a very early age she was enamoured of Gilpin on the Picturesque;[13] and she seldom changed her opinions either on books or men.

Her reading was very extensive in history and belles lettres; and her memory extremely tenacious. Her favourite moral writers were Johnson in prose,[14] and Cowper in verse.[15] It is difficult to say at what age she was not intimately acquainted with the merits and defects of the best essays and novels in the English language. Richardson's power of creating, and preserving the consistency of his characters, as particularly exemplified in "Sir Charles Grandison,"[16] gratified the natural discrimination of her mind, whilst her taste secured her from the errors of his prolix style and tedious narrative. She did not rank any work of Fielding[17] quite so high. Without the slightest affectation she recoiled from every thing gross. Neither nature, wit, nor humour, could make her amends for so very low a scale of morals.

Her power of inventing characters seems to have been intuitive, and almost unlimited. She drew from nature; but, whatever may have been surmised to the contrary, never from individuals.

The style of her familiar correspondence was in all respects the same as that of her novels. Every thing came finished from her pen; for on all subjects she had ideas as clear as her expressions were well chosen. It is not hazarding too much to say that she never dispatched a note or letter unworthy of publication.

One trait only remains to be touched on. It makes all others unimportant. She was thoroughly religious and devout; fearful of giving offence to God, and incapable of feeling it towards any fellow creature. On serious subjects she was well-instructed, both by reading and meditation, and her opinions accorded strictly with those of our Established Church.

London, Dec. 13, 1817.
Postscript

Since concluding the above remarks, the writer of them has been put in possession of some extracts from the private correspondence of the authoress. They are few and short; but are submitted to the public without apology, as being more truly descriptive of her temper, taste, feelings, and principles than any thing which the pen of a biographer can produce.

The first extract is a playful defence of herself from a mock charge of having pilfered the manuscripts of a young relation.[18]

"What should I do, my dearest E. with your manly, vigorous sketches, so full of life and spirit? How could I possibly join them on to a little bit of ivory, two inches wide, on which I work with a brush so fine as to produce little effect after much labour?"[19]

The remaining extracts are from various parts of a letter[20] written a few weeks before her death.

"My attendant is encouraging, and talks of making me quite well. I live chiefly on the sofa, but am allowed to walk from one room to the other. I have been out once in a sedan-chair, and am to repeat it, and be promoted to a wheel-chair as the weather serves. On this subject I will only say further that my dearest sister, my tender, watchful, indefatigable nurse, has not been made ill by her exertions. As to what I owe to her, and to the anxious affection of all my beloved family on this occasion, I can only cry over it, and pray to God to bless them more and more."

She next touches with just and gentle animadversion on a subject of domestic disappointment. Of this the particulars do not concern the public. Yet in justice to her characteristic sweetness and resignation, the concluding observation of our authoress thereon must not be suppressed.

"But I am getting too near complaint. It has been the appointment of God, however secondary causes may have operated."

The following and final extract will prove the facility with which she could correct every impatient thought, and turn from complaint to cheerfulness.

"You will find Captain ——— a very respectable, well-meaning man, without much manner, his wife and sister all good humour and obligingness, and I hope (since the fashion allows it) with rather longer petticoats than last year."

London, Dec. 20, 1817.

Notes

1 In recalling the "pen" in his sister's "hand," Henry Austen ironically invokes the penultimate chapter of *Persuasion,* where Anne discounts examples of female inconstancy in books because the "pen" has been in men's hands.

2 In 1761, Austen's father, George Austen (1731–1805), was presented with the living of Steventon in Hampshire. Four decades later he retired to Bath.

3 In this context, "not wonderful" means "no wonder" or "not surprising."

4 Southampton is an English Channel port in Hampshire.

5 Chawton lies a mile south of Alton, and seventeen miles southeast of Steventon.

6 The novelist and diarist Madame D'Arblay is more commonly referred to by her unmarried name, Frances or Fanny Burney. Maria Edgeworth is best known for her children's stories and novels of Irish life. Both Burney and Edgeworth were held in high esteem in Austen's lifetime and were greatly admired by Austen herself.

7 There is still no conclusive evidence regarding the disease that killed Austen. Tuberculosis, Addison's disease, and Hodgkin's disease have all been identified as possible causes (Tomalin, 287–288).

8 Winchester is twelve miles north of Southampton. Austen is buried in its famous cathedral.

9 On her deathbed, Austen wrote, "When Winchester races first took their beginning," twenty-four lines of comic verse in which she imagines St. Swithin's laying a curse on the annual Winchester races:

> These races & revels & dissolute measures
> With which you're debasing a neighbouring Plain
> Let them stand—you shall meet with your curse in your pleasures
> Set off for your course, I'll pursue with my rain.

(*The Poetry of Jane Austen and the Austen Family,* ed. David Selwyn [Iowa City: University of Iowa Press, 1997], 17–18).

10 In this description of his sister, Henry Austen echoes John Donne (1572–1631) in "Of the Progres of the Soule. The Second Anniversarie" (1612), 244–246:

> Her pure and eloquent blood
> Spoke in her cheekes, and so distinctly wrought,
> That one might almost say, her bodie thought.

(Donne, *The Epithalamions, Anniversaries, and Epicedes,* ed. W. Milgate [Oxford: Clarendon Press, 1978], 48).

11 Henry Austen is eager to present his sister as a model of femininity and refinement. But as Austen's letters make clear, she took a professional interest in her writings and kept a close eye on sales.

12 Austen completed some work on a version of *Sense and Sensibility* around 1795, but it was 1811 before the novel was revised and published. Similarly, she completed an early version of *Pride and Prejudice* in 1797, but the novel did not appear until 1813.

13 William Gilpin (1724–1804) established himself as a leading authority on the Picturesque with a series of books that taught his readers new ways of perceiving landscape. His most celebrated works include *Observations on the River Wye, and Several Parts of Wales* (1782) and *Three Essays: on Picturesque Beauty; on Picturesque Travel; and on Sketching Landscape* (1792).

14 Samuel Johnson, essayist, poet, lexicographer, critic, and biographer, was one of the foremost literary figures of the eighteenth century. His most famous prose works include *The Rambler* (1750–1752), *Rasselas* (1759), and *The Lives of the Poets* (1779–1781).

15 William Cowper (1731–1800) was one of the most widely read poets of the late eighteenth century. He is best known for the *Olney Hymns* (1779) and *The Task* (1785).

16 Samuel Richardson is celebrated for three novels, all of which were written in the epistolary format that he pioneered: *Pamela* (1740), *Clarissa* (1747–1748), and *Sir Charles Grandison* (1753–1754).

17 Henry Fielding (1707–1754), playwright and novelist, wrote *An Apology for the Life of Mrs. Shamela Andrews* (1741) as a satiric riposte to Richardson's *Pamela*. *Tom Jones* (1749) is Fielding's most famous novel, featuring bawdy humor and an errant hero. Richardson replied with *Sir Charles Grandison,* whose hero is a thoroughly good man.

18 The "young relation" is Austen's nephew James Edward Austen-Leigh, who was the son of her eldest brother, James. Many years later he became her biographer.

19 Austen wrote this famous letter from Chawton in December 1816 (Austen, *Letters,* 322–324). Her self-deprecating remarks about her novelistic art taking shape on "a little bit of ivory" are motivated in part by her eagerness to praise her teenaged nephew. It is also possible that she wrote them with her tongue lodged partially in her cheek. Critics, however, have long taken these lines as evidence that Austen herself accepted that—as a female writer—she was "limited."

20 This letter is only known from Henry Austen's publication of it here in his "Biographical Notice."

Appendix C

Emendations and Corrections to the 1818 Text of *Persuasion*

	The 1818 Text	*Emended to*
page 33, line 7	contempt. As	contempt, as
page 38, line 4	the mall	them all
page 41, line 21	she was at	he was at
page 56, lines 34–35	particula inquiries	particular inquiries
page 84, line 14	herright	her right
page 91, lines 20–21	injury receive	injury received
page 93, line 22	to reply	in reply
page 94, line 21	againt it	against it
page 96, line 23	Tuesday.	Tuesday."
page 97, line 15	all that that was	all that was
page 99, line 2	informa tion	information
page 99, line 5	"You	'You
page 99, line 6	again."	again.'"
page 99, line 7	sisters	sister's
page 99, line 8	of being inflicting	of inflicting
page 100, line 19	want,	want,"
page 100, line 19	Something	"Something
page 104, line 14	French rigate	French frigate

page 110, line 6	my dear,'"	my dear,"
page 110, line 6	when he	"when he
page 110, line 36	blesssed	blessed
page 126, line 28	Musgrove, "And no, no,"	Musgrove, and "No, no,"
page 128, line 18	re turned	returned
page 134, line 34	before.	before."
page 135, line 3	for them.	for us.
page 135, line 14	amnsement	amusement
page 159, line 14	behi d,	behind,
page 161, line 34	time.	time."
page 162, line 35	se med arranged.	seemed arranged.

VOLUME 2

page 169, line 21	ame	same
page 171, line 30	now room	room now
page 173, line 22	firs	first
page 179, line 12	well, believe	well, I believe
page 179, line 17	"he never shot"	'he never shot'
pages 179–180, line 17–1	"been quite misunderstood,"	'been quite misunderstood,'
page 180, lines 30–31	"Miss Elliot"	'Miss Elliot'
page 180, line 32	"Elegance,	'Elegance,
page 180, line 33	beauty,"	beauty,'
page 180, line 36	me.'	me."
page 202, line 28	him.	him."
page 204, line 16	iuiagined.	imagined.
page 205, lines 6–7	protegeé	protegée
page 220, line 19	where-ever	wherever
page 221, line 26	"How d'ye do,"	'How d'ye do,'
page 221, line 27	"How d'ye do."	'How d'ye do.'
page 225, line 6	"I wonder	'I wonder
page 225, line 7	at it."	at it.'
page 255, line 8	cou sins	cousins
page 256, line 14	your	yours
page 257, lines 1–2	hnsband.	husband.

page 260, line 18	"Why,	'Why,
page 260, line 18	ma'am,"	ma'am,'
page 260, line 18	"it would	'it would
page 260, line 19	else."	else.'
page 270, line 5	were icher,	were richer,
page 281, lines 19–20	answe	answer
page 282, line 11	friend's account,	friends' account,
page 287, lines 4–5	Harville. "Not quite,	Harville. / "Not quite,
page 287, line 34	again!"	again!'
page 290, line 22	means a are	means as are
page 295, line 15	had began	had begun
page 295, line 22	longer a my	longer at my
page 297, line 6	powerfu	powerful
page 299, line 10	ked at Lady Russell	looked at Lady Russell
page 300, line 17	pendthrift	spendthrift
page 303, lines 28–29	She l d soon	She had soon

Further Reading

Auerbach, Emily. *Searching for Jane Austen.* Madison: University of Wisconsin Press, 2004.

Babb, Howard. *Jane Austen's Novels: The Fabric of Dialogue.* Columbus: Ohio State University Press, 1962.

Bloom, Harold, ed. *Jane Austen's "Persuasion."* Philadelphia: Chelsea House, 2004.

Brown, Julia Prewitt. *Jane Austen's Novels: Social Change and Literary Form.* Cambridge, MA: Harvard University Press, 1979.

Butler, Marilyn. *Jane Austen and the War of Ideas.* Oxford: Clarendon Press, 1975.

Cecil, David. *A Portrait of Jane Austen.* London: Book Club Associates, 1978.

Collins, Irene. *Jane Austen and the Clergy.* London: The Hambledon Press, 1994.

Copeland, Edward, and Juliet McMaster, eds. *The Cambridge Companion to Jane Austen.* Cambridge: Cambridge University Press, 1997.

Deresiewicz, William. *Jane Austen and the Romantic Poets.* New York: Columbia University Press, 2004.

Duckworth, Alistair. *The Improvement of the Estate.* Baltimore: Johns Hopkins University Press, 1971.

Favret, Mary. *War at a Distance: Romanticism and the Making of Modern Wartime.* Princeton: Princeton University Press, 2010.

Freeman, Jean. *Jane Austen in Bath.* Chawton: Jane Austen Society, 2002.

Grey, J. David, ed. *The Jane Austen Handbook.* London: The Athlone Press, 1986.

Harris, Jocelyn. *A Revolution Almost Beyond Expression: Jane Austen's "Persuasion."* Newark: University of Delaware Press, 2007.

Johnson, Claudia. *Jane Austen: Women, Politics, and the Novel.* Chicago: University of Chicago Press, 1988.

Johnson, Claudia, and Clara Tuite, eds. *A Companion to Jane Austen.* Chichester: Wiley-Blackwell, 2009.

Lane, Maggie. *Jane Austen and Lyme Regis.* Chawton: Jane Austen Society, 2007.

Le Faye, Deirdre. *Jane Austen: The World of Her Novels.* London: Frances Lincoln, 2002.

Littlewood, Ian, ed. *Jane Austen: Critical Assessments,* 4 vols. Mountfield: Helm, 1998.

McMaster, Juliet, and Bruce Stovel, eds. *Jane Austen's Business.* London: Macmillan, 1996.

Morgan, Susan. *In the Meantime: Character and Perception in Jane Austen's Fiction.* Chicago: University of Chicago Press, 1980.

Nokes, David. *Jane Austen: A Life.* London: Fourth Estate, 1997.

Poovey, Mary. *The Proper Lady and the Woman Writer.* Chicago: University of Chicago Press, 1984.

Sales, Roger. *Jane Austen and Representations of Regency England.* London: Routledge, 1994.

Southam, Brian. *Jane Austen and the Navy.* London: Hambledon and London, 2000.

Stovel, Bruce, and Lynn Weinlos Gregg, eds. *The Talk in Jane Austen.* Edmonton: University of Alberta Press, 2002.

Tanner, Tony. *Jane Austen.* Cambridge, MA: Harvard University Press, 1986.

Tave, Stuart. *Some Words of Jane Austen.* Chicago: University of Chicago Press, 1973.

Tomalin, Claire. *Jane Austen: A Life.* London: Viking, 1997.

Waldron, Mary. *Jane Austen and the Fiction of Her Time.* Cambridge: Cambridge University Press, 1999.

Walker, Eric C. *Marriage, Writing, and Romanticism: Wordsworth and Austen after War.* Stanford: Stanford University Press, 2009.

Wiltshire, John. *Jane Austen and the Body.* Cambridge: Cambridge University Press, 1992.

Illustration Credits

Lyme Regis, Dorsetshire: A Squall, by J. M. W. Turner, circa 1812. © Culture and Sport Glasgow (Museums). *Frontispiece*

Title page of the first edition of *Persuasion*. Courtesy Houghton Library, Harvard University. *2*

Hugh Thomson, Illustrations for *Persuasion*, 1897. Anne and Captain Wentworth sit on the same couch, divided by Mrs. Musgrove, to whom Captain Wentworth respectfully attends. © The British Library Board, All Rights Reserved. 012624. ee.28. *31, 107*

Haldon Hall, near Exeter, by Francis Towne (1739–1816), 1780. Tate/Digital Image © Tate, London 2009. *35*

Elizabeth Hamilton, by Henry Meyer (circa 1782–1847), after Sir Henry Raeburn (1756–1823), circa 1812. © National Portrait Gallery, London. *36*

Sir Egerton Brydges, from an unattributed engraving. Courtesy Houghton Library, Harvard University. *37*

The prince regent, oil on canvas, by Thomas Lawrence (1769–1830), circa 1814. © National Portrait Gallery, London. *39*

Edmund Burke, after James Barry (1741–1806), circa 1774. © National Portrait Gallery, London. *42*

Title page of John Debrett's famous *Baronetage of England*, the only book that Sir Walter ever reads. Harvard College Library, Widener Library, Br5400 70. *43*

Napoleon Bonaparte on Board the Bellerophon *in Plymouth Sound*, by Charles Lock Eastlake (1793–1865), 1815. © National Maritime Museum, Greenwich, London. *44*

Watercolor of Jane Austen painted by her sister, Cassandra, around 1802. Private Collection. *46*

Thomas Gisborne, by Henry Meyer, after John Jackson (1778–1831), after John Hoppner (1758–1810). © National Portrait Gallery, London. *48*

Mary Robinson, by or after Sir Joshua Reynolds (1723–1792), circa 1782. © National Portrait Gallery, London. *50*

A. Wallis Mills (1878–1940), Illustrations for *Persuasion*, 1908. Sir Walter speaks haughtily to Mr. Shepherd about prospective tenants for Kellynch Hall. © The British Library Board, All Rights Reserved. 12208.t.1. *51*

Lord Nelson, by Sir William Beechey (1753–1839), 1800. © National Portrait Gallery, London. *53*

A military flogging, by George Cruikshank (1792–1878), published 1825. © National Maritime Museum, Greenwich, London. *55*

Charles Edmund Brock (1870–1938), Illustrations for *Persuasion*, 1898. Sir Walter deplores the physical appearance of Admiral Baldwin. Courtesy Yale University Library. *57*

Charles Austen used his prize money to purchase these topaze crosses for his sisters, Cassandra and Jane. Jane Austen's House Museum, Jane Austen Memorial Trust. *60*

View of the south side of St. Domingo, by T. G. Dutton, after W. S. Andrews. © National Maritime Museum, Greenwich, London. *62*

Sir J. T. Duckworth's Action off St. Domingo, February 6, 1806, engraved by Thomas Sutherland (1785–1838), after Thomas Whitcombe (circa 1760–1824). © National Maritime Museum, Greenwich, London. *65*

Frances d'Arblay, by her cousin Edward Francisco Burney (1760–1848), circa 1784. © National Portrait Gallery, London. *66*

David Steel (d. circa 1810), *Original and Correct List of the Royal Navy*. © The British Library Board, All Rights Reserved. RB.a26443. *68*

William Buchan, by an unknown artist, published in 1821. Wellcome Library, London. *73*

Drawing Room Scene, from *The Social Day* by Peter Coxe, engraved by Anker Smith (1759–1819), published 1822 (engraving) (b/w photo), Singleton, Henry (1766–1839) (after) / Private Collection / The Stapleton Collection / The Bridgeman Art Library International. *77*

A young woman plays the harp at an evening party; artist unknown. Mary Evans Picture Library. *78*

Mary Wollstonecraft, by John Opie (1761–1807), circa 1797. © National Portrait Gallery, London. *79*

Shooting Duck, engraved by H. Merke, circa 1809 (color litho), Howitt, Samuel (1756–1822) (after) / Private Collection / © The British Sporting Art Trust / The Bridgeman Art Library International. *81*

Evening Dresses for August 1808, illustration from *Le Beau Monde or, Literary and Fashionable Magazine*, 1808 (colored engraving), English School (19th century) / Victoria & Albert Museum, London, UK / The Bridgeman Art Library International. *82*

Hugh Thomson (1860–1920), Illustrations for *Persuasion*, 1897. Admiral Croft is restrained by the rambunctious young Musgrove boys. © The British Library Board, All Rights Reserved. 012624.ee.28. *87*

The English frigate *Unicorn* in action against the French frigate *La Tribune* off the Scilly Isles on June 8, 1796. © The British Library Board, All Rights Reserved. 10856.i.17. *89*

Charles Edmund Brock, Illustrations for *Persuasion*, 1898. Young Charles Musgrove is carried home after hurting his collarbone. Courtesy Yale University Library. *92*

Samuel Johnson, portrait in oils, by Sir Joshua Reynolds, 1756–1757. © National Portrait Gallery, London. *97*

The Fall of Nelson, Battle of Trafalgar, 21 October 1805, by Denis Dighton (1791–1827). © National Maritime Museum, Greenwich, London. *103*

This 1804 *View of the Royal Navy* identifies the various ships, flags, and military uniforms of the British navy. © National Maritime Museum, Greenwich, London. *105*

Nelson Boarding the San Nicolas *in the Victory off Cape St. Vincent . . . 14 February 1797*, by A. W. Reeve, after W. R. Thomas. © National Maritime Museum, Greenwich, London. *106*

Gosport: The Entrance to Portsmouth Harbour (w/c on paper), Turner, J. M. W. (1775–1851) / Private Collection / Photo © Agnew's, London, UK / The Bridgeman Art Library International. *108*

Maria Jane Jewsbury, engraved by John Cochran, after a painting by G. Freeman. © National Portrait Gallery, London. *111*

An 1821 map of the West Indies by James V. Seaman showing various areas mentioned in *Persuasion,* including St. Domingo, the Bahamas, and the Straits of Florida. David Rumsey Map Collection, www.davidrumsey.com. *112*

An engraving of Maria Edgeworth published by Evert Augustus Duyckinck (1816–1878) in his Portrait Gallery of Eminent Women (1813). © National Portrait Gallery, London. *117*

Charles Edmund Brock, Illustrations for *Persuasion*, 1898. Captain Wentworth removes young Walter from Anne's back. Courtesy Yale University Library. *119*

An 1815 print of a young woman in an autumnal walking dress taken from *La Belle Assemblée*, a magazine "Addressed Particularly to the Ladies." © The British Library Board, All Rights Reserved. P.P.5142. *123*

A miniature of Austen's oldest brother, James, dating from about 1790, when he was twenty-five years old and serving as a curate at Overton. Jane Austen's House Museum, Jane Austen Memorial Trust. *124*

Charlotte Smith, by Samuel Freeman (1773–1857), after John Opie, published 1808. © National Portrait Gallery, London. *127*

Charles Edmund Brock, Illustrations for *Persuasion,* 1898. Captain Wentworth speaks to Louisa, unaware that Anne is near. Courtesy Yale University Library. *129*

Frontispiece from the 1833 *Standard Novels* edition of *Persuasion*, published by Richard Bentley (1794–1871). Harvard College Library, Widener Library, 18475.27.10. *130*

The Midshipmans' Berth, circa 1820 (oil on canvas) (see 216825), DeBerenger, Charles Random (19th century) / © Peabody Essex Museum, Salem, Massachusetts, USA / The Bridgeman Art Library International. *131*

A View of Lyme Regis, by Charles Dibdin (1745–1814), circa 1760–1814. © The Trustees of the British Museum. *137*

The prince regent in a curricle, by Thomas Rowlandson (1756–1827). By courtesy of the Witt Library, The Courtauld Institute of Art, London. *138*

The Assembly Rooms at Cobb Gate, Lyme Regis, attributed to Reed. Courtesy Lyme Regis Philpot Museum. *139*

Sea Bathing at Scarborough, from "Costume of Yorkshire," by George Walker, 1814 / Private Collection / The Bridgeman Art Library International. *140*

Samuel Taylor Coleridge, by Peter Vandyke (1729–1799), 1795. © National Portrait Gallery, London. *141*

Between Lyme Regis and Charmouth, Abbott, John White (1764–1851) / Victoria & Albert Museum, London, UK / The Bridgeman Art Library International. *142*

Engraving of a sailmaker at work, from David Steel's *Elements of Mastmaking, Sailmaking, and Rigging* (1794). Courtesy Houghton Library, Harvard University. *144*

Walter Scott, by Sir Henry Raeburn, 1822. National Galleries of Scotland. *146*

Lord Byron, by Richard Westall (1765–1836), 1813. © National Portrait Gallery, London. *146*

Title page of M. Phillips's book *Picture of Lyme-Regis*, 1817. Harvard College Library, Widener Library, DA690.L885. *151*

Hugh Thomson, Illustrations for *Persuasion*, 1897. Mr. Elliot allows Anne and her party to pass. Captain Wentworth's affection for Anne is rekindled at this moment. © The British Library Board, All Rights Reserved. 012624.ee.28. *152*

A. Wallis Mills, Illustrations for *Persuasion*, 1908. Captain Wentworth kneels with Louisa in his arms after her fall on the Cobb. © The British Library Board, All Rights Reserved. 12208.t.1. *157*

Francis Austen, by an unknown artist. Jane Austen's House Museum, Jane Austen Memorial Trust. *162*

Matthew Prior, by Thomas Hudson (1701–1779), after Jonathan Richardson (1667–1745), circa 1718. © National Portrait Gallery, London. *165*

Hugh Thomson, Illustrations for *Persuasion*, 1897. Captain Wentworth draws his letter from among the scattered papers on the writing desk and leaves it for Anne. © The British Library Board, All Rights Reserved. 012624.ee.28. *167, 289*

A New and Correct Plan of the City of Bath, by G. Manners. Bath in Time. *170*

Camden Place, as engraved by Henry Adlard (active 1824–1869), after William Henry Bartlett (1809–1854). Bath in Time. *172*

Samuel Richardson, by Joseph Highmore (1692–1780), circa 1747. © National Portrait Gallery, London. *177*

Church at Lyme Regis, by Charles Dibdin (circa 1760–1814). © The Trustees of the British Museum. *179*

A. Wallis Mills, Illustrations for *Persuasion*, 1908. Mary Elliot and Captain Benwick walk along the beach at Lyme. © The British Library Board, All Rights Reserved. 12208.t.1. *181*

Tobias Smollett, by an unknown artist, circa 1770. © National Portrait Gallery, London. *184*

Bathwick Ferry below Camden Crescent, from an aquatint by I. Hill, after John Claude Nattes (circa 1765–1839). Bath in Time. *186*

View of Bath, engraved by T. Dixon, 1822. Bath in Time. *186*

Marlborough Buildings, from a steel engraving by J. Hollway, circa 1845. Bath in Time. *190*

Lansdown Crescent, by David Cox (1783–1859), 1820. Bath in Time. *193*

Hugh Thomson, Illustrations for *Persuasion*, 1897. Sir Walter finds that Anne's beauty is returning. © The British Library Board, All Rights Reserved. 012624.ee.28. *197*

Alexander Pope, oil on canvas, from the studio of Michael Dahl (1659–1743), circa 1727. © National Portrait Gallery, London. *202*

The Cross Bath, from an aquatint after John Claude Nattes. Bath in Time. *204*

Charles Austen, by an unknown artist. Jane Austen's House Museum, Jane Austen Memorial Trust. *212*

The Junction of Milsom Street and Bond Street with Portraits of Bath Swells, as drawn and engraved by Robert Cruikshank (1789–1856), 1825. Bath in Time. *217*

Charles Edmund Brock, Illustrations for *Persuasion*, 1898. Courtesy Yale University Library. *219*

Jack in the Bilboes, engraved by William Ward (1766–1826), after George Morland (1763–1804), circa 1790. © National Maritime Museum, Greenwich, London. *222*

A barouche from 1825. Mary Evans Picture Library. *227*

View along Pulteney Street, by John Claude Nattes. Austen and her parents went house hunting in Bath in January 1801. © The British Library Board 199.i7. *230*

New Theatre Royal, from a copper engraving by an unknown artist, 1807. Bath in Time. *232*

The Shipwreck, mezzotint on paper, by Charles Turner (1774–1857), after J. M. W. Turner, 1807. Tate/Digital Image © Tate, London 2009. *233*

The Concert Room or Tea Room at the New Assembly Rooms, by John Claude Nattes. Bath in Time. *235*

Hugh Thomson, Illustrations for *Persuasion*, 1897. Sir Walter and Elizabeth greet Lady Dalrymple and Miss Carteret. © The British Library Board, All Rights Reserved. 012624.ee.28. *237*

Comforts of Bath, by Thomas Rowlandson, 1798. Bath in Time. *239*

Hugh Thomson, Illustrations for *Persuasion*, 1897. The Durands enjoy the concert, open-mouthed and on the edges of their seats. © The British Library Board, All Rights Reserved. 012624.ee.28. *246*

Charles Edmund Brock, Illustrations for *Persuasion*, 1898. Anne is shocked by William Elliot's letter to Charles Smith. Courtesy Yale University Library. *254*

Fanny Knight, from a watercolor by Cassandra Austen. Jane Austen's House Museum, Jane Austen Memorial Trust. *259*

Title page of Thomas Peregrine Courtenay's *View of the State of the Nation*. Courtesy Houghton Library, Harvard University. *266*

The White Hart, by William Lewis, after John Charles Maggs (1819–1896). Bath in Time. *267*

Hugh Thomson, Illustrations for *Persuasion*, 1897. Captain Benwick reads to his fiancée Louisa Musgrove. © The British Library Board, All Rights Reserved. 012624.ee.28. *270*

Charles Edmund Brock, Illustrations for *Persuasion*, 1898. Charles Musgrove and Captain Benwick enjoy a morning together hunting rats. Courtesy Yale University Library. *272*

The Pump Room, by David Cox, 1820. Bath in Time. *274*

Anna Letitia Barbauld, by Sir Emery Walker (1851–1933), after Henry Meyer. Barbauld produced voluminously as an editor and reviewer. © National Portrait Gallery, London. *283*

A youth of the Busby family, by Jacob Fruman. © V & A Images / Victoria and Albert Museum, London. *284*

Unfinished sketch of Jane Austen, by Cassandra Austen, circa 1811. © National Portrait Gallery, London. *295*

A. Wallis Mills, Illustrations for *Persuasion*, 1908. Sir Walter records the marriage of Captain Wentworth and Anne in his beloved Baronetage. © The British Library Board, All Rights Reserved. 12208.t.1. *301*

A landaulette, by an unknown artist, 1816. © Science Museum Pictorial / Science & Society Picture Library. All rights reserved. *302*

First manuscript page of the two cancelled chapters of *Persuasion*. © The British Library Board, All Rights Reserved. Egerton.3038. *310*

Henry Austen, by an unknown artist, circa 1820. Jane Austen's House Museum, Jane Austen Memorial Trust. *322*

Acknowledgments

I would like to thank the Office of Research Services at Queen's University for its generous support of this project. I am indebted to the staff of the British Library, especially Rachel Foss, who kindly arranged for me to examine the cancelled manuscript chapters from *Persuasion*. I would also like to thank the staffs of the Thomas Fisher Rare Book Library, University of Toronto; the Joseph S. Stauffer Library, Queen's University; and the Houghton Library, Harvard University, particularly Susan Halpert. The annotation in this volume has benefited from previous editions of *Persuasion* by R. W. Chapman (1923), Andrew Wright (1965), Patricia Meyer Spacks (1995), Gillian Beer (1998), Linda Bree (1998), Deidre Lynch (2004), Janet Todd and Antje Blank (2006), and William Galperin (2008). For expertise, advice, and support of all kinds, I am grateful to Michael Bawtree, Christine Cox, Mark Gilchrist, Anthony Holden, Sue Rauth, Christopher Ricks, and Alan Samson. Patricia Meyer Spacks and Deidre Lynch read my manuscript with great care and thoughtfulness and rescued me from some embarrassing errors. At Harvard University Press, I am grateful to Matthew Hills, Christine Thorsteinsson, and especially John Kulka, who gave me the opportunity to edit Austen, and whose knowledge and enthusiasm have thoroughly shaped this edition. Larry Krupp once again provided invaluable hospitality during my research time in Boston. James Crowden and Simone Knightley took me on a superb tour of Bath and shared with me their extensive knowledge of the city. James and I also spent a blustery November day in Lyme, where we walked the Cobb and retraced the events of *Persuasion*.

Alastair and Zachary and Carole have provided love and support throughout this project. My greatest debt is to them.